THE ABYSS

A MAX AUSTIN THRILLER - BOOK FIVE OF THE RUSSIAN ASSASSIN SERIES

JACK ARBOR

THE ABYSS
(A MAX AUSTIN THRILLER - BOOK FIVE)

This book is a work of fiction. The characters, incidents, and dialogue are drawn from the author's imagination and are not to be construed as real. Any resemblance to actual events or persons, living or dead, is fictionalized or coincidental.

Paperback ISBN 9781947696105

Edition 1.1

Published by High Caliber Books

Cover art by: www.damonza.com
Bio photo credit: www.johnlilleyphotography.com

USAGE NOTE

In The Hunt, Max Austin's fourth adventure, I introduced a group of men who call themselves the komissariat for the Preservation of the State. The komissariat (for short) is the governing body for four subcouncils, one of which is the Council for Petroleum and Natural Gas, also known as the consortium. These groups form a shadow government that influences commerce, policy, the energy trade, crime, and corruption in Russia.

The word *komissariat* has caused much mayhem in our editing process. In Merriam-Webster, the authority reference for fiction, you'll find the definition under "commissariat": [borrowed from Russian komissariat, borrowed from German Kommissariat, borrowed from Medieval Latin commissāriātus]: a government department in the U.S.S.R until 1946.

I adopted the word from the NKVD, which was the People's Commissariat of Internal Affairs, or *Narodnyĭ komissariat vnutrennikh del* in Russian. This was Lenin's secret police force between 1917 and 1934, and was responsible for political repression, assassinations, and played a large role in Stalin's Great Purge. A student of the Russian Assassin stories will know that the consortium has ties back to the Cheka and the men responsible for starting the NKVD, and so the word is appropriate for this secretive shadow government operating in modern day Russia.

Technically, the komissariat for the Preservation of the State is a proper noun as it designates a particular thing, in this case a club of men not dissimilar from the Illuminati or Freemasons. Ordinarily a proper noun is capitalized. However, according to our research, the word komissariat in Russian is never capitalized, even when part of a proper noun. Therefore I use the lower case form of komissariat to refer to this group even when it seems like capitalization is called for.

Please enjoy the fifth installment in the Russian Assassin series.

Jack Arbor
October 2020
Aspen, Colorado

For Eric. The longest friends are the best friends.

"Betrayal... is my favorite subject"
~Norman Jewison

ONE

Somewhere outside Aspen, Colorado

A twig snapped in the darkness of the trees and Max flinched before he realized Charlie had wandered off. The dog's gray snout appeared a minute later as the Golden Retriever followed them up the trail. Spike, the puppy, bounded ahead, held back by a leash with Kate Shaw at the other end. Lagging ten meters behind, lost in his own thoughts, strode Spencer White, easily keeping pace on lanky legs.

Aside from the crunch of their footsteps and the occasional rodent-induced growl from a dog, the forest was silent. Puffy blankets of snow clung to the jack pines, and the occasional gust of crisp wind pierced their down jackets. Stout hiking boots offered protection from the rocky trail, and their breath came out in puffs as they climbed the steep trail. The low-lying nimbostratus grayed out the sky and promised to dump snow.

It took an hour to reach the shelf of granite that jutted from the cliffside and offered an expansive view of the valley and surrounding mountains. Spencer ventured out on the ledge and surveyed the wilderness. Kate affixed Spike's leash to a tree branch and set out a portable water bowl. Charlie took a drink and laid down and was instantly asleep while Spike looked around, his eyes alert.

Max shrugged off his pack and leaned his rifle against a rock within easy reach. He put out a spread with a large thermos of coffee and a sweet bread-like loaf the Americans called fruitcake. The three friends, comfortable in their silence, took seats while Max poured coffee.

Max held up his mug. "Merry Christmas."

Spencer and Kate touched their cups to his and each took a sip.

The coffee's roasted aroma was deep and rich in his nostrils, but the liquid scalded his tongue and Max blew on the surface to cool it down. He eyed Kate over the rim as steam wafted. Her cheeks had filled in and her color had returned since her harrowing stint of captivity at the hands of the late Victor Dedov. There were still thick veins on her bony hands and her eyes were still dull, despite their best efforts at nourishing her with love, rest, and clean food. She ate voraciously, which was a good sign, but she slept fitfully and refused to sleep alone, preferring to curl up in a blanket and pajamas on the side of Max's king-sized bed. She regularly startled him awake with murmurs, groans, soft cries, and the occasional scream. Along with the small signs of her health returning, she had regained her voice since the outburst on the trail two weeks ago when she'd disclosed Andrei Asimov's hidden message.

After their return from Europe, Kate offered no indication where the komissariat was to meet in January, nor had she revealed the date.

All I can do is stay close to her and hope she tells me. If she even knows.

Kate caught Max's gaze, held it a moment, and looked away. *Were her blue eyes brighter this morning or was it his imagination?* He smiled as she stared at a far-off spot across the valley.

Oblivious to the piping hot coffee, Spencer took a gulp. "You're torturing Alex, you know. Making him wait to open his presents."

Max chuckled. "Delayed gratification is good for him." He gathered up a handful of snow, formed a small snowball, and dropped it into his coffee. In direct opposition to Kate, his friend Spencer was happy and healthy. Kate was safe and under his direct protection, and his purpose in life was restored. The former CIA black ops man would not let his former boss out of his sight again. Hooded but sparkling brown eyes roved from Max to Kate to the trees to the rocks and back again in a restless and calculated surveillance.

The silence around them was disturbed by the flight of a bird that caused a fluffy mound of snow to fall to the ground with a soft *whomp*. Spencer's eyes followed the bird's trajectory into the gray sky. "Do you think spoiling him with those fifty presents will offset the lesson in patience he's learning?" Spencer winked.

"More like twenty. And yes, probably. This parenting thing is tough."

The dull blue-black barrel of a shotgun rested across Spencer's narrow thighs. "You can't buy his love. Trust me. I tried it with my girls. They still don't talk to me."

Max grunted and tasted the coffee. It was the perfect

temperature. The toasted caramel and dark chocolate swirled in his mouth among the licorice and anise. He absently patted his jacket pocket for a pack of cigarettes before remembering he left them on the kitchen table. Arina was vocal about the influence his smoking had on Alex, so Max agreed to cut back. His brain buzzed in a silent cry for tobacco, which he ignored. Instead he took another sip of coffee.

Both men watched as Kate rose and stepped to the edge of the rocky ledge, her footing sure in her Vibram-soled hiking boots. A bulge under her down jacket at her waist hinted at the pistol strapped to her belt.

Spencer speared a slice of fruitcake with a pocketknife, sniffed it, grimaced, and took a bite. "What possessed you to bring this?"

Max shrugged. "I thought all you Americans ate it at Christmas. No?"

Spencer shook his head while he munched. "No one really likes this stuff. The tradition is to regift it."

"Regift? I don't know this word."

The former CIA operative chuckled. "Yeah. It means to give someone else a gift that someone previously gave to you."

Max's eyebrows furrowed. "Why would you do that?"

Spencer smiled. "Good question."

The two men were interrupted by Kate's return. She knelt and snagged a piece of the fruitcake, sat on a rock near Max, and held out her cup for more coffee.

Max watched her swallow and grab another piece. "Boy, for not liking this stuff, you guys sure do eat a lot of it."

With a chunk of cake in hand, Spencer rose, hoisted the shotgun over a shoulder, and trudged down the trail on a ten-minute patrol.

When Spencer disappeared through the trees, Kate leaned her elbows on her knees and grasped her coffee cup in two hands. "Have you heard of the Vienna Archive?"

"The what?" Max was too distracted by the fact that Kate spoke for the first time in weeks to register her words.

She smiled and her eyes twinkled. "I guess that's a no."

"Sounds like something out of a spy novel from the '80s."

"Not quite. It's a name given to a large stash of files that someone stole and hid away. Files that supposedly expose the inner workings of the consortium. Names, financial records, meeting minutes, the like."

Max refilled his coffee. A memory flashed of a video made by his father. It was a message to him from his father that was left in a locket. A locket owned by a woman named Raisa. *They know I've assembled this dossier. They know the keys to unraveling its mysteries lie within the Asimov family.*

Kate held out her cup. "It's a story that's gone around intelligence agencies for years. Every once in a while, a tidbit of intel about the Vienna Archive crops up and the intelligence community gets excited about it. Then it dies away and everyone forgets about it for a while."

Boot steps were heard among the trees.

"No one has ever found it," Kate said as Spencer appeared at the trail head.

"Found what?" Spencer asked.

"The Tsar's gold," Kate stood and stretched her legs. "It was stolen from Tsar Nicholas II during the Russian Revolution. Five hundred pounds of gold disappeared somewhere in Siberia in a fight between the Bolsheviks and the White Forces. Two hundred pounds of it is still missing."

"Is that our next adventure?" Spencer smiled and scratched the top of Charlie's head.

A wet snowflake hit Max's nose, and the sky was filled with flakes that blocked out the sky. He drained his coffee and packed the remaining bits of fruitcake and the thermos into his rucksack before following Spencer, Kate, and the two dogs down the trail. The fresh snow hid their previous tracks, and Max's boots made light crunching noises as he walked. He let his thoughts take over, his focus remaining in that gray area between deep thought and careful awareness of his surroundings. It was a skill he'd learned from his father and cultivated over his twenty-year career as first a KGB officer and then a sleeper agent in Paris. As he walked, he breathed in the crisp air, filled his lungs, and let it slowly out.

The Vienna Archive. His father hid some secret documents and now every intelligence agency in the world was searching for them. *What had his old man been up to?*

The hushed forest was suddenly filled with the sounds of the dogs barking. Charlie and Spike tugged at their leashes and pulled Kate ahead on the trail. She managed to reel in the canines, but their barking continued and Spike threatened to break free from her grasp. Max was jolted from his thoughts and moved to help Kate with the dogs. He stopped in his tracks as the faint sound of gunfire rang through the dense trees.

Three crisp, evenly spaced pistol shots.

Pop, pop, pop.

It was a sound distinct to a particular pistol. A pistol he knew. *That's Arina's Springfield.*

He took a step down the trail. In his periphery, Spencer hoisted his shotgun and stepped closer to Kate, who was busy tying the dogs' leashes around a branch. Her eyes were alive as her hand went to her pistol.

A quiet descended over the forest. Even the dogs stopped barking.

Through the stillness, the chatter of automatic gunfire filled the air.

Max took off at a full sprint.

TWO

Somewhere outside Aspen, Colorado

Pop-pop-pop-pop.

More pistol shots rang out interspersed with the automatic fire.

The gunshots from the pistol were evenly spaced, like his sister was taught. Max recognized the handgun fire as coming from Arina's Springfield .45 compact, a gun she'd fired thousands of times in the barn's makeshift range.

His boots pounded on the ground as he ran along the snowy trail. Slick rocks threatened to pitch him to the ground. Large snowflakes swirled around his head, and he pushed his speed to the brink on the treacherous trail.

The old but well-cared-for Colt Commando was in his right hand. His left arm was out to help him balance as he ran.

Tap-tap-tap, tap-tap-tap.

Automatic fire. Two shooters. Or three.

More gunfire punctuated his footsteps. A root sprang

up and caught his foot, and he stumbled. His boot came down on a layer of ice and he slid for a moment until he caught himself and continued running.

As he rounded a bend in the trail, he slowed to a jog. Through the trees was a clearing with the large log cabin that had been in Spencer White's family for generations. Spencer halted behind him, and Kate stepped off the trail. Smoke billowed in the air, but the tree line hid the source.

The three exchanged hand signals. Spencer took off through the woods, shotgun in hand, around to the far side of the cabin's clearing near the pond. Kate's blue eyes were bright but hooded with concern, and her pistol was out and held in a two-handed grip. She went right to go behind the barn. As Max ran straight down the trail, more pistol shots rang through the forest.

Good girl, Arina. Keep 'em busy. I'm coming.

The trees thinned and gave way to a clearing with the cabin to the left and a pole barn to the right. A small pond glistened in the morning light. A gravel drive made a circle in front of the house before it trailed off into the woods, where it met a forest service road. A waving plume of soot and sizzling embers rose in the air. The strong tinge of smoke hit his nose, and he picked up his speed until he heard roaring and crackling. An inferno engulfed the cabin.

He ignored the fire and searched for the source of the gunshots. His shoulder hit the rough bark of a tree as he took cover, rifle up, and scanned the clearing.

Arina was nowhere to be seen. Two snow-white SUVs idled in the circular drive. Their windows were tinted, and exhaust puffed into the cold air. His finger clenched on the trigger as six men appeared from the burning house, all wearing kerchiefs against the smoke. Dressed in jeans, winter boots, watch caps, knee pads, and down jackets, they each wore tactical vests and wielded assault rifles. Curved mics were attached to their ears. No insignia was visible.

As they emerged, all six men pulled down their face protection. They were tall Caucasians with square jaws who moved with the precision and practice of men who had trained, lived, and fought together for years. Two abreast, rifles up, they swept the yard for targets and danger as they moved down the porch steps and across the gravel drive. One man carried a large duffle bag over his shoulder.

The bag was about the size of a ten-year-old and it wiggled as the soldier grappled to control it.

Alex.

With rage in his throat, Max stepped out from behind the tree and strode toward the two SUVs, his rifle to his shoulder, and fired in three-round bursts.

Two bullets found the lead commando, who fell. The two rear men whirled and dropped to their knees to return fire. The remaining commandos, including the man lugging the duffle bag, sprinted for the waiting vehicles.

Bile rose in Max's throat. *They can't get away.*

He pulled the trigger again and again, pouring slug after slug at the two kneeling men, mindful to keep the fire away from the black bag. Bullets sang over his head and thunked into the trees to his left and right. He put two bullets in one man's throat and shot another in the shoulder. The wounded soldier's rifle chattered, sending bullets into the air, as his arm arced skyward and he spun to the ground. Two more slugs from Max's gun slammed into the man's chest, and he lay still.

The remaining three commandos reached the SUVs and yanked open the doors.

Max dropped to a knee, pressed his cheek against the rifle's stock, and peered through the scope.

One shot. Make it count. As action in his peripherals faded, the target appeared in sharp focus.

The soldier carrying the wiggling package reached the lead SUV and heaved the weight from his shoulder to wrench open the door and hurl the package into the vehicle.

Max pulled the trigger.

The bullet spit from the Colt and clanged into the metal of the open door. Max adjusted and pulled the trigger a second time. A bullet punched through the flesh of the commando's arm, but the wiggling bag was already in the rear seat of the SUV.

Another trigger pull sent a bullet into the soldier's buttock. With a grunt, the soldier fell against the car.

He aimed for the tires. Two shots from the Colt plunked into the gravel while a soldier grabbed the wounded commando and heaved him into the car.

Max rose and fired as he ran.

The roar of a shotgun came from Max's left, and Spencer strode across the open yard, gun to his shoulder, firing buckshot at the rear SUV. A window shattered. A rear quarter panel was peppered with buckshot. To the right Kate ran full tilt along the side of the barn and fired. The lead SUV's windshield cracked from multiple rounds. One of the enemy raised his rifle from behind an open door and squeezed off shots at Kate. She returned fire, sprinkling the open door with bullets.

Had she seen them throw the bound-up Alex into the rear of the first SUV? Max held up his hand while he ran and yelled, "Hold your fire! Hold your fire!"

Kate stopped shooting and swerved to the side of the barn, where she found cover behind a stack of cord wood. A shotgun round from Spencer's gun thumped into the rear of the SUV.

The last commando hurled himself into the lead vehicle as the driver gunned the throttle and the wheels churned on the snowy gravel drive. The SUV fishtailed before it regained control and roared down the drive and disappeared among the trees. The second vehicle bounced over a dormant flowerbed and careened left, tipped onto two wheels, and righted itself before it too disappeared into the trees.

Still Spencer ran and plugged the rear SUV with buckshot until his shotgun was empty. He tossed the weapon and drew his pistol and fired shot after shot until the slide locked back.

Max yelled out a curse as he changed direction and headed for the barn, where their Jeep was parked. In his periphery, Kate dropped to a knee to examine something hidden from view. Sirens rang out in the distance.

"Max! Over here," Kate yelled. "Come now."

Intent on pursuit and blinded by rage and fear for his nephew's safety, he ignored the command. The battlefield narrowed, his vision fogged, and the blaze disappeared. Concern for his sister faded. The growing bedlam of sirens died out. Through everything cut a singular instinct.

Get Alex back.

At all costs.

The intensity of Kate's voice made him falter. "It's Arina."

Damn it.

He yanked up the barn's roll-up door to reveal the burly snout of a Jeep Wrangler.

Kate's voice rang out again, this time cutting through the momentum of his instinct. "She's been shot."

THREE

Somewhere outside Aspen, Colorado

The Jeep's red hood was in front of him. He wrenched open the driver's door but with less enthusiasm.

"Max! She's bleeding out."

Shit.

The keys were in the ignition. He tossed the Colt on the passenger seat.

"She's going to die. Alex is alive, Max. We'll get him back, but your sister is dying."

His fist banged against the steering wheel. *How did she let herself get shot?* He abandoned the Jeep and sprinted around the barn's corner to where Kate knelt in the snow. His heart skipped a beat at the sight.

A blond-haired form lay on the ground surrounded by crimson snow. *Shit, there's a lot of blood.* Arina's pretty face was contorted with pain as red liquid trickled from the corner of her mouth.

With her pistol in one hand, Kate plunged her other

hand under Arina's shirt. "One bullet hole. No. Two. Abdomen." She moved her bloody fingers to Arina's neck. "Pulse is weak. She's losing a lot of blood."

Max bowed his head and pounded the ground with his fist. His rage threatened to consume him as the SUV with Alex got farther and farther away.

The Jeep's engine roared to life and gravel crunched as Spencer backed the vehicle out and around to the group. "Load her up," he shouted. "We gotta go."

Arina's eyes searched the sky, found the side of the barn, and shifted to Max's face. She raised her hand, which Max took in his. Her skin was cold and clammy, her grip feeble. When she spoke, her words were in Belarusian, the language Max and Arina grew up speaking.

"Mikhail. Where were you?"

A stab to his heart.

Her voice was soft, and he leaned close to hear. "Go... Get Alex... back."

A video reel unfolded in his mind as his rage receded. Arina and Alex when they picked him up at the Minsk airport the previous summer, and Max's first glimpse of the boy who captured his heart. The fight with Arina as they drove to their parents' house. The explosion that took their parents' lives. The fight to save Arina and Alex from the clutches of Nathan Abrams. Everything he had done to save them from the consortium's vendetta. And now this.

A tear rolled down his cheek as his forehead touched hers and his body shuddered with sobs. "I'm sorry, sis. I'm sorry I wasn't here."

Her hand, limp and cold, applied feeble pressure. "Find him, Mikhail. Leave me. I'll be okay. Don't let them take him."

More of their life together played in his mind. Fighting

over their mother's borscht. The time when a boy who cheated on her came calling and Max beat him until he ran off, leaving both brother and sister laughing. The vision took a split second, and he clasped her hand and pulled at her arm. "Help me get her up, damn it. Get her in the Jeep."

Someone gripped his arm, and he looked up to see Kate staring at him. "Leave her."

His reaction was immediate and visceral. He put an arm under his sister's shoulder. "Help me, damn you." He clutched at Arina, whose eyelids had closed.

A piercing slap across his face shocked his mind into clarity. Kate's nose pressed close to his as she wound up for another strike. Using a voice honed from years of commanding testosterone-laced soldiers and obstinate field agents, she shouted into his ear. "Her best chance of survival is here. Authorities are on their way. They will give her immediate medical attention. We need to leave her."

Spencer arrived with a blanket, which he laid in the snow.

Max lowered Arina onto the blanket. He leaned over her and put his face close to hers. "I'm sorry, Arina."

A whisper of breath escaped from her lips, and her lashes fluttered. "You must find him. He's all we have."

Something tugged at his arm, which he ignored. When he kissed Arina's cheek, her skin, which was covered in blood and smeared with tears, was cold.

A final yank forced him off his feet and into the Jeep's front passenger seat. Kate piled into the back and slammed the door while Spencer spun the wheel and the Jeep lurched around the far side of the barn. The wailing of emergency vehicles grew louder.

The slap, the encroaching sirens, and his surging adrenaline refocused Max's mind. The two enemy SUVs were a mile or two away by this time and were screaming along any one of the dozen or so forest service roads, dirt tracks, or two-lane highways that crisscrossed the Roaring Fork Valley. He guessed the attackers had done their homework and outlined an escape route over one of the three high mountain passes following old mining trails that provided access to the mountainous regions of central Colorado. The commandos would easily evade the onslaught of emergency vehicles that converged on the cabin.

Max yelled to make his voice heard over the roar of the Jeep's engine. "How many ways out of this valley?"

Spencer's face was red and perspiration dotted his forehead despite the cold temperature. "A lot. Route 82 goes north to the interstate and south to Aspen, where Independence Pass goes over the Sawatch Range to Leadville. Pearl Pass goes between Aspen and Crested Butte, but those big SUVs couldn't take that. A half-dozen other dirt roads and minor mountain passes go east toward Vail and eventually Denver."

"Shit. It will take the authorities time to sort out the carnage before they decide to set up roadblocks."

Spencer snapped his fingers. "I know where they're going."

"Tell me."

"Cottonwood Pass. It's a paved road that runs from this valley, over the Continental Divide, and down into Buena Vista. From there, they might go north to Leadville but they'll probably take 285 to Denver."

"Isn't Cottonwood closed in the winter? They don't maintain it."

"Used to be that way. It's the highest paved crossing of the Divide. Last summer there was a big effort to widen the road and the project stalled but funding was reallocated in the fall. They've been plowing the pass this winter while they finish the project. That route is the fastest way out of this valley. It's the way I'd go."

"They have a big head start."

Spencer gritted his teeth. "I know a shortcut."

––––––––

The Jeep lurched and jounced as Spencer guided the 4x4 up a snow-covered two-track road. Max was amazed that Spencer was able to pick his way through the tight trees. "How do you know where the road is?"

Spencer gripped the wheel with both hands. "I grew up here. Those city SUVs have to stay on paved roads. To get to Cottonwood, they go through Aspen and up toward Independence Pass before turning off. We'll cut off an hour on this Jeep road and get there ahead of them."

"What if we're wrong?" Max mused to himself.

"Shit," Kate said. "What about the dogs?"

"We'll come back for them."

Max checked the mag on the Colt. Six bullets remained. "What's the plan?"

"If my calculations are right, we'll get to the pass before them," Spencer said. "At the top of the pass, the snow is over your head. The plows make a cut for cars, but there is no room to maneuver. We'll set a trap there."

The little group settled into silence as the Jeep made its ponderous way up the mountain. When they emerged from the trees and continued up a slope, there were no other cars. Here above the alpine tree line, the snow was older, dirtier, and thinner. The faint outline of a trail was evident, and the Jeep made better time. When they bounced down a slope and made a hard left turn, the Jeep skidded on wet pavement. Spencer gunned the engine. "This is Route 306."

The road snaked its way up steep switchbacks until the snow rose above the top of the Jeep. Striations were evident in the snow, which had been cut by plows. A brown-and-tan sign appeared that read "Cottonwood Pass, elevation 12,126 feet, Continental Divide." A gap in the snow wide enough for two parked vehicles had been cleared away next to the sign. "The plows open that up to allow cars to pull off if they have trouble," Spencer said.

The sign whipped past as the road curved. When they got to a point where the road was hidden from the top of the pass by the snow, Spencer hit the brakes and pulled the Jeep to a stop so it was at a right angle to the road. "When they crest the pass and hit the curve, they'll see the Jeep and stop."

Max gripped the rifle. "Or try to ram it."

"Two of us will hike back to the pass and wait in the cut."

"You two go," Max said. "Watch your fire so we don't hit Alex." He got out, slung the Colt onto his back, and rummaged in the rear of the Jeep for a small avalanche shovel. Spencer tossed him a handheld radio and stuffed a second one in his pocket. As Spencer and Kate hiked up the road, Max went to work on the snow near the front bumper of the Jeep. The wall of snow was over his head and hard as ice.

As he finished digging a large enough indentation for him to hide in, the radio squawked with Kate's voice. "Two SUVs approaching. High rate of speed."

"Copy that." Max pocketed the radio and hefted the Colt. The cavity in the snow would provide concealment in case the SUVs attempted to ram the Jeep. Snow and ice, however, made for poor cover from bullets. The roar of engines rose in a crescendo before brakes locked and rubber squealed on wet pavement.

Max put the rifle stock to his cheek and stepped out from the hiding place.

The two white SUVs were stopped in the middle of the road, a dozen meters from the Jeep. Bullet holes riddled their side panels.

With the Colt on single fire, Max took aim and pressed the trigger. A hole appeared in the lead SUV's windshield and the driver slumped.

Chaos erupted. A gun appeared from the rear side window of the lead SUV. An engine roared and tires screeched as the rear SUV reversed. A shotgun erupted followed by the *plink-plink-plink* of a pistol.

Which SUV is Alex in?

Max took cover behind the Jeep's hood. The shooter in the lead SUV opened fire and bullets hit the Jeep and sang overhead. His position offered a poor angle on the SUV's shooter, so Max waited.

The rear SUV gathered speed as it hurtled up the incline in reverse. Spencer and Kate were not in sight. Shots ricocheted off the pavement near Max's position. If the rear SUV contained Alex, it had to be stopped.

Max crouch-walked to the rear of the Jeep with the rifle up. Movement came from inside the first SUV. Shadows shifted inside as the man in the rear climbed into the driver's seat. Max aimed at the shadow and fired.

The shadow stopped moving.

Max took off running as shotgun blasts came from up the hill. He emerged from behind the lead SUV at a full sprint. The rear SUV hurtled up the hill, rocking on its suspension as the driver tried to maintain control. A man hung from the side window with a rifle, firing at something to the rear. In a moment, the vehicle would reach the curve.

Max took a knee and raised the Colt. There was time for one shot. He let his breath settle and squeezed the trigger. A hole appeared in the SUV's windshield. The big truck roared backward as if nothing happened. He fired again, but the bullet plunked into the truck's grill.

When the road curved, the SUV plowed into the ice wall with its rear quarter panel. The ice held firm as the truck scraped along the snowbank. Max took off at a run.

Spencer and Kate appeared at the crest of the hill, weapons held up. The shotgun roared and the man hanging out the SUV's side window sagged. Max skidded to a halt and returned to the first SUV. He wrenched open the rear passenger door.

There, on the rear seat, among shards of glass and blood spatter, was a large black duffle bag. It didn't move. Panic surged. *How can he breathe?*

With a snap, Max opened his knife and sliced open the bag. A pile of clothes tumbled out.

A faint cry came from the SUV's luggage area. Max darted to the back and opened the rear door. There, curled in the fetal position, with his hands secured behind him, was Alex.

FOUR

Somewhere outside Aspen, Colorado

"We can disappear in these mountains for a while." Spencer drove with both hands on the wheel while perspiration dripped from his forehead despite the open side window.

Max and Alex rode in the back seat, while Kate sat in the front with her thumbs flying over her phone's keyboard. It was a Blackphone, customized by Goshawk with special security features. The device was untraceable and capable of sending and receiving encrypted text messages and was a newer and slimmer version of the Blackphone carried by Max. The device was a gift from Goshawk after Kate's harrowing rescue from the clutches of Victor Dedov.

After moving the two SUVs with the four dead men into the cutout at the top of the pass, they retraced their route along Spencer's four-wheel-drive road to retrieve the dogs. They had tied them to a tree along a trail that intersected with the 4x4 road and that was far enough away from the cabin to allow them to evade the authorities who swarmed the clearing where the cabin lay in smoldering ruin.

Alex was dazed but otherwise unhurt. With the canines secure in the rear deck, Spencer put the Jeep into gear and turned onto a new trail that led north and deeper into the Colorado wilderness.

Spencer wiped perspiration from his head. "Who were those guys?"

Snow-covered rocky crags slipped by the window as Max tussled Alex's hair. "Can't say for sure. It's a feeling. But they moved like Spetsnaz." Known as fearsome warriors, Spetsnaz were Russian special purpose forces akin to the American Green Berets or the British Special Air Service.

"What? How can you tell?"

"I've operated and trained around them my whole life. Something in my gut."

The bigger question is how did they know where to find us? And who sent them?

They emerged from the White River National Forest and bounced up onto Route 24. To the west, their left, was the swanky ski resort of Beaver Creek. To their right, east, was the former mining town of Leadville, which was known as one of the largest meth-producing areas above ten thousand feet in elevation. Spencer cranked the wheel to the right and the tires spun on wet pavement. The Jeep fishtailed before righting itself, and they sped up a long hill.

Alex tipped his head up to look at Max. "Where's my mom?"

Spencer and Kate exchanged glances in the front seat before Kate turned to catch Max's eye. "Alex..." she began.

Max held up one hand to silence Kate and put the other

on Alex's arm. "Alex, your mom was hurt when you were kidnapped."

The ten-year-old's eyes went wide. "Is she..."

"She's getting medical help. It's serious, but we hope she's going to be okay."

"When can I see her?"

"It's complicated. I hope soon, but it might be a while. For now, you're safe with us and your mom is getting the medical attention she needs. Okay?"

Alex nodded while his eyes filled with tears. He wiped them away and set his jaw, like he didn't want to cry.

Max used a speed dial setting to call Goshawk, the stoic computer hacker currently stationed in her hermetically sealed compound in Paris. She answered with her characteristic demand. "Go."

"We need a safe house." The conversation was broadcast over the Jeep's internal speakerphone, which was hooked to his secure Blackphone by a cable to the vehicle's auxiliary port.

"What the hell is going on?" In the background was typing.

Always the typing.

"We're on the move. Four of us and two dogs. Arina's been shot. Had to leave her behind. Alex was kidnapped. Cabin was torched. We need a safe place to hole up. Can you—"

"Shit, Max. What the hell? Alex was kidnapped?"

"I'm here," piped up Alex.

"We got him back." Max winked at the boy. "Can you help us or not? We have cash."

Outside, snow-laden trees spun by and the occasional car passed going the opposite direction. The other end of the phone went silent, like she put them on mute.

"Goshawk? You there?"

"We don't have anything in the immediate area. All our safe houses are in different theaters. I told you that when you decided to hole up in that cabin in the woods."

"Okay, fine. Can you get us one of those air beans or whatever? Something temporary."

"Airbnb, you mean. Hold on."

Spencer cranked down a window and cold air sucked into the Jeep. His craggy face was beet red.

Kate's brow creased. "Spencer, are you okay?"

The ex-CIA operative nodded.

Goshawk's voice returned. "Bad idea. You have to call the owner, talk to them, make arrangements for the damn key."

"Forget all that. We're coming to Paris. Staying with you awhile. We need to get out of here."

"Negative. You can't come here. Don't call me out of the blue and expect me to conjure up a safe house. I'm in the middle of something, can't help you right now."

The phone went dead.

Max gaped at the phone to see if the call had dropped. *Nope, she hung up on me.* "What the hell is going on with her?"

Spencer slowed the car to the posted speed as they approached Leadville. "I'd offer my sister's house up north, but she might call the cops."

Max tossed the phone on the seat beside him and stared out the window. The wet blacktop stretched into an endless line of gray framed by a blur of snow-covered pines. As a sheriff's SUV roared by in the opposite direction, red and blue lights ablaze, the Jeep's occupants stiffened until it faded away behind them. Frustration surged and Max wanted to find a lead pipe and beat the nearest inanimate object into tiny pieces. Instead, he did the only thing he could think to do. After a deep breath, he grabbed his phone.

The touch of a speed dial made a string of numbers appear on the Jeep's touch screen. The phone number started with a +44, the long-distance code for the United Kingdom.

Spencer groaned. "You're not calling Baxter, are you?"

"Got any better ideas? Because I'm fresh out." Max consulted his watch. It was 8:00 pm in London on Christmas Day.

A series of clicks and whirs filled the speaker as the call was routed through various secure servers. When the call connected, the senior MI6 officer's voice was like sandpaper.

"You better have something good for me or I'm hanging up."

"We need a place to stay."

"What the bloody hell—"

"Four of us. Two dogs. We have to get out of here." A sign indicated they had entered Leadville's town limits.

"The hell you say."

"Your chief offered us any help we need. Our place in Colorado is blown. Literally, it burned to the ground. Alex was almost kidnapped by Russians."

"I don't give a damn what C said. You're not coming back to England if I have anything to say about it."

"Listen, I know you're still angry—"

"I'm beyond angry," Baxter growled.

They approached a gas station, and Spencer yanked the wheel and screeched to a halt by the pumps.

"Callum," Max said. "I wouldn't—"

"I don't want to hear it," Baxter said over the speaker.

Spencer shuffled into the gas station with a handful of cash. The lanky man's right leg dragged with a more severe limp than normal. A dark pool of liquid had seeped into the driver's seat. Kate dragged an index finger along the fabric and held up a burgundy-stained finger to Max.

"Callum, listen. A team of Russian Spetsnaz attacked our cabin and kidnapped Alex. Arina's been shot. We have no—"

"You reap what you sow."

Max gripped the door handle hard enough to turn his knuckles white.

Kate turned in the front seat and whispered. "You know what he wants. Make a trade."

He searched her eyes with his, and she gave a slight nod.

"It's Christmas, for bullock's sake," the MI6 officer growled. "I'm hanging up now."

"Wait. I'll make you a trade."

Outside, Spencer activated the gas pump.

After a pause, Baxter said, "I'm listening."

"I'll trade you what we learned from Kate in exchange for a place to stay."

The phone grew quiet, and the pump outside clicked off.

"How do I know—"

"You can have full access to debrief her. When you're done, you'll know what we know. Everything. I promise."

"Your promises aren't worth the paper I clean my arse with."

Alex snickered.

Placing a hand on Max's arm, Kate moved closer to the Jeep's speakerphone. "Callum, this is Kate. You have my word."

A *harrumph* over the speaker was followed by a long

stretch of dead air. When he spoke, Baxter's words were measured. "Let me be clear. If you arrive here without significant intel, and I do mean significant, you'll be out on your bums. Are we clear?"

"Yes, Callum." Kate winked at Max.

While Baxter issued instructions, Max muted the phone, held out his fist, and whispered to Alex. "You want to fly in a private jet?"

The youngster's eyes lit up and he tapped Max's fist with his own.

When Spencer struggled back into the Jeep with an armful of water bottles and snacks, Max spotted a dark red stain on the operator's jeans.

"Were you hit?" Max asked.

Spencer grimaced as Kate took the snacks. "It's a through and through. I'm fine."

After he dug out a bottle of peroxide from the Jeep's first aid kit, Max doused the wound through the jeans and cut a strip of wool from a blanket stored in the Jeep's rear. He handed it to Spencer, who tied it around his thigh. Once they were underway, Max relayed Baxter's directions. "We need to find someplace called Eagle County airport."

———

It was 1:00 am on Boxing Day, December 26, when the white Gulfstream G500 banked and locked on approach to runway 25 at Eagle County airport. As the airplane glided in, the four humans and two dogs waited in the private terminal lounge. Alex stretched out on three connected seats while Kate fussed over the dressing on Spencer's wound. The two dogs rested on the carpet and lapped at a water bowl supplied by the terminal's night manager. The weapons had been disassembled and deposited in various roadside trash bins, and the Jeep was wiped down and left in the middle of the airport parking lot. They monitored the police band using an app on Max's phone, and so far, no one had reported the two SUVs with the four dead bodies. A bulletin indicated the fire at the White family cabin was extinguished, and an arson investigation would begin in the morning. No mention was made of an injured woman. Max fretted about Arina's status until Kate warned him to act positive in front of Alex.

The private terminal's night manager alerted them to the jet's arrival and escorted the group onto the tarmac where the sleek white jet waited. A man in a parka fueled the aircraft from a tanker. The stairs hissed down to reveal a warm glow inside. A head wearing a captain's hat appeared at the opening. "Come along now, we're on a schedule."

Alex scampered up the stairs and was followed by Kate, who helped Spencer navigate the steep steps. Max followed with Charlie in his arms while Spike almost got tangled in his legs. The plane got underway before everyone was settled. Alex fell asleep in the back with the dogs curled around him. Spencer found a bench where he could elevate his leg.

The jet accelerated and pushed Max into a buttery leather seat. After only a few seconds of rolling takeoff, they were airborne. Max rummaged in a cabinet and found a cache of tiny bottles of gin, Scotch, and vodka. He cracked the bottle of Scotch, sniffed it, and put the cap back.

"You can't do that," Kate said.

"Do what?"

"Open a bottle of airplane booze and not drink it."

"I can if it smells like dirt."

"That's called peat. It gives the Scotch its flavor."

Max opened one of the vodka bottles and dumped the contents into a small tumbler and held it out to Kate, who shook her head. "Tell me about this Vienna Archive," Max said.

After shifting in her seat to check on Spencer, who snored gently, Kate pulled a blanket over her legs and opened a bottle of water. "It's intelligence service folklore that has circulated for a few years. There is evidence that someone has amassed a massive collection of stolen files on Russia. Files that would expose the inner workings of the Communist Party, the Supreme Soviet, the KGB, and more recently, the rise to power of Russia's autocratic president."

"Folklore, huh? Kind of like the Baba Yaga?" Max laughed at his own reference to the Slavic supernatural fairy-tale character. Was this mythical Vienna Archive his father's cache of stolen files?

Kate set her bottle in a cup holder. "I admit, it sounds fanciful—but hear me out. When I was at the CIA, there was a small group of us that started an inter-agency group to compare notes on this Vienna Archive. It was us, the Brits, the Germans, and sometimes the Israelis."

"You're a believer in this archive thing?"

"I am, and so are some prominent intelligence leaders in those agencies. There were simply too many obscure references and random clues. SIGINT, HUMINT, and more recently, with the advent of the NSA's PRISM program, the British Tempora program, and the Germans' Project 6—there is a lot of circumstantial evidence that the Vienna Archive is real. Can you imagine the intelligence coup for whoever finds this archive?" Kate shook her head. "To have access to the old Soviet machine and the inner workings of the Kremlin?"

"Why is it called the Vienna Archive?"

"The director of Great Britain's GCHQ coined it as such after their analysts triangulated on Vienna as a possible location for the actual files."

A niggling feeling crept up Max's neck. "Why are you telling me this?"

Kate lowered her voice. "It's my belief that Andrei, your father, is responsible for the Vienna Archive. There are too many connections, too many coincidences."

"Why am I not surprised?" For the thousandth time, the video Andrei Asimov left for Max hidden in a woman's locket flashed through his mind.

I've known Kate since her days on the Soviet Desk in Moscow and at the embassy in Minsk, in Budapest, in the Czech Republic, and in Belgrade. I found her to be a straight shooter, someone I could trust. She was a natural choice when it came time to divulge my findings.

Max felt the pull to return to the task of unraveling his father's mysteries. "How did you get through the interrogation by Victor Dedov and Nikita Ivanov without revealing this thing, the Vienna Archive?"

Kate shrugged. "Remember, Andrei hypnotized me several years ago. I guess the information couldn't come out without the passphrase."

"Which Arina supplied a couple weeks ago."

"Andrei left explicit instructions that this discussion was for your ears only."

Max nodded and sipped his vodka. "Okay, so maybe the dossier mentioned in my father's video and this Vienna Archive are the same thing?"

"That's my assumption," Kate said.

"Stealing thousands of top-secret files and hiding them away would be treason. And you know how treason is dealt with in Russia."

"Punishable by death." Kate stared out the plane's window.

"And sometimes by death to the traitor's family," Max added. "How much did he tell you about this dossier?"

"Unfortunately, not much." Kate took a pull on the water bottle. "You know what a cipher is, right?"

"It can mean a lot of different things," Max said. "Are you referring to coded messages? Cryptography? Encryption?"

A glint appeared in Kate's eye.

With the vodka glass in both hands, Max leaned his elbows on his knees. "You answered my question with another question."

"Go along with me for a second. Think hand-coded messages instead of computers."

"Like Enigma?" The reference was to the famous encryption machines developed by the Germans and broken by the British in World War II.

Kate shook her head. "Pen and paper. Old school."

"Sounds like Andrei. He hated computers."

"Max, Andrei told me that he hid the archive's location in a handwritten coded message."

Max spread his hands. "So? Where is it?"

"I don't know."

Max groaned.

"All I know is he encoded a message that is for you alone. He did it using a system called a one-time pad. We need to find the correct pad—the key—and we need to find the message. Your father hid both for safekeeping."

"So, we get the coded message and we find the key. We uncover this Vienna Archive thing and barter to lift the death sentence."

"Something like that," Kate said. "You can't just kill everyone."

"As everyone likes to remind me."

"Once this archive of information is unearthed, you can make it public or use it to barter your safety. I get the feeling this was your father's intention."

Outside, the starless sky slipped by the windows.

"But Max..." Kate put her hand on his arm. "There are many agencies searching for this archive. The CIA, the Germans, the Chinese. Most certainly the Russians. Once it gets out that the archive exists, each agency will stop at nothing to find it for themselves. Make no mistake, this is a race among intelligence agencies."

"We better get going. Where do we start?"

Kate's grip on his arm tightened. "I'm waiting for a message. A signal. I expect it any day now."

"What happens then?"

She shrugged. "You'll know when I know." Kate pulled the blanket up to her neck and drifted off.

Max watched as her breathing got deeper. He drained the vodka and stared out the window into the inky blackness.

FIVE

Bath, England

The farmhouse door opened to reveal a dully lit but warm interior and a large woman, with a loose bun on her head and a gray flannel jumper tight against her broad bust, which was covered with a thick apron. Behind the ragtag group on the porch, snow and ice blew sideways and caked the three vehicles parked along the narrow drive.

With one arm around Spencer's shoulder, Max helped the former CIA operative into the farmhouse. During the flight, Kate had cut away the jean leg, applied more of the antiseptic, and covered the wound with a fresh bandage from the jet's first aid kit. Blood had oozed through the bandage and the leg had stiffened. Max led Spencer to a room behind the kitchen prepared with a cot, clean sheets, an IV rack, and other portable medical equipment. There they were met by a Special Air Service medic.

Kate entered with leashes attached to the two dogs, who sniffed the furniture and carpet. She led the dogs to

Spencer's makeshift hospital room behind the kitchen, where Charlie curled up at the foot of the cot and Spike lapped at a water dish.

The farmhouse was a large stone building situated on twenty-four acres and surrounded by a cherry orchard. A dozen paces away sat an outbuilding where a team of Special Air Service men camped, pored over surveillance footage of the grounds, and embarked on patrols around the orchard perimeter.

Max found Callum Baxter standing next to a kitchen stove where a teapot whistled. The senior MI6 man wore his trademark disheveled corduroy jacket, and crumbs clung to his scraggly white goatee. The unkempt look disarmed many, but Max knew the agent's mind was razor sharp and his loyalty to the Crown was matched only by his dogged diligence in the field.

"For the record, I am not happy to see you." Callum Baxter's voice was icy.

"Don't worry," Max retorted. "I won't be here long."

"I trust C's Gulfsteam was satisfactory?" Baxter dropped tea bags into two mugs.

"A step up from that old Lear you fly around in. Have you inquired as to Arina's status?"

The MI6 officer nodded while he poured hot water into the mugs.

"And?"

"She was checked into Aspen Valley Hospital under the name Jane Doe. I'm told she's in critical but stable condition. Except she's in a coma."

"A coma?"

"So we're told. We don't want to appear too interested. She's getting good care. If she wakes, we'll deal with it."

"You mean when she wakes."

Baxter handed Max a mug. "Of course. My mistake."

"Jane Doe? What does that mean? And do you have anything stronger?"

Baxter rummaged in a cupboard and found a green bottle containing a brown liquid and poured them both a finger in odd, bulbous-shaped glasses that resembled snifters but were smaller. "They use that name when the person is unknown. She was found with no identification. Her prints weren't in any databases. Facial recognition turned up nothing. We, of course, kept our mouths shut, for now. Eventually, they'll get it out to Interpol, at which time it might get picked up by the Russians, and someone might put two and two together."

Max held up the glass. "What's with this?"

"It's what the Scots use. Supposed to help it taste better."

Max sipped and grimaced. "It's not working. Tastes like someone dumped some soil and a dead fish in the barrel. Got any bourbon around here?"

"Tom the groundskeeper is Scotch-Irish and a dyed-in-the-wool Scotch drinker. This is eighteen-year-old Laphroaig. Wins all kinds of awards. Don't let him hear you disparaging it—or his little glasses." Baxter fell into one of the rickety reed-seated chairs that surrounded the butcher block table and leaned his head back. "Now about Kate."

"You can debrief her to your heart's content."

"Give me a synopsis."

Max tasted the Scotch again and resisted the urge to spit it out. "My father is playing games. He's jerking everyone around from the grave. He hypnotized Kate to hide some message but didn't give many details. Everyone thought Kate had the answers to some great mystery. Turns out, there wasn't much there."

Baxter's eyes narrowed. "What good does it do you or your father's mission—whatever that is—if there is no action you can take from what he stuffed into her head? Unless you're holding something back."

The alcohol warmed Max's throat and stomach. "Interview her to your heart's content. You'll see."

The MI6 agent seemed to accept that. "This komersortium—"

"Komissariat," Max corrected. "The group's full name is komissariat for the Preservation of the State. Best we know is it's a secret organization of men who wield power over the Russian government."

Baxter scratched his chin. "Sort of like a shadow government?"

"I guess."

The MI6 agent grunted. "So the komissariat must be the source of the real power over the consortium councils. Somehow, your father got himself sideways with these komissariat people, which must be where the death sentence originated. Knowing your father like we do, and seeing how he led you along a path, there has to be more. Either there is additional information in her head, or there's a clue in what she said. Some clue that only you could pick up on. Something coded for your ears only."

Max shrugged. "Trust me, I've gone over her message word by word, and I don't see anything. Perhaps you guys can discern something I can't."

The older MI6 man leaned back in his chair to the point where the chair's spindly legs might shatter under his weight. "Your father probably made it so only you can figure it out." They drank in silence until the front legs of Baxter's chair hit the floor. "We'll find out tomorrow."

———

The farmhouse drifted into silence as the housekeeping duo closed the kitchen and retired to their room. Alex slept in a tiny bedroom on the second floor, and Max passed out on a couch in a second-floor alcove. Baxter had his own room at the far end of the hallway. In the morning, a large MI6 team was due to descend on the sprawling farm grounds and set up audio and video equipment in preparation for Kate's debrief. Outside, pairs of Special Air Service men with automatic weapons patrolled the orchard's perimeter.

Kate cast a watchful eye over Spencer while she made preparations using her Blackphone. Strong painkillers put Spencer into a deep enough sleep where Kate's restlessness didn't wake him. The two dogs dozed at the foot of the cot.

The bullet had penetrated Spencer's vastus lateralis, known as the quad muscle, in the front and had exited the biceps femoris longus, a long, thin muscle that ran from gluteus maximus to below the knee. No major arteries were harmed, and the MI6 doctor said that no nerve damage had occurred. Time would tell if he would make a full recovery.

I'm sorry to leave you behind, old friend.

Kate brought up a secure e-mail window on her phone where she accessed a message. The e-mail had arrived while they were over the Atlantic, and she read it a dozen times since. The sender was anonymous. The message was cryptic, and Kate knew its hidden meaning.

That the autumn season has begun is decided by the appearance of the red dragonfly.

The translated words came from an ancient Japanese haiku and were chosen for a specific purpose. The message triggered a set of instructions that had been planted in her mind years ago. The instructions were hidden there via a hypnosis technique employed by Andrei Asimov. They were commands she was unable to ignore.

This is it. The Vienna Archive is within reach.

After months of convalescence, it was time to get back to work. Everything they worked for over the past several years was on track, and it was time to go.

There was a lightness in her step as she finished her preparations. The Blackphone went into a small backpack along with a bottle of water and a change of clothes. She took no weapons; her travel would be easier without a gun.

Spencer's skin was clammy when she put her hand softly on his cheek. "Forgive me for leaving you behind." When she kissed his forehead, the skin was hot. "Get healthy, old friend."

She stole up the stairs to the alcove where Max dozed. The Belarusian was stretched out under a light wool blanket. His strong jawline and sculpted nose were handsome, but his appearance wasn't the attraction. It was his singular focus on protecting his family. *Is there a sexier trait?* She touched his arm, and as he awoke, his hand jerked to where he kept his gun when he slept.

"It's me," she whispered. "It's time."

He nodded and slid the gun back to his side. "Baxter will be livid."

"Can't be helped."

"Are you sure I can't go with you?"

Kate shook her head. "I must go alone. Besides, the code booklet doesn't do us any good without the message. You must find Andrei's original message."

"I know. I don't have to like it."

"Goodbye, Max. For now." She rose.

"Kate."

She turned back. "Yes, Max."

"Be careful."

She blew him a kiss and padded down the stairs.

After she shrugged on her down jacket, Kate hitched up the backpack and slipped from the room. At this hour, only the Special Air Service guard team night shift was awake. A stop in the kitchen to fill her pack with food. As the second hand touched the twelve mark on her watch, Kate slipped out the kitchen door into the moonless darkness, hugged the farmhouse for a dozen paces, and darted into the orchard. There she was but a shadow as she raced along a row of trees. When she got to the stone wall, she slipped over, gripped the shoulder straps of her backpack, lowered her head, and ran into the darkness.

––––––––

When the farmhouse woke to the aromas of fried eggs, bacon, tomatoes, and coffee, the missing guest wasn't noticed for the first hour. Alex, Max, and the dogs took a stroll through the barren orchard trees to survey the grounds. Baxter busied himself with final preparations for the interview. The housekeeper assumed Kate was sleeping in a second-floor guest room. Breakfast was served, the kitchen tidied, and showers were taken.

It wasn't until the MI6 team arrived from London and set up the video camera and audio equipment that someone asked about the interview subject. "Anyone seen Kate?"

The entire farmhouse was searched. The bedrooms were all empty, and her belongings were missing. Max took Alex on another circuit of the grounds and pretended to look for her. Callum Baxter's howls were heard as far as the outbuilding where the Special Air Service team scrambled to review security footage. It all turned up clean. Kate had vanished.

Max barely hid his grin when Baxter pounded his fist on the kitchen's massive farmhouse table. "You will make her available for this interview."

"I don't know what to say. Your guess—"

"You promised!"

"Well, to be entirely accurate, Kate promised."

The MI6 officer's curses echoed through the farmhouse while Max and Alex took the dogs out for another walk.

SIX

Somewhere North of the Caucasus Mountains

The dirt was dusty and frozen underfoot. What little vegetation once fought to grow on the wind-swept and frost-encrusted field had long given up. Mud, dirt, sticks, and trash from previous training exercises littered the ground and swirled in the wind. To call it a wasteland was to refer to it as a land and that gave it too much credit.

An early morning sky holding dark gray nimbostratus clouds stretched as far as the eye could see. The wind gusts bit into the bare skin of the one hundred soldiers gathered on the field. To the south lay the snow-capped peaks of the Caucasus Mountains with Mt. Elbrus towering above them all.

In the middle of the field stood a roaring bonfire which the soldiers built using wood and motor pool gasoline. The men had jogged to the training field over snow-dusted prairies from the compound's barracks five kilometers to the east.

Each soldier stood shirtless and wore their ragged training fatigues tucked into combat boots. They were all Caucasian, and each displayed an impressive physique with broad shoulders, rippling abdominals, and bulging biceps. Known as *Spetsnaz*, an abbreviation meaning Special Purposes Forces, they instilled fear in their enemies and awe among lesser soldiers.

The sergeant, also bare-chested and carrying a riding crop, led the company through a series of bodyweight movements that included hundreds of push-ups, sit-ups, and Russian twists. As he barked orders, the jagged scar on his face jumped and contorted.

The sergeant called a halt to the calisthenics and ordered the men to attention as a solitary runner arrived.

The runner was identical to the rest of the soldiers except for his age. His bare chest was broad and muscled, his arms strong and sinewy, his neck thick like a weight lifter's. The soldier's gray hair was cropped close, and his chiseled jaw was clean-shaven. No one knew his exact age, but his feats of strength were legendary, as were the challenges he issued to the men under his command. He was rarely bested, and those who beat him knew to keep their tongue. During such feats of strength, his status as a three-star general and director of the Russian military's intelligence directorate was forgotten.

When the leader spoke, his voice boomed out over the plains as if to challenge the icy winds blowing from the north. "Each of you has been handpicked by me to carry out the most delicate of missions. The future of the Russian Federation is in your capable hands."

General Ruslan Stepanov paused for effect. Each soldier stood at rigid attention, face forward. "Your job is to find and capture a single man. This man is a traitor to this country. He is a dog that must not be allowed to walk this earth. He sold himself and our secrets to the West. He turned his back on Mother Russia, and now he helps our mortal enemies. He is the lowest form of life on the planet."

A murmur sounded from the company.

The sergeant took a step forward. "Silence!"

Stepanov felt the adrenaline oozing from his men's pores like a bear's breath in a cold mountain dawn. He stepped closer to the rank and file, hands clasped behind him, and strode along the front rank with his face inches from the warriors' faces while he barked. "This is what you've been training for. This is the moment of truth. The moment where you get to test yourself against one of the best."

A loud boo sounded from the team. The sergeant reared up to bellow another order, but Stepanov silenced him with a short hand wave. The men's enthusiasm was appreciated.

The general strode along the second row of the formation. "Make no mistake. Your target is one of the best the Soviet Union has ever produced. He instills terror in the hearts of his adversaries. He takes life without hesitation and gives no quarter. He is a machine, a man without conscience, born and bred to kill and survive. No man has more records at the KGB institute than your target. This man, a son of Mother Russia, has turned his back on us, and now, we must put him down like the dog he is!"

Ruslan coveted these moments with his troops, walking among the men who did the fighting, the toughest men on the planet. He breathed deep and took their air into his lungs. He smelled the scent of war among their perspiration and he savored it.

"Shortly each of you will be given your orders. Some will go to the West to hunt this man. Others will be stationed throughout Europe in small strike teams, ready to be called upon at a moment's notice."

He turned and strode along the company's third rank. The men's eyes blazed with hatred and fury. In Russia, loyalty was valued higher than all other traits. It was the Russians against the world, and traitors were not suffered.

"When you find this man—and I know you will find him—do not hesitate to capture him, even in unfavorable circumstances. The man or men responsible for finding and taking this traitor will be rewarded. Your families will become wealthy, and you will be promoted to a rank worthy of your skill in the field and your ability to command."

Cheers erupted.

Stepanov put out his palm facedown. "One thing must remain in the forefront of your minds. Something more important than all else."

The cheering quieted, and each man focused on their general.

"You must take him alive. This man possesses intelligence, and we must learn what he knows."

The silence of the steppe was interrupted by whistling wind.

"Now give me a ura!" Ruslan bellowed.

Each man raised his fist in the air and in unison shouted, "Ura!"

After he returned to the front of the company, Ruslan barked at the sergeant. "Sergeant Dikov! Prepare the test."

Sergeant Egor Dikov bellowed orders. Several men moved to the bonfire while the others formed a ragged circle. The general, his chest out, walked to the middle and squatted on his haunches.

Ruslan looked forward to this day all week. Known for his brutal personal workouts and for prescribing vicious training regimens for his troops, he took every chance to leave the bureaucratic confines of the Kremlin and his dilapidated GRU headquarters at Khodynka Airfield to join his warriors in training drills. He was a soldier's soldier and commanded godlike reverence from his men because he trained with them, ate among them, fought alongside them, and tested himself against them. While other Kremlin leaders watched their waistlines expand and their muscles go flaccid, Ruslan kept himself in top physical and mental shape. Because of this, his men would die for him, no questions asked.

The circle parted to let two of the largest Spetsnaz soldiers enter. With gloved hands, each plucked long metal poles from the bonfire and dunked them in a bucket of water, sending steam shooing into the air. The soldiers brandished the poles as they approached.

Ruslan stood and raised his arms to display scar tissue along his torso. He adopted a battle stance with fists in the air, held loosely, like a boxer waiting for the two soldiers to attack.

The fighters circled and wielded their smoking metal pipes. Despite Ruslan's rank and stature, the men would attack with the same ferocity expected of them in battle. Failure to do so meant weeks in the brig.

A red-hot pole thwacked into Ruslan's torso, and he took the pain without flinching. When the second bar hit him in the shoulder, he shook it off and glared at the two men. Whenever he found an opening, he landed a vicious jab or hook that shook his attacker to the bone. They exchanged blows, with strike after strike pummeling him in the side, back, and arms, until he decided they were done.

The next swing hurtled through thin air as Ruslan ducked, stepped in, and launched a right uppercut that hit the soldier in the jaw and sent him sprawling. The general pivoted on one foot, causing the second man's attack to glance off his deltoid. As the soldier regained his balance from the strike, Ruslan jabbed at the man's throat to put him on his knees and peppered punches to the face and neck. The soldier went to the dirt and pounded the ground with his fist to signal defeat.

Ruslan rose to confront the second attacker just as the man swung the iron pipe. He took the strike in his oblique, shifted his weight, and delivered a kick to the soldier's midriff. As the man sagged from the blow, Ruslan landed a series of punches on his neck and face. A roundhouse caught the soldier in the jaw and he dropped and hit the earth in a puff of dust.

"General Stepanov."

The circle of men parted to admit a soldier wearing a full-dress uniform in the Tsar's green. Broad, fit, grim-faced, and flat-nosed, the newcomer observed the melee with a stony face. Behind him was a green military vehicle with a red star emblazoned on its side. A junior aide stood at attention by the driver's side door. The newcomer was Lieutenant Colonel Artur Markov, an elite Spetsnaz turned black ops genius who oversaw the secretive Twelfth Directorate in Ruslan's department.

Markov saluted the general and the two men strolled away from the troops and held a whispered conversation.

"Sir, our source at the FSB confirms Sergei Fedorov holds Asimov's coded message."

Ruslan took Markov's arm. "That's excellent news."

"There's more, sir. The source also let us know that Fedorov has also uncovered the location of Asimov's one-time pad."

Ruslan's mouth curled into a snarl. "Blyat! I knew that

cowardly fuck was holding out on us. He's close to uncovering the location of the Vienna Archive."

Markov's face clouded. "If Comrade Fedorov finds the Vienna Archive first, his power will be unstoppable. He'll take over the council. The komissariat will make him number one!"

Ruslan put his hand on Markov's shoulder. "Calm yourself, Comrade Markov. This is the news I hoped for. He is playing right into our hands. I have a plan. We will kill two birds with one stone. Listen..." He whispered in Markov's ear at length until a smirk appeared on the colonel's face. "Aye, sir. Excellent plan, Comrade Stepanov. The necessary preparations will be made at once."

Leaving Sergeant Egor Dikov to finish with the men, Ruslan joined Markov and the driver in the vehicle, and the three men sped across the frigid plain in the direction of the hulking compound at the base of the distant mountains.

SEVEN

Paris, France

"Do we know her destination?" The question came from Julia Meier, who sat across the table.

"No," Goshawk said. "She's on the continent now. She's being very careful to watch her back. Heading generally east."

"Giving her that phone was a stroke of genius."

"I don't like it." Goshawk squinted at the woman sitting across the table.

"You don't have to like it," Julia said. "Much of what I do is distasteful, but there is purpose behind all of it." The older woman's silver hair was pulled back and held with a lacquer barrette.

The glass of white wine in front of Goshawk went untouched. "You're playing with fire. You know this, right? Max is not going to react well if he finds out."

Julia rolled her eyes. "Let me tell you a little story."

A senior officer with Germany's secret intelligence

agency known as the BND, Julia Meier was also Max's mother and Andrei Asimov's former lover. Goshawk crossed her arms. "It's your nickel. Take as much time as you want."

"Do you know the Bible tale of the twelve Israelite spies?"

When Goshawk remained silent, Julia continued. "After the Israelites were freed from ancient Egypt and were wandering around in the wilderness, Moses dispatched twelve Israelite chieftains to visit the land of Canaan. Canaan was to be the promised land as God had assured Abraham. Moses ordered these twelve men—in what is thought to be the first recorded account of spying—to evaluate the land for population, agriculture opportunities, military strength, civilization, and other attributes. Their mission was to assess their ability to conquer Canaan."

"The first fictional account, you mean?"

Julia waved her hand like she was shooing away a fruit fly. "Ten of the spies returned with a dour outlook. The land cannot be conquered or the land isn't worth conquering, they said. Two spies, however, brought back a positive outlook and urged Moses that Canaan could be taken. What do you think happened?"

Goshawk sipped her wine and peered around the café.

"The Israelites believed the majority. Because the Israelites refused to take the land offered to them by God, God doomed them to wander the wilderness for forty years. A plague struck down the ten disbelievers, while the two spies who believed—Joshua and Caleb—lived through the forty-year penance and entered the promised land. What's the moral of the story, Goshawk?"

The computer hacker shrugged. "If you're a spy, bring back the report your superiors want to hear?"

Julia leaned across the table. "Faith. Spying and the intelligence game require faith and utter devotion to those running the mission." After she tasted her wine, Julia managed a grin. "You'll tell me when Kate is inside Russia?"

Goshawk gave her a tight smile. "It's what you're paying me for."

Julia stood and slid a couple euros under the wineglass. "Sometimes the ends justify the means. You'll see. Besides, you don't think I'd screw over my own son, do you?"

———

Bath, England

Two days after Kate's disappearance from the farm, Max received an unexpected guest. A frigid wind blew from the north and brought sleet on his evening walk with Alex and the two dogs. When he entered the kitchen and stomped his feet on the mat to remove the slush, he was confronted by the last person he expected to see.

"Sir?" It was all Max could manage. *Why is the chief of Great Britain's Secret Intelligence Service here in the kitchen?* The cherry orchard was two hours from Vauxhall Cross in London, where MI6 made its headquarters.

The man known as C—short for chief—rose from the table where he talked with Baxter and shook his hand. Alex stood at Max's side. C bent over to get to eye level with Alex and engulfed the young man's hand in his own. "We're going to do everything we can to get your mother back to you in good health. Okay, son?"

Alex managed a nod and sniffled back a sob. "Thank you, sir."

Max sent the boy off with the dogs as the chief folded his bony body into a kitchen chair.

A bottle of clear liquid sat on the table. The MI6 men had glasses in front of them. C pushed a tumbler at Max. "I hear you're a whiskey man. Can't stand the stuff myself. Raised on gin." He uncorked the bottle and poured Max a finger. "Old family recipe. My brother is in the gin business."

C raised his tumbler and the three men clinked glasses.

Max sipped and tasted hints of juniper and persimmon.

C smiled. "What do you think?"

"It tastes like someone soaked a pine tree in a vat of vodka."

The chief's laughter echoed around the farmhouse as he refilled their glasses. "Is the orchard meeting your needs?"

Max avoided Baxter's stare. "Yes, sir. It's perfect."

"Stay as long as you like. Our agency came into possession of it years ago, and we converted it to a secure location for stashing people and holding clandestine meetings. It doesn't get much use this time of year. A tutor for Alex is on her way, and we're watching Mr. White's injuries closely."

"I'm in your debt, sir."

"Nonsense. It is we who are in your debt. You know better than anyone that the intelligence community doesn't do anything out of the graciousness of our hearts. We all have a calculus that we weigh. Pros, cons. Tit for tat. Quid pro quo. Do we understand each other?"

He wants something in return. "Perfectly, sir."

The chief was an angular man with a hawk-like nose and known for his sharp intellect and unwavering empathy for his people in the field. With bony fingers, he sloshed another measure of the gin into their glasses. "I need some-thing. And I'd appreciate it if we kept it between the three of us for now."

"Sounds intriguing."

"Every intelligence agency is looking for this Vienna Archive of yours."

"Mine, sir?"

"The Americans, the Germans, and the Chinese want it. The Israelis are also looking. The first agency to find it will uncover the largest treasure trove of foreign intelligence since Snowden leaked the NSA's secrets."

Max swirled his drink. "Do you believe this Vienna Archive thing exists?"

The chief tapped a bony finger against his glass so his ring struck the edge. "Either it exists or someone is playing the largest hoax in intelligence history. Every agency has teams of experts searching for it and is devoting vast sums of money to the hunt."

"When I find it, you want me to share it with MI6."

"I appreciate that about you, Mikhail. Your confidence." The chief tossed back his drink and glanced at Baxter, who was engrossed in his Blackberry. "No, that's not why I'm here. You're meant to find it. It was your father who hid it, after all, and you'll decide for yourself what to do with the archive. I hope you share it with us, but I'm not naive enough to think bribes will work. No, I'm here to make a personal request."

"Of course, anything."

The chief let out a deep sigh. "What I'm about to tell you is for your ears only. I'd like to think you and I have earned that level of trust."

"Me too, sir."

"Very good. One of my first successful operations as a

senior officer was when I recruited a source in Moscow. This was... back in the late '80s I think. The man was an odd bird. He wasn't Russian, but he had access to details that only someone placed high up in the Kremlin has. We thought he was a dangle, and for years he passed us a bunch of chicken feed that we figured was supplied by the KGB. We let him think the information was being used but we didn't put any stock in it." C gulped his gin and twirled the empty glass at eye level.

Maybe that's how you get warm gin down. Max took a big swallow and the gin caught in his throat. *Still bad.* He coughed to clear his throat. "What nationality was he?"

"Mongolian."

"I thought you were going to say Romanian or maybe Ukrainian."

"He was a source high up in the Mongolian Embassy staff in Moscow. Relations between those two countries has always been strong, although now that Mongolia is a democracy, Moscow bullies them about. Anyway, eventually things got interesting. The source sent us a small packet of material that wasn't exactly Kremlin specific."

Max arched his eyebrows. "They were consortium documents."

"You're catching on. Yes, and we didn't know what to make of the information. Years later, after a few more deliveries, we put it together. It was our first real inkling that the consortium even existed."

"Now you figure the documents were from the Vienna Archive."

"Quite right, that is our hypothesis. Fast forward, and years later we have a solid profile on the group, partly from our source's intel and also information you've been generous enough to provide."

Despite the taste, the gin warmed Max's mind. "Either this man got his hands on the Vienna Archive or the Vienna Archive owner was funneling documents to your source."

"Exactly. We don't know which."

"Is this source still providing you information?"

"No, and that's the thing. His last delivery was nine months ago. He was on a six-month delivery schedule and he missed the last one. We did some soft inquiries, and it turns out that he's in a Russian prison."

"He got caught. What's his name?"

"We know him as Badū Khan."

"Probably only a few Khans in Mongolia. What can I do, sir?"

"He's probably a lost cause. But watch out for him. If you run across him or any information about him, let me know. Call me directly." C handed him a card.

Max glanced at it and handed it back to him, to which C raised an eyebrow.

"I've memorized the number, sir," Max said.

"Right." C rose from the table and offered Max a hand. "He's somewhere in the Russian prison system. No one knows where. Just one name among hundreds of thousands of prisoners. If you catch wind of any information about him, please let me know."

Max nodded. "Of course, sir."

"I have to return to London tonight." With that, the head of Great Britain's Secret Intelligence Service left Max and Baxter with the half-full gin bottle.

———

The waiting was the hardest part. He waited to hear status on Arina's condition. He waited to hear from Kate. After

Max performed some futile research on his own, the name Badū Khan appeared nowhere. Calls to Goshawk, who normally did this kind of research for him, went unanswered.

With nothing else to do, he spent time with Alex. The youngster took a liking to Tom, the farm's caretaker and a former British Special Air Service captain. The three spent hours walking the grounds, and the older man taught Alex about the different tree varietals, how to harvest the cherries, and even how to evaluate the rootstock. As Max watched them, he tried not to think about how difficult it would be to raise the boy alone. *Don't die on me, Arina. Not sure I can do it by myself.*

He asked for, and was allowed, a bottle of Irish whiskey, which he shared with Spencer. The two men sat near the fire each night, savored the smooth liquor, and speculated about Kate. Spencer had turned melancholy and his wound had become septic, antibiotics were administered, and his IVs reinstated.

A skeleton crew of the MI6 team remained at the farm in case Kate reappeared. Cindy Wallace, Baxter's highly capable analyst, oversaw a small team that included Harris, another familiar face from MI6. Baxter stalked around the makeshift operations center setup in the farmhouse living room, ignored Max, tugged at his goatee, and performed hushed consultations with his staff. Baxter's staff kept to themselves and shared little with Max.

When the break came, it appeared in a way no one expected. Max sat with his feet on a folding table reading through an endless pile of GCHQ reports on the consortium while Baxter paced with his Blackberry glued to his ear. Spencer White reclined with his heavily wrapped thigh propped on a chair also reading from the stack of files. The

clacking of fingers on keyboards was interrupted by an exclamation from Harris. "Callum, a drop from Sable just arrived."

Max's chair legs hit the ground as he looked up from his
report. "Sable? Who is Sable?"

"Damn it, Harris." Baxter's eyebrows narrowed. "Sable
is classified."

The analyst's face turned red. "S-s-sorry, Callum."

Max walked to Harris's workstation. The word *drop*
and the code name *Sable* meant only one thing in the intelligence game. Sable was a source, and the source had
provided intelligence. "Harris, tell me about Sable."

The abashed young man glanced from Max to Baxter
and back again. "I-I-I don't think..."

Baxter put his hand up. "That source is classified,
Max."

Cindy was hunched over a laptop with her nose three
inches from the screen.

"She can't help you either." Baxter glowered. "Not this
time."

Max took a firm hold on Baxter's arm and guided the
senior MI6 man through the kitchen and out the door to the
orchard. The air was still, but the cold bit at his skin. "You
guys are working on something and I want to know what it
is. Cindy's team is assigned to work on the consortium.
Therefore, this source and the dropped intel is about the
consortium. I want to know what it is."

"Forget it."

"You don't deny Sable is relevant?"

"I'm not going to confirm or deny. You're here as C's
guest, damn it. If it were up to me—"

Spencer White appeared in the doorway. He leaned on
a cane with one hand and read from a thick dossier marked

confidential. "Sable. Code name for Lik Wang, Chairman of Sinopec, China Oil, known to be Number Four on the Council of Petroleum—"

"Not relevant, huh?" Max put his face inches from Baxter's nose. "You have a source on the consortium?"

"Where did you get that?" Baxter grabbed for the document.

Spencer eluded the MI6 officer's attempt. "It was in the stack you gave us to read." He read from the file. "Sable approached MI6 in Berlin by slipping a note to the British ambassador's driver while the ambassador attended Mass at St. Hedwig's Cathedral. The source indicated he had information regarding the Council of Petroleum and Natural Resources."

Anger pulsed in Max's forehead. "Were you planning on sharing this source with me?"

Baxter let out a sigh. "Come along. You might as well know." The MI6 officer led them into the house, where they gathered around a table. Baxter informed his team that Max and Spencer were to be read in on whatever information Sable passed in this recent drop.

Max toyed with his Zippo lighter and tried to make eye contact with Cindy, who avoided his glance. *Someone let that file slip to Spencer. This MI6 team isn't that careless.* "How long ago did Sable first make contact?"

Baxter pulled at his goatee. "Several months ago."

Max banged his fist on the table, which made computer gear jump. "You're telling me you've had a mole in the consortium for months and you didn't tell me?"

Baxter smirked. "Yes, that is indeed what I'm telling you."

"What other information did Wang pass along?"

Baxter grinned and crossed his arms over his chest. "That's classified."

Silence descended on the room as Max stared at Baxter. After a few minutes, the MI6 officer smiled. "Consider yourself lucky we have the source, and let's leave it at that. You're read into this communique from Sable, but you're not—and I want to be clear on this—read into our history with Sable. Are we clear?"

Max crossed his arms over his chest. "If I find out you're holding back anything that might help me and Alex, it will end badly for you. I promise you that."

Baxter shook his head and his smiled faded. "You're in no position to issue threats. Harris, give us your report on Sable's latest communication."

A renewed purpose replaced Max's anger. *MI6 has a source in the consortium. This is a huge break.*

Harris stood. "At 0900, we received a signal from Sable indicating he left a drop. One of ours in Berlin retrieved the message from the drop site. Inside was a microSD card taped to a piece of paper. Berlin station sent the contents to us electronically and couriered the original to Vauxhall Cross in the pouch."

Baxter tapped the table with a fingernail. "Skip the bloody details, Harris. What was in the message?"

"Sorry, sir. The microSD card contained a dozen images along with a note. Here are the pictures." After a couple mouse clicks, an image appeared on a monitor on the wall.

The picture was of a balding middle-aged man in a blue suit and red tie with a triangular face in a sickly pallor. He was hunched at the shoulders and gesturing in a wood-paneled conference room full of similarly attired white men.

"Is that who I think it is?" Baxter muttered.

Harris moved the mouse. "I can run it through facial recognition."

"Don't bother," Max said. "That's Sergei Fedorov. Director of the FSB."

"And Number Seven on the consortium," Cindy said.

Harris clicked a few more times, and the monitors showed a series of blueprints and pictures of a large and opulent ski chalet tucked into the side of a tree-covered mountain. The home was six stories in height and supported by gigantic pillars. Warm lights shrouded the chalet in yellow, and three decks offered occupants impressive views of the ski resort. A map with topographic contours and a half-dozen satellite images of the terrain accompanied the pictures.

"Where is that?" Baxter asked.

"That's Courchevel," Cindy said. "A ski resort in the French Alps."

Baxter paced and tugged his goatee. "How did the CEO of a Chinese gas company procure this kind of detail from the ultra-secretive consortium?"

Cindy's fingers punched at the keyboard. "The head of China's Ministry of State Security—Zhao Zheng—is also on the consortium. Number Ten, if I recall correctly. Perhaps they're in cahoots."

"Perhaps. What's the message say?"

Harris summarized. "This communication is in response to our request for intel on the Vienna Archive. There is evidence that the FSB, Fedorov specifically, has the encoded message in his possession."

Max stood and shouted. "So that's what your operation is, the Vienna Archive? And you didn't—"

Baxter raised a palm. "We didn't know this message was specific to the Vienna Archive."

Cindy stood and clapped her hands. "People. Calm down. You can yell at each other later. For now, let's focus. Harris, keep reading." The din in the room faded.

Harris finished his summary. "Fedorov owns the chalet through a number of intermediaries and shell corporations. It's only a stone's throw from the ski resort. He likes to spend two weeks there over the holidays. The note contains guard rotation details and Fedorov's travel schedule. It's all here. Everything someone would need to break into Fedorov's ski chalet."

Max stood and walked to the door. "And that's precisely what I'm going to do."

EIGHT

Courchevel, France

Dressed in a black formfitting down jacket, boots that gripped the ice, and insulated alpine pants, Max made good time along the snow-packed road. Under his coat was nestled an MI6-provided SIG Sauer pistol kitted with a silencer. Leather gloves warmed his hands. A black wool cap was pulled tight over his head. A hard-sided case containing an XAR Invicta folding assault rifle was in his backpack.

The fact that Baxter got this operation through C at MI6—to perform a clandestine operation on French soil—spoke to Secret Service's priority to locate the Vienna Archive. Regardless, MI6 would deny his existence if he was caught.

Puffs of vapor escaped his mouth as Max hiked up the dark and empty road. Scots pines towered like walls on either side of the snow-packed track, and the snow glowed white in the moonlight. His boots made scrunching sounds as he walked. Nothing stirred save for the tree branches waving in a gentle breeze.

As he walked, he thought about his nephew. If Arina died, who would take care of the boy? It was one thing to toss the ball and show him how to ride a quad. It was another to be the sole parent. *Can I do that? Do I have it in me?*

The road curved and climbed up the side of the mountain. Hidden behind the rows of trees and nestled into nooks along the cliff edge were the mansions of the super wealthy. The titans of European industry, descendants of royalty, and scions of oil fortunes maintained second, third, or fourth homes here in the playground of the superrich. The palatial homes resembled small castles designed like chateaus and were spaced out on multi-acre plots so as to not encroach on their neighbors. Access was either by helicopter or long, winding driveways that crawled up steep inclines. Some of the mansions were perched on the edges of cliffs, while others were nestled in protective valleys where the cold air pooled. Max's destination was a home called Le Pettit that offered a spectacular view of the valley while clinging to a rocky outcropping. The home's name was ironic given its gargantuan size.

His thoughts turned to Kate. His father had some role for Kate to play, and time would reveal his old man's plans. How Andrei continued to pull strings from the grave was both frustrating and impressive. *Was she okay?* He pushed thoughts of Kate and Alex from his mind and focused on the mission.

The mansion's soft yellow lights were visible far ahead and above, and once more he reviewed the floor plans he memorized back at the orchard. The home was six stories high, and decks hung from each level. Tall windows lined the front. An open-air swimming pool was on the roof. A four-car garage. Inside a glassed atrium was a second pool and a full spa with steam and sauna. There were ten bedrooms, two offices, a separate but connected guest house, and servants' quarters. Two kitchens, one for the staff and one for the owners. The interior was full of leather, chrome, bearskin rugs, wool throws, exposed wooden beams, and modern appliances. The main living area, a wide-open room with cathedral ceilings and wrought iron chandeliers, was dominated by a gargantuan stone fireplace complete with stone chimney. Stuffed animal heads, of course, hung on the walls. And somewhere in the home was the FSB director, a phalanx of security, and a tiny booklet with his father's message.

A message meant for me.

A roadblock with four parka-wearing FSB security personnel was a kilometer ahead and barred the driveway. Armed guards wearing night-vision goggles manned the various decks and porches of the house. Luckily for Max, the FSB security team relied on the harsh climate and unforgiving geography to provide a natural barrier around the house, which left him free to approach undetected on foot through the rocky forest.

Before he came within direct eyesight of the roadblock, Max ducked off the road, slipped on a pair of folding snowshoes, and set off cross-country. Except it wasn't really cross-country. It was more like winter mountaineering. The terrain suddenly angled upward, so Max used the scrub and foliage for balance as he scrambled through rocks and trees. The snowshoes were compact and flexible with sharp spikes made specifically for backcountry exploration. He made good time and relished the endorphins that resulted from the steady exercise. Soon he was coated in a light sheen of sweat.

He bumped to a stop against the rough granite of a cliff and consulted a handheld GPS device. Right where he should be. His watch showed midnight on the dot. Max toggled his comms and reported in his location. In place of the snowshoes, he attached crampons to his boots and climbed up the rock face. Far above were the stout foundations and pillars that supported the massive home.

The climb was rated a 5.8, he guessed. Steeply angled yet not quite vertical. The granite offered dozens of crags and cracks and tiny ledges for his fingers and plenty of snow and ice for his crampon spikes to sink into. No rope required. It was years since he had done any real rock climbing, but his muscle memory returned easily as he used his legs to propel himself up, relied on his core muscles for stability, and saved his fingers and forearm strength for balance.

Don't look down. The forced concentration resulted in a meditative state that allowed him to forget his worry over Alex's future and Kate's status.

As he moved higher, the ground underneath him sank into blackness. Above was silence—and the man he was here to kill.

Sergei Fedorov, Number Seven on the consortium, and the director of the Russian FSB. A man who had the ear of the Russian president and commanded an estimated two hundred thousand operatives, administrators, functionaries, and spies. A man with immense wealth generated through a vast criminal enterprise. A man whose job it was to keep the Russian president in power.

Focus on the climb. Clear your mind.

Two more heaves upward and he found a resting spot

next to a massive pylon affixed to a concrete foundation. Four stories above was a small deck that jutted from the main building. The crampons slid off and went into the backpack. The assault rifle came out of its case and he snapped it together before screwing on a short silencer. He slung it over his back and wiggled into a harness, affixed a Cynch-Lok around the wooden column, and climbed up the pole.

The open valley yawned below as he cinched up the thirty-meter column. He ignored the height and concentrated on the deck platform above, where a man was on patrol with a shotgun. Lik Wang's intel had been surprisingly specific. Four guards at the roadblock below. One guard on this deck. Three others on three separate decks. Two on the roof. Four inside. A house staff of four, including Fedorov's secretary, two cooks, and a maid. All Russian. All loyal to the FSB director.

When he arrived at the deck overhang, Max let himself hang underneath the deck on the Cynch-Lok. His quads throbbed from the long climb. Wind whistled through the scrub, but otherwise there was silence. He wove thick black webbing over a crossbeam, clipped into the loop, and stowed the Cynch-Lok. He dangled in the air while he listened and waited for an opening.

A bird flapped its wings and took flight from a treetop, which sent snow spilling into the darkness. Max dipped a hand into his jacket and emerged with the SIG.

A footstep crunched over his head.

The snap of a lighter.

A waft of cigarette smoke.

Max hefted the silenced pistol.

NINE

Undisclosed Location

Security for that month's meeting was unprecedented even by the standards set by the Council of Petroleum and Natural Resources. Attendees surrendered their mobile phones, laptops, tablets, watches, and pens. Gorilla-sized men with blank faces and dark suits secured weapons in lockboxes. Wands were used for metal detection, and scanners were deployed to hunt for radio signals. Each council member stood in a wave scanner that produced clear images of his naked body, while security personnel did one last sweep of the council chambers for listening devices.

When the perturbed men finally assembled around the sprawling table, they waited for Ruslan Stepanov to appear. And they waited. Being forced to sit without a phone or a computer was agony. No one spoke.

Something felt off to Lik Wang as he surveyed the room. The sensation niggled at the back of his neck. It wasn't the recording device hidden in the signet ring on his pinky. He had used the ring to secretly document each consortium meeting for the last two years. Zhao Zheng, his fellow council member and colleague from China's Ministry of State Security, assured him the ring was impervious to detection by modern counter-surveillance technology. So far, Zheng's claims had held up. The ring had gone undetected.

No, it was something else. Despite the strict mandate that the meetings take place in person, one council member was permitted to attend this council session via video. The conference phone and video monitor on the table violated every known security precaution. The departure from their standard procedures cast a pall over the room and distracted the men from the other elephant in the room—the five empty chairs, each one a reminder that the Russian assassin still hunted them.

Their chancellor, Nikita Ivanov, was missing and presumed dead. Everyone expected Ruslan Stepanov, Number Two, to assume the council's chancellorship. Andrey Pavlova, Number Three, had disappeared several weeks ago, and everyone figured he was killed by the Russian assassin. He, Lik Wang, occupied the fourth chair, and for a moment, Wang fantasized about the power he would inherit if Ruslan failed to walk through those tall double doors.

Chair five was recently vacated by Russian Army Major Spartak Polzin, who was killed by the assassin in the Turkish desert. Leoniod Petrov, the head of Rosneft, Russia's largest oil company, sat in chair six. Petrov, the classic Russian oligarch, filled out a ridiculously expensive Brioni Vanquish suit with his muscled shoulders.

Chair seven, reserved for Sergei Fedorov, Russia's FSB director, was empty, but an LCD monitor on a stand showed Fedorov's head and shoulders. Clad in a dark suit and red tie, the stoic Russian spymaster smiled as he sipped from a glass of burgundy.

Artur Pipenko, a bookish man of seventy and the head of Ukraine's largest oil and gas producer, sat in seat eight. Beads of sweat glistened on his forehead. Seat nine had sat empty for months. In seat ten sat Zhao Zheng, the man who blackmailed Wang to wear the recording ring. Zheng wore a perpetual dead stare, like he cared about nothing. Seat eleven was recently vacated by Victor Dedov, who was blown to pieces by the same bomb that took down Ivanov. In seat twelve sat the Latvian banker named Erich Stasko. Stasko, the newest and youngest member of the council, fidgeted with the end of his tie.

When the massive double doors finally banged opened, Lik Wang flinched as the imposing Ruslan Stepanov entered. The doors slammed shut and the table shook. As Stepanov strode to the head of the table, shimmers of light reflected off rows of medals and ribbons pinned to his uniform breast. The three gold stars representing his rank on his epaulets glittered in the light from the overhead chandelier. The three-star general leaned on the edge of the conference table with his knuckles and surveyed the men.

Stasko let go of his tie and tapped his finger against the side of the table. Pipenko dabbed at his brow with a hand-kerchief. Fedorov set his wineglass on a table and checked his watch.

Ruslan Stepanov glared at each council member one by one before he spoke. "By the language laid out in section two, subsection five, part B of the council's charter, and rati-fied by the komissariat for the Preservation of the State, I hereby take control of the Council of Petroleum and Natural Resources. As per part C of the same section and subsection, does anyone dissent to my chancellorship? Speak now or forever remain silent."

If a mouse had scurried across the wood floor, the sound would have rung in their ears. Stasko's finger became still. Fedorov smiled into the monitor, reached off camera, and brought a bottle into view, from which he poured wine into his burgundy glass.

The general's gaze circulated around the table again. When the general got to Wang, the Chinese executive returned the stare with a steady look. Cold, gray, and unwavering, the general's eyes probed into Wang's soul. *He won't guess.* Wang held the stare until it shifted to the next man. The room remained still as Stepanov made another tour with his eyes.

Until Fedorov spoke through the monitor.

"Comrade General Stepanov."

A gulp from someone reverberated around the stone walls and Wang guessed it was Stasko.

Stepanov turned to face the screen and crossed his arms.

This won't end well for Fedorov.

On the monitor, the director of Russia's main spy agency slipped his hand into his jacket pocket, removed a flat item in a small plastic cover, and set it on the table in front of him. "Before you slide into that seat, you need to outline your plan to regain the Vienna Archive and eliminate Mikhail Asimov. The man with the best plan deserves to be the head of this council."

Stepanov touched his fingers to his chin and nodded. "Comrade Sergei Fedorov speaks wisely. Indeed, the biggest danger to our existence is the risk that the Vienna Archive becomes public. I dare say this threat poses a graver danger than the lone rogue assassin. I assume, Comrade Fedorov, that you have a plan to offer?"

Fedorov caressed the stem of his wineglass. "Will you submit, Comrade General, to a vote by the remaining seven consortium members? I will outline my plan, and you will do the same. Once both plans are on the table, a simple majority vote will determine who sits in the number one seat."

"This is a fair request." Stepanov sat and crossed one leg over the other. "I will submit, Comrade Sergei Fedorov. Please proceed with your plan."

TEN

Courchevel, France

Boots crunched in the snow when the guard stepped away from the railing. A shower of sparks launched through the air as the man flicked his cigarette into the darkness. Max tracked the footsteps as they trudged to the other side of the deck.

With a push off the wooden column, Max swung himself out over the abyss and caught the edge of the balcony with one hand so he had a view of the far end of the deck. The pistol was in his other hand. The shadow of a man leaned on the wooden railing. The shadow's head whipped around, and a rifle appeared.

Max pulled the trigger twice and twin slugs pounded into the guard's throat. The shadow fell to the deck with a thump. With the pistol clenched in his teeth, Max vaulted over the railing and crouched on the deck.

Nothing stirred. The room on the other side of the black windows was empty. According to the blueprints, this was a guest bedroom. Max crossed the icy planks in a crouch and jiggled the sliding door's handle. Locked tight. A quick search of the dead guard revealed a set of keys that opened the slider. Damp warmth that smelled faintly of eucalyptus washed over Max as he entered the house.

Max pulled the dead guard by the feet into the bedroom and rolled him under the bed. Before he closed the door, he scuffed his feet in the snow to disguise the trough made by the body.

According to Lik Wang's intel, the guards rotated hourly, which meant he had twenty minutes to search the house before another guard might find the dead man. Three strides took him across the plush carpet, where he used the SIG's silencer to edge open the door. Nothing but a dark hallway.

With the pistol in both hands, he stole down the corridor and up a set of stairs.

A toilet flushed, so Max ducked into a darkened room, where he crouched, waited, and watched. Water rushed into a sink and a door cracked open, spilling light into the hallway. A man with stubble flecked with gray and wearing a pistol strapped to his waist stepped into the hallway and killed the bathroom light.

Max shot him twice with the silenced pistol. After a frisk uncovered only a money clip filled with euros, Max pulled the body into the bathroom and closed the door. A search of the rest of the floor yielded nothing.

On the way up a flight of stairs, he stopped midway when he heard voices. The sounds were faint and he was too far away to make out the words. He glanced at his watch. Eight minutes burned.

He continued up the stairs and entered Fedorov's living quarters, which included a lavish bedroom and en suite bathroom, a well-appointed office, a workout facility loaded with the latest exercise devices, and a passage leading to a snow-rimmed outdoor jacuzzi. No one was about.

The next set of stairs landed him in the servants' quarters, where the drone of voices was louder. A bedroom door was closed where the chef and his wife slept. The smell of onions was strong in the industrial kitchen. An empty wine bottle sat on a stainless-steel prep table. He crossed the kitchen to a narrow stairway used by the staff.

Here the voices were clearer, and they filtered down from the room above. One belonged to a man Max recognized as Sergei Fedorov. The second voice blared from a speakerphone. He caught a word here and there but nothing that comprised a sentence.

Floor plans provided by Wang indicated these stairs led to the home's main floor, which contained another kitchen for the owner's use and an open living area.

Max crept up the steps, one by one, careful to test each wooden plank before he put his full weight on it. A warm light shone from the room above. The voices became distinct as he made his way up. A wrought iron railing guarded the servants' stairway. As his head approached even with the flooring, he stopped and peered through the black metal slats.

A cathedral ceiling rose over the room above, supported by thick wooden beams and trusses, and a plush living space extended to his right. A clean and modern kitchen was to his left. Two massive double doors made of stout wood were on the far side of the room. A fire flickered in a huge stone hearth, sending shadows moving along the walls. Near the fire, on a wide leather settee, was a young woman with flowing red hair and porcelain skin who nursed a glass of wine. At the head of a massive oak table sat Sergei

Fedorov, director of Russia's notorious spy organization, the FSB.

Fedorov wore a crisp wool suit and sat with one leg crossed over the other and his hands clasped over his stomach. A cigarette rested in an ashtray, its smoke curling into the air. In front of him on the table was a laptop and a speakerphone.

Max raised the pistol and took a step, but Fedorov's voice stopped him cold.

———

Lik Wang tried to catch Zheng's eye, but the furtive head of China's Ministry of State Security stared at the monitor where Sergei Fedorov prepared to present his plan to find the Vienna Archive and capture the Russian assassin.

The FSB director smiled and steepled his fingers. "As we all know, gentlemen, before Andrei Asimov was killed, he managed to squirrel away thousands of documents detailing the operations and management of this group and our associated councils. This is the true threat to our organization and our livelihoods. Yes, we know Asimov's son is out there slowly reducing our numbers. But let's face it, despite the threat to our individual selves, the council will last into perpetuity even if we all die. Others will simply replace us."

Murmurs spread around the room.

"It's a hard truth to hear, gentlemen, but it's the truth nonetheless. Besides, who can blame the young Asimov? If you knew someone was out to eliminate your family, who can say what actions each of us might take? We trained the attack dog, and now we're surprised when the dog attacks." Fedorov chuckled. "Which is why we need to eliminate the true threat and recover the Vienna Archive. The exposure of that cache of documents will doom this entire organization. As many of you know, I have vast resources at my disposal. The FSB has operatives in every country, moles at the highest levels of our adversary's intelligence agencies. Through such a wide and comprehensive intelligence apparatus, we have come to know several things. First, we confirmed the so-called Vienna Archive exists."

The banker in seat twelve groaned, and Petrov muttered something under his breath.

Fedorov raised a hand. "Second, we know the archive is well hidden. It is secured by a series of hand-coded documents separated and hidden by Andrei Asimov himself. Third, we know many agencies, including MI6, the CIA, the Germans, and probably others, are actively searching for the cache. If any of them find it before we do, it will mean the end of our existence as we know it."

All the heads in the cavernous room nodded except for Stepanov's. The three-star general examined his fingers.

Compelling, thought Wang. *But why does Stepanov look so smug?*

Ruslan Stepanov removed a small knife from his pocket and cleaned under a fingernail. "Is there a plan somewhere in this monologue?"

Fedorov tasted his wine and set the glass down. "Before Andrei Asimov died, we now know he encoded a secret message to his son indicating the location of these files. Knowing Andrei as we do, it's no surprise he made this secret message using an old-fashioned, but extremely secure, technique. It's called a one-time pad and uses a unique set of random characters to make the encrypted message." The FSB director held up the small plastic package he removed earlier from his jacket. "To decode the message, all you need is the encoded note" —he waved the item in the plastic bag— "and the correct one-time pad to decrypt the message. I'm happy to report that the FSB's field operators have uncovered the original message and I have it here in my hand."

Several consortium members grinned and nodded their heads.

"There's more." Fedorov raised his eyebrows. "My team knows where the one-time pad necessary to decode the message is located. It's only a matter of time before the FSB uncovers the Vienna Archive, thus removing the threat to our very existence. Instead of a plan, gentlemen, I submit to you this operation, which is already underway."

———

When Fedorov was finished, Max peeked through the railing again. The FSB director and the woman were the only occupants of the massive living area.

A slow clapping came through the speakerphone.

This Vienna Archive thing is real. Fedorov has his father's original message that shows its location. And he knows where the one-time pad is to decode the message.

Max leapt up the stairs and burst into the room.

ELEVEN

Undisclosed Location

Lik Wang crossed one leg over the other. *This is getting interesting. Fedorov has the upper hand. Unless Stepanov has a better plan, it appears Fedorov is their new chancellor.*

At the head of the massive table, Ruslan Stepanov stood, slipped the pen knife into his pocket, and clapped. The applause was slow, and each clap echoed off the thick overhead beams.

"Bravo," Stepanov called out. "Bravo, Comrade Sergei Fedorov. You appear to have a solid plan. I commend you for recovering Andrei Asimov's message and learning the location of the code booklet. I would consider yielding to your plan, except you forgot one very important thing."

"Why don't you enlighten me, General."

Ruslan Stepanov removed a small satellite phone from his pocket. A lit green LED indicated the phone was active as he spoke into the device. "You may proceed."

Stasko put his hands on the table. Pipenko clutched his

handkerchief with white knuckles. On the monitor, Fedorov's eyes narrowed to slits.

An explosion sounded through the audio feed, and a bright light flashed on the screen. Sergei Fedorov's hair blew back. The LCD went black.

———

Max burst from the stairs and sprinted to the table with his pistol pointed at Fedorov. "The call's over, Fedorov." But his words were drowned out by an explosion that originated from the large wooden double doors.

The redheaded woman screamed as splinters of wood flew through the air and the wineglass in her hand shattered.

A concussion wave hit Max and blew him sideways.

Canisters rolled into the room and spewed smoke that billowed in dark gray clouds. Four commandos wearing gas masks sprinted through the front door while red laser sights danced through the smoke.

Max picked himself off the floor. The smoke rolled at him, and a searing pain filled his throat. Although stunned, his limbs were intact. *The stairs.* He launched himself into the stairwell that led to the servants' quarters. The wind went out of him as he thumped on a step and stopped halfway down. Somehow, he managed to hold on to the gun.

Had they seen him?

Bootsteps sounded above. A yell of pain. Grunts and exclamations in Russian. A scream and the crack of a palm on a cheek.

"Do you know who I—"

A fist thumped on skin and silenced the protest.

Max counted four commandos. Once they tied up Fedorov and the girl, two soldiers would be sent to search the rest of the house. *Time to hide.* He backed down the remaining stairs and into the servants' kitchen, his pistol held up, as his mind raced through his options.

Exfiltrate now and any hope of gaining intel or recovering the message was out the window. Four trained commandos were an overwhelming force, even with the advantage of surprise.

More Russian voices came from up the stairs.

"Clear." The room was clear of any threat.

"Secure." Both captives were handcuffed.

The next voice was vaguely familiar. "You two, search the rest of the house. Me and Fedorov here are going to have a little talk."

Footsteps pounded on the floor above.

Time to go. Max disappeared through a door, ran along a hallway, and took the carpeted steps down. As he ran, his mind spooled through the home's blueprints.

How thorough would the intruders be?

Footsteps behind him.

He made a hard left and entered a room with a wood plank floor containing two washing machines and two dryers, cupboards, ironing boards, and shelving packed with household goods. Behind wire shelves that held cookware and dishes, he found what he was searching for. Recessed into the wood was a handle, which he pulled to open a trapdoor. He jumped into the darkness and tugged the door closed behind him.

As his eyes grew accustomed to the gloom, he stooped to move through a crawl space. At the end, he emerged into a small storeroom where large plastic bins contained canned goods and tins of preserved food. A wooden ladder led up to another trapdoor, which Max opened a crack. No one was in the room above, so he went up the ladder and emerged into the servants' pantry. He had effectively flanked the two soldiers who searched the house.

When he exited the pantry and went into the kitchen, angry voices shouted from above.

"Whoever you are, you're making a grave mistake," Sergei Fedorov shouted.

"We're not. Shut your mouth or I'll shut it for you."

The familiar voice vexed Max. The name was there, hidden in his past, but on the edge of his mind. Many years ago, maybe his KGB training or early days in the Russian Army.

"Voice is active, sir. Working on the video feed now."

The commander addressed his hostage. "General Stepanov would like a word, Sergei."

"That figures," Fedorov growled. "Just like Stepanov to make such a crude move."

Static blared for a second as Ruslan Stepanov spoke over the speakerphone. "We've got the message, Sergei. Now we need the location of the one-time pad. Give us that and we'll let you go."

"Forget it. You're not letting me out of here alive, no matter what I do, so you can go fuck yourself."

The crack of a hand on flesh was followed by a piercing scream. "True, but what about your little redheaded friend here?" The sound of ripping clothes was followed by another scream.

Stepanov's voice crackled through the phone line. "Sergei, Sergei, my old comrade. Must we resort to such unpleasantness? We have Asimov's message. Now hand over the location of the one-time pad and we can all move on. As these men are my witness, I promise there will always be a place for you on the consortium."

"Go fuck yourself, Ruslan."

"So be it. Sergeant, please introduce our FSB friend to how we do things in the special forces."

A fist hit skin. Grunts and sobs mingled with the sounds of physical violence. A chair smashed. The woman screamed.

"We have plenty of time," Stepanov said through the phone. "I'm told all your men are dead. We'll get the information we want eventually. We have many days ahead of us, and you of all people should know what that means."

"Are you sure about that?" Fedorov's voice was low. In pain.

The soldiers must have heard it at the same time as Max. *Thwack, thwack, thwack.* Rotors pounding the air.

"Helicopters." It was one of the soldiers.

The FSB director laughed, which sounded like a gurgle from where Max stood at the bottom of the kitchen steps. "Too late, Stepanov," Fedorov said. "You're out of time. The minute you idiots barged in here, you tripped my remote alarm. Two dozen FSB operatives will have this place surrounded in less than five minutes."

Curses erupted through the phone. "Egor, get outta there," Stepanov yelled. "You know what to do."

Egor. That's it.

Footsteps in the hallway alerted Max, and he whirled to see two men in blue jeans and tactical vests toting assault rifles. The surprised men brought up their weapons as Max fired. One soldier fell into a prep table and sent metal cookware banging onto the floor. The suppressed pistol thumped again, and the second man pinwheeled backward and crashed into a stack of plates.

As the pandemonium in the kitchen died away, shots echoed from up the stairs where Fedorov was held captive. Shouts filtered down, and footsteps pounded on the stairs.

Max sprinted from the kitchen.

————

A soldier appeared at the end of the hallway and Max fired. The man crumpled to the floor. When he got to the spare bedroom where he hid the body of the guard under the bed, Max tore open the glass slider, stepped onto the deck, and vaulted up to the railing. As he balanced on the narrow barrier, he made a quick adjustment to his backpack and tightened the strap on the XAR so the rifle hugged his chest.

A command in Russian boomed from behind him. "Don't move." It was Ruslan Stepanov's team leader from upstairs. The familiar voice.

Max turned.

A hulking Russian with pale skin and a jagged scar along his jaw pointed a rifle at Max's chest. The soldier's gloved finger was steady on the trigger. Muscles rippled under the man's shirt, and a gold hoop pierced his left earlobe. "Step down from the railing, Asimov. It's better for everyone if I don't have to shoot you."

Egor Dikov.

"Hello, Egor," Max said. "Been a long time. Your face healed nicely." With a wink, Max stepped from the railing and plummeted into the dark emptiness.

————

Egor Dikov sprinted to the deck's edge. One foot went out from under him on the icy planking, but he caught himself on the railing. His rifle clanked against the wood as he righted himself.

Damn it.

Beyond the balcony, the darkness opened into empty space. Nothing there. No waving branches. No rocks or snow. And no Mikhail Asimov.

The Russian assassin was in his clutches and he let him go. Ruslan's orders to take Asimov alive caused him to hesitate. Egor pounded his fist on the railing as one of his men came up beside him to scan the darkness below.

"Where'd he go, boss?"

"How the fuck do I know?" Egor kicked at the snow. "Let's go. We need to get out of here."

The helicopter rotors were loud as Egor ran up the stairs, past his two dead men in the kitchen, and into the main room. Fedorov was slumped in his chair with a red hole in his forehead. The young woman lay sprawled on the leather couch, also with a bullet through her forehead. After he checked the two victims' pulses to ensure they were dead, Egor patted his pocket where the plastic-wrapped package was stowed. The successful mission to secure the document almost made up for missing Asimov.

Egor followed the soldier outside where his driver sat in an idling SUV. The men hung on while the vehicle sped through icy curves to put as much distance between them and the helicopters as possible. Egor stared into the darkness as they drove while visions of his past haunted him.

I've waited a long time for this, Asimov. It's only a matter of time.

————

The landing was bad. Worse than Max anticipated. The chute deployed perfectly, but a wicked cross draft blew him sideways into a strand of pines as he neared the landing zone. Branches ripped at the chute and his clothes and drew blood. A crushing pain coursed up his left arm when he hit a tree. Pine needles raked his face as he plummeted to the ground, which he hit with a force that knocked the wind from his lungs.

He gasped for breath as he crawled through the knee-deep snow to rest against the granite wall of the cliff. While he filled his lungs with air, he took stock. His left arm was limp, and pain radiated through his shoulder and into his spine. He rolled his head to crack his neck. His fingers worked well enough to find the tactical snowshoes in his pack, but it took a couple tries for his numb hands to get them affixed to his boots. When he stood, dull pain radiated from his left quad muscle. He shoved it from his mind as he placed one foot in front of the other.

No Spetsnaz unit would sit idle. Roadblocks would be set up around the perimeter, and soldiers would comb the woods in search of a black parachute. *Time to move.*

He skirted the open field, followed the tree line, and stopped next to the mark he had carved into a pine tree's bark. Hidden under a camouflage netting was a snowmobile. He cranked the starter and the 200-horsepower engine purred under mufflers modified to mask the roar. The pain in his thigh flared as he swung a leg over and nudged the machine into the field. He followed the tree line up a ridge and through a trail in the trees. After he sped over a dozen ski runs, the woods opened up to reveal a small lake and the tiny ski village of Le Praz, where he traded the snowmobile for a four-wheel drive SUV.

He held the SUV on the snowy road at a reasonable

speed and reached for a cigarette before he realized he had none. *Damn it.* The ache in his thigh, the hot poker in his arm, and the scrapes and bruises from the landing intensified the nicotine craving. He dug into his pocket and dry swallowed two little white pills to help the pain.

As he raced north, the events of the night consumed him. The consortium meeting where Stepanov asserted his authority. The commandos who broke in on Fedorov and stole the encoded message booklet.

Why had Lik Wang's intel directed Max to the chalet at the same time as Ruslan Stepanov sent a team to interrogate and kill Fedorov?

Coincidence?

Unlikely.

And how do I recover the message from Ruslan Stepanov, a Russian three-star general?

TWELVE

Somewhere in Russia

The lights winked out as the soft velvet hood slipped over Ruslan Stepanov's head. The grip that pinned his arms back was unyielding but not rough. Course rope was spun around his wrists and bound his arms behind him. A hand, firm but not aggressive, urged him to take a step, which he did.

In a twenty-five-year career distinguished by Red Army medals for feats of valor, operations that provided presidents and general secretaries with unprecedented military intelligence, and an unblemished record of political maneuvering in a cutthroat bureaucracy, Ruslan Stepanov, a three-star general, had not experienced the fear he felt now. Not in the hundreds of physical battles with men younger and stronger than himself. Not with numerous loaded pistols pointed at his head. Not during the countless waterboardings, electro-shock therapy, and other brutal training methods at the KGB academy. Not even when his late ex-wife held the razor-sharp chef's knife to his throat.

Nope.

The fear he experienced now was fear he had never known.

A sheen of perspiration covered his forehead, and his armpits were damp under his uniform jacket. The step he took was on a rubbery leg that threatened to pitch him to the ground. His bowels were watery and loose, and he concentrated on keeping his sphincter tight. *Lock it down, Ruslan. You may have to be carried out of here, but you will not soil yourself. Lock it down.*

The next two hours, if that was even the duration of time, were a blur of stumbling progress through endless corridors, a silent car ride characterized by the overpowering scent of Russian tobacco, and a humiliating strip search by an anonymous pair of latex gloves. He endured it all with a velour hood on his head. During the cavity search, when he was forced to relax his anus, he thought he might lose it. Ruslan Stepanov, the first incoming chancellor to be sworn in with feces running down his leg. Mercifully, his bowels held, and he was led along another series of carpeted hallways.

He knew they were carpeted because he was still naked, and the wool fibers were soft on his bare feet. The air was warm with a strong aroma of mildew and skunk, smells he associated with his late parents' home.

They had to be close. *Chest up, Ruslan. You are not a coward. You fear nothing. Not even these men, who can snuff out your life, the existence of your whole family, your lineage, with the sweep of a pen.*

The grip on his arm brought him to a halt. Two more hands grasped his bare shoulders. Abruptly, the hood was removed, and as the bright rays of yellow light pierced his retinas, he jammed his lids shut. Even with his eyes clenched, the bright light permeated his vision, and it was all he could do to concentrate on the booming voice that pierced his eardrums.

"Ruslan Stepanov! What brings you to the hall of the Bolshevik?"

What do I say? There had been no coaching. The disorientation from the long hours in the hood and the piercing lights had rendered him dumb.

"Ruslan Stepanov! Speak your piece or be gone with you."

The voice was amplified and disguised by a machine.

"Yes, yes. I'm here." Ruslan dug his thumbnail into his skin.

"We know you're here. We can see you. State your business with the komissariat!"

This hadn't started well. Was there required preparation no one had informed him about? Did he miss a memo? *Get yourself together.*

"Ruslan Stepanov, at your service," he bellowed in his most commanding voice. "I submit my application for Chancellorship of the Council of Petroleum and Natural Resources, subcouncil to the komissariat for Preservation of the State. Per komissariat bylaw twenty-three, subsection Roman numeral II, parts A and B, titled Succession of Chancellorship. The former chancellor has perished at the hands of the enemy, and the council remains leaderless."

His words hung in the air. Is this the end? Were his instincts wrong? Had he missed a step in his preparations? The silence dragged on and doubt crept in. Was a gun pointed at his head? Was he about to die? Greater men than he had appeared in front of this council, never to be seen again. His groin clenched, and gas roiled in his bowels. *Lock it down, goddamn it. Lock it down.*

"Ruslan Stepanov." The voice was softer but still mechanized.

The spotlight clicked off, and his vision was filled with black spots. Soft material caressed his skin as a robe was placed around his shoulders. There was a tug as a sash was tightened around his waist. His vision returned.

A great mahogany desk towered over his head like a judge's bench. He stood before it on a plush red shag rug, alone in a pool of pale light from overhead. The walls of the room were bathed in shadows. Two men sat at the bench while a third spot remained empty. Both men wore crimson robes, but Ruslan's legs went weak again at the sight of their masks.

The silver-gold iron of both masks glinted in the spotlight. Each mask had almond-shaped eye holes and an elaborately carved set of mustaches under a squat nose. The masks were attached to pointed helmets topped with a spike. A neck gaiter of chainmail hung from each mask and disappeared under the men's robes. A vision of one of the men rising and swinging a broad sword with two hands to separate his head from his neck flashed and disappeared.

"Indeed," the man sitting at the center position said, his voice hollow behind the mask. "Nikita Ivanov is dead. Or might as well be."

Ruslan let the voice die away, unsure of how to respond.

"You have distinguished yourself," said the voice. "The komissariat recognizes your leadership and your accomplishments, and your background has been sufficiently vetted. Your little operation against Comrade Sergei Fedorov was a stroke of genius. By the power vested in me, Kommissar for the Preservation of the State, presider over the council of three, I hereby promote you to the chancellor-ship of the Council of Petroleum and Natural Resources, subcouncil to the komissariat for Preservation of the State. The appointment is effective immediately."

With renewed confidence, Ruslan bowed slightly. "The honor is mine, and I humbly accept."

The robotic voice blared. "The petroleum council is in shambles." A chainmail-gloved fist hit the bench with a crack. "The Asimov boy has made us look like fools! Ivanov was weak."

With his hands clasped in front of him, Ruslan summoned more courage. "I agree," he shouted. "Ivanov made a mockery of things. Under my leadership—"

"Enough false bravado, General," the voice thundered. "Between Andrei Asimov's betrayal, Ivanov's ineptitude, and the Asimov boy's actions, our position in the world petroleum market is at risk, which puts the future of the komissariat at risk. Indeed, the balance of power on the world stage is at risk. It cannot continue!"

The robed figure at the center of the bench pounded on the desk again with a metal gauntlet. "The very existence of the council is at risk for the first time in one hundred years. A cancer grows in the core of our beautiful country, the same tumor that created that damned *perestroika*. The cities and towns of the hinterlands are rotting from corruption and crime. The world changes around us while we weaken. The younger generation want opportunities and jobs while the Russian president grows weak and our coffers grow smaller from the sanctions brought on with his reckless actions. He is losing his grip, growing older, weaker. The people want reforms." The masked man said the last word like he was spitting bile from his mouth.

Ruslan dropped his gaze to the carpet.

The man in the center chair rose to his feet, his red robes rustling and chainmail creaking. "The people of Russia must be placated to prevent another *glasnost*. It's no longer sufficient to trot out progressive candidates before threatening them with corruption charges. It's no longer enough to present a false strength to the world. This nation needs new leadership."

Ruslan lifted his head. "Yes, sir. I completely agree. How can I help?"

The voice rose an octave. "Now we are getting somewhere. When Andrei disappeared, he took with him a cache of information with the potential to wipe out everything we've built. Everything we stand for is at risk of crumbling before us."

"The Vienna Archive," Ruslan said.

"Records of our existence," the voice bellowed. "Minutes from our meetings, our financial transactions, member rosters. Documents outlining our operations, our structure, and even how we select members." The man under the chainmail and mask fell back in his chair as if exhausted from yelling. "He must be stopped, or we're all finished. Do you understand me?"

Does this man have all his faculties? The komissariat is presided over by a madman.

"To compound matters, we've learned through our contacts at the FSB that various intelligence agencies around the world, including the British and the Americans, are aware this cache of information exists. They've dubbed it the Vienna Archive." The last two words were spit out of his mouth. "Of all things."

Did he even hear what I said? "Sir, why Vienna? Is this a clue to its location?"

"If I knew, would I be here talking to you?"

"Of course not, sir."

"You have distinguished yourself by recovering Andrei Asimov's message that pinpoints the location of the archive. All that is left is to uncover the decoding booklet. The one-time pad. Are we clear?"

"Very clear, sir." Ruslan projected his voice. "I have a plan underway."

"I expected you might. And this Asimov boy?"

"One hundred of my best soldiers are ready to take him as soon as he surfaces."

"Excellent. One more requirement."

"Anything, sir."

"We need the Asimov boy alive. You may kill the rest of his family, but you must take Mikhail Asimov alive."

"Of course, sir. It will be done."

"You have thirty days. Thirty days before we wipe the slate clean and start over. Do I make myself clear?"

"Sir? Start over?"

"With a new chancellor!"

Sheer force of will allowed Ruslan to remain standing, and he managed to bow at the hips. As he straightened, the lights disappeared when the velour hood was draped over his head. Strong hands gripped his biceps and guided him from the room, through a door, and along a hallway. Eventually, he was stripped of the robe and forced to dress in his uniform without the benefit of sight. No words were spoken as he was led through more corridors and into a waiting car.

Thirty days to capture Asimov or I'm dead.

THIRTEEN

Vienna, Austria

Flurries swirled as Kate stepped through the transom of the small church outside the city's famous walking district. A fine blanket of snow coated the cobblestone sidewalk, the church tower, and the buttresses above, and dulled the noises of the city behind her. Her surveillance detection effort took hours, and as she stepped into the ambulatory the fatigue caught up with her.

The Blackphone buzzed in her pocket and she removed the device to see a message from Max.

Baxter is livid. Safe travels. Check in after Vienna.

She chuckled and typed a reply. *Baxter will get over it.*

The e-mail she received while at the cherry orchard gave her three possible dates and times for the meeting. Travel delays between England and Austria meant she missed the first two. Tonight was her last chance.

Inside, the church was blustery cold like someone had left the door open. Towering columns lined both sides of the nave, and a wide aisle threaded between rows of wooden pews. The high alter stood on a dais, and an intricately carved fan vault covered the ceiling far overhead. A stone baptismal font was in the corner, opposite an elaborately carved confessional. No candles were lit, but the smell of wax and incense was heavy. A check of her watch revealed it was the appointed time.

Kate circled the interior of the church. Seeing no one, she pulled aside the confessional's heavy velour curtain and stepped into the tiny enclosure. A faint musty odor and heavy incense assaulted her nostrils. As she sat on the oaken bench, she suddenly wished she had a weapon.

She didn't wait long. A scrape came from the other side of the confessional's wooden screen, followed by a long, choking cough. When the spasm was finished, hacking and spitting erupted. *I should have worn a mask.* "Everything okay over there?"

Fabric rustled and was accompanied by more sputtering until the confessional melted into silence. She peered through the wooden screen but saw no clues as to the other occupant. When the voice came, it was low and soft and muffled by the curtain, so she leaned closer to hear. "Do you have the code phrase?"

Kate repeated the phrase that appeared in the message she received while at the cherry orchard. "That the autumn season has begun is decided by the appearance of the red dragonfly."

"Thank you for coming, Kate."

"Are you going to tell me who you are?"

"If I planned to reveal myself, would we be meeting in a confessional?"

She bit back a retort and waited for the voice to continue.

Another long, hacking cough was followed by the sound of someone spitting. "Here is the message I've been asked to relay. Professor Leonhard Euler at Saint Petersburg State University has the one-time pad. Andrei Asimov gave it to him for safekeeping. You are to visit him at once. He will not know who you are. You are to give him this passphrase. I will only repeat it once. Are you ready?"

"I am."

"The red dragonfly exists because it exists and for no other reason."

"What's the significance of the red dragonfly?" Kate asked.

More coughing erupted from the other side of the screen before material rustled and a door clicked shut.

Kate was alone in the silence.

———

Goshawk's lacquered fingernails clacked on the keyboard as she typed out a brief message to her client, Julia Meier.

After a night at the Vienna Ritz-Carlton, subject made a stop at a church for ten minutes. Might be part of an SDR or she might have met someone or retrieved a dead drop. Subject currently on a train to Budapest.

Goshawk hit send and the encrypted e-mail system did its thing. When the notification system indicated the e-mail was sent, she padded into the kitchen and heated water for green tea. It was one of the many substances she used to calm her nerves. *The ends justify the means. You're right, bitch. But will you be happy with the end?*

———

France

The sway of the train jostled Max awake. A hint of euca-lyptus and orange petals caught his nostrils, and he blinked at the bright daylight. For a split second, the blue interior threw him.

Where am I?

It came back to him in a rush. He jumped on a train at Valence as part of the surveillance detection route after the botched operation in Fedorov's chalet. Stepanov has his father's message that shows the location of the Vienna Archive. To get to Stepanov, he needed Goshawk. *Time to figure out why Goshawk is avoiding my calls.* The train would deliver him to Paris in six hours.

The refreshing scents became overshadowed by the dull aches in his thigh, arm, and shoulder. He looked around while he flexed his muscles and rolled his head.

The source of the fragrance was a woman who sat across from him. Statuesque and poised, she radiated an aura common to runway models. It was the kind of air reserved for those told their beauty was rare enough to warrant enormous sums of compensation. A paperback was in her hand.

Up all night, in a gun battle, covered with mud and snowmelt, he didn't smell like a bed of roses. He inspected the woman from the corner of his eye.

Her long black hair was swept back and held under a wool beret. Full lips were painted dark red. High cheek-bones were punctuated with a pert nose, and her large eyes hinted of the Far East. Impossibly long lashes flicked with each blink as she read. An olive-skinned thigh peeked from under a wool skirt, and her wool overcoat was a color that matched the lips. Silky fingers capped with dark red polish held the paperback so the title was hidden. Young in age but aged in experience, her jaw was set in a mask cultivated to ward off public encroachment.

Outside his window, the French countryside flashed by. This close to the Mediterranean the fields were winter-brown and without snow. A memory appeared, and he drifted back in time. It was of one of his first operations after graduating from the KGB academy and took place in Warsaw in the middle of the winter. A lanky and ravishing brunette Russian woman with translucent white skin and a deep décolletage sat on a barstool in the Bristol Hotel toying with an olive-laden toothpick in a martini. Next to her stood a pudgy Londoner, martini in one hand, his other hand buried in the woman's lap, his wedding ring be damned. The Londoner was an unimportant man in an important firm on an unimportant business trip to Warsaw. The sting was a trial for both the woman and for Max, her handler.

Max had sat in a corner of the bar with a clear view of the woman and the Londoner. His job was to take notes on the woman's performance and to make sure she followed through with the job. He felt like a pimp, which he didn't much like, but he also didn't care. He was young, had something to prove, and wished it was his own hand buried between the woman's legs. *Ah, youth.*

It was a traditional honeypot operation, with the woman as the bait. The Londoner fell hook, line, and sinker. Two martinis ensured he followed her to a hotel room that was equipped with hidden video and sound equipment. Max sat in the next room and recorded the Londoner's grunts and bleats and plaintive attempts at pleasuring the young woman, who in turn played her part with boisterous gusto. Later he informed the Londoner that he was now owned by the KGB. It was a thrill to complete his first operation, even if the unimportant businessman never provided useful information to the KGB.

Even now, on this train, he savored the taste of that adrenaline rush back at the Bristol.

Is the woman in the wool beret a civilian or a trap?

His stomach rumbled.

Another glance at the woman, who now held the book so the title was visible. *Passage of the Red Dragonfly.* The book was unfamiliar to him.

What are the odds a beautiful woman randomly appeared in the seat next to him?

He left his seat in search of the dining car.

FOURTEEN

France

Outside the wind howled and snow swirled in the gusts. When Max got to the dining car, it was mostly empty. A couple paid their tab and left before a short, fat waiter wiped down the table. Max slid into a booth and sat with his back against the wall so he could watch the entire train car.

For the hundredth time, he reached for cigarettes. Old habits stick around. Instead, he removed the Zippo lighter from a pocket. The lighter was dinged and scratched with an aged patina from years tumbling around in pockets. Embossed on the outside was the red and green image of the Belarusian flag. The lighter was a keepsake from Max's grandfather, and it grounded him and reminded him of home. He ran his thumb over the ridges of the etched design and wondered if he'd ever see home again.

The door at the end of the train car slid open, and the woman with the wool beret sauntered in. After she stopped to scan the dining room's occupants, she walked up to Max's table. To his complete surprise, she shed her overcoat and slid in across from him.

"Buy a gal a glass of wine?"

Before Max could reply, the waiter approached wearing an apron wrapped around his large belly.

"Uh, a bottle of burgundy, please." Max also ordered two servings of a classic French stew with braised beef and carrot.

As the waiter departed, the woman folded one manicured hand over the other. "Can't smoke on trains in this country. Shame what's become of France."

Max shoved the lighter into his pocket. "I quit smoking. Can I help you with something?"

She shrugged. "Despite your, ahem, disheveled state, you look like a man accustomed to women inviting themselves to your table." The woman's French was perfect, except for a hint of an Eastern European accent.

"And how do you arrive at that conclusion?"

"Your actions betray you. You walk with purpose. You resemble a laborer, but even with the rips and stains, your labels are expensive. Behind the tussled appearance, intelligence simmers. You're dirty for a reason, and you can't wait to get to a shower and clean off the filth."

Alarm bells chimed.

"That's quite a profile you've worked up."

"You're an enigma, Mister..."

"Green. Jacob Green. At your service." Max extended a hand.

She pursed her lips and shook her head when she took his hand in a soft shake. "You don't look like a Jacob."

The waiter saved him by delivering the stew and pouring wine.

His stomach rumbled, so Max tore off a hunk of crusty bread and dug into the stew.

The woman watched with a bemused grin and toyed with her food.

When the stew was half gone, he slowed and wiped his mouth. "What do I look like?" He ripped off another piece of bread and slathered it with butter.

With pursed lips, she tilted her head. "I'd say Andrei, or—"

The bread was halfway to his mouth when he stopped.

The smile vanished from her face. "What is it? Did I say something wrong?"

"That's my father's name. Did you know my father?"

White teeth flashed as she smiled. "Nope. I guess you're Romanian. Andrei is the most popular male name in that country. Lucky, no?"

Watch it. Max dabbed another slice of bread with butter. "And you know this how?"

"I'm a writer. Well, I dabble. Nothing published. My protagonist is Romanian, and I almost named him Andrei."

"And what did you name him?"

Her eyebrows shot up. "My character? Why, I named him Gabriel instead."

"Gabriel. The archangel. Good name for a hero. And you are?"

"Gabrieli Rokva, at your service." Her glossy lips curved in the right places.

"I see." Max grinned. "Well, Gabrieli, it's my pleasure to make your acquaintance. Despite your excellent French, you are not French, dare I say?"

She widened her eyes and frowned. "And how do you know this?"

A shrug. "You haven't been the least bit sarcastic since I

met you."

Her mouth hung open. "How—"

"Rude?" He laughed. "I have many French friends. I love this country. But one cannot deny the fact that the French are a sarcastic people. Besides, Rokva isn't French, either."

She hid her grin behind her wineglass. "I'm Georgian, actually."

"That book you were reading earlier," Max said. *"The Red Dragonfly?"*

"Passage of the Red Dragonfly. It's translated from Japanese into French, but I think it's missing something in the translation."

"What's it about?"

"Death. Someone recommended it to me."

Max's skin prickled. "What about death?"

"Well, not only about death but about the transformation associated with death."

"What transformation?"

"I'm only halfway through, but apparently the dragonfly is meant to mysteriously appear at moments of death to signify the transformation from our worldly emotional dramas to the freedom of death. In Japan, the red dragonfly is sacred and is meant to convey comfort during the passage into death, love, and the afterlife."

"Death sets us free from burdens of life."

"Something like that."

An alarm klaxon sounded, and the train slowed abruptly. Her wineglass slid and she snagged it with surprising dexterity, but not before some of it sloshed on the table. Max held his own glass when the train lurched, and he caught the wine bottle as it flew at him. The waiter scurried past, cursing under his breath.

Gabrieli creased her brow. "What's going on do you think?"

He shrugged. "Probably weather related." The train slowed even more until it shuddered to a halt. Thick snow blew in swirls outside the dining car windows, and wind buffeted the train car. "At least we have a bottle of wine to keep us company."

She shifted and put a leg up on the bench so her back rested against the window. Max couldn't shake the feeling she didn't like having her back exposed. *My imagination again?*

"*Fait chier!*" The fat waiter cursed as he rushed along the aisle.

Max caught his arm. "What's the problem with the train, monsieur?"

There was more cursing as the waiter threw up his hands. "A train derailed ahead. Freight train, luckily. But alas." More curse words as he bustled off.

They exchanged glances, and Gabrieli's finger tapped a fast beat on the table.

"What is it?"

She waved her hand, but her full wineglass sat forgotten. "It's nothing. I just need to be somewhere." She flashed a smile as her eyes roved in constant motion. "I'm on a schedule."

A derailed train. A beautiful woman. Coincidences? If you were going to attack a train in the middle of a modern country, how would you do it?

As if in answer, the doors at each end of the dining car burst open and two hulking commandos appeared, rifles up, red laser sights flashing.

Gabrieli's face went white.

FIFTEEN

France

The dining car was empty, save for Gabrieli, Max, and a hulking soldier at each end of the car. They resembled the men who invaded Fedorov's house. Caucasian males, weathered faces, red lips, bulging muscles. Wraparound sunglasses. Heads covered by wool caps. Cargo pants and light jackets. Compact assault rifles and sidearms.

Spetsnaz.

Time slowed.

To her credit, Gabrieli didn't scream. Instead, she pressed her back into the side of the train car and hyperventilated with wide eyes.

Both doors were covered by the soldiers. Presumably additional soldiers patrolled outside the train. Likely on the roof.

That's how I'd do it.

Standard escape hatch in the ceiling and rows of windows that could be broken or opened. Trapdoors in the floor for storage. And something most civilians didn't know —panels that allowed access under the train. His SIG in its holster. Two laser sights on his chest.

Yup, both laser sights were on him. Dead to rights. He put his hands on the table, his right close to his jacket where his SIG was nestled. His only solace was if they wanted him dead, he would already be dead.

Their first mistake.

The soldiers advanced at a crawl, rifles clutched against their shoulders, steady in gloved hands.

The booth where he sat might offer cover. The backs were upholstery over metal and might prevent bullets from piercing or may deflect the projectiles. But any sudden action might draw shots and Gabrieli was in the direct line of fire.

He stayed put, taut and ready, and waited for the soldiers' next move.

A bang sounded from one end of the train car, and the pudgy waiter bustled in, still cussing and complaining. The sound of the doors clanging open was a like a gunshot in the silent car.

Both laser sights disappeared from Max's chest. *Sloppy training.* The soldier with his back to the waiter spun and pulled his trigger. Bullets spit, and the waiter's white shirt and apron were peppered with holes. A wine-colored blossom spread over his chest as he staggered back.

The second soldier's rifle left Max's chest at the distraction. When it returned, it didn't find Max.

"Get under the table," Max hissed as he pitched himself at the floor while yanking the SIG free.

He landed on his back in the aisle and pulled the trigger twice at the commando who killed the waiter.

The SIG's bullets found the man's face and throat and

cut off a scream as a chunk of his neck disintegrated and a bloody red hole appeared in his cheek. He hit the floor, dead.

Train cars resembled airplane fuselages, in which Max had trained extensively. The momentum of his dive carried him across the aisle, and his head became wedged underneath the booth across from where he and Gabrieli had sat. His back was against the booth's pedestal, and he was prevented from firing on the second soldier. So he scrabbled with his feet to propel himself backward.

He sensed rather than saw the second soldier turn. He felt rather than heard boot steps on the train car floor. Max pictured the man's hands tight on the rifle, panning left to right, searching for the threat. While turtled on his back under the table with the SIG held in both hands and pointed at the walkway between the tables, Max dared not move. Any sound would give him away.

A step.

Silence.

A squeak in the train car floorboards from another footstep. Max glanced across the aisle expecting to see Gabrieli huddled under the table, but she wasn't there. He pictured her frozen in place on the bench, a deer caught in headlights, while the rifle barrel arced at her and a bullet spit, displacing the air, and plowed into her forehead.

More silence.

Until a creak sounded and a boot appeared.

Max pulled the trigger and the man's lower leg exploded. Few men, even those hardy souls trained by the Russian military's finest special ops programs, would be able to hold a rifle, let alone aim it, while experiencing the shock of a disintegrated tibia. With the SIG up, Max wormed up to the bench seat, spotted the soldier's torso, and fired. And fired again.

The bangs of the pistol rang loud in the close quarters.

The commando careened backward, his arms pinwheeling, as the rifle clattered to the ground. Max's aim was off, and the bullets found the soldier's shoulder and stomach. He jumped to his feet and pointed the pistol at the man's head as a trickle of blood formed at the wounded man's mouth.

"How many more, damn it?"

The question was greeted by a gurgle and a laugh.

Max kicked at the soldier's wounded leg. "Help is on the way. You don't have to die. How many more men are outside the train?"

The man sputtered.

Max put the heel of his boot on the man's shattered ankle and shifted his weight. The soldier screamed.

The man flexed his good leg in an attempt to scooch along the aisle on his back, except Max's weight on his foot prevented him from moving. After two futile pushes, his leg went slack. Blood pooled on the thin carpet.

"You're bleeding out. Tell me what I want to know and I'll give you something to stop the blood."

The man spit and droplets of blood flew from his mouth until he fell into a violent cough.

A glass-shattering scream erupted. He whirled to see Gabrieli behind him, palms clenched to her face, mouth agape as she stared at the bloody soldier.

With his gun in one hand, Max grabbed her around the shoulders with the other hand and propelled her away from the still-breathing soldier. As they stepped over the dead man at the far end of the train car, her body went slack.

"Hush." Max put a finger up to her mouth. "They would have killed us."

Gabrieli nodded and clenched her fists to her throat.

Max put his hand on her cheek. "I have to get out of here. You need to stay. When the police get here—"

She swatted his hand away. "No! You have to take me. Don't leave me."

"I can't take you. There will be more men. They're after me. When I'm gone, you'll be safe."

She shook her head wildly. "They're after me too."

What?

Best he could tell, these were the same Spetsnaz that killed Fedorov. Probably the same crew that invaded the Colorado cabin. They tracked him this far, caused the freight train to derail ahead, and used the cover of night to infiltrate the train.

"You have to take me with you. Please! I'll explain. Just don't leave me here." Fear masked her face as tears streamed down her cheeks, creating little channels in her makeup.

Damn it.

Urgency made his decision for him. "Come on." He grabbed her and yanked her along the aisle to the train car door and wrenched it open to access the gangway between the cars. He slid the door open to the next train car and kept the SIG pointed ahead. The car was empty. No civilians. No Spetsnaz. The door slid closed, and they stopped in the ganway between the train cars.

How many men were outside? Did they have enough to cover both sides of the train? If he had a small squad, Max would place men on top of the train in order to watch both sides.

He opened the door and blowing snow swirled in. Nothing moved in the dimly lit winter landscape.

After he jumped into the snow, he swung her to the ground by her waist. With Max leading, they hugged the train car and scrambled over snow-covered railway ties. Any commandos on top of the train should miss them because of the narrow viewing angle. Speed was their friend, but stealth was important. Max kept a grip on her hand to help her over the terrain. Glances to their rear revealed nothing. There was no pursuit.

The train had stopped in the middle of a field, where the open expanse was covered in a smooth blanket of snow and crisscrossed by several lines of trees. A road ran parallel to the train tracks several kilometers away, and dark structures were visible far in the distance.

As the fleeing duo reached the last car, Max led Gabrieli away from the train on a beeline to a row of trees a dozen meters away. Their boots sank into muck and slush as they ran. At any moment, Max expected shots to ring out. When they reached the darkness of the woods, they fell against a tree for a rest.

Gabrieli's chest heaved as she gripped a branch and leaned on Max's arm.

Can't stay here. "Can you keep going?"

A quick nod.

The air near his head was displaced as a bullet plowed into the trunk an inch from his temple. Bark splintered and struck his cheek. More bullets whizzed by.

"Come on." He grabbed her around the waist, and they ran through the trees as bullets cracked and hummed around their heads.

SIXTEEN

Somewhere in France

Max led her deeper into the trees where the snow was untracked and crusted over with ice. Post-holing through snow up to their calves slowed them, but the dense trees covered their movements. The attackers chose their site well. The train had stopped in the middle of nowhere. They needed to find civilization before the men behind them tracked their footprints through the snow. Trained and fit Spetsnaz would eventually outlast them and kill them both.

Soon Gabrieli fell against a tree and grasped a branch as her lungs heaved. Max urged her on, and she ran but stumbled and fell.

"I'm not going to make it," she cried. "Go on without me."

Instinct told Max this was a bad idea. This woman didn't sit next to him on the train randomly. With a grunt, Max hefted her into a fireman's carry and took off through the forest. At first she protested but settled in as he wove through the trees.

Carrying her across both shoulders allowed his free hand to hold his gun. His aim would be off with the unwieldy weight on his back, but he could walk like this for hours. He could not, however, run faster than a team of fit commandos through the snow with a hundred pounds on his back. If they didn't find cover soon, they were dead.

A bullet whizzed by. A slug burrowed into the tree next to him. Bullet after bullet sang by his head. He zigged around a tree, stepped over a fallen tree trunk, and urged his legs to pump faster. They emerged from the trees onto a road, where he dropped Gabrieli to her feet. A cluster of buildings was to their right. A glance back. No moving shadows. With no cover available, the two ran hand in hand.

Although covered with snow, the road was plowed and offered a smooth surface. It curved to their left, away from the tree line. They slowed to keep their footing and turned into a driveway. A brick farmhouse sat on a large lot surrounded by a fence with a barn on a rise behind the house. The house was dark.

They followed a plowed track to the barn, and Max wrenched on the door to slide it open. He looked back at the road and thought he saw shadows. With heaving chests, they tumbled into the darkness and pulled the door shut.

Both braced their hands on their knees to catch their breath. As his vision adjusted to the darkness, Max spotted rows of farm implements, including field cultivators and grapple rakes, an old tractor, and something that made him grin with relief.

An old pickup truck.

———

The fugitives' tracks ended at the road. Although covered with snow, it was recently plowed, which made footprints more difficult to discern. Egor Dikov held up a fist and the man behind him halted. Time was not on their side. Any moment, the bodies of his two commandos on the train would be found and an alarm would go out. Ideally, they'd be far away from this area when that happened. Instead they were a kilometer from the train with their quarry nowhere in sight. The traitor had been in his sights for the second time. Letting him get away this time was unacceptable. Fury drove him.

To the left was nothing but darkness offset by a fresh covering of snow over a field that glowed dimly in the sparse moonlight. The road stretched out into the murk. Egor knew from his reconnaissance that the road led to a small farming hamlet. Nothing moved, and he glanced the other way as he squatted to examine the ground. Concealed among the tire tracks, gravel, and ice, were the faint outlines of footprints, one large, one narrow. They led in the direction of a huddle of buildings on the edge of the field.

With the fresh scent of the hunt, Egor signaled to his soldier and they took off for the farm. A fast jog brought them to the farmhouse porch. A barn was behind the house, along with several outbuildings, any of which offered a suitable hiding place. They didn't have time to search the entire farm.

With a curse in Russian, he grabbed the farmhouse's door handle with a gloved hand. Unlocked.

Egor stepped into the dark interior. It smelled of yeast mixed with mildew, and an ancient floorboard creaked gently under his foot. After giving his partner the signal to clear the main floor, he took the stairs up slowly to ease the sound of his footsteps. The upstairs was comprised of one large room dominated by a massive bed, where two forms lay under blankets. The blankets rose and fell to the rhythm of the forms' breathing. Egor watched and waited. A moment later his partner appeared next to him and shook his head.

If Asimov and the girl were in the house, they were well hidden and entered without waking the farmer and his wife. More likely, they were in one of the outbuildings. Still, he had no choice. He nudged the farmer's fat cheek with his rifle barrel.

After a more aggressive nudge, the man awakened and gasped as Egor held a gloved finger to his lips. A piercing scream rang out as the farmer's wife sat up to see two hulking soldiers in her bedroom.

Egor's rifle flashed as he crushed its buttstock to her temple. She fell back into the bed, limp and silent.

The farmer, who by now was fully awake, cried out and reached for his wife.

Egor put a restraining hand on his partner's shoulder and he pushed his rifle into the man's face. "Truss 'em."

A minute later the farmer and his wife were secured with plastic cuffs. A quick round of questioning in halting French convinced Egor the man never saw Asimov or the girl.

Both soldiers took the stairs to the ground floor and walked to the old wooden barn. With their rifles up, Egor covered his partner, who reached for the sliding door's handle.

The roar of a big engine erupted from behind the door.

———

The truck growled to life when the wires cracked a spark. Max gripped the wheel, gunned the engine, and jammed it into gear. Next to him, Gabrieli hunched in the passenger footwell, shaking in fear.

The old truck jumped ahead, and Max spun the wheel to point the hood at the barn door. The gas pedal hit the floor, the front grill hit the wood plank door, and they burst through in a shower of splinters. Wood rained down on the truck and obscured his view as Max wrestled with the wheel.

A shadow loomed in front of him, and the truck thumped against a heavy but elastic object. Another shadow flashed in Max's periphery. The truck lurched, and Gabrieli screamed as they rolled and banged over an object in their path.

The windshield spiderwebbed as bullets ripped through it, missed him, and plowed into the vinyl bench. Max goosed the accelerator. "Stay on the floor!" The shadow moved, and Max brought his pistol around and fired.

The truck's rear wheels snagged on the object, and Max floored the accelerator and they lurched free. Tires spun for purchase on the snowy drive, and the truck hesitated as if suspended in a split second of inertia. Max looked left in the moment the tires spun. A soldier stood near the barn with his right cheek pressed against a rifle stock. The soldier's face glistened in the moonlight. A jagged scar ran from the man's eye, across his left cheek, and along his neck before it disappeared under his collar.

Egor Dikov.

As the truck wheels spun on the snow, bullets hammered into the side of the truck. Gabrieli yelped, and Max muttered a few encouraging words to the truck.

Plunk, plunk, plunk. Bullets sprayed the length of the

truck's rear quarter panel as the Spetsnaz team leader brought the rifle around.

Another glance at Egor Dikov, who was now running as he fired. Max brought his pistol around, but he was too late. In a split second, bullets would spray across the door and plunge through the thin metal.

The truck wheels caught on a bare spot of gravel, and the vehicle leapt ahead. Stones and rocks sprayed, and the lightweight rear end of the truck fishtailed before the snowy field blurred in movement. More bullets plinked into the truck's tailgate, and the soldier was left behind. As Max guided the truck down the drive and out into the road, his last impression of Egor Dikov was his scar pulsing with blood, his eyes glaring in hatred.

SEVENTEEN

Dijon, France

The town was asleep as Max guided the truck into the ancient city of Dijon, the capital of France's Burgundy region. Their route through the small city meandered through side streets, and at this hour, Max saw no pursuers. They abandoned the truck in the rear of a church parking lot between a pair of shuttle buses and set off on foot.

They trudged in silence on ice-covered cobblestones as the little town came awake. Tiny bakeries emitted the strong scent of yeast and bread while café after café offered steaming coffee. Laborers carried their tools, and the occasional suit-clad man hurried by. Gabrieli gazed longingly into each coffee house as Max dragged her along, anxious to get to a more permanent shelter.

Max pulled Gabrieli through a corner doorway and into the Grand Hôtel La Cloche Dijon. The empty lobby was warm, dimly lit, and lined with plush blue chairs. The owner was a former KGB collaborator and owed Max a favor.

The two stumbled into a large suite with soot-colored carpet, a massive bed, and two bright orange wing chairs. Gabrieli hugged herself while Max closed the drapes and flicked on a gas fireplace. Over the bed was a massive charcoal drawing of a bare-chested warrior wielding a sword in battle with a muscle-bound cat baring huge fangs.

Max wedged the door with a chair and pointed the SIG at Gabrieli. "I need answers."

She gasped. "But—"

He waved the gun. "Remove your clothing."

Her mouth hung open. "What?"

"You heard me. Off with your clothes."

She didn't move.

"Do it or I'll do it for you."

She undid the sash on her wool coat with trembling fingers. "But why?"

"I don't trust you. You appeared next to me on the train out of the blue. You followed me to the dining car. Commandos appeared and miraculously didn't shoot you. You could have stayed at the train, but you begged me to take me along. You didn't tell me why." He waggled the gun. "Do it."

With her eyes downcast, she dropped the coat on the bed and kicked off her mud-covered boots. Next she removed a thin leather belt. Her shaking hands made it difficult for her to undo the clasp on her wool trousers. The silk blouse was undone one button at a time to reveal bare olive skin, no undergarments. The wool pants fell with the wiggle of her hips, and she stood naked except for a sheer thong.

She clasped her hands in front of her. "Satisfied?"

"Nope. Off with the panties."

Her mouth was pursed in anger, but she pulled the thong off and dangled it from a finger. "Hope you're enjoying yourself, you fucking pervert."

Max waved the gun. "Spin around."

The underwear dropped to the carpet. She spun to reveal a heart-shaped posterior and glanced back at Max with narrowed eyelids. "Want me to spread 'em?"

"Not necessary. Dump the contents of your bag on the bed and step away."

With the grace of someone comfortable in her own skin, she emptied her purse. A compact, a wallet, some lipstick, a package of tissues, and a smartphone fell onto the duvet. A roll of cash held with a rubber band dropped after she shook the purse.

"Take the battery out of the phone."

"It's an iPhone, you asshole. Can't remove the battery."

"Toss it here."

She flung it at him, and he let it hit his chest while he held the gun steady. He knelt, kept an eye on her, and raised his gun to slam it down on the phone but stopped when she shrieked.

"Wait!"

He raised an eyebrow.

"You're going to want that."

"What do you mean?"

She pointed at the device. "There's a message on there."

"A message?"

She crossed her arms over her chest. "It's for you."

She's a courier?

He slid the phone into his pocket and waved the gun at the items spread out on the bed. "Dump the wallet out on the bed. Open the compact and lipstick."

With a wary glance, she did as instructed.

"Step over to the window."

As she stood by the curtain with her arms crossed, Max searched through the purse contents and examined the roll of euros. "That's a nice wad of dough." After he was satisfied that there were no weapons, tracking devices, or recording electronics, he put the gun away. "You can get dressed."

She strode by him and into the bathroom, where he heard the shower running. She stuck her head out the door. "Get us something to eat, will you? I'm starving."

Max stiff-armed the door and barged into the bathroom as she stepped into a frosted glass shower stall.

"Tell me about the message, Gabrieli."

Her only answer was splashing as she sudsed her hair and skin.

He left the bathroom door open, ordered a continental breakfast and coffee from room service, and sat in an orange wing chair. He craved a cigarette. A pack of smokes and a gold lighter sat among the contents of Gabrieli's purse. He snagged one and held it between two fingers and wavered. Finally, the scent of the tobacco did him in. He held a flame to the end and sucked in the acrid smoke. Calm instantly washed over him.

Guilt flashed, but he ignored it and removed the woman's mobile phone from his pocket. After toggling it on, the device requested a six-digit pin. He made a couple half-hearted attempts that failed. Frustrated, he tossed the phone on the bed and blew out a cloud of smoke.

Gabrieli padded out of the steamy bathroom in a terry cloth robe as Max accepted the cart of food at the door. He wheeled it over while she sat cross-legged on the bed. Her wet hair was in a tangle over her shoulder and she attempted to comb it with her fingers as she nibbled on a muffin. Max poured coffee from the carafe into two mugs.

"I thought you quit," she said.

"There's something about being attacked by commandos while trying to protect a mystery woman that makes me crave a cigarette."

She sipped from the mug. "I decided in the shower that I don't blame you."

"I don't care what you decided. I want answers."

After finishing the muffin, she tasted a thin slice of ham. "You're not eating."

"What's the damn message? Your phone is locked. And while you're at it, who's sending the message?"

She smirked as she ate. "I've never been forced to strip without getting anything out of the deal."

After a sip of coffee, Max forked a slice of goat cheese into his mouth and chewed. "Damn it, Gabrieli. I'm out of patience."

She patted her hair dry with a hand towel. "You were right not to believe me. But it's not like you think."

She rose from the bed, untied the robe, and let it drift to the floor. Long, toned legs rose to meet a muscled stomach, which gave way to breasts with nipples pointed up, taut and hard. "I'm not here to hurt you. I'm here to help." With the grace of a tomcat, she slipped between the sheets and snuggled into the pillows. "Why don't you get cleaned up," she murmured. "I'm going to doze."

Max yanked down the sheets to reveal her naked, olive-toned body. She grabbed at the covering, but when he clutched her wrist and twisted, she fell face-first into the bed and yelped.

"I'm out of patience, damn it. What's the message? Who's it from?"

"Okay, okay. I'll tell you. Let me up."

Max let go of her arm. "Look, I wish I had time to lay around a luxury hotel suite with a beautiful woman. I don't."

Now on her knees, she batted her long lashes. "I get it."

He touched her arm. "Are you hurt?"

"I don't know." While flexing her elbow, she bowed her head as a tear appeared on her cheek.

He sat on the edge of the bed and caressed her bicep. "I'm sorry. I..." Next thing he knew, she was cradled in his arms, wracked with sobs.

The crying slowed and she sniffled. Her arms snaked around his neck and she pressed against him. She fumbled at his pants as they kissed, tentative at first until it turned urgent. His shirt came off, and she pushed his pants down around his thighs and straddled him. Once he was inside her, she rose and fell in a crescendo, her back arched, breasts upturned, until a moan escaped her lips. At one point, she bit hard on his lip and he tasted blood before a second wave of pleasure took them both. Finally they collapsed, spent, and lay in each other's arms.

They stayed with their bodies intertwined for a long while as he smelled her hair and caressed her shoulder with his fingers. Eventually she stirred, and her fingers went to work on his chest, drifting south, until they found him aroused. Their lovemaking was slow, tender, and long, and after, she pushed away and went into the bathroom. When she returned, she sat naked and cross-legged on the edge of the bed and bit her lip. "That wasn't supposed to happen."

"Not part of your assignment?"

Her shoulder dropped as she glanced away. "Don't shoot the messenger, okay?"

He shrugged. "As long as you're truly just the messenger."

"Do I seem capable of anything other than delivering a message?"

"Hard to say what you're capable of."

"Fair enough. But believe me when I say I'm just the mail carrier here."

"Why don't you begin by telling me who sent you? Who is the message from?"

Gabrieli sniffed. "It's from your father."

EIGHTEEN

Dijon, France

After everything his father had orchestrated from the grave, the revelation wasn't a surprise. "My father's dead."

"I know he's dead."

"Explain."

"I worked for your father. I mean, I still do, sort of."

"Belarusian KGB?"

She shook her head. "No. I'm part of a small team your father assembled before he died."

Max stood from the bed and refilled their coffee mugs. "What kind of team?"

"People he trusted."

Max found his clothes and pulled on his pants. "Is this team still in place?"

"In a manner of speaking."

"What does that mean?"

Gabrieli tasted her coffee. "There are only two of us left that I know of."

He shrugged into his shirt, smelled it, grimaced, and retrieved his gun from under the pillow. "What happened to the rest?"

"Let me show you." She fetched her mobile phone, tapped in a six-digit code, tapped a few more times, and presented the phone to Max.

The display showed a document in Russian and Max pinched and zoomed to read.

Mikhail, if you're reading this it means I am dead and time is of the essence. Our enemies are close, and you must move with speed and precision. I have set events in motion that will illuminate traitors in our midst and simultaneously unveil our enemies. As the stakes are higher, so too are the threats. Our enemies will detect the threat and will take ever greater risks to protect the sources of their power. You must proceed with great caution.

As you know, I managed to secret away thousands of documents that explain the operations of the komissariat, its associated councils, their relationship with foreign govern-ments, and even key figures in the Kremlin. The cache includes membership rosters, budgets, financial transactions, ownership records, and meeting minutes. It will also bring to light the inner workings of this so-called shadow government and surface those foreign governments and interest groups who profit from the komissariat's success. Trust me when I tell you this dossier is unlike any cache of intelligence files ever assembled.

This is why all the world's spy agencies will stop at nothing to secure it for themselves. The Americans, the Chinese, and the Germans all covet these files for the obvious leverage it will provide them over the Russians. The Russians, of course, will seek to uncover the files in order to root out the scourge that has become the komis-

sariat. The komissariat wants these files to protect their power.

You must retrieve this cache before any other group. Before my death, I placed a number of safeguards in place to ensure these files didn't fall into the wrong hands. For obvious reasons, I cannot outline those safeguards here. My agent, however, will put you on a path you must follow in all haste.

By now I hope you will not trust that this message is legitimate. In order to prove authenticity, my agent will provide you with a passphrase."

Max looked up. "You have a passphrase?"

Gabrieli smiled and held up the book with the red dragonfly on the cover. "This is it."

"I'm supposed to know it?"

"No. You're supposed to take it and the message. Later, someone will give you the same passphrase."

Max turned back to the phone. *One of my associates needs rescuing, Mikhail. If you've come this far, then you must find this man. He is the only one who can help you find the files. My agent will provide you with what you need. You are singularly equipped to liberate one of my closest and deepest friends.*

Mikhail, everything rides on your success.

-Your father.

Max offered the phone back to Gabrieli, who held up her palm.

"You can swipe to see the rest of the files."

Max swiped. On the screen was an image of a bald-headed man with swarthy skin and narrow eyes with deep wrinkles at the edges squinting into the sun. His cheeks were rosy, and his smile was missing several teeth. A gold hoop was in his left earlobe. There were four more pictures of the same man. He wore tattered work clothing and displayed arms covered in multicolored tattoos.

"I give up. Who is he?"

She crooked her finger and he surrendered the phone. She tapped a few more times and handed the device back. "He's our team leader."

The screen showed a document in Russian Cyrillic. Max pinched and zoomed to read it better. The upper left corner contained a logo and two black-and-white pictures of the same man in the upper right. One image showed him from the chest up, facing the camera. The second was a profile shot. The document's title was *Federal Penitentiary Service Inmate Internment Record*.

The name field read *Badū Khan*.

————

Max plopped into an orange wing chair and toyed with Gabrieli's box of cigarettes. His mind screamed for more nicotine, but he resisted. "That's it?"

With the sheet held to her chest, Gabrieli held out two fingers. "Can I get one of those?"

Max tapped out a smoke from the packet, held it to his lips, lit it with his Zippo, took a draw, and handed it to her as he blew out smoke. "Who is that man?"

"I don't know anything about him," Gabrieli said.

"Tell me about this team. Who is on it?"

"That's the thing. We are very compartmentalized." She waved her hand at the phone, which Max still held. "Once Andrei was killed, someone took over. The communications continued. We use a series of encrypted e-mail inboxes. Whoever is in charge hands out assignments, distributes the funds, and gets us any credentials we need. I assume Andrei left someone in charge, I just don't know who it is."

"And you follow the instructions without question?"

Gabrieli shrugged. "The money shows up in my account. The assignments appear just like they always did. Andrei told us that in the event he was killed, the team would continue to function. I have no reason to doubt."

"How did you get this?" Max waved the phone.

Gabrieli shrugged. "The assignment came through the normal channels."

"Show me."

"Per protocol, I already destroyed the message."

Max stared at her, and she shrugged. "It's the truth."

If even half of what Gabrieli said was true, someone was pulling strings. Kate departs to hunt for the one-time pad after receiving a secret message. This woman—she says her name is Gabrieli—delivers him a message supposedly from his father. He fished out a cigarette and lit it. The smoke filled his lungs and the nicotine helped him think.

I should inform C. But he hesitated. If Badū Khan was his father's associate, then either he was leaking documents to MI6 against his father's wishes, or he was sending the documents under his father's instructions. *Before I report into MI6, it would be better to find out which is true.*

He examined the prison form. Prisoner intake was dated six months ago and indicated Badū Khan was imprisoned at Zurgan, a military prison. The prison was familiar. Located in a closed town on the western edge of the Siberian steppe several hundred miles from anywhere, the facility was cloaked in secrecy. It was the kind of place the Kremlin sent people to disappear. Max had visited several times in his capacity as KGB field operative. Remote, dank, and secure, Zurgan was easily forgotten.

The sheet slipped to her waist as Gabrieli leaned over to flick ash into a coffee cup. "Did I do good?"

"You did great." Max smiled. "How did you know what train I'd be on?"

Smoke wafted as they sat in silence, and the question hung between them. With a flick of her finger, Gabrieli deposited ash into the glass, huffed out a breath, and muttered in a soft voice. "It was texted to me."

"By whom?"

"I don't know."

"What did the text say?"

"What trains you were on. Sort of like a play-by-play."

How on earth? Something niggled in his mind, but the thought eluded him.

"How did you meet my father? You must work for some intelligence agency."

She punched his arm playfully. "How did you—"

"But you're new to the game. Trustworthy and effective but junior. My father saw potential."

She crossed her arms over her chest.

Max touched her shoulder. "You did exactly what you were supposed to do. No one planned for you to get caught up in the crossfire between me and those Russian thugs."

A sparkle appeared in her eye. "I was just supposed to deliver the message. What gave me away?"

Max shrugged. "You took the strip search well. It was like you expected it. How you're sitting on the bed. Confident, sure of yourself, which means you're right where you're supposed to be."

"Aren't you going to ask me which agency?"

"You'd lie."

"I was forbidden from sleeping with you, you know. That wasn't part of it."

Shaking his head, Max laughed. "No, you weren't. They were counting on it."

Gabrieli hit him with a pillow. "Is everything in this business lies over lies over lies?"

"Pretty much."

She pulled his hand and he floated into the bed. Her hands tugged his shirt over his head and fumbled at his pants.

The gun fell to the floor as she wrestled off his pants. Her mouth nibbled on his chest and moved slowly along his stomach, and he succumbed to the heat of her breath on his skin. As she climaxed under him, she whispered in his ear, "You better see me again."

She fell asleep, her damp hair on his shoulder. After she drifted off and he confirmed she was asleep, he wormed out from under her, found his clothes, and dressed quietly. After a last look at her face, Max slipped out the door.

Goodbye, Gabrieli. You can't go where I'm going.

———

Russian Border with Belarus

Even as the Cold War thawed, many of Kate's old contacts from her days as CIA station chief in the Soviet Union were still alive. On both sides of the Russian border, former spies, operators, and civilians who her team worked with to gather intelligence and move clandestinely around the old Soviet Union still made their life. While much of the network had disappeared to the onslaught of time—people moved, houses were sold, key figures passed away—remnants of her old relationships persisted, even now.

As she traveled from Vienna to Prague and from Prague to Warsaw, calls were made, signals left in the proper spots, cash was exchanged, and credentials were retrieved. Which explained how Kate managed to get herself on an eastbound Russian train with a Canadian passport.

Wrapped against the cold in a tight-fitting wool jacket, gray wool cap, and hiking boots, she scratched an opening in the frost caked on her window. Through the murky glass flowed the off-white and flat winter countryside of Western Russia. The tracks threaded through the bleak and snow-covered countryside between Smolensk on the Belarusian border and Moscow. Huddled between the frozen metal of the train car and an obese babushka who reeked of onions, Kate kept her nose buried in a guide-book. The credit cards in her wallet were fake, and she relied on a wad of Canadian and US dollars and a handful of wrinkled euros. A hidden compartment in her backpack contained two passports held by a rubber band along with supporting documents and credit cards. There was no home base support, no satellite overwatch, and MI6 had no idea where she was. Relying only on her sparse network of old friends behind the Iron Curtain and her own wits, Kate's pulse pounded with the thrill of the operation.

The operation brought back fond remembrances of her time on the CIA's Russian desk. It was a different era back then. Clear lines were drawn between good and evil. Democracy against communism. She had been far away from the politics at Langley and relied on skills honed in the field. She chalked up hundreds of successful missions on behalf of those in Washington, only to be cast away like a criminal by the machinations of a corrupt director. The anger burned deep. But another emotion was there: the need for absolution. If she returned to Langley with the Vienna Archive, her sins might be forgotten.

She let the thought linger as the dead fields slipped past the window. Then she dismissed it. Loyalty was paramount. Her loyalty to Andrei, and in turn to Max, was sacrosanct. *Right?*

The secure Blackphone was a boon. She typed a quick text update to Max to let him know she was okay and stuffed the phone into her pocket.

The conductor appeared, his face a stoic mask, and she provided her passport, complete with entry visa, and her train ticket with Moscow as her destination. For good measure, she handed him an e-mail printout with reservation details for the InterContinental Hotel in Moscow. The conductor probably didn't read English, but it was the sort of arrogant mistake a Western traveler in Russia might make. The conductor frowned as he snapped a small tear in her ticket and returned her paperwork.

There was no way to know if she passed. That was the thing about Russia. You never knew until the KGB thugs showed up. Outside the window, the featureless landscape clacked by as the train took her deeper into Russia.

———

Subject crossed Russian border at Kurgan via rail. Based on material found on subject's phone, destination is InterContinental Hotel in Moscow.

Goshawk hit Send, cinched her silk robe, and walked up the sweeping mahogany stairs to the master bathroom. She turned off the faucet, gave the tub a swirl so the suds formed, hung the robe on a hook, and sank into the scalding water.

Let the water cleanse me of my sins.

A glass of burgundy sat on a windowsill that was actually a live digital image of the Paris skyline. She picked up the book that rested next to the wineglass. The title was *Master and Margarita* and was written in Moscow by Mikhail Bulgakov between 1928 and 1940. Hidden away for years to keep it from Stalin's purges, the manuscript was finally published uncensored in 1973. It tells the story of a woman, Margarita, who sells her soul to the Devil to gain the master's release from a psychiatric ward, where he interned himself after critics attacked his literary work.

Fitting.

————

Somewhere North of the Caucasus Mountains

The rapid *clack-clack-clack* of two cane shinais striking each other grew louder as Colonel Artur Markov strode along the stone-floored hallway to his boss's office. Abrupt attack shouts sounded from both combatants, and as Markov rounded the corner and went through the door held open by Stepanov's attaché, he witnessed a spectacle he had seen many times before.

The sensei, Stepanov's teacher, was dressed in body armor that covered flowing black robes and a protective mask. The sensei wielded the bamboo sword with a speed that made the weapon invisible to the naked eye. Ruslan, bare-chested but with his face covered by an identical protective mask, defended himself from the sensei's onslaught. Both men's feet slid across the stone floor in a blur.

As Markov watched from the corner, the sensei barked an attack cry and struck Ruslan's arm and torso with an unbridled ferocity that left more red welts among those already present on the general's body. Stepanov struck back with a flurry of his own, which the sensei easily parried before launching a counterattack that left more wounds on Stepanov's torso. When they were finished, both men bowed and removed their masks. The teacher, a stout Japanese man, instructed Ruslan on an attack sequence before he bowed again and departed.

"Colonel Markov, thank you for joining me," Ruslan said. "Would you like to take a turn with the shinai? I fear my skills are not yet where I would like them, and I could use the extra practice."

Markov held up a small package wrapped in plastic.

"Ah, yes. Andrei's infamous message." The three-star general wiped his face on a towel. Sweat covered his pink skin, and the welts where the sensei had struck him stood out in bright relief. "And how is Sergeant Dikov after his misadventures in France?"

"He burns with the obsession to find Asimov. I am confident his energies are up to the task."

"Despite the failures?" Stepanov rubbed his hands on the towel and unsealed the plastic envelope. "He had the Asimov boy in his clutches not once but twice, only to let him escape." The general withdrew a tiny, flat booklet and set it gingerly on the table.

"Yes, sir. Asimov's appearance in Courchevel was a surprise. On the train, Egor's overconfidence led him to miscalculate the assault and use only four men. He prioritized minimal impact instead of overwhelming force. He won't make that mistake again, sir."

"He best not or it will be his last mistake. At least we

have Andrei's coded message." With a smile on his face, Ruslan thumbed through the booklet. "A bunch of gibberish without the decoder, is it not?"

"Correct, sir."

"And where are we on the operation to secure the code booklet?" Stepanov slipped the pamphlet back into the cellophane envelope and placed it in a desk drawer.

"Everything we discussed is in order. I received word from our contact in Germany that Ms. Shaw crossed into Russia earlier today. I depart for Saint Petersburg first thing in the morning to ensure our assets are in place, but I wanted to deliver this package first. For safekeeping."

"I know you will not disappoint me, Comrade Markov. Send updates as the plan unfolds. You are dismissed."

NINETEEN

Dijon, France

Who the hell is tracking me?

As Max trekked along a frosty street, visions filled his mind from the hunt for Kate when the mysterious operative named Kira managed to track him. He never learned how she did it. Now someone was tracking him again.

How the hell are they doing it?

The town was mostly empty this early in the morning. Max walked behind a tall man in a wool overcoat carrying a briefcase and wearing a scarf. A mobile phone was pressed to the man's ear. After looking both ways, the businessman jaywalked across the street and fumbled at the entryway of a café as he tried to open the door with the case in one hand while holding the phone at his ear.

Max, intent on a warm croissant and coffee from the same café, stopped dead in the middle of the street. A taxi horn blared, and Max jumped to the curb.

The mobile phone.

Something clicked in Max's mind.

Goshawk is avoiding my calls.

He dug the secure Blackphone from his pocket. With a bare hand numb from the cold, he examined the device. The phone itself was a solid piece of electronics. The outer shell was made from a black carbon steel alloy and offered extreme impact resistance. Little effort went into the device's ergonomics and the edges were sharp, the corners pointed. The front glass panel was made from a military-grade version of Corning Gorilla Glass and could withstand a drop from ten stories. A mini-USB port allowed for data input and output, and its battery held a charge for a week. The device was heavy enough to shatter a plate glass window. Inside, the Blackphone's electronics were state of the art, encrypted, and had been heavily modified by Goshawk for even more security, which included a custom modification to prevent the cellular data transmissions from being tracked by cell towers.

Had she modified the phone in ways she hadn't told him? After the events in Cyprus, Goshawk had gone over the device with a fine-toothed comb and upgraded the electronics and security algorithms. No one had touched the phone since. *Was the phone compromised without her knowledge?*

A rumble came from his stomach, and Max entered the café, where he ordered a coffee and two croissants. As he stood in line to pay, he pinched the bridge of his nose.

What if?

Gabrieli, mobile phone in hand, bides her time at Gare de la Part-Dieu train station awaiting instructions.

Goshawk tracks the phone's location and deduces what train he is on.

Gabrieli sits up when her phone dings with an incoming

message. He's arriving on the 11:27 from Chambery Challes due to arrive at Lyon Part-Dieu at 13:00. Departing Lyon to Montpellier on the 17:04. Gabrieli hurries to board the train and finds a seat across from the disheveled but ruggedly handsome man who matched the picture on her phone.

Is that how it happened?

There was no other explanation. Not even MI6 knew his surveillance detection route through France. He devised it as he went and compartmentalized the information. It helped keep him safe, and it helped pinpoint leaks.

He dialed Goshawk's number. After a dozen rings with no answer, he hung up.

With a heavy heart, he hefted the phone. Nothing short of a sledgehammer would destroy it, so he did the next best thing. After paying for his food and wolfing down the two pastries, he exited through the café's back door and stopped next to a dumpster. With a glance in either direction to ensure he was alone, he wrapped the phone in the greasy croissant bag and shoved the sack deep under a mess of coffee grounds, bacon grease, and rotten vegetables in the trash bin.

As he left the alley in search of a vehicle to hot-wire, he felt naked.

———

The Otam 80 series yacht raced across placid blue waters powered by four Caterpillar C32 diesels that put out 1670 hp each. Even at the yacht's top speed of fifty-eight knots, it was a forty-hour trip through the Greek isles, into the Sea of Marmara, past Istanbul, and out to the Black Sea. From there the Tunisian captain would point the prow east until they landed at a secluded beach north of Batumi, Georgia.

All roads led to Badū Khan. Between C's request for a favor and the message from his father, it was clear what he had to do. Besides, there was something his father knew that no one else did. It made Max realize the message delivered by Gabrieli had to be legitimate. Max had knowledge of Zurgan's inner workings and an inventory of the prison's weaknesses. During his stint in the KGB, Max had been assigned to a team tasked to assess Russia's military prisons for vulnerabilities. The assignment was the outcome of a political battle between the KGB director at the time and the man who oversaw the prisons, a two-star general named Morozov. The grapevine reported that Morozov's daughter spurned the KGB director's son, and the audit was payback. Such is the way the bureaucracy worked in Russia. Max had an encyclopedia's knowledge of Zurgan's vulnerabilities, weaknesses that had remained unaddressed for the past decade.

He and his father were one of a select few who knew about these vulnerabilities. The only problem was the weakness needed to be accessed from the inside. And that meant Max needed to get himself admitted to the prison as an inmate.

In addition to the well-stocked galley and crew of three, the boat captain provided Max with a change of clothing that included a thick sweater and a wool cap. Max sat in the bridge, sipped coffee, and smoked while the ocean unfolded before him, his thoughts drifting to his father. Larger than life, Andrei Asimov attracted friends like the boat captain, a man who attached their loyalty to the individual instead of his country. Through a carefully orchestrated set of constant favors, Andrei cultivated friends like gardeners tended their gardens. Now, even years later, those investments paid dividends.

Childhood in Andrei Asimov's household was characterized by short, intense moments with his father that were interrupted by long periods of his father's physical or emotional absence. The old man had been a mythical creature in Max's life. Nicknamed *The Bear*, Andrei handed out exotic gifts from foreign lands and conducted intense teaching moments before he disappeared again for weeks. When Andrei trained Max in the finer arts of subterfuge, espionage, and tradecraft, it was done over his mother's strenuous objections. Now, years later, Max wondered what he would have become if he hadn't been trained as a spy.

Arina went to school to be a lawyer before her marriage to one of Andrei's up-and-coming KGB agents. When Alex was born, her life became centered around the boy.

Arina. If she died, what would happen to Alex?

It was too horrible to contemplate, and so he pushed the thought from his mind as the yacht captain, a light-skinned Tunisian with a scraggly white beard, handed Max a mug of coffee. After twenty years of navigating the northern Mediterranean, the Tunisian knew its waters better than most. Tall and wiry, he wore a wool cap and heavy shirt with the sleeves rolled up to his elbows. Since they left Marseille, the captain said little to Max. When the Tunisian held out a cigarette, Max hesitated but relented. There was nothing else to do. The two men drank coffee and smoked in silence as the gray water slipped by.

When they passed the Maiden's Tower in the Bosporus straight on their way past Istanbul and into the Black Sea, Max toggled the captain's satellite phone. He dialed the number provided by Gabrieli. After he was routed through two equally gruff male voices, he landed with an all-business female voice who had asked for the passphrase.

Passage of the Red Dragonfly.

After that, the stoic woman's voice returned with a time and a location marked by GPS coordinates, which he memorized. "After that time window, there will be two more windows where he'll be available. Do not miss one of those times." The phone went dead.

Max made a few travel arrangements before he disappeared into his cabin, a cocoon of pillows and crisp cotton sheets. After locking the door, he slid the SIG under his pillow and drifted off to sleep.

———

The year was 1992 or thereabouts. The twenty-first class of the Red Banner Institute, Moscow's ultra-secret training camp for KGB operatives, was grouped outside in the quad, each man stripped to his underwear. The compound was encrusted by a layer of ice and snow, and the ever-present gray skies held a low ceiling of cumulus clouds. A sharp wind blew, and Max's skin turned numb as he stood at attention in a row of men. The starting class of one hundred and fifty men had been winnowed to twenty-three, soon to become twenty-two. The hardy group huddled there that day were the survivors of a three-month-long training course designed to force all one hundred and fifty men to quit. One man shivered uncontrollably while another fell to his knees, where he was left to cower on the ground.

A sergeant barked a command directed at Max and another man. It was a favorite game of the ex-military sergeants who ran the KGB program. Strip the men bare and force them to fight one another. Undaunted, Max stepped alongside a large broad-shouldered and square-jawed career soldier and former Olympic boxing champion named Egor Dikov. Egor had proven himself a leader of men, an adroit thinker, a student of military history and theory, a crack shot, and a capable fighter. Here, at the end of the six-month training period, the KGB officers pitted the two strongest trainees against each other to see who would emerge victorious.

Like he studied all his enemies, Max closely watched each and every fellow trainee and knew their strengths and weakness. And he knew Egor's.

A signal was given, and the ogre-sized man launched a fist at Max's face, but Max was ready. Max bobbed his head to evade the strike, moved inside, and landed a series of jabs on Egor's ribcage. Egor grunted and a short silver blade appeared in his fist, which was against regulations. With a swipe, Egor sliced the knife across Max's chest and drew blood. Max jumped back and circled out of reach. Immediately, Egor thrust the knife and swiped again.

Egor liked to strike first and hard to throw his opponent off and grab a quick win. But Egor's endurance was low, and he tired easily. Max avoided that thrust and the one that followed. On the next swipe, Max struck the attacking arm with his left fist and sent a fast uppercut at Egor's nose, which burst blood in a spray. The next instant, Max weaved, avoided the knife, and danced away.

The two men went back and forth as the trainees yelled and jeered. Max, faster and nimbler, struck quick and jumped out of reach as Egor swung the knife. Faint lines of blood appeared on Max's abdomen twice, but the wounds were superficial.

The burden of adrenaline showed on Egor's face and hampered his movements. Max kept up the barrage of strikes and evaded the knife until finally Egor slowed and Max snagged Egor's arm. He used the big man's weight and momentum to swing him around and bend his arm at the *wrong angle, and Egor dropped the knife. With his grasp tight on Egor's wrist, Max grappled him to the ground, where he landed punch after punch on the man's face, neck, and head. In a moment the sergeant would stop the fight.*

A glint of silver on the ground caught Max's eye, and he snatched up the knife. "Draw a knife on me, will you?" he growled. With his elbow jammed into the side of Egor's neck, he pressed his opponent's face into the gritty dirt and dragged the knife blade deep along Egor's jawline, who screamed until the sergeant yanked Max away.

It was the last time the trainees saw Egor. Rumors circulated that Dikov washed out of the KGB training program and landed in the Spetsnaz while Max graduated at the top of the Red Banner Institute's class of twenty-one students.

TWENTY

Moscow, Russia

The InterContinental Hotel was a squat but contemporary glass and yellow brick affair centrally located near the Kremlin. Kate read somewhere that it was built on the former site of the Hotel Minsk, which was fitting. Upon arrival, she transformed herself from a traveling student to a visiting professor by picking up a dozen mix-and-match blouses and suits, a wool overcoat, and a few scarves in Moscow's famed GUM shopping district.

Now, she sat in the hotel's P-Square lounge and sipped a vodka martini. The drink was the choice of her persona, an assistant professor from New York's Columbia University on a junket to Moscow before visiting Saint Petersburg on business. After she good-naturedly fended off an advance from an overweight Russian in a loud suit, she removed the Blackphone from her handbag.

No message from Max. The last note had been from somewhere in France after the failed Fedorov mission.

There was a quick update that Ruslan Stepanov now had the coded message and it was more imperative that she secure the code booklet.

Nothing since.

Not to worry. He was probably on a surveillance detection route before heading to the cherry orchard. She switched off the device, paid for her drink, and went to her room.

———

Subject still in Moscow. Heading to St Petersburg on 9:00 am train from Leningradski station in Moscow.

After she sent the note to Julia, Goshawk took a half-empty bottle of French Chardonnay and walked barefoot into her bedroom, where she curled up among the heavy blankets with her book.

———

Utsera, Georgia

For a Russian marked as a traitor, or a Belarusian in this case, there are two ways to get into Russia. The first is to use a fake identity at a main port of entry. Most immigration waypoints use facial scanning technology, which can see through most disguises. For this reason, Max chose a safer but much longer method. The route included an overland car ride through the country of Georgia followed by a handoff to friendlies who would usher him over a remote border on a road used primarily by Chechens and Georgians.

Because of an increase in terrorist activities by Chechens, the Russians had stepped up patrols on the northern side of the border between Georgia and Russia. Still, better to take a chance with soldiers than an entire immigration bureaucracy. Max preferred visible enemies.

An earthenware bowl of steaming stew sat on the table, its steam wafting across Max's face. Crusty bread and a mug of beer sat within easy reach. Across the one-room shack was a broad-shouldered woman in a smock laboring at the sink while next to him a gnarled man in a woolen cap sat hunched over his own bowl.

The old couple was part of an underground network used to smuggle locals in and out of Russia. Max, bundled in a wool overcoat, watch cap, and heavy boots, had appeared in their kitchen under cover of darkness, placed an oilskin-wrapped bundle of cash in the old man's hand, and settled in for a meal. The old woman's stew was famous among the dissidents and guerrilla fighters that used this route to cross the border. Max and the old man conversed in low tones using the local Georgian dialect.

"What of the Russian patrols?" Max asked.

"More frequent." The old man chewed a piece of meat. "And more brutal. Killed a student last week on his way home to visit his grandparents. Claimed he was conspiring to plant a bomb."

"Why now?"

The old man's rheumy eyes searched the darkened room before he sipped his beer. "The Russian president is weakening, so he invades Crimea and starts picking fights with the Chechens."

Max shook his head. For decades, and through two invasions, the Russian president had used the Chechens as scapegoats for oppression. Of course, the Chechens didn't do themselves any favors when they committed acts of terror on Russian soil. As with most things, the truth of who was to blame was a muddled jumble of fact, propaganda, and emotion.

The pickup truck got him at 12:00 am local time. The wife had long gone to bed, but the old man stayed up with Max and smoked and talked. They shook hands before Max climbed into the truck's cab, where he was surprised to see his old friend Doku, a former Chechen fighter and ally of his father. Months ago, Doku had helped Max locate and apprehend Usam Islamov, a longtime bomb maker and perpetrator of the West Brompton terrorist explosion that killed fifty-six innocent civilians.

Max jerked his thumb at the empty truck bed. "Where is everyone?" A standard border crossing involved a truck full of men bristling with weaponry.

The truck bounced over a snowy wooden bridge with Doku's hands gripping the wheel. "Better to keep a low profile these days. Processions of pickups draw attention."

"Any weapons?" Max asked. "Or are we going in naked?"

The Chechen jerked his head to the rear of the extended cab, where under a blanket was an old and scarred AK-47. As Doku engaged the four-wheel drive, Max gave the rifle a once-over and grunted his approval. Boxes of 9mm parabellums and 39mm Russian short cartridges for the AK sat in the rear footwell. Max busied himself reloading his SIG as the truck jounced over the rough track.

"Glove box," Doku said. "Per your request."

In the glove box was a dented and scratched mobile phone. A SIM card was taped to the back.

"New SIM," Doku said. "Should be untraceable, but

just to be sure, keep the SIM out of the phone until you need it."

Max pocketed the mobile. "Copy that."

Outside, the truck's dim headlights reflected off fresh snowfall and a road hemmed in by Scots pines. The only tire tracks on the road were from Doku's recent descent into Utsera. They ground upward in four-wheel-drive, gaining elevation, and Doku wrestled the wheel around switchback after switchback.

Like Colorado.

Max listened and smoked as Doku filled Max in on the former freedom fighter's family. His teenaged son had taken an interest in Doku's business, and his daughter was in the top of her class and couldn't be pried from the ballet studio. The stories hit a nerve, making him wonder whether Alex would ever get a chance at a normal life. As Doku described his sedate and domestic homelife and boasted about his children's accomplishments, Max watched the trees slide by in the darkness. *I can't be a single father.* There was no question of his love for Alex. The strength of that emotion was undeniable. But if Arina didn't emerge from her coma, the prospect of raising Alex alone sent panic coursing through his veins. *And what if I'm killed? What happens to Alex then?*

He gritted his teeth and pushed the thought from his mind as his father's gruff reminder pulsed through his subconscious. *A distracted soldier is a dead soldier.*

It took two hours of climbing to reach the summit, where the road turned into a narrow double track with no room to pass. The truck hugged a rugged cliff on Doku's side, and a sheer abyss opened under Max's window. There was no room for a misstep, and Doku's fists were white on the steering wheel as the Chechen drifted into silence to concentrate on navigating the treacherous road.

The box of French smokes had two left. Max tapped one out and offered it to Doku, who shook his head. "At least the Russian patrols won't come this high. Have we officially crossed the border?" The cigarette's tip flared at the touch of a flame from his lighter.

"Unsure," Doku muttered. "I'd check the GPS but I'm a little busy."

The truck shuddered as the front wheel slid off a snowy rock and the vehicle lurched at the drop-off. With a deft touch of the wheel, Doku maneuvered the truck back onto the road, and Max groaned in relief as their hood angled down and they descended to the Russian side of the mountain range. Max gripped the rifle with one hand while he flicked ash through a crack in the window.

The sheer drop-off disappeared as the road entered a plateau, and a measure of tension left both men. "Stay sharp," Doku said. "We're entering military patrol territory."

"What are the patrols like?"

The old Chechen fighter shrugged. "Anything from four-wheeled quads to army trucks to these new Typhoon mechanized infantry vehicles. Depends."

Max stubbed the cigarette out on the sole of his boot and stuffed the butt in his pocket. "Got any smokes?"

A head shake from Doku. "I quit that stuff. My kids nag me about it. They claim they want their old man around awhile."

"I figure I'll die of something else long before I get lung cancer," Max said with bravado he didn't feel.

They crept along in four-wheel drive for another hour and descended two thousand feet in elevation until the road widened and turned dry. Doku disengaged the axles and they sped up. Two more hours and they'd be safe at Doku's home on the outskirts of Grozny, where Max hoped to catch a nap and a bowl of hot breakfast.

"Shit." Doku glanced in the rearview mirror. "We've got company."

Max craned his neck to see out the back window and counted two pairs of headlights bobbing in the darkness, approaching fast.

This late and this close to the border meant one thing: Russian military.

TWENTY-ONE

The Caucasus Mountains

"Shit, shit, shit." Doku muttered under his breath as he wrestled with the wheel and stomped on the gas. The pickup truck swerved as the rear wheels spun in the mud.

"Where'd they come from?" Max cranked down his window to look behind them. Two heavily modified SUVs bounced over the undulating ground about a hundred meters back. Headlights and roof-mounted off-road lights lit up the road. "Faster, damn it."

Minutes later, the two SUVs caught them and stayed a dozen meters from their rear bumper. An amplified voice spoke in Russian. "Under orders of the Russian Army, bring your vehicle to a halt."

"Don't stop," Max said as he crawled into the narrow space in the rear of the extended cab. He slid open the rear window and stuck the AK-47 through the opening. "Keep it steady."

"Yeah, right," Doku yelled over the sound of the truck's whining engine. The truck bounced over the rutted road.

The tone of the old fighter's voice made Max hesitate, and a vision of Doku's new life floated through his mind. His large family in Grozny. The business Doku ran to support his kids and parents. His daughter in ballet shoes. A new, stable life contrasted from his former life as a militant. The faces of Arina and Alex appeared in his mind, and Max fired the rifle.

Bullets sprayed at the lead SUV as Max pulled the trigger. Slugs found the SUV's windshield and knocked out a headlight and a fog light. He let go of the trigger when the thirty- round magazine was empty, dropped the mag, and rammed home a full one. The gunfire slowed the pursuers, and the SUVs faded back fifty meters.

Trees flashed by in the wavering headlights. The pickup jounced over ruts as Doku wrestled with the wheel.

"Stop the truck," Max yelled. He ducked back into the front seat and put his hand on the door handle. "I'm getting out."

"No way," Doku shouted.

Max cracked the door. "No choice."

Doku slowed the truck. "What are you doing?"

"Go home to your family. You didn't sign up for this. I'll take care of these guys." Max stuffed three fresh magazines into his pockets and secured the SIG in a jacket pocket.

The pickup slowed even more as Doku's resistence wavered.

"If you don't stop, I'm going to jump out." Max pushed the door open while looking for an open area without trees and a soft cushion for the landing.

"They'll follow me."

"No, they won't. I'll make sure of that." An open glade

appeared on his side covered with fluffy snow, and the pickup truck slowed to a crawl. "Call you later."

With the AK-47 clutched tight, Max jumped, hit the snow, and rolled.

The smooth blanket of snow was thinner than he guessed. His shoulder plowed through the snow and hit the frozen ground with a jolt. As he rolled, his arm hit a rock, nearly dislodging the gun from his grip. In his periphery, the pickup's wheels spun, and the rear fishtailed before Doku disappeared around a curve in the road.

Adrenaline coursed. His shoulder throbbed. Max popped to his feet and dashed to the road, rifle up. With the stock pressed to his cheek, his numb index finger curled around the trigger. The two SUVs were nearly upon him as he squeezed and fired automatic bursts at the oncoming vehicles. The AK chattered and the gunfire reverberated around the still woods. Bullets found the hood and windshield of the lead vehicle.

The driver of the Russian military SUV wrenched the wheel and the big truck careened off the road and into the field, where its front wheel hit a hidden ditch. It pitched and tipped on its side and plowed into the snow.

With the rifle now pointed at the second vehicle, Max squeezed the trigger. Bullets sprayed the windshield and grill as the SUV headed right at him. He kept the trigger compressed until the last minute when he hurled himself out of the truck's path. Rolling, he came up on one knee, rifle stock jammed into his shoulder, and fired.

Bullets peppered the back of the retreating truck as the SUV bucked and swerved and plowed into a snowbank. The AK clicked on an empty magazine. Max dropped the magazine and slammed home a new one. Soldiers spilled from the rear of the vehicle, some staggering in the road, a couple operational.

A Russian soldier dressed in winter camouflage raised a rifle with unsteady hands. A second soldier, blood trickling from a wounded forehead, fumbled at his holster and attempted to free his handgun. A third dropped to his knee with a raised rifle.

No cover. Open fields stretched on both sides of the road. No one moved in the first vehicle. There was a brief moment of calm while the enemy shifted into position and Max reloaded. Staying on a knee to minimize himself as a target, he leveled the rifle and depressed the trigger. Bullets sprayed the side of the SUV until one hit the man whose gun was caught in the holster. The bullet's impact pushed the soldier backward and his arms flailed as he landed in the snow. A second burst found the kneeling shooter, who spun from the round's impact, and his rifle chattered into the air. The third soldier, who took a position behind a door of the vehicle, returned fire.

Bullets churned up the mud to Max's left, and he rolled to his right to reduce the shooter's angle. Now the soldier had to leave cover in order to find an angle around the vehicle's rear.

Max leapt to his feet and fired as he ran at the Russian Army SUV. Bullets plinked into the rear quarter panel as the soldier sought cover behind the vehicle. A slug hit his calf and he screamed, dropped the rifle, and clutched at his leg.

As the AK's magazine clicked empty, Max reached the vehicle. He tossed the rifle, drew his SIG, and shot the writhing soldier. The truck's driver was sprawled over the steering wheel with blood covering his face and uniform. Max checked his pulse. *Dead.*

He whirled and dashed to the other vehicle. It rested on its roof, wheels still spinning. With his pistol up, he bent and looked through the side window. Two soldiers were in the front; the rear was empty. The men didn't move. To be safe, Max fired a double tap into each and returned to the road.

The quiet was interrupted only by the ticking of the hot engines. He patted down the soldier with the calf wound and pocketed cigarettes, a butane lighter, and a wallet.

A crackle followed by a voice in Russian came from the SUV's interior. Max found a satellite radio on the floor of the passenger side and toggled the talk button. "Da."

"What's your position?"

He clicked the talk button. "Hold."

A Russian military-issued handheld GPS unit was on the truck's floor. Max snatched it, woke up the screen, and peered at the tiny map. The middle of nowhere.

Two choices. Walk or commandeer the SUV. Walking to Grozny—130 kilometers over mountains and dirt roads—was a multi-day journey. Military patrols would increase once this carnage was discovered.

The truck was Russian green in color with a faint camouflage pattern and well marked with the ubiquitous red star of the Russian Army. A string of holes ran along its rear panels and bullets had pulverized the front grill, and the engine had stalled.

Max yanked the dead soldier from the driver's seat, used the man's jacket to clean the blood from the vinyl seats, and climbed inside. He jammed the transmission into park and cranked the key. The engine roared to life. He yanked on the four-wheel drive lever to engage the front axle before putting the transmission in reverse. All four wheels spun for a moment before they caught and the truck lurched onto the road, where he jammed on the brakes. He left it to idle and jumped out. The Russian soldier he shot in the calf lay to his right.

About the right size.

After peeling off the soldier's uniform, Max shrugged it on and adjusted the camouflage pants so the hem was shoved into his combat boots. The soldier's uniform was snug over his civilian clothes, but that was nothing new to an army with a notorious shortage of uniforms. The man's field insignia was the two silver stars of a lieutenant and the name patch read *Smirnov*. He put the dog tags over his head and tucked them under his shirt, pocketed the wallet and identification, and pulled the standard-issue khaki wool cap over his head.

Before he jumped into the driver's seat, he used a rock to scrape off the identification number from the vehicle's side panel and used a screwdriver from the onboard toolkit to wrench off the license plate. While bending under the front fender with a flashlight, he found the GPS transmitter, pried it off, and pulverized it with the rock.

The army vehicle would ensure the locals gave him wide berth. If he ran into another patrol, the momentary confusion might give him an advantage. He hit the gas and left the battle scene behind him.

TWENTY-TWO

Rostov-on-Don, Russia

The nine-hour drive north over dark, icy roads was arduous, and Max fought the need for a cigarette the entire way. Doku's comment echoed in his mind, and in a moment of courage, Max dumped the cigarettes he picked up from the dead Russian soldier. Now he fought the urge to buy some.

As he crossed the Rostov-on-Don city limits, he used Doku's burner phone to map the meeting spot. The GPS coordinates showed a location in an industrial section of the city. Probably some warehouse or abandoned lot where they could meet without being seen.

He left the Russian Army SUV in Grozny and hot-wired a Toyota pickup. A nighttime raid on a used clothing donation center produced boots, jeans, three shirts, and a winter jacket. With a passenger seat strewn with food and bottles of water, Max motored northwest along secondary roads. The trip was an hour longer than using the highway, but this way he avoided denser traffic and random traffic stops.

He had arrived at the city of over a million people on the Don River, two hours before the appointed meeting time. Max found a late-night gas station and bought some cheap toiletries and made an attempt to clean himself up before refilling his coffee and arriving at the location early. He sipped the hot but weak beverage as he surveilled the meeting spot from a dark corner.

The GPS coordinates did in fact lead to a warehouse surrounded by a tall chain-link fence topped with barbed wire. A fleet of black SUVs and sedans were parked in the front lot. The vehicles' drivers sat inside the cars smoking or gathered in small groups talking with their breath coming out in small puffs in the cold air. He counted twelve vehicles. The gate was open.

He left the car on the street and walked through the sliding chain-link gate, past the chauffeurs who eyed him warily, to a side door. There, two ogre-sized men frisked and wanded him, and he dumped his phone and pistol into a metal box, which was locked and placed on a shelf next to a dozen similar boxes. With an ogre at each shoulder, he was led down a dark hallway that smelled of fresh paint. Two more doors and corridors, and the three men emerged into a dimly lit room, and Max was startled at the scene.

Three round tables were surrounded by men in suits who all smoked either a cigarette or cigar. A haze hung at the ceiling and rekindled Max's nicotine craving. Women wearing black smocks sat at each table and dealt cards from a shoe. Stacks of chips, some small, some large, were in front of each man. Three statuesque, mostly nude women threaded through the tables to deliver drinks. The tinkle of music came from hidden speakers. Max did a quick scan, but he didn't recognize any of the men except General Fyodor Bakunin, who sat at the far table immersed in the game.

Unsure of what to do, Max watched the action from the side of the room for ten minutes before one of the dealers stood and announced a break. Men filed past on their way outside to check phones or use the bathroom, and General Bakunin rose to his feet and beckoned Max with a finger.

Calling Bakunin a large man was an understatement but labeling him fat was inaccurate. Tall, broad-chested, and wide, with a large head on a muscular neck, General Bakunin wore a suit with the tie loose. Wrinkles at the corners of his eyes gave away his age, but otherwise he might be able to wrestle a bull to the ground.

The general dismissed the two guards, held a black cloth aside, and ushered Max through a short passage and into the spacious warehouse. Light glowed from high over-head and their footsteps echoed in the empty space as they walked.

"You're among friends here, Mikhail. Your father joined this game on occasion. While we were happy to see him, he invariably cleaned us all out." The general chuckled and drew in a deep breath. "I'm sorry about his passing."

Max shook his hand. "Thank you, General. I under-stand you can help me."

Bakunin placed a roast-sized hand on Max's shoulder and they stopped to face each other. "I told Andrei I'd do what I can. But I admit I have reservations about this plan."

"I've had reservations about everything since my father died, but so far he hasn't led me astray."

"Still..."

Max shifted his feet and caught movement at the far

side of the empty warehouse where a guard patrolled. "Can you do it?"

"Of course. But you have to understand. Once you're in Zurgan, you're on your own."

"I get that."

"To accomplish this without raising flags in Moscow, you'll have to enter the prison as what we call a reserved status. It's a prisoner classification reserved for people we want to, ahem, make disappear. The paperwork makes you anonymous. This is designed so no one at the prison leaks the prisoner's name. It also means the prisoners are treated poorly, especially by the warden."

"I can take care of myself."

"If you're even a fraction of the man your father was, I agree. But still..." The general gazed at the ceiling before he steered Max back in the direction of the poker room. "I have to get back to the table. A warning to you, son. Once you're in, there is nothing I can do to help you. I might be able to get you released, but it will take time. Things happen in that prison that are unspeakable—"

"I'm aware. I've been there several times. General, there is one additional thing I need."

The general crossed his arms. "I'm listening."

When Max told him, Bakunin was silent while he considered the request. "You're asking for a lot."

"Haste is required."

"Right." The general let out a breath and placed his hand on the back of Max's neck. "You'll need to hit the time window precisely. There will be only one shot."

"I understand, sir."

"I'm doing this because I promised Andrei. I admit I never thought it would come to this." He pressed a piece of paper into Max's hand. "Wait at this address. To preserve the charade, the takedown will not be gentle."

With the warning ringing in his ears, Max memorized the address on the paper as he walked through the parking lot to his truck. When he was in the cab, he held a flame from his Zippo to the slip of paper and dropped it in the ashtray.

———

The address was in a low-rent neighborhood on the outskirts of Rostov, far away from the glitz of the upscale shopping areas near the river. Here air pollution from petroleum refineries covered everything in a dingy film and the homes were cinder block and the vehicles were rusted. It was just another one of the hundreds of failed Soviet public housing experiments that littered Eastern Europe and Russia.

The sky brightened a shade of gray as Max wiped down the interior of the truck and left it in the driveway. The home's front door was locked, but the rear opened into a kitchen with cracked linoleum and broken cabinet doors hanging open. A rodent scurried out of the light as Max entered. A search of the house yielded nothing of interest, except for a handful of Western paperback novels and a stack of Russian literature in an upstairs bedroom. He smiled when he found a copy of Russian folktales by Alexander Afanasyev. The stories were his father's favorites, and the old man used to read the fairy tales to Max and Arina when they were children. Max thumbed through the tattered book half expecting to see an inscription with his father's name. Had his father cooled his heals in this safe house while reading Afanasyev's tales?

With the book under his arm, Max returned to the kitchen. A bag of coffee grounds was in the cupboard, and Max wiped mouse droppings from a pan and heated some water. He dumped coffee grounds into the water and let it brew. When he sipped, he felt the grit of the grounds, but the coffee was strong. It was a trick he learned in the army, and Spencer had once told him Americans called it cowboy coffee.

He took the cup and the book into the living room, where he sat and read as the sky's color shifted in shades of gray and cars left for work and citizens walked to the bus stop. Max set the pistol on a side table within easy reach. A wall clock that ticked off the seconds was the only sound in the room. *The coffee in prison won't be as good as this.*

As the clock hands clicked to 8:00 am, there was a crash and a bouncing object in the rear as the kitchen window broke and something landed on the floor. The window on the front door smashed and two hissing canisters bounced across the carpet. One landed next to Max's chair. The metal cans poured a white-gray cloud into the room, and Max's throat constricted and his hand instinctively went for the gun.

Is this really necessary?

Four dark-clad shapes wearing gas masks burst through the front door and ran into the living room. Two more black shapes appeared from the rear, and six red laser sights centered on Max's chest.

A deep voice in Russian issued a command. "Don't move."

Max froze.

"Hands up."

He put his hands in the air and let the pistol swing free on his index finger.

TWENTY-THREE

Rostov-on-Don, Russia

A man dressed all in black and wearing a gas mask plucked the gun from Max's hand while the rest of the assault team held compact assault rifles with red laser sights trained on him. The caustic chemical stuck in his throat and made him cough.

The men were efficient. His arms were secured behind him with plastic cuffs, and he was frog-marched through the shattered front door and into the frigid air, where he sucked in fresh oxygen. As he was dragged along the sidewalk, he blinked hard to clear his vision enough to take in his captors.

They wore identical uniforms with black tactical pants, shiny boots, and black flak vests with no insignia. Wool caps covered their heads and their faces were obscured by the gas masks. They moved as if they were well trained, but they weren't Spetsnaz. For one, they were all shapes and sizes; two tall men, a couple shorter figures, and one who wore a large spare tire around his gut. Spetsnaz were known for uniformity and fitness—no overweight members allowed. For another, their weapons were vintage Russian and well worn. The Spetsnaz were armed with the latest in modern weaponry imported from Germany. These men screamed local police. One man frisked him and removed his cash and his lighter.

The lighter. *Shit*. It was a vintage Zippo with a Belarusian flag burnished on the side. Months before it was given to Max by his late grandfather, and he prized it like a family heirloom. He should have left it at the cherry orchard.

The police officer handed the cash and the lighter to a beefy man in a suit with a pink face, who flicked the Zippo open and closed it with a *ping*. "You won't be needing this where you're heading," the man said as he slipped it into his pocket.

While Max stood on the sidewalk, the pink-faced man walked up to him and put his nose inches from Max's chin. "I don't know who you are, but I know this." The man swung his knee and connected with Max's groin, and Max folded and nearly crumpled to the ground. A fist hit him in the gut and another crushed down on his back. "Behave yourself and there'll be no trouble. Cause problems and these men here will have some fun rearranging your face. Get it?" The pink-faced man in the suit rubbed his knuckles on a handkerchief as two policemen propelled Max down the sidewalk and out to the street. A black van sat with its engine at idle, spewing diesel fumes into the air. Another truck sat down the block.

He landed hard on the cold floor of the van's deck and his ankle was shackled to cold, hard metal. All he saw from his vantage point on the metal deck were four pairs of boots, two on either side. "You guys gonna at least let me sit up?"

The only response was a hard kick to his side. The

driver ground the gears and found the right spot between the clutch plates, and the truck lurched ahead.

———

Time blurred as the truck ride turned into an airplane trip, after which came a ride in a second truck. The airplane was a decaying Antonov An-70 retrofitted for cargo. There the guards let him sit upright on webbed seating, his back against the fuselage, which was more comfortable than lying on the back deck of the truck, except his hands remained zip-tied behind him. It felt like the airplane ride was between two and three hours, but he couldn't be sure.

The second truck ride was short and took place in a light blue bus retrofitted for security. Bars crisscrossed the windows, and his hands, now in handcuffs, were secured to reinforced hooks welded to the vehicle's frame. Four of the black-clad guards rode with him and laughed, smoked, and told stories in Russian. Through the bus windows, dark and featureless plains stretched to the horizon. No city lights were visible, and if mountains were in the distance, he couldn't see them.

After a short ride, the bus bounced over a series of speed bumps and roared through a tall fence topped with barbed wire. Through the bared windows, several towers were visible, each with rifle-toting men.

"Welcome home," one of the guards snickered.

Max winked at him, and the man's smile vanished.

After the bus ground to a halt, Max was yanked to his feet by two guards. Another removed the shackles from the bar and bent his arms behind him to resecure the cuffs. He leaned over at the waist as two guards levered his arms up behind him and forced him to walk along the bus aisle. He stumbled down the bus steps, where a prisoner hand-off of sorts was made.

Four burly guards in greenish-blue camouflage uniforms and tight-fitting ushankas—the Russian fur caps with ear flaps—with the insignia of a gold leaf crossed with an ax and sword, received Max. Two of the newer guards flanked him. Each threaded an arm though his and forced his wrists up while his shoulders were pressed down so he was forced to walk in a hunched over position—what he called the *prison walk*. The prison walk, he knew from his KGB audit of the facility, was designed to exert maximum leverage over a prisoner while preventing them from mapping their surroundings. He craned his neck and caught a glimpse of a large cinderblock building painted baby blue.

Zurgan Military Prison.

Secret even from most of the Russian government and hidden away from the world, the Zurgan Military Prison was located in a closed city north of the Caucasus Mountains. Dozens of so-called closed cities exist in Russia, each serving some military or nuclear purpose, and are sealed off from foreign visitors and the majority of Russian residents without security clearance. Many such cities are left off Russian maps. Zurgan itself was founded in 1947 when a plant was constructed to produce highly enriched uranium and nuclear weapons. Like many closed Russian cities, Zurgan was also home to various other secretive government and military facilities, like the military prison.

The military penitentiary, also known by those that lived and worked around it as Penitentiary Number Nine, was one of a dozen such facilities where the Russian government stowed its most dangerous threats against the state, which included oligarchs who fell out of favor with the Russian president, activists, and journalists. Similar to

America's Guantanamo Prison, the military stockades operated outside the Russian legal system. Running under the
strictest of security classifications, those souls entering such
facilities were seldom ever seen again.

As Max was propelled through a double set of doors,
along a cold concrete corridor, and through a gate, Max
suddenly appreciated the trouble he was in. His clothes
were ripped off and he stood naked while an ogre-sized
male with the cauliflower ears of a boxer probed his orifices
with a latex-clad hand.

A simple bit of trivia about Zurgan prison popped into
mind.

No one has ever escaped.

When the guard pronounced Max free from contraband, a pile of black clothing was tossed at him. He stepped
into a black jumpsuit made of coarse cloth with white
stripes on the arms. A brimless cap, black with white stripes,
fit loosely on his head. The clothing he wore when he
arrived was shoved into a clear plastic bag by an orderly.

Two giant-sized guards flanked him and shoved him
back into the same hunched-over position he entered the
prison with. It was in that position that Max received his
first visit with the warden.

A door clanged open somewhere and footsteps sounded
on the tile before a pair of shiny combat boots appeared in
his field of vision. "Welcome to Zurgan, my friend. I call
you my friend because I'm unaware of your real name. It's a
rare prisoner incarcerated here whose identity is hidden
from me, and you, my friend, have joined that singular
group."

"And who the fuck are you?"

Silence fell over the room, and a loud chuckle sounded.
"Well that, my friend, is a good question. My name is

Colonel Turgenev, but you may call me Boss. I run this place."

"Turgenev, huh?" Max spit on the ground. "I know that name. Wasn't your father run out of the army for taking it in the ass by one of his lieutenants? I'm guessing fondness for cock runs in the fam—"

The kick connected with the underside of Max's chin and sent stars through his vision. He collapsed to the floor.

Max laughed and spit blood. "Truth hurts, doesn't it, Turgenev? I'll bet you go around the prison here letting your inmates fuck you in the ass—"

A fist hammered into the back of his head, causing his vision to waver. While the guards fought to hold him upright, the colonel's red face was visible for a second as he scowled at Max.

It was a bluff, of course. Max had never heard of Turgenev, but now he knew his face.

The guards regained control and forced him to his knees while pushing his face to the concrete.

The colonel's voice bellowed in Max's ear. "I see my friend here is going to be trouble. Give him a dose of the hole to remind him where he is." The polished combat boots snapped a turn and disappeared.

Iron gates rumbled open, and he was marched into a pale white hallway while still bent at the waist. Here the scent of bleach was strong, and a prison orderly with a mop stepped aside as Max and the two guards marched by. The tile floor was nicked and scraped but clean. Both guards' ham-sized hands remained on the back of his neck and forced his head closer and closer to the floor. As he marched in the prison-walk position, the boots of a dozen or so guards appeared along the wide hallway.

Another iron gate receded long enough for the procession to move through. He counted two more gates before he was halted and maneuvered so the top of his head banged against the wall next to a pale green iron door. Swift kicks connected with the insides of his feet to force his legs apart.

Keys rattled, a steel bolt banged, and dry hinges squealed. Pain shot though his shoulders as his arms were wrenched up and he was propelled through the door into a dark room. Momentum carried him through the tiny space and he slammed into a wall as the door clanged shut.

He fell against a wall to catch his breath as a narrow window opened in the metal door.

"Hands." The demand came from outside the door.

He turned so his back was against the door and thrust his hands through the tiny window.

A guard grasped the cuffs and yanked so Max's wrists were wedged against a sharp steel edge. "Now listen up. We call this the hole. You know it as solitary confinement. You eat in there, you piss in there, you shit in there. Sleep in there, if you can. It's dark all the time. If you're lucky, we'll play you some of that German hate metal."

Max's hands were released and the cuffs removed. When he withdrew his arms from the tiny window, he rubbed his wrists and felt viscous liquid. *Blood.*

A cover slid over the opening, a bolt fell into place, and Max was sealed into pitch darkness.

TWENTY-FOUR

Zurgan Military Prison

The room was pitch dark and stank of body odor, an astringent cleaning fluid, and decaying meat. And urine and feces. It was an overwhelming mixture of odors that Max immediately ignored. KGB training included days and weeks at a time in solitary confinement and he knew all the tricks to staying sane.

The first thing he did was pace off the dimensions of his cell, which he found to be four feet by six, or the size of a double bed.

At least I can stretch out on the ground, corner to corner.

Gradually the darkness faded as his eyes became accustomed. A metal urn about the size of a medium vase lay on its side. It stank of shit and piss but was at least empty. He placed it in one corner that would become his latrine. If this solitary confinement was in a facility that was part of the Federal Penitentiary Service, he would be allowed ninety minutes of exercise in the yard and afforded harsh lighting by which to read or write. The lighting, which would click on at 5:30 am and off at 9:00 pm, would help him mark the time. He expected no such luxury in a military prison, so he stretched out on the cold concrete floor. The fatigue of his travels took him into a deep sleep.

Instead of using the lights to mark time, he did so with meals. A rap on the metal door woke him in time to receive a tin tray with a bowl of gruel. He ate every bit of the sodium-saturated soup containing spongy meat and the cake of fried potatoes, and he drank all the sour milk from the tiny cardboard container. The vile food made him retch but it stayed down.

Ritual was one key to maintaining sanity. When the meal was done, he worked up a sheen of sweat performing a long, slow set of bodyweight exercises. After the push-ups, planks, sit-ups, and scissor kicks, he did another round. And another, and another, until he couldn't move his abdomen and his shoulder muscles were knotted. He squatted over the pot to defecate, urinated, and performed what toilet he could, which was limited to cleaning underneath his finger-nails with the nails on his opposite hand. After he finished his breakfast, fitness, and toilet, he sat cross-legged on the concrete floor and meditated.

Or tried to meditate.

He struggled to maintain focus as nicotine withdrawal made his mind jumpy and visions danced in and out of his thoughts.

How are you, little Alex? How can I help you when I'm incarcerated like this?

Arina, Arina. Please wake up. I'm sorry, my sister.

What is this team my father assembled? Who are they? Why is Badū Khan so important?

What would my father do in this situation?

Will Kate be successful and recover the one-time pad?

How will he find Ruslan Stepanov and his father's message?

Why did Goshawk abandon me?

Answers to the questions eluded him as more questions filled his head.

The constant reminder to follow his breath helped him remain grounded and made him aware of his thoughts. Better to be aware of them—like he was positioned up in the corner of the room watching his thoughts happen—than let the fears, depression, and worry consume him.

Lunch appeared, and he repeated the routine. Eat, fitness, toilet, meditate. Dinner and the same round of activities. Even if he didn't need to urinate, he went through the motions. The amount of fitness helped him fall asleep for a few hours each night. He counted seven breakfasts, seven lunches, and seven dinners before they came for him.

When the door panel slid open and the guard demanded his arms, he stuck them out and endured the manacles. The door creaked open, he blinked against the light, and he was prison-walked through two rumbling gates of iron bars painted white. Once again, his head was banged against a wall and his feet were forced apart. Another bolt unlatched—this one had an automatic click he associated with a magnetic control buried somewhere in the wall—and he was thrust into another cell. No words were spoken as the door clanged shut, but he knew enough to slide his arms out the opening in the door so the manacles could be removed.

New digs. This room was lit with flickering fluorescents high above and painted a dingy white. A rectangular window large enough to fit his arm through was along the ceiling. A dented metal commode sat in one corner next to a sink. A cot lay along a wall with a thin mattress and a tattered wool blanket. The floor was a grimy tile that might have been white back in the sixties. He washed his hands and face with a tiny bar of soap and stretched out on the mattress and was soon fast asleep.

It was during his first foray into the prison's general population where his abuse of the warden paid off. He sat at one of the metal picnic tables bolted to the floor, alone with his tray of food, when a large man bent over and banged his tattooed fists on the table. The tray rattled and milk sloshed over the sides of the plastic cup. The prisoner was obese in a way that made his head disappear into his shoulders, but he had a self-assuredness about him. Two skinny youngsters, faces covered with tattoos, stood like guards behind him. An indecipherable tattoo was etched into the man's neck. Max smelled sweat as the fat prisoner snatched a hard roll off the tray with a meaty paw. "You eating this?"

Max tensed but remained seated. The rules of prison fights were simple: Do as much damage as possible in the short time before the guards arrive. A fist to the fat man's throat followed by a yank of his face into the table. Use the split second of surprise to rise to his feet and jam a finger into the fat man's eye socket to rip out his eyeball. The encounter was about to end poorly for the fat man when a voice cried out from across the room. "Vlosi!"

Max held the fat man's stare.

"Vlosi! Don't you know who that is?"

The voice was closer now, and Max took him in using his peripherals. The newcomer was short and approached on bowlegs. A broad chest stretched his prison uniform and his sleeves were rolled up to reveal elaborately colored tattoos along his arms. Long black hair laced with gray was tied in a ponytail and red-rimmed eyes peered out from crinkled and yellow-brown skin. A sparse beard grew on his chin and when he smiled, several teeth were missing.

Badū Khan.

The hair was longer but the Mongolian face was unmistakable.

The newcomer slapped the table. "Vlosi! This is the new guy who called the warden a cocksucker and did a week in solitary."

The fat prisoner, apparently named Vlosi, stared at Max for a beat before a wide grin appeared on his fleshy face. "That right? You're that guy, eh?" He straightened up and tossed the hard roll onto Max's tray, where it bounced and landed in the bowl of gruel. "Eat up, friend. You're going to need it." Laughter erupted from the fat man as he walked away.

Max let out a breath. Another stint in solitary would be painful. He stood to greet the tattooed man, but the short Mongolian had disappeared.

———

Somewhere North of the Caucasus Mountains

"He's where? How on God's green earth did you let that happen?"

Lieutenant Colonel Artur Markov, the recipient of the tongue-lashing, stood in front of the desk. The army-uniformed attaché stationed at the door winced.

Ruslan Stepanov, clad in fatigue pants tucked into spit-shined combat boots, his chest bare and covered in a sheen of sweat, plucked the Kizlyar blade from its sheath on his belt and embedded it into the mahogany surface of his desk with a *thunk*. With a wave of his hand, he dismissed the attaché, who disappeared out the door. Ruslan grabbed a towel and strode to the row of broad windows that faced south, in the direction of the Caucasus Mountains. To the left of the windows ran a row of bookcases the length of the wall. "Speak, damn it!"

Markov cleared his throat. "How he ended up at Zurgan is something we're still working on, sir. We believe he entered the country through the mountains of Georgia. Six days ago one of the army's patrols encountered a pickup truck crossing the border. The unit was decimated. One of the army's SUVs was found in Grozny. We're getting the intel now, but it looks to be the work of Asimov."

The general returned to the desk, yanked the knife from the wood, and ran a thumb along the blade's matte finish.

The colonel shifted his weight from one leg to the other. "From there, he disappeared and ended up at Zurgan."

The general removed a leather strop from a drawer and began to hone the knife. "What is the source of your information?"

"We have a man on staff at Zurgan Prison, sir. Asimov was admitted as an anonymous prisoner. Our source recognized Asimov or we'd still be in the dark."

"Anonymous, huh? That requires someone very high up." Ruslan tested the knife on his arm hair. Was it good luck that Asimov suddenly appeared a few hundred kilometers from his compound? Or bad luck?

"Do we have any idea who jailed him at Zurgan? I mean, this is irregular. Anyone in leadership at that prison who knows who he is would have him transported to Moscow immediately. He'd disappear into the bowels of Lubyanka faster than a cheap hooker can get you off, Artur."

To hide his grimace, Markov hung his head. "We're working on it, sir."

"You'd have to be someone high up in the Russian military to make this happen."

"Zurgan Military Prison is part of the Southern Military District."

"That's General Mikhail Bakunin's command," Stepanov said. "Can't imagine anything like an anonymous prisoner happens at Zurgan without his knowledge."

"I agree, sir."

"Get me our dossier on Bakunin." Ruslan shrugged on a clean white T-shirt.

"Aye, sir," Markov said. "It will be done. There's something else."

Stepanov positioned himself in front of a standing mirror and buttoned up a uniform shirt. "Tell me."

"We have people inside."

"Inside?"

"Yes. Inside Zurgan."

"Explain."

"Two years ago, a squad of ex-Spetsnaz started their own private contractor business. Protection assignments for former Russian military commanders who were selling weapons on the illicit market."

Ruslan tugged to straighten his shirt. "I remember something about that."

"Well, it went badly for them. One of their clients got himself into trouble with the South Africans. He was picked up, interrogated, and held for some time. In a bid to free their client, these four ex-Spetsnaz killed a few civilians in Johannesburg and got caught. One thing led to another and they were extradited home, and the Kremlin stuffed 'em into Zurgan."

Ruslan spun to face his underling, his brow furrowed. "You're telling me this why?"

"Well, sir. We can get to Asimov in the prison."

"And do what with him? Shiv him in the shower? Did my orders to take Asimov alive not get through your thick skull?"

Markov hung his head to avoid the general's gaze.

"What is it, Comrade Markov?"

"May I speak frankly, sir?"

"You may."

"This requirement to take Asimov alive is a problem, sir. Sergeant Dikov is operating with one hand tied behind his back."

The knife thunked into the desk, and Ruslan stepped around the desk to grasp Markov's blouse with both fists. "We take him alive, do you hear me? If Dikov can't do it, I'll find someone who can. Are we clear?"

Ruslan got himself under control and smoothed out Markov's uniform. "No one touches Asimov in that prison, do you understand?"

Markov nodded.

"You're dismissed, Colonel Markov."

————

As Artur Markov exited his boss's office, he tugged at the collar of his uniform shirt and straightened his tie. Ruslan Stepanov was cracking under the pressure. Why was this requirement to take Asimov alive so important? The general wouldn't say. They had Andrei Asimov's message, and it was only a matter of time before they had the one-time pad to decode the message. Once they had the Vienna Archive,

Ruslan's ascendence was secure. The old man's blind spot would get them all killed.

Markov removed his mobile phone from a pocket and dialed a number. When the other party answered, Markov issued an order.

The man on the other end responded. "It will be done."

TWENTY-FIVE

Zurgan Military Prison

After the scene in the mess hall, there was no sign of the tattooed Mongolian. In a prison of nine hundred, where the inmates were kept locked down for twenty hours a day, mingling was almost nonexistent. Days and nights blended together in a rhythm of meals, exercise, and reading. Unlike civilian prisons, this one ran with a military-induced order designed to prevent conflict between inmates. Each prisoner was allowed four hours out of his cell each day. One for shower and breakfast, one for lunch, one for recreation, which Max used in the gym or the yard, and one for dinner. Otherwise, prisoners were confined to their cells. Inmates rotated through cleaning detail, and disorderly conduct was dealt with swiftly and harshly. Although cigarettes were available for a steep price on the prison black market, smoking was prohibited, and Max chose to abstain. Despite the prison's squalid conditions, he slept well, shed five pounds of fat, and put on ten pounds of muscle through fanatical workouts.

Like most prisons, Zurgan had its own black market. If you knew who to ask, drugs, special food items, and even women were available for the right price. Also like most prisons, commodities emerged as a means of exchange in Zurgan. In a prison where smoking was banned, two food items emerged as a barter system between inmates: canned sardines and packages of ramen noodles. Both had a long shelf life and the added benefit of nourishment in an institution where the food was bland and unimaginative.

After a few days, the cellblock's pecking order became apparent. Vlosi was in charge, and he had a cadre of inmates under his command who performed tasks, smuggled contraband, and whispered information in his ear. Among the network of flunkies who worked for Vlosi were prison orderlies and even a few guards.

One guard in particular on Vlosi's payroll was the muscle-strapped boxer with the cauliflower ears who had performed Max's cavity search. This became apparent one afternoon when Max heard the rap of a baton on metal and looked up as the door latch gave and the door opened an inch. He sprang to his feet, ready for anything, when a hiss came from the hallway and a head appeared through the doorway. It was the craggy-faced guard with the ears misshapen from years of boxing. "Message from Vlosi," the man whispered.

Max moved to the door.

"There's a contract out for you," the guard said. "Four guys, former army. Watch your back."

"Why are you—"

The door slammed shut, and the bolt clicked into place.

―――――

On Max's fifth day in the general population, twelfth day as Inmate Number 59783, a prisoner was found stabbed to death in his cell. Word passed among the prisoners that Vlosi had ordered the killing and one of his minions had carried out the task. The dead prisoner was an orderly and a known favorite of the warden. The motive was unknown, although one old-timer whispered to Max in between bench-press sets that Vlosi had a standing feud with the warden and the dead prisoner was a message to Turgenev that the fat man could reach anyone at any time.

Tension in the cellblock rose. Guard rotations increased. Despite the prison's military order, an attack might come at any time and in any place. A well-placed shiv jab while waiting in line for chow. Two men could pin your arms back in the shower as a third man stabbed you repeatedly with the sharpened end of a spoon. Max remained vigilant, stayed an arm's length away from the prisoners at all times, and relied on his sleep skills, honed over years of operational readiness, to rouse himself instantly if anyone set foot in his cell at night.

―――――

Most prison body care goes on at the integrated commode and stainless-steel sink in the prisoner's cell. Inmates are allowed fingertip toothbrushes, tiny pieces of plastic that fit over an inmate's finger with bristles on one side, that are impossible to make into a shank. Shaving is accomplished via a safety razor: a single tiny blade in a hard-plastic case designed to be tamperproof. The razors have a short, soft, flexible handle and are distributed for one hour. Any missing blades are noted and investigated.

The shower is the real adventure. Unlike in the federal penitentiary system where men shower twelve at a time in a large open room under the watchful stares of a guard unit, the Zurgan Military Prison has individual shower stalls with thin plastic curtains for privacy. Each man is assigned a ten-minute window every other day, and if you missed your slot, you were out of luck until your time rolled around again. Prisoners were allowed a bar of soap and a towel in the shower room, nothing else.

Max made it a habit not to miss his allotted time. With the curtain open, he soaked in the cold water, lathered, and rinsed while facing the shower room's entryway. That morning, no other prisoners showered, which wasn't odd enough to alarm him.

As he lathered up, the far door to the shower room opened. Normally, this wasn't remarkable, as prisoners moved in and out of the shower room regularly. Except four prisoners entered at the same time. All four wore their black-and-white striped prison jumpsuits.

Not good.

After rinsing his hands in the shower water, Max stepped into the center aisle, a rubber-floored section of the shower room that ran between the two rows of stalls. Once again, the confined space might work to his advantage.

And he was going to need every advantage. All four men were similar in appearance. Each wore their gray-speckled hair cropped in a buzz cut. Square-jawed, broad-shouldered, and lean, the crew liked to lift in the cellblock's weight room. They resembled the Spetsnaz Max had trained with during his time in the KGB, like the men who invaded their Colorado cabin and the men on the train in France.

Two men blocked the door while two others came at Max in formation, one staggered behind the second. Hands flashed from underneath their jumpsuits and homemade weapons appeared—hunks of sharpened metal with tape wrapped as a handle—and they were on him.

Behind him was a cinderblock wall and empty shower stalls on either side. In close combat, Max was at a huge disadvantage as both men could shove the knives into his abdomen with repeated ferocity and disappear before leaving him to bleed out on the rubber floor.

The lead man bull-rushed and thrust the shiv.

Instead of meeting the charge, Max sidestepped into the vacant shower stall where the narrow walls made it so only one man might attack him at once. With one bare foot on concrete and his other foot braced against the tile wall, Max lashed out with an open left palm and caught the rushing man in the side of the jaw.

The prisoner grunted, turned, and thrust his knife again. Max parried, but his foot slipped on the sudsy floor, and he barely struck the man's arm. The blade nicked Max's side and drew a thin line of blood. The attacker was fast, and the knife flashed in another thrust. Max side-stepped, but his hip hit the shower faucet handle and sent hot pain shooting up his side. The knife cut into his side and a flare of blood spattered across his oblique. The man lowered a shoulder and plowed into Max in an attempt to take him to the ground.

As he met the charge, Max's feet fought for grip and he barely managed to stay upright with his back braced against the tile wall. The knife swipe caught his deltoid. As warm pain flooded his side, Max trapped his attacker's thrusting arm with his armpit and clamped on. With the knife held at bay, he jabbed a finger at the attacker's eye.

And missed.

He jabbed again and missed again.

A mighty heave allowed the attacker to free his knife hand, and he struck at Max's face. Max caught the attacker's wrist with two hands but slowly sank toward the floor as the man's weight overcame him. Slowly, the attacker's knife was lowered toward Max's neck. Any moment, Max's hand might slip from his wet grip on the attacker's arm, and the knife would plunge into his esophagus. As the man's meaty body pressed Max into the ground, the knife got closer and closer to his neck.

A commotion came from outside the stall. It was a series of footsteps, grunts, and the slapping of wet skin. His attacker's attention wavered for a split second.

It was enough.

With his foot planted against the corner of the wall and the shower stall floor, Max brought his other knee up and connected between his attacker's legs. Simultaneously Max jerked down and out and plunged the knife into the surprised man's chest. The blade was too small to be fatal in one strike but it was all Max needed. He yanked the knife free and jabbed upwards. This time the knife sank into the base of the attacker's throat and severed the carotid artery. Blood erupted and sprayed the walls of the shower stall and covered Max with a warm thickness. The blood mixed with the soapy water to make the floor slick as ice.

Max wielded the shank as he stepped from the stall. The attacker was left to writhe on the shower stall floor with his lifeblood slowly slipping down the drain. What he saw surprised him.

One of the former Spetsnaz lay on the ground with a

dull red puddle of blood under him, his eyes glazed. A second prisoner lay in the fetal position with a large gash in his head. The remaining attacker stood poised with a home-made knife clenched in one hand, the other hand outstretched for balance, in the classic stance of a street fighter.

The tattooed Mongolian stood naked with his wet stringy hair plastered to his face and blood spattered on his chest. He balanced on the balls of his feet and studied his opponent with a toothless grin.

Max's appearance caused the attacker to dash for the door. The Mongolian's leg flashed out and tripped the fleeing man, who sprawled onto the rubber matting.

In two strides, Max was on the man and thrust the knife repeatedly into his torso, chest, and neck. With a final swipe, Max dragged the blade across the thug's neck.

Max turned to see the Mongolian man step into a stall to rinse off the blood. Max did likewise and wrapped a towel around his waist. After wiping the weapons clean, the two men left the knives on the floor and departed. In the hallway, Max turned left in the direction of his cell, and Badū Khan made a right.

TWENTY-SIX

Zurgan Military Prison

The rap of a baton on his door rousted Max from the depths of *Doctor Zhivago*, a book that was banned from schools when he was a youngster and was now popular in Russia.

"Get up," an unseen voice growled. "We're going for a walk."

Alarm bells went off in Max's mind. Dinner was over, lights-out was soon. There was nowhere to go. The attack in the shower was only yesterday.

"Hurry up, pig. Don't make us come in there and get you."

He stood and stretched as the door popped open with a click. Two guards stood in the hallway. One was tall, his Adam's apple bobbed as he spoke, and he held a Taser. The other was the cauliflower-eared guard on Vlosi's payroll. He held a metal baton and his brows were scrunched tight. Both men's jaws were set, but their gaze shifted as if they were breaking a rule or three.

The guards at Zurgan wore no name tags or identification, a policy designed to prohibit fraternization between guards and the prison population. Cauliflower Ears pointed down the hall with his baton. "Move. We don't have much time. And no funny business, or we'll beat you like the pig that you are."

Max stepped into the corridor. Cauliflower Ears was two paces behind him, while the guard with the Taser walked last, but offset so he had a direct shot with the electric weapon. An attack now may allow him to take out Cauliflower Ears, but the second guard's electrodes would instantly incapacitate him.

Better to see what this is about.

Instinct told him someone paid the guards to make this happen, which explained their nerves.

They proceeded through two iron gates, operated by a guard in a plexiglass booth, and made three turns before they arrived at a nondescript door set into the concrete wall. While Adam's Apple stood three feet back, Cauliflower Ears used a set of keys to unlock the door. The guard poked Max with the baton. "Move."

The door opened into a dim corridor, its ceiling lined with pipes and conduit, the floor caked with dirt, and the walls rough cinder block. The only light came from bare bulbs strung along a cord high up on the left.

Max glanced back at the two guards, who urged him ahead. "Go, pig."

The door banged shut behind them as the procession walked through the corridor, Max in front. After twenty paces, voices were heard ahead. Cauliflower Ears poked him with the baton, so Max picked up his speed.

A scream came from around a corner in the hallway.

The guard behind him struck a swift blow to his buttocks with the baton. "Move it."

After he turned the corner, Max stopped short. The obese figure of Vlosi was on his hands and knees in the center of the corridor, a pool of blood under him. His prison uniform was torn, and its white stripes were saturated with crimson. Two hulking figures stood over him, one with a metal baton, the other with a switchblade knife. The man with the baton repeatedly struck Vlosi on the back with wicked strikes. The prisoner cried out at each hit.

The attackers, both prison guards, looked up at the interruption. They each wore the standard-issue camouflage uniform pants and T-shirts, which were soaked in sweat. The man with the baton wore tiny glasses, while the guard with the knife filled out his T-shirt with beefy muscles. Another glance behind. The hallway was empty.

What the hell?

The guard wearing the tiny glasses took one last lash at the back of Vlosi's head and the fat man collapsed on the ground. He moved at Max, baton held up and a sneer on his face. "What the fuck are you doing here, prisoner?"

Good question.

The two burly guards approached with weapons raised. "Yeah," the man with the knife said. "You made a big mistake."

With his hands raised, Max took two tentative steps back.

"Not so quick, prisoner." Baton pounced and swung the club.

The narrow hallway made it so only one man could effectively attack. Max shifted his weight and the baton glanced off his shoulder. He brought up an open palm and stepped into his attacker. His arm snaked around his opponent's neck, and he squeezed to cut off the man's air. The momentum allowed Max to pivot the baton-wielder around in time to absorb his fellow guard's knife attack. The blade sank into the first guard's abdomen, and the man screamed. As the bleeding guard sank to his knees, Max snatched the metal baton and swung.

It was a weak attack, but the ball tip of the metal rod caught the knife wielder in the arm. A flick of his wrist and the baton struck the attacker's forearm. Even though the first rule of prison fights is to do damage quickly, here, away from the cameras and guards, he had a minute to get some answers. "You want to live, drop the knife."

A snarl came from the guard as he thrust the knife at Max's chest.

The attack was clumsy. Max danced back, avoided the blade, and swung the metal rod. The baton connected with the attacker's wrist and the switchblade clattered to the floor. A backhand with the baton hit the guard's knee and his leg buckled, but somehow he remained upright. A third swing crushed the guard's hamstring and this time he toppled. Max stepped over him and wound up for another whack.

"Wait, wait!" The guard thrust out his hands, palms out. "Hold on."

The plea made Max hesitate. Blood pooled under the first guard's stomach as he lay curled in a fetal position. The knife glinted a few feet away against the wall. Max pointed the baton at the guard's face. "You move, you die. Get it?"

The guard nodded rapidly, his hands still up.

Max snatched the knife and closed the blade. There were no pockets in the prison uniforms, so he stuck the knife in the waistband of his undershorts. With an eye on the guard, Max checked Vlosi and found his pulse strong.

The stabbed guard wasn't so lucky. That man's pulse was a weak flicker, and the puddle of blood on the concrete grew larger.

"Your friend is going to die," Max said.

"What do you want? I'll do anything. I can get you privileges. Special treatment. You want a girl? Drugs? I can get—"

The baton arced and thwacked into the guard's shin. Howls of pain rang through the corridor.

"I want answers," Max said. "Why are you attacking this man?" He pointed at Vlosi with the baton.

The guard was silent, so Max swung the baton and struck the man on the shin a second time.

When the guard stopped screaming, Max raised the baton again.

"Orders, man. Orders."

"Orders from who?"

"Turgenev, who do you think?"

"So why am I here?"

"I don't know!"

Someone wanted me to help Vlosi.

This was a precarious position. If he was found here among the carnage, the prison staff would assume Max was the aggressor. If he left both guards alive, assuming the knife victim lived, they would make Max's life miserable, and may even have him killed.

A groan came from Vlosi as he awoke. The fat man rubbed the back of his head and tried to stand. "What the fuck?" Vlosi put a hand on the wall for balance, staggered, and finally found his balance. Blood was on the floor and on his uniform. He took in the scene with the wounded guard, the second guard on the floor, and Max standing with the baton.

"Your knife wounds are superficial," Max said to Vlosi. "They were toying with you before they killed you."

The fat man staggered a step. "You need to get out of here."

Max hesitated. "You sure? You don't look well."

"You can't be here," Vlosi said. "Go."

Max pointed the baton at the knife victim. "That one isn't going to make it."

Vlosi let go of the wall and put his hand out. "None of 'em are gonna make it. Now get outta here."

After he handed Vlosi the baton, Max withdrew the switchblade and slapped it into the fat man's hand. He stepped over the pooled blood and disappeared around the corner. When he emerged through the door and into the brightly lit hallway, he found Cauliflower Ears and Adam's Apple.

Cauliflower Ears patted him down while the other man held the Taser. After Max was proclaimed clean, the three men made their way through two iron gates and back to Max's cell, where he was unceremoniously shoved through the door. The lock clicked into place.

What the hell just happened?

————

The weight room was large by prison standards and contained a half-dozen benches and barbells, racks of dumbbells, and stacks of metal plates. The equipment might have dated to the 1960s and was rusted and corroded. Ordinarily, there were six to ten prisoners watched over by two guards and security cameras. Today, favors were called in and payments were made, and when Max entered, the cameras were dark and the room was empty of prisoners and guards. The door opened and Badū Khan strode in alone.

"We have five minutes at the most," Max said. Max sized up the man he was sent to rescue. The Mongolian was short and bowlegged, and when he smiled, dark holes appeared where his teeth should be. Tattoos covered his arms, and despite the pallor many prisoners developed from prison life, his face was perpetually rosy. What was this man's relationship with his father? Time later for pleasantries—this meeting had one objective.

The two men spoke in whispers, and Max stepped close. "You like to read?"

The Mongolian cocked his head.

"Books. You like to read books?"

"Sometimes."

"Can you be in the library tomorrow at 11:45 sharp?"

Badū nodded once.

"Don't be late. Timing is critical."

The door opened, and Cauliflower Ears walked in and gave them an almost imperceptible head waggle. Max and Badū exited the weight room as the green LED on the security cameras winked on.

———

Vlosi reappeared in the prison general population two days after the attack, haggard but still in command. Max was on his usual stroll around the perimeter of the yard. His hands were stuffed deep in his jacket pockets and his head was down while his eyes roved over the handful of prisoners who shared the exercise time slot. The sun was hidden behind low clouds, and his breath came out in little puffs.

The only explanation for how Max ended up in the

back hallway at the same time the two guards attacked Vlosi was Cauliflower Ears acted to save his boss's life. Regardless, it offered an opportunity. Max caught the fat man's eye and made a slight movement with his head.

The fat man was trailed by two skinny and heavily tattooed inmates. With a wave, Vlosi dismissed the two bodyguards before he fell into step with Max. "You did me a solid the other night."

Max kept his gaze forward. "I need something in return from you and your crew. I think you'll like it."

"Name it."

Max described what he needed, and Vlosi laughed hard enough that his jowls shook. "You're right. I like it. When?"

Max named the date. "Make the arrangements."

"Consider it done." There was a spring in the big man's step as he peeled off and summoned his bodyguards for a whispered conversation.

TWENTY-SEVEN

Zurgan Military Prison

The next morning the prison felt ripe with tension. As Max went through his morning toilet routine followed by a slow walk to the mess and the standard breakfast of paste-like hot cereal, brown banana, and milk, there was a pensiveness throughout the cellblock. Guards' faces were stern, set, and grim. Inmates kept their heads down, and conversation was muted.

It must be my imagination.

A flood of thoughts bounced around Max's mind like a hungry monkey as he slowly ate. Max was knowledgeable about Zurgan prison operations and a few of the security protocols from when he was part of the audit team. The visible barriers, the roving guards, the towers manned by rifle-toting sharpshooters, and the multiple rows of fencing were the tip of the iceberg. Infrared was used to search for tunnels in the grounds surrounding the prison. Motion sensors were rigged around the perimeter. All deliveries coming into and shipments going out of the prison were searched and scanned for heat signatures. Despite the decrepit condition of the prison, no expense was spared on security.

Max was about to rise and return to his cell when the immense shadow of Vlosi fell on his table. The big man stopped long enough to toss a crumpled candy wrapper onto Max's tray and mutter a few words. "Good luck today, homes. After this, we're square, ya hear?" He moved off with his enormous girth barely contained in the extra-large prison jumpsuit. Two skinny men, their skin pale as a sheet, trailed after their boss.

Max deposited his tray and walked to his cell, where he fell on his bunk and tried to read. *Doctor Zhivago* was done and he was a quarter through *A Hero of Our Time*, first published in 1840 and what some call the first Russian psychological novel. Full of beautiful descriptions of the Caucasus, the story followed the womanizing and freedom-seeking exploits of a young army officer, who was often described as fiction's first antihero. Max's mind wandered and he found himself rereading passages over and over again. He tossed the novel aside and watched the clock.

Time in prison was an enigma. Inmates had all the time, but time was measured in small increments. Time to sleep, time to shower, time to roam the yard. Limited time to shave before razors were collected and accounted for. Three times a day, inmates were required to be in their cells for the count. Every cell had a clock, and clocks were pervasive around the prison, hung high on every wall, wired to a central time-keeping server managed in the administrative offices. Time in the army and the KGB had conditioned Max to wait, so he waited.

It was a five-minute walk to the library, but to leave

himself wiggle room, he departed his cell at 11:25 am. The library was centrally located at the confluence of three cell-blocks, and special approval was required to exit the cell-block and walk the ten-meter corridor to the cramped storeroom the warden had converted to a library. Max made the walk daily, and the guards were accustomed to his library visits. Two bored guards at the lock-off allotted him ten minutes and he strode through the gates as they clanged shut behind him.

Just as all hell broke loose.

Klaxons rang out that shattered his ear drums. He turned, stomach in his throat, expecting to see the two guards running at him with clubs extended. Instead the two guards emerged from their secure room and drew their weapons, but faced away from Max.

Smoke poured down the hallway from the direction Max had come.

As the smoke enveloped the two guards, four inmates appeared with lengths of cloth over their faces. One wielded a shotgun and the other three carried lengths of pipe with taped handles at one end and nails glued on the business ends. The inmates set upon the guards with weapons flying. As the guards cried out, the smoke completely engulfed the guard shack and rolled at Max.

Max sprinted for the library, where he burst in to find two guards incapacitated and Badū Khan, his face obscured by a cloth, standing over them. Without a word to the Mongolian, Max pulled a folding table to the middle of the room and grasped a second table by the middle and swung it up so it stood on the first. He vaulted to the top of the table and pushed at an air grate in the ceiling.

Badū tossed him a wad of material, which Max fastened around his face to cover his nose and mouth, and handed him a weapon belt from one of the incapacitated guards. Max fastened the belt around his waist and checked the MP-443 Grach pistol, which was Russian military standard issue. There were also handcuffs, an extendible metal baton, and a radio.

Max grasped the edge of the hole in the ceiling and clambered through. The smell of smoke came from down the airshaft as he helped Badū hoist himself up.

A decade earlier, when Max and the KGB team had performed their audit, they identified this airshaft as one of six weaknesses in the building's security. The arrogant warden ignored their recommendations and now it was going to hurt him.

With the Mongolian behind him, Max scrambled along the airshaft on his hands and knees. Billowing black smoke filled the duct, and he fought back the urge to cough. They made two left turns and a right before Max stopped and pushed up on a grate. He propelled himself up and out of the passage.

The grate opened into a storage room. The walls were covered by stout metal shelves, which held a range of boxes with labels indicating paper goods such as toilet paper and paper towels.

Max grasped the top of a shelving unit, climbed up, and pushed on a trapdoor in the ceiling, which gave way to reveal a metal ladder. "Gotta move, we're running late." He disappeared up the ladder.

Cold air hit his skin as Max emerged through the trapdoor. They were on the roof of the prison with a view of the compound below. The sound of a battle was all around. Alarms blared and gun blasts came from the depths of the prison. Guards ran to and fro across the courtyard while smoke billowed from dozens of broken windows.

His battle-trained ears heard the helicopter before it appeared. The four rotors of a Russian Kamov Ka-60 chopped at the smoky air while the fantail hummed quietly. The bird, known in Russian military circles as a *Killer Whale*, slowed to a hover twenty feet over the prison roof as a rope with two harnesses dropped from the sky.

Right on time.

The Mongolian wasted no time strapping in.

Max glanced at the guard towers and saw two men in each, their attention fixed on the prison riot below. The Killer Whale, with its fan tail and muffled rotors, descended from above, where the guards least expected it, and had not yet captured their attention. He fastened the harness straps between his legs and around his torso, and the Mongolian made a circle in the air with a finger. The two men lurched off the ground as the helicopter rose in the air, and Max felt himself gliding through the frigid air.

Shots came from the towers as the guards saw the aircraft rising with the two men floating beneath. Max guessed the tower guards had two types of rifles: the AK-74M standard-issue assault rifle and at least one sniper rifle per tower. 39mm bullets from the assault rifles flew around them in a hail of lead, but the AKs were notoriously inaccurate at this distance and the bullets flew past the soaring helicopter. The sniper rifles would already be deployed in reaction to the riot, so it was only a matter of time before one or more of them were hoisted skyward. As if in answer to his concern, a large-caliber bullet sang by his head and plunked into the underbelly of the helicopter.

The bird's winch whirred and groaned under the weight of the two men. As Max's head approached the underside of the helicopter, a slug pounded into the chest of a man in an olive flight suit who waited with an outstretched arm. The man was propelled back into the cabin while a blossom of blood appeared on his chest. Max found a handle on the underside of the bird and hoisted himself into the cabin, where he fell to the metal floor before scrambling to lend the Mongolian a hand.

A 55mm bullet from a sniper rifle penetrated the under canopy of the Killer Whale, ricocheted off the cockpit's dash, and impaled itself in the pilot's neck. Blood spurted, the pilot slumped, and the bird went into a tailspin.

Max was flung away from the trapdoor and landed with his back against the fuselage. With his harness still around him, Max lurched to the cockpit, flung himself into the copilot's seat, and grabbed the stick with both hands.

Blood covered the instruments but he couldn't spare a hand to wipe it clean. The ground rushed at them as the bird spun lazily and out of control. Underneath them was the white expanse of a snowy field several hundred meters from the prison.

His muscles strained and his hands were slick with blood as Max fought with the controls. Slugs pounded into the fuselage as the prison guards fired round after round at the plummeting bird. With his teeth clenched and jaw set, he slowly managed to gain control of the bird. As the white field rose up from underneath them, the helicopter leveled and the spin stopped. He jammed the stick forward and the bird skimmed along the ground on a vector away from the prison walls.

Luck was not on their side. A bullet plunked into the engine compartment, the craft shuddered, and they lost altitude. The ground hurtled at them while Max fought the controls with both hands.

"We're going to hit. Brace for impact."

TWENTY-EIGHT

Somewhere North of the Caucasus Mountains

The crash felt worse than it was. Max fought the controls until one wheel hit the ground. The landing gear crumpled, and the aircraft tipped until the rotors dug into the ground and snapped off. The fuselage tumbled along the ground and mangled the side panels. Anything that wasn't strapped down flew around the interior, which included the tattooed Mongolian.

When the bird came to a rest, Max shook off the shock of the impact and blinked blood from his eyes. Pain radiated from his head like a halo.

No time.

Panic and adrenaline helped him move. He shrugged out of the seatbelt and surveyed the interior of the heli-copter. The Mongolian groaned from somewhere in the rear. The dead pilot, who wore a Russian military uniform in white-and-gray camouflage, was to his left. Max yanked on the dead pilot's boots, jacket, and pants. There was limited time until prison authorities showed up, but Max rummaged for a first aid kit, some rations, and a few water bottles and tossed them into a leather flight bag with a shoulder strap. Badū appeared and stumbled through the wreckage until he found the dead copilot. After wrestling with the corpse, the Mongolian shrugged on the dead man's uniform and slipped on his boots.

Where had General Bakunin found the pilots? Max assumed they could not be tied back to the general.

Not my problem right now.

After a search, Max found two Russian Army standard-issue AK-74M rifles and a few magazines. The "M" stood for modern and signified an updated version of the AK-74. One of the rifles was kitted with a 1P29 universal sight. Max clambered out of the wrecked helicopter, tossed a rifle to Badū, and started across the tundra with the Mongolian on his heels. The snow was knee-deep with a thin ice crust on top. Each step required him to lift a leg high, set it on the hard surface, crash through the crust, and posthole through six inches of dry snow. A sheen of sweat covered his skin, and he shivered when the wind blew from the north.

A glance behind and the Mongolian stayed close. The shorter man used Max's boot holes in the snow and smiled a toothless grin. "Let me know when you want me to lead."

Their destination was a tree line and a road Max spied from the air two klicks from the crash site. West. Away from the prison. A thin line of smoke curled from the trees, which meant civilization, food, and perhaps a vehicle.

Out here in the snow-covered Siberian plain, they were easy prey to a Russian military equipped with airplanes, heat sensors, dogs, snowmobiles, and platoons of men. Their tracks away from the chopper wreck were clear, as was their destination.

He focused on each step. Place the boot. Crash through the ice. Take a step. Repeat. They reached the road without incident or any sign of pursuit. In both directions, the empty road disappeared into a gray-white horizon. A stand of trees extended away from the road, and the thin line of smoke wafted from somewhere in the timber.

They walked down the snow-packed street a hundred meters before setting off through the trees. Here the snow was thin and the earth was bare in spots, which allowed them to set off in one direction and double back on dirt in an effort to throw off their pursuers.

Before long they broke through the trees and into a clearing where a log cabin sat nestled in a white field. The building's metal roof was covered with a foot of snow, and the entire structure listed to the side. A dilapidated porch ran the length of the front where two decrepit rocking chairs sat. A row of cordwood was stacked along one side, and a pile of tree trunks hacked into one-foot lengths lay near a stump that had a long-handled ax embedded in it. Smoke curled from the roof's stovepipe.

A faint noise sounded in the distance.

"Do you hear that?" Badū whispered.

A helicopter.

Max nodded to his new friend before he snagged the ax from the stump and stomped up the roughhewn steps to the porch.

———

The Spetsnaz commando Egor Dikov rode in the rear compartment of the Hind Mi-24 attack helicopter, his attention glued to a tablet balanced on his lap while his thick fingers tapped, pinched, and zoomed. Around him were five handpicked men, each with a full kit, body armor, night-vision gear, and assault rifles. The soldiers wore regulation winter uniforms, with wool underwear and a white-and-gray camouflage pattern. Thick wool caps, goggles, and gloves completed their cold weather gear. Two men smoked while others tried to catnap.

The attack bird hit an air pocket and dropped a few feet before it steadied itself. Egor caught the tablet before it hit the deck and resumed his study of the map. The crash site was marked with latitude and longitude coordinates. Intel from Markov's sources at the prison indicated the helicopter wreckage contained two dead crewmen and one set of tracks that led west, away from the wreckage. He switched to a view that showed satellite imagery and searched the surrounding countryside. There was a road, a line of trees, and several houses in a loose scatter. The tracks led in the general direction of houses. After toggling his mic, he gave the coordinates to the pilot and resumed his scrutiny of the map.

Just like in France. The assassin on foot in the snow. Except this time I have a helicopter.

His prey was headed for one of the houses closest to the crash site to scrounge for weapons, clothing, and food. And a vehicle. It wasn't genius—it was survival. *It's what I'd do.*

Outside the helicopter window was forlorn whiteness and nothingness. A gray void. Absently, he touched the decades-old scar that ran along his jawline.

Time for payback.

TWENTY-NINE

Somewhere North of the Caucasus Mountains

Max kicked and the door gave way in a shower of splinters, and he came face-to-face with the double barrels of a shotgun.

Behind the shotgun was the oldest man he had ever seen. Rheumy eyes were set deep into a thickly lined face and his mouth formed a toothless snarl. Fingers misshapen from rheumatoid arthritis grasped the gun, one hand on the forestock, the other around the grip. A finger with a long yellow nail pulled tight against the first of two triggers.

Which is older? The man or the shotgun?

The shotgun had a break-action hinged barrel that allowed for reload. The stock and forend were made from walnut, and the receiver was engraved with intricate swirls and swoops. The gun was steady, but the old man's gaze roved between Max and the Mongolian, who had followed Max up onto the porch.

It took Max a split second to disarm the old-timer. As

the old man's eyes shifted to the Mongolian, Max batted the barrel to the right and stepped left while sweeping the old man's legs out from under him. As the frail man went down, Max caught him by the tunic with one hand and plucked the shotgun from his grasp with the other. With the gun's barrels pointed at the ground, he eased the man to his feet and escorted him to the couch. "We're not here to hurt you."

Badū tossed over a length of rawhide, which Max used to lightly tie the old man's wrists. When the homeowner was secure on the couch, they searched the cabin.

"Can't help but feel bad ripping off this old guy," the Mongolian said as he stuffed cans of food into a ratty canvas knapsack.

There were no additional weapons, but Max swept a couple dozen shells of buckshot into his pockets. "Someday we'll pay him back. Tell yourself that, anyway."

The thumping of rotors grew louder.

"They stopped at the wreckage," Max said. "Won't be long before they figure out where we went. Roadblocks are already up, and they're scrambling at least one airplane with gear that can search for heat signatures." He put a dull and rusty hunting knife in his pocket before exiting through the back door.

A carport sheltered an old Russian Army transport. The bulbous hood was painted blue, and the backend was converted to a flatbed. Max swung up to the cab and found the key on the dash. He jabbed it in the ignition and turned. Nothing. After two more cranks, the old truck fired up. He let the engine run, dropped down from the cab, and found six full gas cans, which he secured to the rear bed with jute rope.

Max entered the kitchen, where he found Badū. The Mongolian flung matches, a rusty knife, and a few more canned goods into his bag. In another cupboard, they found twelve bottles of water in a wooden crate, which Max slung up to his shoulder.

"Your chariot awaits," Max said.

"I heard the engine crank. Let's go."

They exited the cabin, and the Mongolian clambered up to the truck's passenger side, tossed the bags into the footwell, and held on as Max ground the gear into first and bounced the truck over the rutted track and onto the road.

The thumping of the helicopter grew louder.

————

The truck groaned, wheezed, and shimmied. The bald tires slipped and slid on the icy roads, and more than once, the large vehicle threatened to hurtle off into a snowy field as they rounded corners. Badū's fist was white as he gripped the door handle.

Max accelerated as they hit a straightaway. If his sense of direction was correct, they were headed south. The white ice of the road blended into the white fields on either side which merged into the gray skies, giving the impression they were hurtling into a cloud bank.

"The further south we can get, the better." Max gripped the wheel with two hands but inspected his new friend. Despite the harrowing escape, the Mongolian wore a smile on his face and had a glint in his eye. "Is your name really Badū Khan?"

"It is. I'm a direct descendant of Batū Khan, also known as Sain Khan, the great grandson of Genghis Khan and the founder of the Golden Horde."

Great. I rescued a madman. "Well, congratulations, Badū, founder of the Golden Horde. Are any of your horde going to sweep down on their horses from those mountains and rescue us from the Russian Army, which is probably tracking us via satellite?"

Badū snorted. "Unfortunately not. Catherine the Great finally defeated us 1783."

"But really? You're a direct descendant of Genghis Khan?"

"Indeed, I am. And you are Mikhail Asimov, son of Andrei Asimov."

"You knew my father."

"I did." Badū peered out the window. When he spoke, his breath came out in little puffs and the window briefly fogged up with each puff. "You know that Russian school-books teach that the Mongol invasions and occupation brought nothing but suffering, pain, rape, and humiliation. The reality is the Mongols taught the Russians a thing or two about centralized government, military expansion, and autocratic rule."

Max fought to keep the truck upright while they hurtled around a corner.

"The Russian president is a khan," Badū went on. "What he says is rule, law. What he says is done. What has evolved in Russia is not communism but an autocracy similar to China. Ironically, both Russia and China were once under Mongol rule and now they've evolved to similar ruling styles." Badū turned to Max. "Did you know that China recently amended its constitution to allow its president to remain in office for life? Do you think the current Russian president doesn't also want the same?"

The truck skidded, and Max let off the gas to control the vehicle. "This is an illuminating history lesson, but how did you know my father?"

"Do you know the siege of Jalalabad?"

Max downshifted to maneuver through an S curve and searched his memory. "1989, I believe. The mujahideen, supported by Pakistani intelligence, attacked Jalalabad, which was held by the Russian-supported Afghani army. The mujahideen failed to take the city. Perceived by many as a Russian victory."

"Precisely. Your father and I were in Jalalabad together."

"But you're Mongol."

"Mongolian," Badū corrected. "And yes. The Mongolian General Intelligence Agency partnered with the KGB on an attempt to remove a local warlord."

It was Max's turn to laugh. "Mongolia has a spy service?"

"Of course. It's one of the oldest in the world. Started in 1922."

"Wait—" Max glanced over. "So... you're part of that agency."

"Watch it!" Badū clutched at the door handle as the truck skidded and tires collided with a bank of snow.

Max fought with the wheel and righted the truck.

"I was," Badū said. "Before that I was in the 330 Special Task Battalion, which focused on counterterrorism."

"What was your specialty?"

"Sniper." Badū smiled a toothless grin.

The next question was delicate, so Max put some thought into how to ask it. Somewhere between C's information that Badū leaked Vienna Archive documents to MI6 and his father's trust in the man was the truth.

Badū broke the silence. "Right now, you're wondering if you can trust me."

"Right."

"Andrei saved my life," Badū said. "Not in the traditional way, like I was bleeding and he put a tourniquet on my leg. No, it was more subtle." The Mongolian held out his forearm. It was covered with bright red, yellow, and green tattoos of fierce battle scenes.

"I have a friend you should compare tattoos with," Max said.

"Look again." Badū moved his arm to allow a closer inspection.

There among the blood-soaked swords and fierce Mongolian warriors were dozens of scars. The distinct pattern of needle marks.

"Those look old," Max said.

"They are. I haven't shot anything in five years. Before that, I was in a dark place." The Mongolian talked while he gazed out the side window. "It was my work. Too much killing. Death. It was all I knew. I turned to the junk. Finding money to stuff more heroin into my veins consumed me. It was the only way to forget..." His voice trailed off, and the blankness of the gray snow trailed by the window. When he looked back over at Max, there were tears in his eyes. "And then Andrei found me. He got me some help. And gave me a job. Once again, I had a purpose. Andrei was my only family."

"He became your father," Max said.

"Yeah, which probably sounds weird to his son."

"Nah. Andrei was like that."

"If your son was in prison, unlawfully, what would you do to get him out?" Badū asked.

An image of Alex in a cell sent cortisol coursing through his bloodstream, and Max didn't reply.

"Besides," Badū said. "You need my help to break into Stepanov's compound and retrieve the one thing that will help you find the Vienna Archive."

THIRTY

Somewhere North of the Caucasus Mountains

The search of the six farmhouses near the crash site didn't take long. Egor divided his team into three teams of two men and each team performed cursory searches of the six farmhouses. The radio call came when the third team found the old man trussed in the cabin. "They're in a blue truck, boss."

"Did he see which way they went?"

"Negative."

"Weapons?"

"One shotgun. One knife."

"Copy." Egor dialed the satphone and got through to General Stepanov.

"Report," barked the general.

Egor spoke calmly. "I'm not seeing any Russian military out here. It's almost like we're the only ones out here searching. What's the status on roadblocks and the thermal imaging?"

"None"

"Sir?"

"No army search party has been mobilized."

Egor scratched his head. Ten paces away, his men stood in a circle and smoked cigarettes. One man told a joke and the others laughed.

"He's headed south," Stepanov said. "Stay behind him and flush him south."

"How—"

"Because he's coming here." The transmission ended, and Egor scratched his head. *You cagey old fuck.*

With a glint in his eye, Egor twirled his finger in the air, indicating to his men to board the Hind. His five commandos boarded the bird as her rotors stirred up a swirl of snow. Peering westward down the desolate road, he pictured a desperate Asimov hunched over the wheel of an old truck, fear of pursuit gnawing at him. Egor settled back onto the edge of the Hind's doorway as the bird lifted and spun to the northwest. Even though Egor saw nothing in the sea of white below that resembled a speeding truck, he knew.

The target is out there.

Your time will come, Asimov. And when it does, I'll be there to welcome you to the afterlife.

———

"So the story is true?" Max eyed the gas gauge as the indicator bounced around near empty.

The Mongolian peered at Max. "What story?"

"You were on my father's team. It was your job to leak bits of the Vienna Archive to MI6."

"It's true. How is C?"

"He's worried about you."

The Mongolian grunted. "He's just disappointed the trickle of documents dried up."

The engine sputtered and the truck lurched. Max brought the vehicle to a stop and Badū leapt out to empty one of the gas cans into the truck's tank. As he waited, Max scanned the sky for any sign of airplanes. Seeing none meant nothing. The Russian Army was probably tracking them via satellite. The road was empty. They hadn't encountered a vehicle since departing the old man's cabin. Something was off.

Why was there no evidence of a pursuit?

It was there. Invisible.

When Badū climbed back into the truck, Max steered the truck back onto the road. Badū broke out a bag of cured venison, and the two men talked while they munched on the hard meat.

"What do you know about the Vienna Archive?"

Badū laughed. "Wonder who started calling it that? Ruslan Stepanov killed Sergei Fedorov and stole your father's message to you that indicates the location of the hidden files."

"Correct. But how do you know this?"

"You think I can't get information in prison?" Badū watched the landscape sliding by. "Stepanov has a compound down near the Caucasus Mountains. It's where he trains his little army of Spetsnaz. If he has the message, he'd keep it there. Guarded by a hundred men, it's the safest place to hide it."

"What if he's already decoded the location and is retrieving the files?"

"He doesn't have the one-time pad." Badū smiled. "Yet."

"Do you know where the archive is?"

"I do not." Badū smiled. "I only know its location is outside of Russia and is not easy to get to."

He's lying. "Tell me about this compound."

"It's a former monastery about a hundred kilometers from Grozny on the edge of the Caucasus Mountains."

"What do you know about its defenses?"

"The building is ancient. It began as a fort before it was converted to a castle. Eventually it fell into disuse until a flock of monks turned it into a monastery. About a decade ago, Stepanov turned it into a compound to house and train his personal army of elite Spetsnaz."

"He kicked out the monks?"

"Apparently."

"That's cold."

For a minute, the thumps of a helicopter emerged over the roar of the truck's engine. The telltale sound came from the rear. The two men exchanged glances. After ten minutes, the thumping of the rotors disappeared.

"They're pushing us south," Badū said.

"Into a roadblock."

"No," Badū said. "To Stepanov's compound."

Max frowned. "Why?"

"They know we're coming. And it's exactly where they want us."

THIRTY-ONE

Saint Petersburg, Russia

A dirty blue-and-white bus groaned by and sprayed slush and mud on the sidewalk of the Palace Bridge. The deluge forced Kate to sidestep and hug the bridge's green metal railing. A stream of cars and buses trundled past in a slow procession under an inky gray sky whose clouds threatened precipitation. Kate blended into the straggle of pedestrians who were bundled in wool coats, thick fur caps, and scarves over their faces.

The silence from Max was worrisome. She chose not to call Baxter and endure his harangue. Calls and text messages to Goshawk went unanswered. With no way to get information without blowing her cover, she endured the silence and trusted Max was okay. Such was the nature of her profession.

Dressed in a smart tailored wool overcoat, wool suit skirt, leggings, boots, and crisp top, she dodged another spray of slush and hurried from the bridge, made a left on

University Embankment and, with the river Neva on her left, found her way to a side entrance of the long red-brick building with white-painted trim that housed the main offices of Saint Petersburg State University.

Inside was only slightly warmer than it felt outside. She removed her gloves and presented herself to the pale-faced guard behind an elaborately carved reception desk. The business card she handed over described her position as an assistant professor of mathematics at Columbia. "I am here to see Professor Leonhard Euler." She spoke in halting Russian. "I apologize, I'm still learning your beautiful language."

The guard didn't smile.

After a long delay that involved several telephone calls, she was directed to a flight of expansive stairs. The guard pointed with two fingers like his hand was a pistol. "Second floor."

The hallway was empty, and her boots echoed on the marble floor as she began up the steps. A handsome broad-shouldered man wrapped in a long coat pattered down the stairs as she walked up. Rimless spectacles were perched on a flat nose. The man was hatless and his hair was cut high and tight. His posture and manner screamed military.

The man ignored Kate as she took the stairs two at a time.

The hallway at the top was covered in a parquet floor of orange oak. Glass and wood cabinets covered the wall to her left while rows of arched windows allowed a pale gray light to cast shadows along the ornately inlaid wood floor. The university was established by Peter the Great in the early 1700s and it looked as if the interior hadn't been updated since. She found the right door and rapped with her knuckles.

It was opened by a man who could only be described as sallow and wispy, like the wind might blow him away. Red-rimmed eyes peered through Coke-bottle lenses that gave him the appearance of a bug. A few strands of white hair flew around a cone-shaped head.

"What do you want?" He spoke in fluent Russian, although the man's heritage was Swiss. A riff of jazz came from the interior of the office along with a plume of sweet pipe smoke.

A glance up and down the hallway and no one was in sight, but Kate knew from her days as CIA's station chief in Moscow that there were eyes and ears everywhere in Russia. She bowed and presented her fake card from Columbia University with both hands. He moved to take the card but she reversed it so he could view the back, where she had written the code phrase in red ink. *The red dragonfly exists because it exists and for no other reason.*

The professor's face blanched like he saw a ghost. "Wait here."

He reappeared a moment later with a parka sized for a giant. With her arm in his grasp, he propelled her along the hallway, down a flight of back stairs, and out through a side door.

When they reached the street, she said in a low voice, "I must congratulate you, Professor Euler, on the paper you presented at CERN last month. It was breathtaking in its scope."

His reply was to grip her elbow tighter and push her through an intersection and into a long, narrow greenway that ran along the edge of the university. The open spaces were covered in gray snow.

With a hurried glance over his shoulder, the professor

leaned close, his grip now hurting her elbow. "Did you send someone earlier?" This time he spoke English.

The question stunned Kate. "No, of course not. Why—"

"A man showed up not thirty minutes ago and said the pass code. I gave him the... uh... package."

A shot of hot blood coursed through Kate's veins. "This man. What did he look like?"

"Oh no," Professor Euler moaned. "What have I done? Andrei—"

"Professor Euler. It's okay. How could you have known? The man had the passphrase. It's not your fault."

Grabbing his temples with both hands, the professor cried out. "Oh, God. Oh, God. Andrei, I let you down."

The professor's moans got progressively louder. Two students, their oversized backpacks bouncing on their behinds, hurried along the snowy path. Kate let them pass before spinning the tiny man around to face her. "What did this man look like?"

The professor sputtered. "Uh. Medium height, broad shoulders. Like an Olympic lifter."

"Shit. Long coat, eyeglasses? Flat nose?"

"Yes, yes. That's him."

The man hurrying down the steps.

She left the professor standing alone in the snow and sprinted back into the red-brick building where the surprised guard stood at his post. "Where did the man go just now? He had on an overcoat. No hat. Black hair?"

The guard stared at her.

"I'm sorry." Kate put her hand on the desk. "He left something behind in Professor Euler's office. I need to make sure he gets it back."

The sentry touched the log book but peered around the empty hallways.

After rustling in her purse, Kate held up a thumb drive. "It's important he get this back."

The guard consulted the logbook. "Do you mean Professor Borodin?"

"Yes, yes, that's it." *The only other human that's graced these halls in the past three hours, you numbskull.*

"Yes, let's see." The guard traced his finger along the entries in the logbook as Kate strained to see over the desk. "He arrived twelve minutes ago and spent five minutes with Professor Euler—"

"Yes, I know. Thank you. But which way did he go? I need to catch up with him."

With his hand in the shape of a pistol, the guard pointed to the west doors. Kate dashed off. To her back, the guard yelled, "Ma'am, he asked for directions to the Vasileostrovskaya metro stop. Maybe—"

Kate punched out the door and lost the rest of the guard's sentence. She conjured up a memorized map of St. Petersburg's metro system, turned left, and sprinted through the campus buildings before emerging onto a busy street. There she careened left past a towering Christmas tree decorated with red, yellow, and blue balls, and almost caught her thigh on the wrought iron fencing surrounding the gun metal gray statue of a man leading two horses and a blue tram. When she reached the entrance to the metro, she took the escalator steps three at a time, handed over the correct number of rubles to the booth attendant, and hurried to the platform where a smattering of pedestrians waited for the next train.

As she peered up and down the platform, she covered her face with a light scarf. Maybe the man had mentioned the metro to the guard in an attempt to throw off a pursuit and was now settled into a warm cab. There weren't many dark-coated men on the platform, and she threaded through groups of students in colorful jackets and housewives carrying their shopping bags.

There.

At the end of the platform. The man's hands were shoved into the pockets of his dark blue wool coat. Hatless despite the cold. Rimless glasses and a flat nose.

It was the man who passed her on the stairs.

THIRTY-TWO

Saint Petersburg, Russia

A rumble and a whoosh of air came from the tunnel, signaling the approach of a train. As the breeze ruffled her hair, Kate sidled closer to her quarry. The man in the blue overcoat was unhurried, although he glanced around the platform several times as he stood with his back against a wall. Somewhere buried in his pockets was the item Andrei had left with Professor Euler for safekeeping.

A red and silver train groaned to a halt and the doors swished open. Her target shifted aside as a hoard of students emerged before he entered the train. Kate stepped aboard the train one car down from the man in the blue overcoat and moved to the connecting door, where she watched him grip a steel bar as the train got underway.

Unlike many of the riders who took advantage of the metro's ubiquitous free Wi-Fi and plastered their faces to their devices, the man in the blue overcoat did nothing. He remained motionless and faced the door, but Kate observed the man's eyes as they roamed around the train car.

When the automated voice indicated they approached Gostiny Dvor station, the man in the blue overcoat leaned in the direction of the door. It was slight but noticeable under observation. *A trained operative but not that well trained.*

As the train ground to a halt at the busiest station in Saint Petersburg, he stepped on the platform and disappeared into a throng of people. Kate followed and managed to keep him in her sights as he approached the stairs that would take him either up and out to the street or down to the blue line.

As the man took the concrete steps down, a vision appeared in her mind: the same man on the stairs at Saint Petersburg State University, his right hand inside his jacket like he was placing something in the inside pocket.

An idea.

It was risky, but the crowded station afforded her an opportunity she may not get later. At any moment, the man might pass the package to another pedestrian or emerge from the station and jump into a waiting car or taxi. She couldn't afford to lose him. The risk was necessary. She removed her scarf, tucked her curly hair under her hat, and took the stairs down two at a time as if she were late for a train.

At the landing she stopped and searched the tops of heads in the crowd. A moment later she spied the man in the blue overcoat picking his way through the thick crowd. After crossing the steps at an angle, she shot into the pack and squirmed around commuters until she was ahead of her quarry. She ducked to wrap the scarf around her head gypsy style, and reversed course. The man in the blue overcoat walked right at her.

I have one shot.

With her eyes on the crowd in front of her, she avoided looking at him as they passed. As their shoulders jostled, she snuck her hand into his left inside coat pocket, felt a flat object, grasped it between forefinger and thumb, and plucked it out as she wormed by.

A right turn followed by a left, and she ducked behind a tall standing sign that offered metro users a system-wide view of the routes. The scarf went into her bag and she shook out her hair. The pilfered item went into her bag under the scarf as she emerged from behind the sign. As she peeked over her shoulder, the man hurried to the end of the platform.

Oblivious.

A train approached and the doors hissed open. The man stepped inside and the train departed.

She shrugged on her wool coat as she took the stairs two at a time. Outside, where two busy roads intersected, she flagged a taxi and ducked into the warm back seat to begin a long surveillance detection route. As the cabbie bitched about the traffic, the weather, and his wife's borscht, Kate withdrew the stolen item from her bag.

It was about four-by-three inches and as thick as twenty sheets of thin paper. Encased in a plastic baggie, the pages were dogeared and yellowed, and the cover was maroon like a Russian passport but devoid of markings. She removed the pamphlet. The first page showed rows upon rows of Cyrillic characters in five-character groupings. Even with her fluency in Russian, the words were gibberish. She reinserted the pad into the plastic, hid the package inside her shirt where it was secured by her bra, and watched the traffic for any surveillance.

A grin appeared on her face as she pictured the man in the blue overcoat as he arrived at his destination, patted his breast pocket, and realized the item was gone. In Russia, men lost their lives for lesser offenses.

The operational win was a fleeting emotion, the jolt of dopamine from an addiction. As she performed a lengthy surveillance detection route and hopped on a train to Estonia, the pride was replaced with something she didn't expect.

Hope.

This is why I agreed to work with Andrei a year ago.

Back then, while with the CIA, her operational objective was to secure the Vienna Archive for the Agency. Pretend to go along with Andrei's scheme until the archive's location became known. But since meeting Max, her emotions became jumbled.

Was the one-time pad her ticket back into the CIA's good graces? Or was she on team Asimov? The thoughts nagged at her as she went from the taxi to a subway and back out to another taxi. Even as she crossed the border into Estonia and drifted asleep, the conflicting emotions tormented her.

———

What would happen if I didn't send the message this time? Maybe the ends justified the means, but whose ends mattered?

Goshawk stood on a small wooden platform she had built on top of the warehouse she called home. It was a small deck, maybe four-by-four meters, with a wooden railing. A handful of green plants were in wooden boxes attached to the railings. A bottle of rosé sat within arm's reach. The views took her breath away.

Here above the city she loved, she liked to breathe in the scents of the bustling metropolis. Diesel fumes, the smell of paint thinner that somehow pervaded the city, and wafting odors of trash reminded her of real life. Some of her best thinking happened here, and the outside air, as polluted as it sometimes was, helped reset her mind after endless hours of computer time.

Clouds threatened moisture, and she shivered against a sharp breeze in the light wool sweater and jeans. She drained the cold rosé by chugging straight from the bottle and used the ladder to return inside. There she opened a new bottle of the same wine, draped a wool throw over her shoulders, and woke her computer.

Maybe someday he'll forgive me.

Her fingers flew over the keyboard. *Subject has recovered the prize. Currently en route to Germany through Estonia. Stay tuned for real-time updates as she approaches Berlin.*

The tub was no longer sufficient to calm her angst. Bottle in hand, Goshawk walked wearily up the steps to her bedroom suite where she opened a small overnight bag and tossed in a few belongings for her upcoming trip. Soon it will all be over.

When the case was full of her travel necessities, she opened the dresser's top drawer and removed a small, flat leather case, a bent metal spoon, a syringe, and a baggie of powder. Her clothes dropped to the floor. Naked, she sat on the bed, tied a rubber tube around her calf, and found a spot between her toes where she poked the needle. Slowly she eased in the syringe's plunger and sank back into the pillows as the drug washed over her mind.

THIRTY-THREE

Somewhere in the Caucasus Mountains

Through the scope attached to the AK-74M assault rifle, the monastery evoked lost memories of majestic structures with its colorful walls, towers capped by onion domes, and open wards. Now the compound lay in decayed ruins. Weathered stone walls formed a pentagram punctuated by fortifications at the corners. The towers had pointed roofs that held bare flag poles where sentries stood with long rifles and scopes. A worn track in the snow led to a triplet of arched doorways that made up the main gate. Behind, the complex rock cliffs jutted up on two sides of the pentagram to provide a natural barrier to the west and northwest.

From their vantage point high up on a rock outcropping, at least five buildings were entrenched between the walls. A long five-story hall dominated the center of the compound. Next to the hall stood a tower topped by a corroded and weathered onion dome. A smaller building with a carved cross stood near the front, and three more narrow buildings skirted the perimeter. The balance of the interior was made up of snowy courtyards, vacant paddocks, and stacks of cordwood. Military transports and a hulking helicopter sat in a corner. Outside the walls, windblown plateaus stretched north, east, and west. A few klicks east was a bare plain of dirt and scrabble with a big fire pit and nothing else.

A desolate place.

The scope was attached to one of the nicked and scarred AK-74M assault rifles they found in the downed helicopter. Despite its appearance, the weapon would fire. If the Kalashnikov was known for anything, it was reliability. Not accuracy.

"Any other intel about this place?"

Badū grunted. "Like I said, at any one time, the compound might house up to a hundred soldiers. Some are current Spetsnaz permanently attached to Stepanov as security detail. Others are retired soldiers co-opted into his private army. I guess it depends how many he's got deployed around the globe instead of barracked here."

"Any idea which building Ruslan stays in?"

"None."

Through the scope Max picked out a handful of men on patrol along the wall's perimeter, dressed against the elements in camouflage similar to what he and Badū wore. Otherwise the compound was devoid of movement. "Assume motion sensors and extensive surveillance cameras. Ideas?"

Badū grunted. "Repel down the cliff under cover of darkness."

"You must have some rope squirreled away in your pocket." Max remembered the last compound he broke into. "Any tunnels?"

"No clue."

Four hours of surveillance yielded no action in the compound and no ideas. There was no sign of Ruslan Stepanov.

Another extended silence stretched into an hour.

"Why are you here?" Max asked.

"Where else am I going to go?"

"No. I mean, what's your role in this?"

"You're asking if you can count on me."

"That's exactly what I'm asking."

"You can. My reasons are my own. But yes, you can count on me."

"In that case, here's our plan." Max told him.

———

The alert came from the front gate at exactly 3:03 a.m. Egor was instantly awake, pistol in hand. The radio on the floor next to his cot squawked, but the message was not what he expected.

"Boss. We got an unidentified male approaching the front gate."

Egor toggled the mic. "Vehicle?"

"Negative, sir. On foot."

What the hell? "Description?"

"Um. Ordinary-sized male, sir. Dressed in Russian Army winter fatigues."

"Describe his face, soldier." Egor wore his uniform to sleep, and now he swung his legs out from under the warm wool blanket.

"His face is covered, sir."

"Shit." After he yanked on his boots, he shrugged on his jacket, holstered a pistol, and strapped his rifle to his back.

Every instinct screamed at him to order his soldier to shoot the visitor.

An icy blast hit his face when he stepped from the barracks where he slept and trudged across the open ward to the building that housed the front gate. He stomped up the stairs and joined his sergeant on the rampart that overlooked the snowy track that led to the front gate.

Sure enough, about five meters from the wall, bathed in the harsh light of a spotlight, stood a military-aged male wearing Russian Army fatigues in the distinctive white-and-gray camouflage pattern. A scarf covered the man's face, and a gray wool cap was pulled tight on his head. The visitor appeared weaponless. Egor grabbed the bull mic from his sergeant and bellowed into the mouthpiece. "Identify yourself!"

The visitor didn't move.

"He's not talking, boss."

"I can see that," Egor snapped. Into the bullhorn, he ordered, "Identify yourself. If we have to come out and get you, you're going to regret it."

Nothing.

"Shit. Get that piece of dog turd in here."

The sergeant issued a command. Two gorilla-sized Spetsnaz slung their rifles over their backs and trudged down the steps. A minute later, the oversized doors creaked and groaned as they trundled open. Egor's heart was in his throat as he watched the motionless soldier below. The man had not moved. Soldiers stood on the ramparts with their rifles trained on the mystery man, and the snipers in the towers also had him in their sights, yet Egor's stomach was seized in knots.

What the hell kind of stunt is this?

The two soldiers appeared below, walking abreast. As

they approached the mystery man, the stranger neither tensed nor stirred. He stood there, legs shoulder-width apart, gloved hands by his side.

One of his men said something to the stranger before the other patted him down. Egor held his breath as his man searched the stranger's legs and torso, but there was nothing. The two Spetsnaz grabbed the stranger roughly by the shoulder and pushed him in the direction of the keep's massive open doors.

It wasn't until the three men disappeared into the entryway below that Egor realized his mistake.

I never saw his face.

———

The soldiers led the stranger into the tunnel.

The oversized wooden entry doors to the keep gave way to a dim tunnel under the stone wall before it opened into the courtyard. Barricaded doors, unopened for decades, lined the tunnel. A second set of immense wooden doors stood open to the courtyard.

The moment the trio was under the shelter and out of the direct line of sight from the sentries on the walls, a small, dull blade appeared in the stranger's palm. The knife arced through the darkness and swiped across one soldier's bare neck, and a gush of blood spattered on the walls. The stranger hurled the knife and impaled it into the lead man's throat. Both soldiers' hands went to their necks as they gurgled and sank to their knees.

The stranger plucked the AK-74M from one of the dying soldiers, ripped the pistol from the man's holster, and melted into the shadows.

"It's a trap," Egor blurted as he sprinted down the carved stone stairs.

Staccato gunfire erupted from the tunnel below and one of his men in the courtyard fell.

Egor yanked his pistol free as he ran. "Pin him in the entryway. Go, go!"

Men scattered. Some fanned out through the courtyard. Others spread along the wall and scanned the interior of the compound.

While holding his pistol in a two-handed grip, Egor reached the foot of the stairs and stopped with his shoulder to the stone wall. The tunnel's opening was around the corner. To his horror, he watched another burst of gunfire from inside the tunnel catch a soldier's leg as he ran across the ward. With his pistol trained on the dark opening where the intruder was, he toggled his mic. "Grenades, damn it. Someone bring grenades."

By now his men had formed into a defensive position with six rifles trained on the opening. He knew at least three snipers in the towers had line of sight to the main doors leading into the courtyard. More men scrambled from the barracks.

A soldier named Yuri sidled up to him and tapped him on the back. Two Soviet-made F1 fragmentation grenades, nicknamed *limonkas* after their yellow-green color, were in his hand. Egor grabbed one, yanked the pin, glanced at Yuri, and counted down with his fingers. Yuri pulled the pin on the other grenade.

As Egor counted to two on his fingers, blood spattered the side of his face when Yuri's cheek exploded as a heavy-caliber slug ricocheted off the stone wall. Yuri collapsed and the live grenade slid from his hand, bounced on the ground, and came to rest a meter from Egor's position.

Decades of war-bred instinct took over, and Egor simultaneously flung himself away from the live grenade and attempted to hurl his own grenade into the dark hole of the keep's entryway. *Where did that shot come from?*

Three events happened concurrently. Yuri's grenade exploded and sent a shower of stone and dirt at Egor's head. Egor's grenade bounced off the jamb of the entryway and careened back out into the ward, where it exploded harmlessly. A sniper round found the head of a second Spetsnaz, who collapsed in front of him.

Sound became muffled as the action around him slowed. With his ears ringing, Egor saw a third soldier go down from a sniper round and knew they had a big problem. While they were focused on the stranger in the keep's entryway, a second man must have penetrated the walls and overpowered one of his sniper posts.

Dazed from the grenade, and blood oozing on his cheeks, Egor looked up to see a fourth soldier fall from the sniper. What was happening? His mind was foggy, so he stayed in a crouched position with one knee on the ground.

A fifth Spetsnaz took a bullet in the neck. Egor's limbs didn't move, even when his stunned senses screamed to run. The courtyard was clear of his men, who all sought shelter from the sniper.

The stranger emerged from the entry tunnel in a crouch walk, a rifle up to his shoulder. It was like the slow-motion reel of an action flick.

The bodies of the five dead Spetsnaz were all that remained in the keep's open yard. And Egor. He knelt on the snow and mud, unable to move.

The stranger stood in front of him. The rifle was

pointed at his head. Egor had stared down the barrel of many a gun, but this time it felt different. The stranger's face was unmasked.

The coal-black eyes of Mikhail Asimov, the Russian assassin, stared at him from behind the barrel.

THIRTY-FOUR

Somewhere in the Central Ural Mountains

The sniper rifle cracked. From the corner of Max's eye, the head of an enemy soldier, who stood watch in one of the towers, dissolved into a fine spray. That soldier would soon be replaced with another, so he needed to get to cover. To his right was a large stack of cordwood. To his left was the snowy field of the open ward. No Russian soldiers were in sight.

Except the one on a knee directly in front of him.

Blood dripped along the soldier's jaw and his uniform was in tatters. Mud encrusted his face and tiny rock shards were embedded in his skin. Vacant eyes stared at Max from under a ripped olive-green stocking cap. The man's bare left hand hung by his side, the fingers twitching. The soldier's lungs heaved to breathe. Hyperventilating. Classic signs of post-traumatic stress. That he was able to remain upright was a testament to the soldier's fortitude. The man was familiar, but all the Spetsnaz resembled each other.

"Stepanov! Where is Ruslan Stepanov?" Max shouted in Russian as he approached with his rifle pointed at the soldier's chest.

No response. A blank stare.

The chatter of AK-74M bullets erupted from the stack of wood to his right, and he sensed rather than saw chips of stone fly from the battlement tower where Badū was holed up. In a matter of seconds, the battle-hardened Russian special forces troops would recover from their shock and mount a counterattack. When that happened, Max needed to be hidden from sight.

"Where is Ruslan Stepanov. Where is General Stepanov?" Max yelled at the soldier, who peered back with a dead stare.

No response.

Max held his rifle pointed at the man's chest as he approached and barked the question again. They were both exposed, out in the open field of the keep. Rifle fire might resume at any moment.

The soldier's vacant eyes locked onto Max as he approached. A long, jagged scar became visible through the dirt, blood, and mud on the man's face.

Egor Dikov.

Max slung the rifle over his back and drew his pistol. With the man's lapels in his fist, he pushed the pistol barrel against the soldier's neck and jerked him to his feet. Max forcibly marched the stunned man through the snow to one of the outbuildings, where he kicked in the door and flung his captive to the dirt floor.

"Where is it, damn it!" Max slapped the soldier hard on the face and hit him a second time. "Where is the one-time pad? Where did Ruslan hide it?" He hit his captive over and over until the man cried out.

"Stop," Egor panted. "We don't have it."

With his fingers curled into a fist, Max punched the soldier in the face. The soldier's nose burst, and Max saw only red, his mind lost. All the pent-up anger and frustration from the previous month cascaded out of him as he beat the soldier. Blood spattered, and the man rolled on the ground to protect himself.

"I'm telling you," the Russian bellowed. "Stepanov isn't here. He's in Moscow."

A rifle crack from outside was followed by the rattle of AK-74M fire. Bullets hit the wooden door. Another shot from the long gun. And another. Max stopped, his gloves soaked with blood, and the soldier crumpled on the floor.

More sniper-rifle fire was followed by chatter from the AKs. The Spetsnaz had rallied. Soon the soldiers would breach the door and enter the room.

Max yanked the Russian commando to his knees and placed the pistol against his temple as the wooden door burst open. Two burly Russians stood in the opening, rifles up.

"Back up," Max shouted. "Or your man dies."

The soldiers hesitated.

"Shoot him," Egor panted.

"You do and my finger twitches, sending a bullet into this man's brain." Egor's status might prevent the soldiers from shooting. "Now back up."

The two soldiers were frozen in place.

"Shoot him, damn it!" Egor shouted. "This is Asimov, the traitor. The man who kills him will be rewarded by General Stepanov himself."

Max hauled his prisoner to his feet, used him as a shield, and backed deeper into the room. He kicked aside a stool and knocked over a wooden table as he maneuvered through an open door and into a hallway. Max flung the soldier around and pushed him down the corridor.

A soldier appeared in front of them, rifle up, and hesitated at the sight of Egor. Max shot him with the pistol.

"You can't escape, Asimov. There are too many of my men. Eventually, we'll overwhelm you. Drop your gun—"

"Shut up," Max rapped Egor's temple with the gun butt. They emerged into a kitchen. Pots and pans hung on racks, stacks of flour and rice sat on the floor, and three industrial-sized gas stoves lined one wall. With a shove, Max forced the Russian's cheek onto a burner and cranked on the gas. Flame leapt up and licked the man's face, and he screamed.

"Tell me where the message is," Max yelled.

"I don't know what you're talking about," the soldier screamed.

Max kept Egor's face pressed near the flame.

"One last chance, Dikov. Where did Stepanov hide my father's message? I know you took it from Fedorov. I also know Stepanov hid it here for safekeeping."

"Ruslan isn't here! He's in Moscow. He has the message with him." Max pushed the man's face into the fire, and Egor's screams filled the kitchen until Max pulled him away. A ring of burned flesh was etched into the man's cheek opposite the scar.

While shaking Egor Dikov by his collar, Max put the gun back to his captive's head. The soldier's gaze was unfocused. The smell of scorched skin filled the kitchen.

"I'll... I'll take you to his office. You can see... There is nothing."

Max yanked the man to his feet. "Let's go."

With one hand on Dikov's collar and the other holding the pistol to his neck, Max followed the Spetsnaz officer down a hall, up two flights of stairs, and down a corridor to a set of large oaken doors. Egor fumbled with a set of keys and managed to get the door open.

Frescoed ceilings towered over their heads, and a massive desk stood close to long, narrow windows that looked out over the dark plains. Tall bookcases lined the walls to their right, and a weight rack was to their left. Various fighting equipment was neatly arranged around the room, including a set of Japanese katanas and a rack that held Ruslan's bōgo, the armor he wore while sparring. Weapons from around the world lined the walls.

Max used a belt from a folded stack of karategi—the traditional Japanese karate practice uniform—to secure Egor's wrists behind his back. With the dazed Spetsnaz motionless in a chair, Max searched the office. The desk contained the basics and nothing else. A laptop power cord was attached to a plug. Ruslan must have taken the laptop with him. A Russian tactical knife was in a drawer, and underneath the desk, Max found a loaded Makarov pistol in a partially hidden recess. He pocketed both weapons.

Satisfied the desk was empty, Max turned his attention to the bookcase. It was stoutly constructed of dark oak like the desk and took up an entire wall. The shelves were packed with books and free of dust. The collection was a mixture of English language and Western literature, but many were not in good condition. At the far end of the bookcase, near the desk, were a set of glass-enclosed shelves. Each glass partition was secured with a small, silver lock. The collection behind the glass was all Russian literature, and the spines were in excellent condition.

He scanned the titles, more out of curiosity than anything. It would take hours to search the bookcase for the message. Hours Max didn't have. As if in reminder, the sound of automatic gunfire rattled through the window.

Time to go.

His eye caught on a title. It was on a shelf at shoulder height, on the end, closest to Ruslan's desk. The book was a thick volume of Russian fairy tales, and it triggered a memory.

His father sat by a roaring fire in the stone fireplace at the home where Max grew up. The family was gathered around. His sister liked to sit cross-legged at his father's feet while his surrogate mother sipped wine while curled in a leather wing chair. Max, six or seven years old—he couldn't remember exactly—preferred to lay on the settee with his eyes closed and let his father's story-telling voice wash over him.

Andrei read many stories to the family in this way, but one stood out as their favorite. *Narodnye russkie skazki*, or *Russian Fairy Tales*, was a compilation of almost 600 folk-tales collected by Alexander Afanasyev in the late 1800s. Afanasyev didn't write the stories but had published the collected works.

Now Max stared at the spine of one of Afanasyev's volumes.

Coincidence?

With the butt of the pistol, Max smashed the glass and removed the book from the shelf. Its soiled linen cover was noticeably worse for wear than the rest of the volumes in the glass enclosure. A prickle of déjà vu went up the back of his neck. Even the texture of the cover was familiar. When he opened the book, he almost gasped. Written along the top of the cover, in his father's distinctive scrawl, was an inscription to his mother.

To my beloved Katherine. Love always, Andrei.

———

Max flipped through the book but discovered nothing hidden among the pages. Other than the inscription, the margins were devoid of notes. Several of the pages were tatty, but none of the folds were fresh.

Why does Ruslan Stepanov have his father's book in his collection?

Did his father know this and send Max and Badū to the compound to collect the book? It sounded fantastical, but his father had acted more bizarrely in the past. He had hypnotized Kate and hidden a video-recorded message in a locket around his girlfriend's neck. What other surprises did his dead father have in store?

A gun battle erupted outside. This time, all the gunfire was the distinctive rattle of the AKs.

Time to go.

Max shoved the book into his jacket, near his chest, and stepped to the window. Muzzle flashes blinked like fireflies. He grabbed Egor by the jacket, pressed the pistol against his neck, and pushed him out the door and down the stairs. A Russian soldier appeared, brought his weapon around, and fell against the wall when Max shot him.

He left the Spetsnaz soldier leaning against the wall and pushed open the door with the barrel of his pistol and surveilled the keep's dark courtyard. Lit only by the moon, a group of four Russians were out in the open, firing, advancing on a position to Max's left where a heavy truck sat. Bullets plinked off the truck's armor as the soldiers advanced.

Max turned to Dikov, whose head lolled to the side. "You're losing a lot of blood. If I'm lucky, you'll bleed out. If you're lucky, maybe you'll survive."

The Spetsnaz crumpled to the floor as Max peeled out the door and crouch-ran to the shoulder-height stack of chopped wood. He holstered his pistol, aimed the AK, and squeezed off a three-round burst. One of the enemy soldiers stumbled. Another burst missed as the remaining men spread out. A gun muzzle appeared from behind the truck and fired, also at the Russians. *Badū*. Pinned out in the open and caught in the crossfire, the Spetsnaz scattered.

After he acquired a target with the rifle, Max picked off an enemy soldier and Badū hit a second before the last man disappeared behind a building. The courtyard descended into silence.

Badū's head appeared from behind the heavy truck. Max used hand signals and Badū nodded. On the count of three, Badū left the safety of the truck and scampered across the open field while Max covered him. There was no enemy fire. The short Mongolian fell in next to Max behind the wood pile.

"Any luck?" Badū asked.

Max peered closely at the Mongolian spy's face as he removed the book from his jacket. "Is this what we came for?"

Badū's face was blank. "A book? Is the message in there?"

Max shoved it back in his jacket. "No. The message isn't here. Ruslan has it with him in Moscow."

"Shit." Badū, with his rifle up, left the safety of the wood pile and took off along the dark side of a building with Max on his heels. Two more Russian soldiers fell before the two men rounded a corner to see the hulking shape of a five-bladed helicopter. The stubby wings and hull-like fuselage indicated the bird was a Sikorsky S-61. American made, venerable but long-ranged, if Max's memory served him correctly.

"Cover me," Max whispered. "I'll get this thing fired up."

Badū took a knee with his rifle aimed at the courtyard as Max yanked open the door and lunged into the cockpit. Smells of cigarette smoke, body odor, and mildew assaulted his nostrils. *Smells like the bird has been flown recently.*

As he strained his memory, he flipped toggle switches. First the battery. He skipped the anti-collision lights to remain dark as long as possible. Next was the inverter, followed by the DC generators. He started engine one by moving the mixture lever forward and holding the starter button down and repeated those steps with engine two. Turbo whined and the aircraft shuddered as the rotors lumbered to life.

Ping. Clang. Bullets plunked into the side of the helicopter.

Badū opened fire and the AK chattered over the drone of the engines.

"Let's go! Let's go!" Max shouted.

Badū jumped into the helicopter's open side door and kept the trigger pressed. When the Mongolian's ass hit the deck, Max guided the twelve-thousand-pound bird into the sky. Badū fired the AK until the monastery faded into the darkness below.

THIRTY-FIVE

Somewhere over South-Eastern Russia

Badū plopped into the copilot's seat and slipped on a pair of ear cans. Max wore an identical set and concentrated on steering the helicopter on a southeasterly course. The two men talked through the onboard audio.

"What's the fuel gauge say?" Badū asked.

"Full," Max said. "I recall the range on these birds is about four hundred fifty nautical miles. Grozny should be within easy reach."

"Why Grozny?"

"Friends. We can get over the border to Georgia."

After he studied a chart, Max entered the appropriate coordinates into the onboard avionics. Outside the windows the sky and earth merged in an inky blackness.

"So you know nothing about the book I found in Stepanov's study?"

"I swear. Andrei mentioned no book."

Here in the cockpit Badū's face was lit by the multicolored LEDs from the helicopter's flight panel and Max searched his face. The former spy's eyes danced from the thrill of the gunfight. Max removed the book and handed it to Badū. "Ruslan had one of my father's books in his collection."

Badū flipped through it and paused when he read the inscription. "Katherine was your mother?"

"My surrogate mother." Max explained that his true mother was Julia Meier, his father's longtime lover.

Badū closed the book and stared out the window while he ran a finger up and down the linen spine.

"I swear on the grave of my ancestors I have no idea what this means. Andrei never mentioned it."

Turbulence buffeted the Sikorsky and the two men rode through it with a stony silence. When the air smoothed, Badū spoke. "Probably not a coincidence."

"No, it's probably not."

"So let me get this straight. You were part of a team assembled by my father before he was killed?"

"Correct."

"Who else is on this team besides Gabrieli?"

"I'm not at liberty to say. We made a pledge in the beginning not to reveal the team's existence or its members."

"Before my father was killed."

"The pledge superseded death of the team's members, Andrei included."

"How'd you end up at Zurgan?"

Badū let out a breath. "I don't know exactly, but I was one of a couple of Andrei's people that were gathered up and stuck in prison. It's what they do in Russia."

"This was before Andrei's death?"

"Yes, months before."

"Who's in charge of this team right now? Someone is calling the shots."

"Search me. I don't rightly know."

The two men lapsed into silence as the helicopter chugged through the darkness.

————

Moscow, Russia

"Let me see it." Ruslan Stepanov held out his hand.

Colonel Markov walked next to his boss as they crossed the glossy shine of the Grand Kremlin Palace's ornate floor. Intricately carved domes held massive chandeliers high overhead. The walls and doors were gilded with gold and gleamed in the harsh light. Red velour chairs that no one sat in lined the walls. Both men wore dark gray wool suits, Ruslan with a red tie and Markov with a blue one. The cavernous hall was filled with men and women in suits and military uniforms.

From the breast pocket of his suit, Markov removed a flat package encased in plastic and held it out.

Ruslan's stoic face hinted at a grin before he masked his elation. About three inches by four inches, the sheer, flat envelope encased a thin booklet with a maroon cover and about twenty pages. The two men stopped in an alcove away from prying eyes.

Years of work, planning, and sacrifice. Here in the sacred halls of the Kremlin that represented so much prestige and authority was the perfect place to behold the source of his own burgeoning power.

After he unsealed the plastic, Ruslan slid the pad of

paper out and held it lightly in his fingers. The cover was devoid of letters or markings. The papers were several decades old, so he carefully pried open the cover and saw a thin page full of Cyrillic characters organized in a grid. The random letters were boxed in groupings of five. There were eighteen pages, all with different sets of random characters. He closed the booklet and slipped it back into the cellophane wrapper before putting it into his jacket pocket.

"Excellent work. And the rest of the operation?"

Emotion was uncharacteristic of his subordinate, but now Commander Markov's face brightened as he described the mission. "Like clockwork, sir. She fell for it all the way. Picked my pocket in the train station and disappeared with the fake one."

Ruslan clapped his commander on the shoulder. "Excellent work, Comrade Markov. An operation worthy of your skills. And the tracker?"

Prior to the mission, Markov's team of experts had secreted a tiny, flat tracking device in the cover of the fake one-time pad. The device was limited to four days of battery life, but by then the damage would be done. "My team is watching her movements as we speak. So far it appears she has not found the tracker."

"And where is she heading?"

"Difficult to say. She's well trained and is making a long surveillance detection route. I'll report in as soon as we know."

"Do that. Despite our acquisition of the decoding pad and all the power it will bring us, the final step of the Kate Shaw operation is critical to bringing an end to Mikhail Asimov."

THIRTY-SIX

Munich, Germany

Fatigue sank in as Kate stood in the immigration line at Munich's International Airport. Despite naps on the previous three flights, exhaustion clouded her mind. It was the kind of tired where she could sleep for two days straight, wake up to a tall cup of black coffee, and still have a foggy brain.

The travel, however, provided perspective. She no longer toyed with the idea of returning to the CIA. Like Gollum's ring, the recovery of the one-time pad tempted her to violate her values. The last year had changed her. Yes, the initial objective had been to turn Andrei into a CIA source and nab the Vienna Archive for the Agency. With the one-time pad in hand, redemption pulled at her, but another emotion percolated below the surface. It was a closeness to Max, and even now she had trouble admitting it to herself. Deep affection, bordering on love. Was it love? She didn't know. Love wasn't an emotion with which she was acquainted. If Max secured Andrei's message, and they recovered the Vienna Archive, he could put the consortium business behind him. Only then Max might have enough space to let her in.

The lack of communication from Max concerned her. After three calls to Goshawk went unanswered, Kate called Cindy, who reported they hadn't heard from Max in a week.

He can take care of himself.

It was the mantra that sustained her.

Ahead of her at the immigration officer's booth stood a family of travelers, all with bulky backpacks and ball caps with American sports insignias. The male gesticulated and spoke loudly and heads turned to watch. The stoic immigration officer shook her head until the older female traveler made an exclamation, rummaged in her backpack, and yanked out a piece of rumpled paper. The officer's stamp kerchunked three times and the harried family was on their way.

This was the last flight leg of Kate's journey to Vienna. The trip included a train from Saint Petersburg to Minsk and a flight from Minsk to Budapest, where she stayed a night and explored the Hungarian National Gallery before boarding a flight to Rome. She ate and drank her way through the Eternal City and dropped into her business class Lufthansa seat and fell asleep for the short flight to Munich. Through the entire surveillance detection route, her nerves were on edge as she guarded the little pad of paper secreted in her brassiere and watched for any sign of a tail. Mercifully, there was none.

The immigration officer beckoned and Kate stepped to the window. The young woman's blonde hair was tucked under a cap and her muted blue uniform was starched and pressed. Kate adjusted her backpack and slid her Canadian passport under the plexiglass divider. The officer barely glanced up while she typed furiously and ran the passport through a scanner.

As the officer scrutinized the passport's picture, Kate thought through her next move. A train from Munich's airport would take her into Munich's Central Station, where she'd hitch another train to Salzburg, Austria. There she planned to cool her heels and ensure she wasn't followed before driving a rental car to Vienna.

Kate tensed when the immigration officer's eyes narrowed. An overwhelming instinct came over her to run.

The takedown was swift.

First the blonde officer behind the plexiglass screen picked up a telephone and murmured some words. A split second later a burly young man with a crew cut and black uniform complete with badge and sidearm gripped her biceps. "Please come with me, ma'am."

"Why?" She forced the panic down. "Is there a problem?"

Two more uniformed officers with sidearms, flak vests, and automatic rifles appeared and took positions in front of her and behind her.

The officer with the crew cut increased his grip on her arm. "Come with me, ma'am. We'll get it straightened out."

The two officers watched with hands on their weapons as Kate allowed herself to be led away.

———

Munich, Germany

. . .

Despite the long duration without contact with anyone in authority, Kate was treated well by German immigration. The official led her to a small, windowless beige room with a metal table and two black chairs. Her backpack was confiscated over her strenuous objections, but a bottle of water was left for her on the table. High overhead, fluorescent lights buzzed, and the only window was a narrow pane of reinforced glass in the door, blocked by the dark shadow of an armed guard.

With nothing else to do, Kate stretched out on the thin carpet and closed her eyes. She used the cold bottle as a neck pillow rather than filling her bladder. Nowhere in any of her possessions was there a link to her old life as Kate Shaw, CIA officer, wanted in the United States for treason. They hadn't taken her fingerprints—once they did, they'd obviously know. Unless facial recognition technology was used, the Germans didn't yet know her true identity.

Somehow her fake Canadian passport was flagged. She held on to a tiny hope that it was a clerical error, a computer glitch, or a random search, except officials would make a thorough search of her backpack and find the two other fake passports and assume she was a spook or foreign agent. At that point, all hell would break loose. A long interrogation by the BND, Germany's spy agency, would be followed by incarceration in a German federal prison. Maybe she could barter with the code book nestled in her bra. With that slight hope, fatigue won and she fell asleep.

A foot nudged her awake, and she blinked against the harsh fluorescents as a silhouette stood over her.

"Hello, Kate."

The voice was familiar.

As she propped herself up, the woman came into focus. Kate's pulse settled as a friendly face appeared.

"Julia." Kate got to her feet. "What a surprise. How did you—"

"Hand it over." Julia Meier put out her hand.

"What? Hand what over?"

"You know what I'm talking about. Hand it over and we'll help make sure you get back to that cherry farm outside London."

Kate stepped back until her butt hit the wall. Why was Julia Meier here, in German immigration, demanding Kate hand over Andrei's code booklet?

"Now, now, Kate." Julia's face brightened into a smile. "You did good, venturing so far into Russia to retrieve it for your friend Max. But now it's time to hand it over to us. We'll take good care of it."

Kate crossed her arms over her chest. "Why don't we go together and give it to Max?"

The smile vanished as Julia put her hands on her hips. "Kate, there are two ways this plays out. Either you hand over the one-time pad and you walk out of here a free woman or we forcibly remove it from you and start extradition procedures back to the US. I know a certain CIA director who would be eager to get his hands on you. Now what's it going to be?"

That's when Kate knew she would never walk out of here a free woman. Instead the Germans planned to send her back to the US to face the music. She was a bargaining chip, and an expensive one at that. Meanwhile the Germans secured the code booklet for themselves—one half of the solution to the Vienna Archive.

At Kate's hesitation, Julia issued an order to the guard. "Search her."

With a sigh, Kate withdrew the flat pad of paper in the plastic covering with the maroon cover and tossed it onto the table. "I thought Germany was a friendly country."

Julia's face lit up when she picked up the package. "You figured wrong." She walked from the room.

As the door slammed, Kate sank to the floor and put her head in her hands.

THIRTY-SEVEN

Munich, Germany

The mobile connection was encrypted, routed over secure servers, and patched through a proprietary broadband tunnel established by the German government for high priority calls only. It was one benefit of working in her own country.

"I have it," Julia said into her phone. "She went without a fight." Julia chuckled, which caused her driver, an agency rookie named Valter, to glance at her in the rearview mirror. Outside the smoky glass was snarled Munich traffic.

"And where is she now?" The voice on the other end was stoic, deep, and gravelly. It was the voice of her immediate superior, Frederick Wolf.

"In a holding cell. As soon as Washington agrees to our demands, she'll be on a flight home."

"When do you meet with Stepanov's people?"

"Tomorrow. I still don't think he's going to agree to our

deal. They might prefer the Vienna Archive remain hidden rather than share the details with us."

"Perhaps," Wolf said on the other end of the line. "If they balk, we'll move to plan B. I'll meet you at the safe house tonight, and we can go through it again."

"Ma'am, we have a tail." Valter's voice was low.

With her hand over the phone's mouthpiece, Julia said, "What is it?" A relative newcomer to the BND, Germany's federal intelligence service, Valter had only driven for her three times. The job was simple; ferry her and the package from Munich's airport to her safe house in Bad Tölz, a bucolic town an hour south of Munich in the Bavarian hills.

Is the tail related to the one-time pad? It couldn't be.

As he threaded his way through rush-hour traffic, Valter's eyes roved between the rearview and side mirrors. "Black Sprinter van three vehicles back. Been with us since the airport."

"Frederick, I'll see you tonight." She tapped to end the call, stowed her mobile phone in her handbag, and touched the flat package sealed in plastic in her handbag. A SIG P365 sat on the seat next to her and she set it on her lap. "Probably a random tail who picked us up at the airport. Intelligence agents sometimes hang out at airports to watch for various dignitaries to practice surveillance."

"Yes, ma'am."

"Why don't you make a couple of evasive moves and let's see what happens."

The silver Mercedes accelerated and made an abrupt right turn onto a four-lane boulevard with leafless trees lining the center greenway. Another series of turns put them on the opposite side of the Isar River from the Mandarin Oriental Hotel. Winter dusk settled over the city and many of the cars around them had turned on their lights. Several more turns took them into a seedier section of the city. Valter slowed the car as the traffic turned sparse. "I don't see them anymore, ma'am."

Even though tails are a common and often harmless occurrence in her profession, the Sprinter van shook her. "Let's do an SDR, Valter. Just to make sure. I don't want anyone—"

A large object smashed into the side of the Mercedes, and the jarring impact caused the pistol to drop to the floor. She bent to retrieve the gun. "Shit, Valter. Get us—"

Before the young driver could react, a second crunch came from behind and Julia's head snapped into the headrest and the world blurred as the car stopped.

Four black-masked heads appeared through the haze, two on either side of the Mercedes. Thumps of silenced rifle shots sounded and Valter slumped as blood spattered the front windshield.

Things moved in slow motion. Julia lifted the SIG and pointed it at a blurry target. With her hand wavering, Julia squeezed off two shots.

The glass next to her spiderwebbed as a large object hit the safety glass. Another hit, and the window fell in on her. A gloved fist pummeled her face, and she almost dropped the pistol. An attacker gripped her wrist and wrenched, and the pistol fell from her grasp. The hand on her wrist gripped tighter while another hand grabbed under her shoulder and she was yanked through the window.

As Julia thumped to the pavement, she managed to get a view of her attackers. All four men wore black material covering their faces and black tactical vests. They carried small HK MP5 9mm submachine guns rigged with suppressors.

Who are they?

A hood went over her head as she was jerked to her feet and shoved into the waiting van. Tires churned as the vehicle took off. The whole snatch took less than sixty seconds.

Plastic cuffs bit into her wrists as a needle was jammed into her arm. She had one last thought as everything turned gray. *Did they grab the handbag?*

––––––

Undisclosed Location

The mood in the room was buoyant. Ruslan Stepanov, three-star army general and director of Russia's Military Intelligence Directorate, stood resplendent at the head of the table, his dress uniform pressed, his boots polished, and enough medals on his left breast to sink a battleship. Stepanov's crew cut shone from oil and his white teeth glowed in the room's murk. A large caliber pistol rested in a polished side holster. As he talked, he stalked the head of the table like an animal on a hunt.

As Stepanov crowed about his accomplishments like a man running for office, Lik Wang bit his lip and tried to figure out how to extricate himself from his predicament. Across the table, Zhao Zheng glared at him as if he could see through Wang's cranium and read his thoughts.

Well, you can't, Zheng.

What would become of him now that Stepanov and his cronies had won? Fedorov was dead, and Andrei Asimov's message and the accompanying code booklet had been recovered. All that remained was for Stepanov to recover the Vienna Archive and his position of power would be cemented. Once that happened, Zheng would put even more pressure on him.

How much longer can I do this?

Only one chair was empty among the twelve that ringed the massive black oak conference table. New members took the place of those who were recently killed. There was an army general and a Russian navy admiral, both wearing full-dress uniforms, and an oligarch dressed in a ridiculous purple silk sport coat and red cravat. To Stepanov's right sat a Russian Army lieutenant colonel named Markov, who everyone knew was one of Ruslan's closest confidants.

Wang's leg bounced uncontrollably. Anxiety burned the back of his neck and made his heartbeat erratic. Stepanov had failed to follow protocol. By the consortium's bylaws, with the death of Number One and Number Three, Lik Wang should have been promoted to Number Two. Instead, Ruslan had installed Markov as Number Two and the Russian Army general as Number Three.

What does it mean?

A massive LED screen was attached to the wall at the foot of the table. Right now, it displayed a dark screen, but memories of the attack on the FSB director Sergei Fedorov played though his mind.

Wang twirled his diamond pinky ring. As Ruslan Stepanov spoke, the device in the ring recorded every sound in the cavernous room.

"Today marks the culmination of my work over the past three weeks," crowed the three-star general. "The plan we executed has finally borne fruit." He worked a clicker and an image of two documents appeared on the screen.

On the screen's left was a short handwritten message in a spidery scrawl. It was in Cyrillic, of which Wang had a working knowledge, but the writing was gibberish. The other was a tiny booklet of onionskin pages, also showing rows and rows of Cyrillic in five-character groups.

Stepanov paced. "The paper on the left is an encrypted message written by Andrei Asimov to his son, Mikhail. The booklet on the right is called a one-time pad, which is an old and anachronistic method of coding messages. The principle is simple—you use the pad to encrypt a message. The receiver of that message has to have an identical decoder pad."

The oligarch spoke up. "Why is it called a one-time pad?"

Ruslan frowned. "The system was used in World Wars One and Two. It was highly secure, but to remain secret, each random set of characters could only be used once. Each pad was discarded after one use."

Ruslan Stepanov strutted around the corner of the table, down the opposite side from Wang, and pointed at the massive screen. "The code booklet was recovered after a complicated operation performed by Colonel Markov. We lured an agent of Andrei's—a former CIA officer named Kate Shaw—into a trap and secured the one-time pad required to decrypt the message."

The oligarch in the purple suit spoke up again. "And the message?"

"As longtime consortium members witnessed, we recovered the message from Sergei Fedorov." Stepanov glared at the oligarch. "Comrade Sergei Fedorov, I'm sorry to report, had his hands in too many illicit deals. Arms sales, tax evasion, even the unlawful killing of several journalists. Our office was asked by the Kremlin to arrest Comrade Fedorov. When we did, he resisted and was shot in the process. Unfortunate, I know. Luckily for all of us, we recovered the message from Fedorov's possession before it was stolen by our enemies."

Lik Wang rubbed his thumb on the table edge. *Did Stepanov outright lie to rewrite history?*

The oligarch slapped the table. "Enough with the theatrics. What does the message say? Where is the Vienna Archive?"

A cloud passed over Ruslan's face, and Wang bit back a grin. This oligarch's tenure on the consortium might be the shortest in history.

"The message provides the location and coordinates of Andrei Asimov's hidden cache of files. The files he stole from the komissariat. The files that we've searched for now for several years. The files that Asimov held over our collective heads. The files that Asimov's son has searched for. The files that have the opportunity to put down the komissariat. The Vienna Archive itself."

You mean the files that will propel you to a seat on the komissariat.

The admiral raised a finger. "But what of the assassin? Once he learns we refilled the seats on the council, our names will be added to his list."

Stepanov paced around the table and stopped behind the oligarch's chair. He set a hand on the back of the man's chair.

"I'm glad you asked, admiral. Mikhail Asimov also seeks this so-called Vienna Archive. We will dangle the location of the files so he will be unable to resist. When he sticks his head up, we'll—"

The admiral slapped his hand on the table. "How will the Asimov boy come to know that we have these items?"

Ruslan Stepanov paced around the table to stand behind Wang's chair and placed his hands on Wang's shoulders. "I'm glad you asked, admiral. Because, you see, we have a secret weapon." The grip on Wang's shoulders clamped down like a vice, and he sank deeper into the chair. As panic washed over him, Wang tried to catch Zheng's eyes, but the Chinese spymaster fidgeted with his tie clip.

"Our friend here, Mr. Lik Wang from Shanghai, also Chairman of Sinopac Oil, has a special relationship with the British Secret Service. Don't you, Mr. Wang?"

The grip let up and cold steel pressed against Wang's neck.

Ruslan Stepanov racked the pistol's slide and the *crunch-crunch* echoed around the chamber. "Number Four here has been providing recorded information of our proceedings to the British, and by extension I assume, to the Americans. You do know the penalty for treason, don't you, Mr. Wang? Ask the Asimov family how their deception worked out for them."

Wang's throat was too constricted to talk, his skin prickled with heat.

"If you wish your family to remain alive, Mr. Wang, you'll do exactly as I tell you. Do you understand?"

Wang nodded and his gaze found on an object on the far side of the room. The object went in and out of focus. *Has that always been there?*

"Excellent." Ruslan strode to the front of the room, the pistol still in hand. "Mr. Wang will deliver a specific message to the British, who will in turn supply it to Mikhail Asimov. When Asimov appears in the specified location, we'll kill him. With Asimov dead and the files back in safe-keeping, we can take our time before we get to the youngest Asimov." The chairman spread his arms, right hand still holding the pistol. "How long can a ten-year-old elude us without his protector?"

"What makes you think Asimov will take the bait?" It was the oligarch in the garish sport coat again.

Stepanov smiled. "Excellent question. Because we have someone he wants, someone he won't be able to resist rescuing. Would any son refuse to rescue his own mother?"

Smiles broke out around the table. As the meeting broke, Wang sat still, his eyes glazed and focused on a single object on the far wall. Men gave him a wide berth as they filed from the room. Wang saw none of the angry and disapproving stares. Instead the item on the wall came into focus. It was an ornate carving of a crow, the symbol of death in China.

That symbol hadn't been there before. Stepanov put it there. And he missed it.

THIRTY-EIGHT

Helsinki, Finland

The white SUV ground to a halt in a tight alley between a soot-covered white building and a dumpster that overflowed with fish heads and rotting lettuce. In front of them, a block away, a second SUV blocked the alleyway. A third SUV was behind them. Their driver, a pale young man with bloodless lips, jerked his thumb. "The door next to the dumpster."

Max slid out and sucked in the frigid air. The opposite passenger door chunked shut as Badū appeared next to him. The alleyway was empty. This was the kind of meeting one didn't refuse. It was also the kind of meeting where an impressive amount of security was in place, even if you couldn't see it. Ice crunched underfoot as Max opened the door and entered the building's steamy warmth.

The last few days were a blur of travel. Doku laughed when Max put the helicopter down in the Chechen's large backyard. "What am I going to do with that thing?" Doku yelled.

A truck ride over the mountains and into Georgia was followed by a series of flights originating in Tbilisi that culminated at Heathrow. Max's intention was to return to the cherry farm and connect with Kate and Baxter. Instead, he and Badū were met at Heathrow by a phalanx of blue-suited MI6 men who redirected them into a familiar-looking white Gulfstream G500 that whisked them to Helsinki. Max's questions went unanswered while Badū stoically enjoyed the jet's creature comforts.

Now he and Badū stowed their clothing in lockers and wrapped themselves in fluffy towels. They padded along a hallway lined with a wooden walkway reminiscent of a Japanese bathhouse. Another door led into a cedar-lined room about ten feet by ten feet. Along one wall was an open fire with a pile of rocks suspended above. Standing next to the fire was the room's only occupant.

Naked and covered with a sheen of sweat stood C, Britain's chief of spies. Tall and gangly, his skin had a youthful elasticity despite the man's advanced age. As the two men walked in, C spooned a ladle of water over the rocks and watched as steam poured into the room. "Please, sit," he said, motioning to the cedar bench along the back wall.

"All your safe houses taken?" Max asked. While C shook Badū Khan's hand, he got the distinct impression the two men knew each other better than either were letting on.

"Budget cuts, I'm afraid." C sat in a corner. With his elbows on his knees, C looked down his crooked beak to survey the two men. "I'm glad to see you both still alive."

Heat washed over Max's skin, opened his pores, and

sank into his bones. Until this moment, he hadn't realized how weary he had become.

"Sauna has a long history in Finland," C said. "Finns like to say the sauna is the poor man's pharmacy. Woman used to give birth in the old smoke sauna rooms because the soot-covered walls made them the most sanitary place in the house."

Grunting, Max adjusted his towel. "It also helps prevent anyone from smuggling in listening devices."

"That too."

"Does Callum know we're meeting?"

"He does. I left him at our embassy to prep. There is much work to be done."

"Has something happened?"

C pressed his fingertips together. "We received a communiqué from Sable."

Max wiped water from his head. "I'm sure whatever he has to say can be ignored. I don't trust that guy any farther than I can throw him."

"He claims to know the location of your father's files. This so-called Vienna Archive. Ruslan Stepanov revealed the decrypted message to the consortium."

Max studied the long, narrow face of the MI6 man. "Has to be a trap."

"We agree, which doesn't bode well for Sable, I'm afraid." After standing, C ladled water over the red-hot rocks. "There's something else."

"Tell me."

"Sable claims Stepanov has kidnapped Julia Meier."

A rock dropped in Max's stomach. "How—"

C avoided eye contact with Max. "We've reached out to our friends at the BND, but so far they are silent."

"What else did Sable tell us?"

"You're to appear at a certain address in twenty-four hours' time. Alone, of course. Ruslan Stepanov wants a trade. You for Julia. And it's not optional. If you don't go, she'll die."

"Sable is definitely blown."

"That's our assessment as well. Stepanov used him to deliver the message."

"What's the address?"

"It's to be provided by our source only thirty minutes before you're to appear. Of course, the address is to be sent to you and you're not to mention the address to anyone or the woman dies."

"Of course."

"Max, you have my word that all the resources at my disposal are on this. We'll do what we can to help."

"Did they give any indication of where this address is? Do I need to get on a plane?"

"It's here in Helsinki."

———

After showers, Max and Badū caught a ride with C to the British Embassy. Located on a peninsula of tree-covered land on the southeast corner of Helsinki, the diplomatic compound was next door to the French, kitty-corner to the Americans, and backed up to a greenway crisscrossed with walking trails. Today, in the dim light of winter, the pale pink four-story villa that dated back to 1918 and housed the ambassador and staff was quiet. The men were whisked through the austere office building which sat at right angles to the residences and into a cramped operations room with a dozen men and women hunched over laptops. In one corner, his back to the wall, chair on its rear legs, sat Callum

Baxter talking into his Blackberry. Cindy, resplendent in a crisp blouse and dark skirt, gestured wildly at her laptop screen as Harris looked on. The room grew silent when the three men walked in.

"Report," C demanded. "Where are we?"

Cindy marched to the front of the room, toggled a clicker, and presented an image of a pad of onionskin paper along with a single sheet with torn edges. The pad showed rows of Cyrillic characters in groups of five. The contents of the single sheet were digitally blurred except for a header of spidery handwriting in faded ink that read, *To my son, Mikhail.* "This image was provided by our source on the consortium."

Max raised his hand. "How did the source make contact?"

Cindy frowned. "He used a chat room on the dark web. One he's used before that we monitor. The image was encrypted and sent through the chat board's direct messaging function."

C broke in. "Any luck in un-blurring the message?"

"None yet, sir, but a team in London is working on it. The pixels themselves were blurred. Instead of adding a layer to the image—"

"How about authenticity?" Max stepped closer to the monitor. "This is the first time I've seen this specific one-time pad. It looks like the other ones I've used in the field while with the KGB." His focus shifted to the single sheet of paper. "The handwriting resembles my father's, but of course that could be easily faked."

Cindy tapped a pencil against her palm. "The hand-writing was analyzed by a team at Vauxhall Cross and appears to be authentic. We believe they left it unblurred in order to establish bona fides. As for the one-time pad, it matches archived images MI6 has from WWII of KGB cipher booklets. Vauxhall has proclaimed them both authentic, to the best of our abilities."

"Excellent," C said. "Proceed, please."

Harris clicked, and the image was replaced with a screenshot of a message in a chat window. It read: *Heed these instructions, for any deviation will result in the death of Julia Meier. Mikhail Asimov is to make himself available, alone and without tracking devices, on Monday, 24 January, in the city of Helsinki, Finland. Thirty minutes before the appointed time, you will receive instructions. Asimov must be alone and weaponless, must not be watched, and must carry no communication or tracking devices. Any failure to follow these specific instructions will result in Julia Meier's untimely death.*

Another click, and a short video played showing Max's mother, Julia Meier, in a small, dark room. She sat on a soiled mattress with her knees tucked under her. The videographer barked a command in Russian and she lifted her gaze. A newspaper was tossed on the mattress next to her and she picked it up.

Max peered at the monitor. "Is that a German paper?"

Cindy signaled Harris to pause the video and it stopped with Julia Meier holding the newspaper. "We've confirmed the newspaper is authentic and dated yesterday. It's a morning edition of the *Süddeutsche Zeitung*, one of the largest newspapers in Germany. It's published in Munich."

The room grew quiet.

"Analysis," barked C. "Any weak links, openings? Anything we can use? Anything with the voice in the video?"

Baxter rubbed the back of his neck. "Nothing. We ran

it. Twenty- to thirty-year-old Russian male voice. No matches in the computer."

"There isn't a lot to go on," Cindy said. "We've reached out to the BND—Julia's agency—but they're not saying much. They asked for copies of the video."

"Which we're dragging our feet on," Baxter said.

C put his hands on his waist. "Okay, what's the plan? Send Max in alone?"

That's how it usually goes. Max sighed. All this techno-wizardry and all these people and it would come down to him.

"Not exactly, sir." Cindy held up her hand. "Before we get the next message, we're thinking Max might be able to help us narrow down where his father might have hidden the cache of files. If we can beat Stepanov to the files, we can have a surprise waiting for them."

C chuckled and settled his gaze on Max. "Thin, but a good idea. Can't think of another angle, can you, Max?"

"I've already considered, and I can't think of anything." Max crossed his arms across his chest. "Much of the time my father was operational, we weren't in contact, especially while I was in Paris. Historically, as you know, Helsinki was neutral ground during the Cold War. Espionage has a rich history in Helsinki since the city is so close to Saint Peters-burg and the country shares a fourteen-hundred-kilometer border with Russia. He had many reasons to visit Helsinki, and I know of no personal or professional contacts he has here."

"Okay, keep at it, people. We're used to long odds. We'll figure something out."

"Tell me about it," Max muttered.

———

Max leaned the chair he was sitting in against the wall on its rear legs. His eyes were closed and his arms were crossed over his chest. The din of the operations room rose and fell as he attempted to corral his scattered thoughts.

"Ahem." Baxter cleared his throat. He stood in front of Max with his Blackberry in his hand.

Max opened his eyes. "Are you still using that old Blackberry? Do they even sell those things anymore?"

"Whenever the tech brings around the new iPhone, I seem to be away from the office."

"Sure you are. What do you want?"

"I have news from the US."

The front chair legs hit the floor as Max opened his eyes. "Tell me."

"Arina is awake from her coma."

"That's great news, right?"

"There are implications to her...ahem...condition."

"What do you mean?"

Baxter stuffed his hands in his pockets. "Well, comas are complicated—"

"Tell me, damn it."

"She's lost her memory."

Max leaned the chair back against the wall.

Baxter dragged over a chair. "I'm told by our medical team here that short-term memory loss is common. I'm getting the information secondhand from my contacts at the CIA. Cindy suggested that Arina might be faking. If the CIA learns her true identity, there's no telling what they might do, so Arina might be putting on a ruse. As it is, she's got a long road to recovery and perhaps her Jane Doe status is best."

"Will someone from MI6 be able to talk with her?"

"Not right away. As I indicated before, we don't want to tip our hand. I'll keep you apprised."

"Do that." Max closed his eyes.

———

When Harris raised the alarm, Max, Cindy, and Baxter were no closer to a plan than when they started. Takeout containers of food littered the tables, and the room stank of body odor and chow mein and Peking duck. "The message from Sable arrived."

The analyst made a couple keystrokes and the note appeared on the overhead screen. Baxter called C, who raced into the room.

Be at Market Square in ten minutes and await instructions. Heed the previous rules. Otherwise the woman dies.

"Predictable," C said. "That market is crowded, even on a cold day. They'll isolate you and observe to make sure you're alone."

Cindy tapped a pen against her palm. "We'll have a satellite watching your every move."

"I can blend in," Badū said. "I'll be twenty feet away."

"We should go." Baxter walked to the door. "We need to get people in place."

Max put his feet on a table. "We have time. I'm going to be fashionably late."

THIRTY-NINE

Helsinki, Finland

Even in the middle of January, Market Square at the harborside in Helsinki bustled with tourists on the hunt for souvenirs and locals doing their grocery shopping. Dressed in a bright red down jacket, a black watch cap, and jeans, Max ambled along the cobblestones with his hands stuffed in his empty pockets. To his right were the murky green waters of the harbor, and to his left were a row of colorful tents protecting trinkets and food items. Dry flurries floated from light gray clouds that Baxter said might interfere with satellite tracking. Next to the market the white SkyWheel turned slowly with tourists crammed into its blue-and-white cars. He craved a cigarette to give his hands something to do.

So far no one in the market roused suspicions. A flicker of panic flared when Max thought they had abandoned him because he was fifteen minutes late.

No way. They want me too badly.

The market was small and the harbor bordered one side, a car park on another, and a four-lane road on a third. A stubby pier housed a sightseeing line and a ferry service. Despite the warnings, C ordered a surveillance detail of MI6 agents to ring the block in a wide perimeter. Badū, dressed in a black jacket and wool cap, perused the wares in the market stalls and, true to his word, never strayed more than twenty feet from Max's side.

An abrupt jostle from behind startled him, and a man in an overcoat shoved a small package into his hand. Before Max could react, the man pedaled off on a bicycle, hunched over, his face hidden by a hood. Max let him go—MI6 would track him.

The package was a padded manila envelope sealed with tape. He ripped it open to find a stubby mobile phone, what those in the trade called a *burner*. It was charged enough for a single use and was untraceable. The phone was on, and it vibrated with an incoming call as he removed it from the package.

"You're late."

"Sue me." Max stood with the phone to his ear and slowly surveyed the market. A man sat on a bench tapping furiously on a mobile phone. A woman pushed a baby stroller while holding a phone to her ear. Two pensioners strolled, each with their hands clasped behind their backs. There was no one who might be the caller.

"We accounted for your little mind games. Good to see you're wearing such a visible jacket."

"Where to? The metro?" They would force him to perform a surveillance detection route designed to either illuminate or lose his MI6 watchers. The Helsinki metro would easily elude the satellite overwatch.

"Walk to the SkyWheel. Hold on to the phone, you'll need it again." The transmission ended.

Max pocketed the phone and shoved the envelope into a trash can, where MI6 would pluck it and subject it to endless hours of forensics scrutiny, after which they'd find nothing. It took him three minutes to thread through the car park and amble past the Allas Café to the bus terminal next to the towering SkyWheel.

The phone buzzed. "Keep walking and enter the Katajanokka Terminal."

It took exactly nine minutes to walk from the SkyWheel past the Scandic Grand Marina Hotel, skirt the fenced container storage lot, and enter the terminal building, where crowds from an incoming ferry swarmed. The phone vibrated in his pocket.

"Purchase two tickets—one to Mariehamn and one to Tallinn. Ditch your jacket in a restroom trash can. In locker R-5 you'll find another coat along with a hat and a new phone. You're to drop this one off the side of the ferry."

———

In the operations room at the British Embassy in Helsinki, Baxter, Cindy, C, and the rest of the team watched the red-jacketed form of Max enter the Katajanokka Terminal building. The satellite image showed two ferry boats docked along the wharf.

"Where do these ferries go?" Baxter barked.

"There are two lines," an analyst read from his screen. "One goes to Tallinn, Estonia, the other to Mariehamn, which is a ferry stop on a Finnish island. Looks like Mariehamn is a waypoint to a dozen Baltic locations including Stockholm and Latvia."

Cindy clicked and a map on a wall monitor zoomed in to show the ferry routes emanating from the Katajanokka Terminal. One dotted line curved west through blue waters until it terminated at Mariehamn. Another went due south to Talinn, Estonia, directly across the Gulf of Finland from Helsinki. "We're going to lose him."

"Thanks for stating the obvious," Baxter growled. "Get the satellite over those boats and watch for a red jacket. Maybe we'll see which ferry he gets on."

The satellite hovered over the terminal, and everyone watched for a sighting of a bright red jacket, but none appeared. First the Tallinn ferry pulled away, followed shortly by the boat to Mariehamn.

The operations room grew quiet as the team gradually ran out of things to do. A brief flurry of activity followed the appearance of the plain manila envelope but that generated no intel. All the air evaporated from the room when Badū radioed in. "I found his red jacket in a bathroom trash can. He must have traded it out for a different coat. No sign of him, I'm afraid."

————

Stockholm, Sweden

Max spent much of the ten-hour trip from Helsinki to Mariehamn on the top observation deck hoping that MI6's satellite might somehow pick him up. The new jacket was dark gray, and the ball cap was black, and he blended in among the tourists and commuters who filled the boat. He dined voraciously at one of the ferry's excellent restaurants and drank coffee after coffee from the café. To entertain himself, he watched for surveillance but gave up. This team were professionals.

After he pitched the first phone over the railing, he kept the newly supplied burner turned off. It wouldn't acquire a signal out here in the Gulf of Finland and he didn't want to drain the battery. Besides, there wasn't anywhere to go other than the ferry port. With nothing else to do, he curled up in a chair with a view of the ocean and fell asleep as early darkness descended.

Arrival announcements woke him, and he glanced out the window to see the lights of Mariehamn off the starboard bow. After flicking on the burner phone, he made his way off the boat and into the low-slung off-gray terminal building.

The phone buzzed. "I hope you got some rest. You're going to need it."

"Where to?"

"Take the 2:25 to Stockholm. Await instructions." The transmission ended.

FORTY

Stockholm, Sweden

The ferry docked at the Viking Terminal in the Stockholm borough of Södermalm at the pitch-dark time of 6:55 pm. Max stepped from the boat to the dock and made his way through the terminal building and out to the curb, where he was met by three black Sprinter vans, their windows tinted dark. The door to the middle van slid open and, per previous instructions, Max stepped inside.

Three men greeted him, a hood was jerked over his head, and rough hands frisked his body. The burner phone was taken from his pocket. Plastic cuffs were cinched onto his wrists. No one spoke. The overpowering smell of cheap cologne filled the van.

"Someone is trying to compensate for something," Max said. "Can someone roll down a window?"

His request was ignored. The van made a right turn, a left, and another right. The interior of the van was silent until a radio squawked with a Russian voice. "The package has arrived."

The van traveled for another fifteen minutes before they stopped. The door opened and Max felt tepid air. *I'm inside a building.* He was hustled over hard concrete by four strong hands. The hood was yanked off, and he blinked against the pale light of fluorescents. A small Learjet was to his left, and an airplane hangar roof towered overhead.

Ruslan Stepanov stood ten paces away. Ramrod straight, arms by his sides, Stepanov wore a severe gray suit and a red tie under a wool overcoat. Oil glistened on his white flattop, and white teeth shined as he smiled.

A hulking man exited the jet and stomped down the plane's airstairs to stand next to Stepanov. This man wore a motorcycle jacket, and his face sported a jagged knife scar on his left cheek and a hideous burn on his right that looked fresh.

Max smiled. "How's your face, Egor?"

The punch to his kidneys took him by surprise, and Max keeled over but was held up by the two men at his side. As Max recovered, another man deplaned from the private jet. He wore a blue wool overcoat, and his nose was flat and bent like it was broken numerous times. The newcomer stood near the jet and watched.

Stepanov walked over to stand a meter from Max. "Well, well. If it isn't the world-famous Mikhail Asimov. In the flesh. Thank you for coming. I guess no one can resist rescuing their own mother."

"I'm not here to rescue her," Max said. "I'm here to relieve you of my father's files, which you stole."

Laughter reverberated around the hangar as Stepanov made a show of holding his side. "Indeed."

Egor Dikov glared at Max.

Stepanov clasped his hands together in front of himself. "You are an entertaining man, Mikhail. But we shall uncover these files together. I can assure you they are the property of the komissariat for the Preservation of the State, and we take their theft seriously. It was your father who stole them, and it is your family who will pay the price for his betrayal."

"It is the consortium members who are paying the price. As soon as I kill you, I'll keep picking them off until there are none left."

The laughter died away, and Stepanov dismissed the comment with a wave of his hand. "You're merely removing the weaker members, those who were associates of our late leader. I can assure you those men have been replaced with my closest confidants, men whose strength cannot be matched."

"Don't worry, Ruslan. I'll get to them. It's just a matter of time."

"Given your current predicament, it's unlikely. I understand you and Egor here are acquainted." Stepanov raised a gloved hand to Egor's face, who glared at Max. "You're going to wish you killed him when you had the chance. When you and I are done, he has some special treatments in mind for you." As Stepanov laughed, Egor stared at Max.

Ruslan gestured at the vans. "Shall we? My advance team has visited the vault prepared by your late father. They report the cache of files was well hidden, but they've been unearthed and are waiting for our arrival before they are revealed. I left strict instructions that you and I, Mikhail, will be the first ones to view them in all their splendor."

"Release Julia now or I'm not going anywhere."

Stepanov grimaced. "Egor, show our friend here what happens if he refuses to follow along."

The Russian Spetsnaz soldier formed a ham-sized fist and rammed it into Max's stomach.

As Max gasped for breath, another fist pummeled the back of his head, and he went to his knees. As he was jerked upright by his two guards, another fist slammed into his chest, followed by another punch to the gut.

His body convulsed and he fought for air as he was thrown back into the van, where he lay curled on the floorboards while the procession got underway. No hood was provided, but his vantage point from the floor afforded him little clue as to their location or destination.

Stepanov's voice came from the front. "I know some important people, Mikhail, who will be glad to see this little charade of your father's come to an end. He was once one of us, a man with considerable power who did much to advance the Soviet cause. I'd almost go so far as to say he was a legend. It's too bad, really."

The van droned on through the darkness until they turned onto a rutted road. The men rolled with the bumps as they drove another ten minutes. When they stopped, he struggled to his knees and two of Egor's men dragged him out of the van.

A blanket of clouds hid the starlight and turned the area around them pitch black. The road underfoot was dirt and fields stretched in all directions. As his vision grew accustomed to the darkness, several outbuildings materialized, one in the shape of a barn. Another was a low-slung building made of glass, like a greenhouse. A wintery gust turned his cheek to ice.

As the men exited the van, three halogen lights on tripods snapped on thirty meters away next to the entrance of the greenhouse. Prodded on by his guards, Max followed Stepanov and Egor along an ice-crusted track leading to the glass building, where four men greeted them. Two leaned on shovels while two held automatic rifles. Piles of dirt formed a dozen waist-high mounds and an equal number of holes lined the edge of the greenhouse.

"Been digging awhile?" Max snickered.

At the men's feet was a dirt-encrusted metal box, its lid still secured by a small padlock. A pickax lay nearby, and a metal detector leaned against the greenhouse wall.

The flat-nosed man in the blue overcoat stepped forward. "The farm is owned by a series of shell companies. We're still unwinding the ownership structure. If Asimov had outside help to hide these files, we want to find out who it was."

"Agreed." Stepanov nodded once. "Thank you, Colonel Markov. I trust the box has been tested for traps?"

"We looked for heat signatures, X-rayed the box, and tested for bomb residue. We found nothing. It's clean, sir."

Stepanov squatted next to the box and attempted to move it. "Heavy, no?"

One of the men with the shovels grunted. "Took three of us to haul it out of that hole."

The three-star general rattled the padlock and motioned to Egor, who produced a pry bar. With an abrupt wrench of the metal bar, the lock fell from the box. Ruslan looked up at Max as he wiped dirt from the top of the container. "Just like your father to bury the files in a field."

"We're not in a field," Max said. "The field would be over there."

Egor swung the crowbar and hit Max's shoulder, sending searing pain through his body.

Stepanov raised his hand while his attention remained on the box. "That's enough for now, Egor. I want Asimov awake and coherent as we open the box. Later you can do whatever you want."

The general ran a gloved hand over the box as if he were petting a small animal before he lifted the lid. With a rusted creak, a crack appeared before the heavy top slammed back in place. The general stood for better leverage and heaved the lid and let the metal top clang to the ground. In unison, everyone leaned over to see better. The box contained stacks of papers and files but no details were visible in the shadows cast by the halogens.

Stepanov stuck his hand in the box and emerged with a handful of manila files. He opened one, glared at it, and let the pages slip from his fingers. "Is this a joke?" The general dropped to his knees and pulled file after file from the box, examined each, and whipped them away. After he examined a dozen, he reached in and took two handfuls of the paper, stood, and flung them into the air as he screamed in frustration. "Is this a joke?"

Papers fluttered to the ground. A dozen were visible as they swirled in the wind, and Max smiled.

Every one of the sheets of paper was blank.

FORTY-ONE

Farmland outside Stockholm, Sweden

No one moved as hundreds of papers swirled in air. The guards and the men with the shovels were frozen in place. Egor groaned. Markov cursed.

Blank pages littered the ground as Stepanov rifled through the remaining contents of the box. He tossed files and papers until the container was empty, and he ran his hands around the interior. He tried to lift the box, but it was too heavy. One of the shovelers moved to help, but Stepanov pushed him away. The general's movements were frantic, his face a mask of hatred. He grabbed Max by the jacket. "What's the meaning of this?"

Max shrugged. "My father never trusted anyone, so..."

"Where are they, damn it! Where are the files?"

Max chuckled. "Maybe it's all a hoax. Maybe there are no files."

Veins in the Russian general's temples pulsed, and his arms shook while he grasped Max's jacket.

"Boss, you might want to see this." A man holding a shovel in one hand pushed a document at Stepanov. It was a single sheet of lined paper.

Ruslan snatched the document.

Max craned his neck. The page contained a few faint lines of Cyrillic in tight, neat handwriting, but he couldn't read it from his vantage point.

Illuminated by the halogens, crimson crept into Stepanov's face. He wadded up the paper, threw it on the ground, and jabbed his finger at Max's chest as he spoke to Egor. "Do whatever you want with him. But don't leave him alive."

Summoning two of his guards, and with Colonel Markov in tow, Ruslan Stepanov stalked to his vehicle and climbed into the passenger seat. Men loaded in, the engine fired up, and the SUV spun its wheels and made a wide turn before it sped down the road with its headlights bouncing. Taillights flashed once as it turned onto the main road and disappeared into the darkness.

All this energy chasing after this message from his father had been for naught. Even if he and Kate had secured the one-time pad and the encrypted message, it would have led to a remote farmhouse in Sweden and they would have found the same thing—a box full of blank papers. This meant the cache of files is still out there somewhere. If it even exists.

Max wriggled his wrists to test his bonds. Egor stood and looked at the box, stunned. The two men with the shovels shuffled their feet. Two soldiers, both brawny Spetsnaz, stood with their hands on their weapons.

Egor recovered his composure and slammed his fist into Max's head. Bright stars flashed in his vision. Another punch landed on his jaw, another on his temple, and he dropped to his knees before he toppled onto his front. As he fell, Egor's scarred and burned face, aflame with hate, flashed in his peripheral vision.

A kick landed on Max's face and another boot planted itself on the back of his head. Next came the shovels as the men took turns hitting him on his back and legs with the spade ends. He curled into a fetal position, but it did little to protect him as the blows rained down on him.

The action paused when Egor ordered two of his soldiers to pull Max to his feet. Strong hands grasped him under his arms and a vicious kick landed on his shin before he was able to find his footing on the hard-packed snow.

"Hold his head still," Egor said. The gargantuan Russian soldier with the bull-sized shoulders stood with his feet planted and produced a long fixed-blade knife. Egor raised the knife so the halogen lights gleamed on the honed steel. The Spetsnaz sergeant held the blade to Max's jaw and drew the tip across the skin. Blistering pain bloomed over Max's face and blood flowed down his throat. With his nose an inch from Max's, Egor spoke through clenched teeth. "See my face? You did this. How do you like it?"

Hysterical laughter overtook Max and cut through the pain from his jaw and the aches in his body. "Looks like an improvement to me."

With a flick of the blade, Egor carved a tiny chunk of skin from Max's left cheek. "How about we improve your face, you fuck." Another twist of the blade and a one-inch cut appeared along Max's jaw. Egor worked the knife and another gaping wound appeared on Max's cheek. Pain engulfed his face as warm, viscous blood ran freely along his neck. The Spetsnaz soldier wiped the knife on Max's jacket sleeve. "If you were going to survive, that would turn out to be a wicked scar. Too bad you will die."

Egor's gauntlet-sized fists slammed into his chest, stomach, and head. A shovel swung and caught the back of his legs and he went to the ground, where dirt mixed with his own blood to cover his face. The shovels thumped on his back and legs as he lay there, his arms up to protect his head. The butt of a rifle bounced off his head and stars flew through his vision. A boot connected with his face where Egor carved up his jaw, and the pain made his consciousness dim to gray.

Somewhere, among the ringing in his ears and the clangs of the shovels, Max sensed another sound. It was lower in resonance, almost guttural. It was a sound he had heard many times in his long career and a few times recently.

The beating let up as the other men also heard the sound, and Max was left to lie on the ground as he faded in and out of consciousness. Voices in Russian cut through the fog of agony.

"Shit, we need to get outta here."

"We're not leaving him. Get him into the van. Now, damn it."

"There's no time."

"Put him in the van or I'll shoot you myself."

A curse in Russian.

He was dragged along the ice and rocks. The sound grew louder. It was a thumping sound that could only mean rotors beating the air.

"Move it. Faster, damn it."

Several hands grabbed him and heaved, and he jolted as he hit the van floor. The engine growled to life and the vehicle shook as men climbed inside. Wheels spun and the van got underway, slow at first before it picked up speed.

Sirens sounded in the distance, and the rotors grew louder.

The van shuddered to a halt as automatic gunfire sounded, and the shots were deafening in the small confines of the van. Casings plinked on the metal floor as the smell of cordite filled the interior and singed Max's nostrils.

Should I do something?

Voices in his mind screamed for him to move, to mount an assault on the van's occupants, to take out the automatic weapons. His body disobeyed his own orders and he remained huddled on the van floor with his back wedged in a corner.

A voice over a bullhorn issued commands, first in Swedish, then in German. The voice repeated the commands as the sirens grew louder. The words were indecipherable through the murk in his brain.

The Spetsnaz fired barrage after barrage, and return fire hit the van. *Plink, plink, plink.* Bullets penetrated the sheet metal. Max curled himself into a ball as the slugs careened around him. Someone in the van cried out in pain, followed by a curse in Russian. The gunfire from inside the van slowed.

More commands over the bullhorn.

Cursing in Russian.

The interior of the vehicle grew quiet. The van door slid open and Max sensed men exiting.

Minutes of commotion and yelling in German followed until he heard a distinctive and familiar growl. "He's here. In the back of the van."

Hands jostled him, and he watched shapes moving through blurred vision.

"He's in bloody bad shape," the voice said. "Get the medic."

Consciousness wavered in and out. He became vaguely aware of a stretcher and an IV that was jammed into his arm before he felt the sensation of being lifted into the air. As the rotors droned overhead, he drifted off into a swaying darkness.

FORTY-TWO

Two events made headlines around the globe in the twenty-four hours while Max wavered in and out of consciousness in a private Stockholm hospital room. Only a tiny segment of the intelligence world even noticed the two were connected.

A Learjet touched down in Moscow at a tiny airstrip reserved for Kremlin elite. Except on that wintery night in late January, instead of his usual security detail, General Ruslan Stepanov was met by a row of four black SUVs. Complete with glossy clear coat over reinforced side panels and thick, bulletproof tinted windows, each vehicle was flanked by three men in Russian military fatigues and wielding automatic rifles. An old man, who stood ramrod straight and wore the traditional Russian rabbit-fur ushanka hat, waited near the hood of the second vehicle.

"I'm protected," Stepanov protested as he was searched, cuffed, and shoved into a seat in the third SUV.

"No longer," the old man in the suit informed him.

The column of SUVs roared off in unison on a direct line to Lubyanka, the yellow-brick neobaroque building that housed the FSB's main headquarters. Lore was that prisoners who entered Lubyanka never left. Alive, anyway. The myth wasn't entirely true. Most prisoners were interrogated and tortured there and later moved to one of several military prisons or work camps around Russia.

As the speeding convoy crossed the Garden Ring, using the lane on Petrovka Street reserved for high-ranking government vehicles, a small Kremlin-issued press release was distributed to government agencies and news outlets. The release was short and garnered almost no public interest.

Vice-Admiral Dmitry Ostrovsky is hereby appointed Head of Russia's General Staff's Main Intelligence Unit after the retirement of the former head, General Ruslan Stepanov, due to health concerns. The Vice-Admiral's appointment is effective immediately.

In a room deep under the stadium-shaped building on Hubble Road in Cheltenham, England, that housed the Government Communications Headquarters, Britain's version of the US National Security Agency, a computer notification dinged. A programmer turned from her tea to examine the latest finding by her artificial intelligence computer algorithm. Her job was to tune the AI system to be more accurate. She was responsible for producing CYBINT or what she preferred to call DNINT, or digital network intelligence, via a complex set of bots that crawled the internet searching for keywords. She left the interpretations of the intelligence to others.

The millennial-aged woman, dressed in a long skirt and cashmere jumper, wore cat-eye glasses perched on an expertly crafted nose. She was MIT educated and was a direct descendant of a family of dukes, but she cared little about the trappings of her heritage and was utterly devoted to her work. After a few clicks, the programmer read the headline about the newly appointed head of Russia's Military Intelligence Directorate and digitally tagged the clipping, checked her algorithms, and hit a button to send the snippet to various subscribers: agencies and teams across Britain's wide swath of government installations who cared about news and events in Russia. Each agency employed analysts who might interpret the information differently depending on their objectives and aims.

Satisfied her program behaved appropriately, the programmer sat back and sipped her cup of Earl Grey tea.

In the hallway of a clean and efficient hospital in downtown Stockholm, Cindy, who refused to leave until Max showed signs of recovery, saw the notification. When she read the tiny bit of information sent by the GCHQ, her breath caught and she rushed into the hospital room to show her boss, Callum Baxter, who sat at Mikhail Asimov's bedside.

———

In Berlin, Germany, a short man walked along a snowy sidewalk, oblivious to the events in Russia. Had Lik Wang known of Ruslan Stepanov's demise, he might have altered his course of action. But he didn't know.

One more thing to do before it ends.

One last good deed.

Do the good deeds make up for all my sins?

The Buddha claimed so, but in his long life, Lik Wang had committed many sins. Would this last thing even the account?

I doubt it.

Still, it must be done.

Besides, nothing matters as long as my family is safe.

Dirty ice water sloshed over his cordovan leather Brunello Cucinellis as he crossed a street, but he was beyond caring. Two men followed him, back there in the darkness. Tall and white-skinned, heads with black hair unadorned by hats. Leather jackets in this weather. They resembled Russians, but of course Wang had trouble distinguishing Germans and Russians.

An old-fashioned film canister was grasped in a sweaty hand and shoved deep in a coat pocket. Secreted away in the two-inch gray container was a microSD card wrapped in brown paper so it wouldn't rattle.

Before he made the drop and left the signal that the dead drop was in place, Wang needed to lose the tail. Espionage was not Lik Wang's trade. Instead he had risen to the top of China's largest oil and gas company via raw intellect, gritty courage, and foxlike cunning. Sure, he had executed many of his own operations at the expense of coworkers and competitors, and those operations earned him the reputation as a ruthless executive.

The past year, however, had found Wang performing an increasing number of ultra-risky spy games. He recorded the consortium's meetings and funneled information to MI6. He was blackmailed into performing the former by his own country's head of espionage and fellow consortium member. The latter was his own doing. *Call it restitution.*

Now the grim reaper was here for payment. He completed Stepanov's instructions to the letter, but still there was only one outcome for betraying the consortium.

On the block ahead, a taxi disgorged its occupant, a short, raven-haired woman in a leather biker jacket and black watch cap. Lik ducked into the cab's open door and tossed a hundred-euro note at the driver before mentioning an address. "Go."

Three taxi rides and two underground train trips convinced Lik he had eluded his pursuers. *For now, anyway.* He yanked the collar of his wool coat around his neck and adjusted his Hermès scarf as he ducked into an alleyway. Truck tracks ran through otherwise pristine snow. Wires crisscrossed overhead, metal roll-up doors lined the brick walls, and blue-and-white graffiti covered a row of dumpsters. A vending machine offering beer sat in a corner, its neon sign casting blue light over the alleyway. With a glance over his shoulder, Wang stopped and pretended to peruse the beer selection. The alley was empty in both directions.

He stooped next to the vending machine and counted ten bricks up from the ground, dug a manicured fingernail into the grout, and wiggled the brick loose. He slipped the film canister into the hole and pressed the brick back into place.

As he straightened, the small form of a female wearing a leather jacket and black watch cap appeared at the far end of the alley. His skin prickled and he slipped on the snow while he hastened the opposite way. *I've seen her before.*

When he looked over his shoulder, she was gone.

Almost at a run, Wang exited the alley and headed for the entrance to the underground train station. No one was about. Before he started down the stairs, Wang thumbed a text message, hit send, and stuffed the phone into his pocket.

I've done my best. That's all anyone can ask.

It was his last thought before the bullet pierced his skull to the rear of his left temple, which caused him to somersault down the steps. He was dead before his body came to a rest on the dirty concrete.

The programmer on Hubble Road was engrossed in writing a particularly complex set of instructions for her artificial intelligence algorithm when the notification dinged. With a sniff of frustration, the woman adjusted her glasses and read the flashing message.

Man slain in Berlin's Neukoelln neighborhood was recently identified as Mr. Lik Wang of Shanghai, China. Mr. Wang was in Berlin on business, according to representatives from Sinopec Oil, the Chinese state-run company where he was chairman. Survived by his wife and three children, Mr. Wang was known for his philanthropic activities...

Someday, the analyst knew, the manual review of the high priority hits would be unnecessary. Until the higher-ups trusted the artificial intelligence, she was required to read each and verify its distribution. We wouldn't want some gray-haired bureaucrat to get his knickers in a twist, now would we? The analyst pressed a few mouse buttons and the article was tagged, archived, and distributed.

Cindy dashed into Max's room and found the spy awake and conversing in low tones with Callum Baxter while Badū Khan sat cross-legged on a vinyl couch. The MI6 officer had a hand on Max's shoulder in an attempt to prevent him from getting out of bed. As Cindy entered and distracted her boss, Max stood. His gown parted and when he bent to retrieve his pants, she smirked at his white buttocks. Her gaze lingered until shame overtook her and she averted her eyes.

The three men looked at her as she blurted the news. "Lik Wang is dead."

Baxter's shoulders sank and he fell back to lean on the bed.

Max frowned. "Any news of Julia or Kate?"

Cindy nodded. "Last night we received a text message from Mr. Wang that he made another dead drop. The message came through his old channels instead of the new chat room. We believe his choice to use the old channel means the message is authentic, er... not from Stepanov. And since Stepanov has been replaced as director of the GRU—"

Max yanked on his pants and searched for a shirt. "What was in the drop?"

"We dispatched an agent from Berlin station who recovered a microSD card. The information on the card is being processed in Berlin now and will be transmitted shortly."

His gown fluttered as Max opened a cupboard. With a yank of a string, the gown dropped to the floor. Cindy gasped at the black and blue bruising of his back, neck, and torso. After he shrugged on a T-shirt, Max faced her. "Possible to get some fresh clothes?"

Unable to contain the flush in her cheeks, Cindy stammered, "Yes... Yes... Of course." She fled the room in search of her mobile phone.

FORTY-THREE

British Embassy, Stockholm, Sweden

If the Soviets designed a building on behalf of the British, it would be the concrete block-like embassy building at Skarpögatan 6-8 in Stockholm. Situated on a tree-lined street between the embassies of Japan to the north and Norway to the south, the British Embassy was squat, gray, dingy, and uninspired. It might be mistaken for one of the hundreds of Soviet-era apartment complexes situated around any Eastern European city.

Its interior was no better appointed than the exterior. In an austere conference room on the third floor, a small group of analysts and operatives huddled around a handful of laptops. The team sipped weak coffee and eyed the water-stained drop ceiling with distrust.

Sable's message from the Berlin dead drop had just arrived from Berlin station. Cindy operated the computer, which mirrored her screen to a display on the wall, while Max and Badū hovered. C was in London on urgent business. Baxter received a call and was pacing in the hallway with his Blackberry stuck to his ear.

Cindy briefed the team. "The messages we received from Sable last week about the fake cache of files at the farm outside Stockholm came through an internet chat room. The chat room was a new communication channel requested by Sable, who said he wanted something faster than a dead drop. Now we know why. Sable was discovered by the consortium and coerced to send the chat room message that ultimately resulted in Max's trip to Stockholm."

Harris chuckled. "At least Sable got the last laugh."

"Except now he's dead." Cindy frowned. "Stay focused. The last time this dead drop was used was several months ago. We believe his use of the old dead drop signals an untainted message, so to speak."

Cindy clicked the mouse to navigate through a document folder tree. "The dead drop contained a single microSD card wrapped in brown paper and shoved into a film canister."

"Who uses film anymore?" Harris asked.

"Can you open it, for Pete's sake?" Max unwrapped a stick of chewing gum and popped it into his mouth.

"Right, sorry." Cindy double clicked and the message appeared.

Julia Meier was snatched outside Munich. She is being held in a safe house outside Salzburg in Anif, Austria.

Good luck. This will be my last transmission.

. . .

Along with the message was a physical address written in German. Cindy opened a browser and mapped the address. Max peered at the screen on the wall that showed the tiny hamlet of Anif was twelve kilometers south of Salzburg.

"We need to alert German and Austrian authorities," Baxter said.

Max shook his head. "We do that and it will take days to mount an operation. She'll be dead by then."

"She might already be dead," Baxter said. "Once Stepanov disappeared in Russia, his men probably shot her and vanished. They'd erase the evidence."

In his heart, Max knew Baxter was right. "Only one way to find out."

———

Baxter, Cindy, Harris, and the rest of the MI6 team took a short Lear ride from Stockholm to London and settled into their offices at Vauxhall Cross while Max and Badū caught a commercial flight to Salzburg. Despite Max's protestations, Baxter alerted the German BND, who in turn brought in the Austrian Bundesamt für Verfassungsschutz und Terrorismusbekämpfung (BVT), which acts as that country's domestic intelligence agency. While Max and Badū winged south on a two-hour commercial flight, Germany and Austria activated their law enforcement teams and established surveillance on the Anif address.

Baxter called in a favor, and Max and Badū were picked up from the Salzburg airport in a black BMW sedan and whisked south on the 150. The two blue suits who escorted them south were chatty, but Max clammed up when he realized they were pumping him for information.

The BND, when presented with intel on the whereabouts of its missing senior officer, moved fast, and when the two men arrived at the command post, a one-kilometer perimeter was set up around the home. A half-dozen black vans were parked in a semicircle outside an empty school gymnasium while suited agents barked into mobile phones. Julia was a BND legend, and the agency would use all their resources to rescue one of their own. Satellite imagery was pulled and scrutinized for signs of occupants at the identified address. Utility companies were called. Ownership records were examined. Max counted at least twenty tall, fit men and women with sidearms and tactical vests.

At the center of it all was Frederick Wolf, the granite-faced BND officer who was Julia's supervisor. Even now, Max felt a pang of anger from his experience with Wolf when the man was undercover as an assistant to Wilbur Lynch. Subsequently, Wolf had tried to recruit Max and Spencer White, both of whom spurned Wolf's offer. Max reminded himself that Wolf had his mother's best interest at heart and accepted the intelligence officer's hand.

"We're glad you're here," Wolf said. "I know Julia will be happy to see you. Do me a favor and stay back as an observer. Let my team and the Austrians do our thing. Do we understand each other?" The senior BND officer eyed Badū, but Max refrained from introducing the Mongolian.

"What are we waiting for?" Max asked.

"We want to know what we're getting ourselves into," Wolf said. "If there's a squad of heavily armed commandos in there, we'd like to know that first."

Max accepted a Styrofoam cup of coffee from a staffer, and he and Badū listened to a briefing by one of Wolf's lieutenants.

"The house remained empty for months until recently. Utility use—electricity, gas, internet—was almost nothing.

The house is owned by a shell corporation, and a team back in Berlin is still tracing ownership. They're hitting a lot of brick walls. The utilities are paid from an offshore account in Panama. Again, a dead end. Still, it has all the hallmarks of a safe house."

"You said until recently?" Max asked.

All heads swiveled to look at Max. Wolf scowled.

"Getting to that," the BND man held up a finger. "Satellite imagery showed the arrival of a van and a sedan seven days ago. Their arrival coincided with a spike in electricity and internet usage. Two days ago, those vehicles disappeared and haven't been seen since."

Max stepped closer to Wolf. "That matches with Stepanov's disappearance in Moscow." More angry glances from the BND team. His coffee was cold, and he'd probably have to help himself this time.

"The house has remained dark since," a BND staffer reported.

"Great, let's go." Max dropped his cup in a trash receptacle and left the group.

"Max!" It was Wolf. The officer ran to catch Max and grabbed his arm.

Mistake.

With a pivot and deft shift of his weight, Max flipped Wolf, who landed on the ground with a *whomp*. Shouts erupted from the agents. Pistols appeared and slides were racked. Max ignored it all and crossed the street with Badū on his heel.

The house was situated on a quarter acre of densely treed land. A thin crust of snow blanketed the front lawn, and Max's boots kicked up powder as he stalked up the sidewalk. Behind him, men deployed with assault rifles and a helicopter's rotors thumped overhead.

The home's front door was stout oak, and the handle was locked. A bay window was to the right, covered from the inside with curtains pulled tight. Badū handed him a rock and Max pitched it through the window, kicked in shards of glass, and vaulted over the sill and through the opening. The living room was devoid of furniture and nothing moved. Badū appeared next to him, and they set out to search the house.

They found no one, but there was evidence of recent inhabitants. Canned goods and empty tin cans were in the kitchen, and dirty dishes were piled in the sink. Half-smoked cigarettes lay in makeshift ashtrays. Magazines with nude women and guns and motorcycles were strewn about, and a deck of cards was on a table.

"They left in a hurry." Max's heart grew heavier as they satisfied themselves the house was empty.

"Out back," Badū yelled from the rear, where he looked through an open door to the backyard.

There were dozens of boot prints in the snowy back-yard. The tracks led to a small green-roofed building situated next to a row of trees twenty meters from the house. Double doors, painted a faded blue, were on the front of the shed. Max dashed across the snow and found a padlock securing the doors.

Wolf appeared, an order was issued, and a crowbar was produced. One of the German intelligence men did the honors and two others yanked open the door while Max stood at the entry.

As his eyes acclimated to the darkness inside the shed, a form about the size of a body took shape. It lay in a fetal position on a thin mattress among a slew of yard imple-ments and tools.

Heart in his throat, Max knelt next to the body and

gently rolled it over onto its back. He sensed Wolf over his shoulder. When he saw the face, his mind caught up to what his heart already knew.

Silvery hair spread out on the soiled mattress and framed the beautiful face of his mother. Julia Meier.

Out of habit, Max placed his finger on her neck. There was a faint pulse.

"Get a medic," Max yelled. "She's alive."

———

The orange-and-white Austrian ambulance sped north, siren blaring, lights flashing. In Austria, even the ambulances are Mercedes, and the van made good time up the 150 on its way to the University Hospital in Salzburg.

Julia lay on the stretcher with a set of IVs administering liquids, nourishment, and vitamins. A paramedic sat next to her, and Max sat next to the paramedic. Wolf, Badū, and a skeleton BND team followed in black vans.

Other than severe dehydration and ravenous hunger, Julia appeared uninjured except for the purple and yellow bruise on her face. Max learned during a quick debrief that Julia remembered little about her abduction and subsequent captivity. Her captors kept a mask over her head and didn't speak around her.

Julia reached a hand out to Max, who took it but didn't smile. He asked the paramedic to give them a few minutes, and the woman moved through the opening to the front passenger seat.

"Why'd you do it, Julia?"

She ignored his question and avoided his gaze.

"Why, Julia?"

"You should know by now." Julia spoke in a monotone.

"The good of the state outweighs the good of the individual."

"What happened to family?"

"You're too focused on the consortium. Just like your father. You can't see the big picture."

"What's the big picture?"

"You think the world's petroleum resources are going to last forever? The archive provides details Germany needs to safeguard and procure oil and gas for generations to come. I'm looking out for the future of Germany. Can't you understand that?"

"What about Alex's future? And mine? I'm your son, for God's sake."

"The good of the many outweighs the welfare of the few."

"Bullshit. That's propaganda someone drilled into your head. Did you ever love him? Or was everything between you just a mission for German intelligence?"

Julia turned her head away. When she turned back, her eyes were moist. "We made the plan together, your father and I. We agreed that he would steal the documents and funnel them to me in Germany. The German government would use them to disband the komissariat and the councils. Those files were supposed to be mine. But when he was killed, I found out..."

"What, Julia? You found what?"

"The ones he gave me were fake." She sniffled. "He betrayed me." Her eyes narrowed. "So spare me your sermons."

"The box was empty," he said. "Maybe he didn't know who to trust."

A tear rolled down Julia's cheek, and Max took her hand.

The paramedic called out from the front. "We're two minutes from the hospital."

They rode in silence until the ambulance stopped and the rear doors opened. An orderly in blue scrubs pulled the stretcher, and Julia's hand slipped from his grasp.

Max stepped from the rear of the ambulance as Badū approached. The Mongolian took him by the arm and led him away from the hospital and through the parking lot where a long black Mercedes sat idling. "Since we're in Austria, how about a side trip to meet the team?"

FORTY-FOUR

1st District, Vienna, Austria

The long black Mercedes rode low on a modified suspension that supported a reinforced chassis, steel-plated side panels, solid rubber tires, and bulletproof glass. A burly driver in a suit jacket and craggy features drove with one meaty fist on the wheel while the other clutched a .45 automatic. An identical bodyguard, the driver's brother, rode shotgun and also clutched a .45 automatic.

Max rode in the rear passenger compartment with Badū Khan next to him. The Mongolian was silent on the ride between Salzburg and Vienna and refused to answer any of Max's questions. Unlike in Germany, where vast sections of the autobahn had no speed limit, the highways in Austria were limited to 130 kilometers per hour and so the trip took just under three hours.

Max stared out the window at the snow flurries. The Mercedes windows were so thick they distorted the view. The snow swirled in darkness sprinkled with the multicolored lights of the city, which looked like they were viewed through raindrops instead of bulletproof windows.

After a circuitous route through the city, which Max guessed was to shake any surveillance, they sped along Parkring with the Wiener Stadtpark on their left and took a series of abrupt lefts and rights before they turned into an underground garage. An elevator ride took them up to the penthouse, where two more bodyguards waited in an antechamber. Badū gestured at a door and Max pushed it open.

"After you," Badū said.

Warm air washed over Max as he entered. The hallway was painted in cream, the floor was parquet oak, and the lighting was dim. An antiseptic smell and the faint odor of bleach reminded him of a hospital. A faint tinkle of Mozart came from deeper in the apartment. As he strode along the corridor, a tall woman in a red dress appeared at the end of the hallway. The high cheekbones and almond eyes were immediately recognizable. A shawl was around her shoulders, and Gabrieli approached with a finger to her lips.

"Shhh, he's sleeping."

"Who—"

"Come. I'll show you."

A gruff voice barked out from the room at the end of the hallway. "Mikhail? Is that Mikhail?" A stream of coughs was followed by hacking and spitting.

That voice. It can't be.

Gabrieli took Max's hand and led him into warmer light. To the left was an expansive and modern kitchen, while the right opened into a living area with high ceilings, elaborate crown molding, and huge oil paintings by the masters. Black velvet drapes were closed tight over floor-to-ceiling windows.

The music came from a pair of standing speakers. A woman with a sharp nose and pale skin stood at the kitchen sink. Against one living room wall sat an elaborate hospital bed complete with two IV stands, vitals monitor on a stand, and its occupant propped up on pillows.

A raspy, phlegm-laced voice interspersed with fits of wet coughs projected through the cavernous apartment like a megaphone. "Mikhail, my boy. Come over here."

Like he was floating through a blurred tunnel, Max walked over the silk rugs that littered the wood floor until he reached the side of the hospital bed.

How is this possible?

Andrei Asimov's shaggy head, gaunt but still massive, rested on fluffy pillows. An oxygen tube was wound around his ears, but the nose piece hung free. An IV with clear fluids was attached to a thin arm. The form under the light blanket was a frail version of its former self. Max held onto the bed's metal rail so his shaky knees wouldn't give way.

"I know, it's a shock," Andrei said. "I don't have much longer, son, so get over it." A fit of coughing overcame the former spymaster, and the sharp-nosed woman rushed over to wipe his mouth until Andrei shooed her away. "Damn woman," he muttered.

Max forgot Gabrieli stood at the end of the bed and Badū was somewhere behind him. "How... I mean, what happened? Our house was bombed. You..."

Andrei pointed at a chair. "Pull that over, son. I don't have long, and I have things I must tell you. Events have evolved now to where you must come to know the truth, no matter how difficult."

Badū approached, took Andrei's hand in both of his, and withdrew without speaking a word.

"I'll leave you two to chat," Gabrieli said. "I'll be in the next room if you need anything." The silk dress swished as she smiled at Max and left the room.

"That woman has a real future in this business," Andrei said. "Emma! Bring us some of that vodka."

Emma glared at them, so Andrei shouted a string of curses. "Damn it, woman, I only have days left to live. I want to share a drink with my son." Under his breath, Andrei whispered to Max. "This one, however. Her days are numbered."

Emma approached with two crystal tumblers and a green-labeled bottle full of clear liquid. Max took the bottle, offered the nurse a smile, set the alcohol on a table, and helped Andrei sit up. Andrei's hand shook as he held the glass and Max poured them both a finger.

"To your health," Andrei said. They clinked glasses and his old man tossed back the drink. "Ah, that's good."

Emma retreated to the kitchen while Max poured another shot for them both.

"I think that woman is the daughter of Satan," Andrei muttered.

"She's just doing her job, Dad." *That word feels surreal.*

"Yeah, well, who's in charge here? No cigarettes. No red meat. I draw the line at alcohol. It isn't going to make a bit of difference. My number is up. Who knew it would end this way? In a damn hospital bed with tubes stuck in me. Drag that stool over. This might take a while. I need to stay alive long enough to explain everything."

Max perched on the stool and touched his father's arm. *Not a hallucination.*

"Now let me look at you, son."

Max tried to smile, but emotion welled up. Love conflicted with anger and confusion at being deceived.

"Ah, you look good, son. Except for that scar."

"Egor Dikov."

"That old prick? Jesus, I hope you put him out of every-one's misery."

"He's locked away somewhere in the Swedish justice system."

"Well, good riddance." Andrei held up his glass. Max clinked his glass to Andrei's and they sipped. The vodka reminded him of his childhood, when the bottle sat on the table at dinner like red wine in a French household.

Andrei closed his eyes as he swallowed. "The bomb at the house was an unfortunate necessity, Mikhail. The komissariat had just proclaimed me persona non grata, and I had to take drastic action to protect myself."

"But what happened to Mom?"

A groan from Andrei morphed into a spasm, and Emma rushed to hold a cloth next to Andrei's mouth. The cloth was red when she removed it, and Emma shot Max a glare. Max took the cloth from her and draped it on the metal rail.

"It was a heart-wrenching decision, son. But your mother... By now you know Julia is your true mother. Katherine was compromised."

"Compromised?"

His father's big, black eyes held Max's. "She crossed over. She worked for the komissariat. Gave them intel on my whereabouts and actions."

"What? Why?"

"It was difficult, Mikhail. Even with...my relationship with Julia, I loved Katherine. When I found out she was... It broke my heart."

"But, why would she do that?"

"We'll never know for sure, but I suspect they offered her safety in exchange for the information. Or threatened her. Once I was out of the way, she'd be in the clear. Who knows? Maybe it was her way of getting back at me for Julia."

"You planned the bombing, which took out Katherine and staged your own death."

Andrei's face darkened. "To be more accurate, Victor planned the bombing. I found out about it and used it to my advantage."

"Was Julia aware you were alive?"

"She suspected."

"You didn't trust her, did you? That's why you gave her the fake documents."

"She told you about that?" Andrei's face turned slack. "It broke my heart, Mikhail."

After another spasm, Emma brought over a plastic cup with a straw. When the nurse left, Max held the cup so Andrei could drink. "When I explain the whole thing, you'll understand."

"Does the Vienna Archive even exist?" Max asked.

Andrei reached out to pat Max's arm. "It's funny how we make these names up. The Vienna Archive. They were closer than they thought." A coughing fit took over, and the old man spilled vodka on his bedclothes.

When Andrei was able to talk again, he spoke in a hushed tone, and Max had to lean close. "So far, you've only learned what I've intended for you to learn. It was for your own good, Mikhail. I knew if I had any hope of ending the consortium once and for all, you would need to be my weapon. My options were limited while I was in hiding. I was already sick when the bombing happened. I risked exposing myself to our enemies. I know these past months have been difficult on you, Mikhail, and I can only hope someday you'll forgive me."

Max touched his father's arm. "You did what you had to do."

Andrei glanced at Emma, who worked at the kitchen sink, and lowered his voice so Max had to lean even closer. "By now you know of the existence of the komissariat along with the operational councils for energy, defense, finance, and economics. You know these bodies are a shadow government operating with autonomy to carry out the aims of the komissariat leadership, a secretive group of men with ties to Lenin's secret police, the Cheka. You know this group's aims are to protect and enhance the Bolshevik power base in Russia and around the world. You know the komissariat's mission is in opposition to the formal government in Russia and the president." As he spoke, Andrei's voice became stronger.

Max refilled both glasses with a splash of vodka. "What I still don't understand is why this komissariat wants us all dead."

"You're going to want another hit of that vodka before I explain."

Max raised his eyebrows. "Sounds ominous."

Both men drank, and Max watched his father watch Emma.

When he spoke, Andrei's voice was a whisper. "You see, I was once a member of the komissariat. I sat on the komissariat council of three."

FORTY-FIVE

1st District, Vienna, Austria

The confession landed with a thud, and the room swirled like a whirlpool. Max steadied himself with the bed's steel railing and stared at his father. A man he thought was dead until thirty minutes ago. A man who always had another surprise in store.

What else are you going to reveal tonight?

"That's right, Mikhail." The glass was steady in Andrei's hand, almost as if the vodka held the sickness at bay. "Our family is descended from the Cheka. Your great-great- grandfather, my great-grandfather, was Felix Dzerzhinsky. Felix had one son officially but raised another son out of wedlock, a boy named Dmitri. That illegitimate son took the surname Asimov when Dzerzhinsky initially disowned him. The two later reconciled, and Dmitri Asimov was given a high-ranking position in Stalin's army. Later Dmitri Asimov became a charter member of the first komissariat established when Stalin died.

"Wait. Dmitri Asimov is my great-grandfather? Your grandfather? And Yuri Aristov, whose real name was Mikhail Asimov, your father, was Dmitri Asimov's son?"

"Yes. As you know, Stalin's death was a pivotal moment in Soviet history. The central committee established a collective leadership so no one might gain the kind of power Stalin had. The gulags were reformed, the Korean War ended, political prisoners were released, and many other reforms were put in place. The komissariat was formed by the hardliners to counterbalance the central committee's reforms. The Bolshevik hawks wanted a return to Stalin's ways."

Andrei's breath rasped as he leaned back into the pillows. Max held the oxygen tube to his father's nose. "When Dmitri died in 1968, I took his place on the komissariat."

"Why didn't Yuri—I mean, your father, Mikhail, take the spot?"

"As you know from your talk with Yuri in the States, he took a different path. He was not as committed to the komissariat and focused on his career in the army. Eventually, events took their course, and Yuri made the decision to defect to the CIA."

"So, what—"

"Right. What happened? What happened is, I grew disillusioned with both the komissariat and the Soviet Union. The Berlin Wall came down, and things in Russia went crazy. Overnight, men became billionaires, our president asserted himself, the komissariat grew weaker, and the mistake of communism became obvious." A wistful Andrei Asimov sipped his vodka. "I saw how communism failed, and I saw how the new regime in Russia failed their people. The only hope was to eliminate both the komissariat and the Russian president and replace it all with a true democracy."

"That's a lot for any one person to take on."

"I had the means. The evidence of the komissariat in their archives was enough to take them down and prompt the Russian people to stand up against their government."

"What's the connection between the komissariat and the Russian president?"

"That is a good question, Mikhail. There are a lot of things I still don't know. For example, I don't know who the komissariat's leader is."

"What? How is that—"

"Possible? One of the ways the komissariat preserves its power is through secrecy. Only a handful of very powerful men know who runs the komissariat."

Max sipped the vodka. "Some think the komissariat is now in the hands of someone else. A clandestine power foreign to Russia."

Andrei's big head nodded. "You and Badū have become acquainted. I'm glad about that. You can trust him with your life, Mikhail."

"So it was you who orchestrated the prison break through General Bakunin?"

"Yes, but more on that later, Mikhail. We don't know the relationship between the komissariat and the Russian president. As you know, the president is a very powerful man. Some believe he couldn't be in power without sanction from the komissariat. Others believe the komissariat is a tool for the president."

"So why the death sentence?"

"As my discontent grew, I collected evidence of the komissariat's operations and stored that material away in a secret hiding place."

Max looked around the apartment for a stack of boxes. "So this Vienna Archive exists?"

The glint in Andrei's eye returned. "I'd have given millions to see Stepanov's face when he opened that empty box in Stockholm."

Max grinned. "He was livid."

Andrei chuckled. "He deserved that. The komissariat gave him a deadline to find you and the files. He failed and that sealed his fate. If he's not a corpse in Lubyanka's basement, he soon will be." After handing his empty glass to Max, Andrei bent over to rearrange the blanket, covering his legs.

Max helped his father pull the covering over his chest. The old spymaster took the opportunity to close his eyes, and the room grew silent except for chopping sounds from the kitchen and the faint Mozart from the speakers.

Don't die on me, damn it.

Max was about to prod his father awake when the old man's eyes popped open.

"The files, son, are well hidden." The old man's gaze darted around the apartment and rested on Emma. He lowered his voice to a whisper. "Only I know their location. If I die, that knowledge will die with me."

The damn Vienna Archive exists.

"What's your intention?" Max asked.

Andrei erupted into a fit of spasms, and this coughing episode was so violent that Emma ran over to hold a cold cloth to Andrei's forehead. When he recovered, Andrei sent Emma away and sipped water from the plastic cup.

"Where were we? Ah, yes. You were wondering why the komissariat issued the death proclamation on the Asimov family. Well, you see, Katherine found out what I was doing. She overheard something, probably a phone call between me and Julia, and reported me to Victor, who aspired to a komissariat seat for himself. Imagine how this sat with Victor. He was my boss at the KGB, but I had ultimate power because I sat on the komissariat. I was one of the three." When Andrei grinned, his eyebrows went up and down.

"Victor didn't like that," Max said.

"No he did not. Victor thought by turning me in, it would bolster his own stature. I believe what happened is the komissariat made an investigation, uncovered little but found enough to implicate me. Or maybe my past deeds came back to haunt me. Whatever the reason, I was summarily released from the komissariat. All of this took place while I was traveling in Europe. Luckily, I was tipped off before I returned. Otherwise, I'd have suffered the same fate as Ruslan Stepanov, and I might still be buried in a cell in the basement of Lubyanka. Staging my own death was the only thing I could think to do. You see, the komissariat's policy, which dates back to Lenin's secret police, is that traitors are sentenced to death along with their entire family."

"It's meant to discourage turncoats," Max said. "This is still the culture in Russia."

A nod from Andrei. "Right. This is why Moscow will chase traitors to the ends of the earth. Berezovsky, Poteyev, Yushchenko. All of them killed because they turned their back on Russia."

"Tell me about the komissariat."

"I figured you'd ask. And I'll tell you. But just like you can't put an end to the consortium by killing everyone, you can't kill off the komissariat."

"People keep telling me that," Max said.

"They're right. The organization is designed to live into perpetuity even if its members are eliminated. The only

way to end the komissariat and the bounty on your head is
—" This coughing fit ended in another blood-soaked rag,
this one a deeper red than the first.

"Lung cancer, Mikhail," Andrei said when he could
talk. "Of all the things to finally get me." Andrei rested his
head on the pillows while Max held the straw to his lips.
When the cup was half empty, he pushed the straw from
his mouth. "Vodka."

Max splashed some in Andrei's glass and refilled his
own. "You were saying something about the only way to end
the komissariat and the bounty on our heads."

"Ah, yes. Right. Two things, both of which must be
done simultaneously. It's my belief that the only way is to
publicly reveal the existence of the komissariat. Its main
source of power is its secrecy. Once the contents are
divulged, there will no longer be a legitimate shadow
government able to exert pressure behind the scenes."

"And the second?"

"Money. You must cut off the source of their funds.
Without the secrecy and the funding, they will be
impotent."

"And the best way to expose the komissariat is to reveal
your files."

"Yes, but it must be done in a particular way. You can't
just give the files to the *Financial Times* of London."

The noises in the kitchen died down. Emma's back was
to them as she cut food on a cutting board. "Where is the
archive?"

Andrei's sigh was deep and generated a loud hawking
noise from his throat, and he spit up a wad of blood-soaked
phlegm into a cloth. "Before I tell you..."

Max groaned inwardly. *Enough already.*

Andrei waved him closer.

Max hunched over with his ear close to his father's mouth.

"You can only trust a few people," Andrei whispered. "Because I needed to keep my secret hidden, I assembled a small team of people. This team is all you have."

"Gabrieli and Badū?"

Andrei nodded.

"General Bakunin?"

"General Bakunin is not a formal member of the team."

"Are there others?"

"There are."

As if on cue, there was a disturbance at the door and footsteps sounded in the hallway. Max turned and his mouth dropped open.

Tall and resplendent in a Burberry wool coat over a flowing black dress was Goshawk.

———

"Hello, Max." Goshawk smiled coyly.

Andrei's hand tightened on Max's arm. "Do not blame her, Mikhail. She was acting on my explicit instructions. I knew we had a mole on our little team, and I suspected it was Julia. The whole elaborate plan with the fake one-time pad was to flush out the traitors. I needed to see who was with me and who wasn't. I guess we found out." The pain in his voice was evident. "I loved Julia, Mikhail. And now I wonder whether she ever truly loved me or if I was just a source to her."

Goshawk deposited her coat on the back of the couch and retrieved a bottle of white wine from the refrigerator before perching on a stool within easy reach of the vegetables Emma cut.

"Anyone else on this team I should know about?" As Max asked the question, a face popped into his mind. "Kate Shaw."

Andrei smiled but shook his head. "Ah, yes, poor Kate. Every team needs a foot soldier. She played a necessary role."

"Does she know you're alive?"

"She does not. Despite Kate's treatment at the hands of the CIA, I predict her loyalties will be soon tested. You cannot trust any of the so-called intelligence agencies. I know you've been hanging around with the British, and their chief is the most morally sound of all of them. But each of them—the KGB, CIA, MI6, and the German BND— have their own agenda. They all want the archive. They perceive it to be the key to Russia's petroleum strategy, and they're right. As you have found out, the fight for natural resources outweighs almost all other considerations. Wars have been fought over natural resources since the beginning of time and will continue to be until we destroy this planet."

"And Goshawk's role?"

Andrei smiled at the tall and tattooed computer hacker. "She was necessary in our ruse against Julia."

Max caught Goshawk's eye and saw moisture there. A thought sprang to mind. It was the answer to a question that had plagued him since Baxter rescued him from the farm in Sweden.

"Someone had to tip MI6 off to where I was in Stockholm." Max turned to his father. "You're the only one who knew where the box was buried."

"I alerted Baxter to your location," Goshawk said. "I'm sorry for doing what I did. It was the only way to test Julia's allegiance."

"And Kate's, it sounds like," Max said. "Julia failed the test. Kate passed."

Andrei squeezed his lids shut, and Max sat with him while he rested and avoided Goshawk's gaze. When the old man's eyes opened, Andrei pressed a small SD card into Max's hand.

"What's this?"

"Shush." Andrei's eyes darted to Emma, who watched them from the kitchen. His voice went a decibel louder. "You think I want to carry boxes of paper around with me?"

Max scrutinized the tiny memory card. "This is it? The whole archive? Is this the only copy?"

"As far as you know." Andrei laid back into the pillows and closed his eyes.

"Hand it over!" The shrill voice shouted from the kitchen where Emma pointed a pistol at Max. "Do it or I swear I'll kill both of you!"

Andrei's eyes opened. "I knew it. That damned woman. I told you. Evil as Satan."

Max palmed the SD card. "Why don't you come and get it?"

"Toss it on the ground and step back." The pistol swung to point at Goshawk. "Or the woman gets shot."

Max did as he was instructed.

"Now get on your knees."

As Max knelt, Emma's eyes went wide, and she moved her pistol and fired just as a second gunshot roared next to Max's ear. Emma staggered against the counter, a red bloom appeared on her blouse, and the pistol fell to the tile. Slowly she sank to the floor as Goshawk rushed around the counter to kick the gun away.

Two guards sprinted into the room with Gabrieli and

Badū on their heels. A hand went to Gabrieli's mouth as she pointed at the hospital bed.

Max turned. His father held a Russian-made Makarov 9mm. A satisfied smile was on his face. A maroon stain spread on his bedclothes near his chest. Max went to the bed.

"Mikhail."

The pistol fell from Andrei's hand, and Max stuck it in his waistband before taking his father's hand. "Dad, what have you done?"

"Never trusted that bitch."

"But—"

His father's grip tightened on Max's hand. "Mikhail. The memory card."

Max motioned to Gabrieli, who fetched the card from the floor and handed it to Max. "It's right here, Dad."

The old man chuckled. "There's nothing on it. You don't think I'd have the whole thing on me, do you? I'm an invalid, for God's sake."

"So it doesn't exist?"

"Of course it exists, my son. And you have everything you need to find it. All the clues. Only you can figure it out. It was the only way to keep it safe."

Max searched his memory. "But..."

The old man's grip loosened. "It's okay, son. I can't lay here in this bed any longer. Better this way."

Andrei closed his eyes as his last breath escaped his lips.

Max bent to his father's ear. "I love you, Dad."

FORTY-SIX

Fairfax County, Virginia

Kate Shaw was permitted to ride in the small private jet unencumbered by restraints, although three corn-fed CIA agents were never more than four feet away.

During the flight over the Atlantic, she tried to sleep but instead played back the events that had transpired to make her a fugitive from her old employer. The mysterious death of her old CIA boss and longtime friend, William Blackwood. The ascendance of Piper Montgomery to the director's office. Montgomery's actions to demote Kate and eliminate her team. The mole who was never caught. Kate's abduction by the CIA and subsequent incarceration at a black site in upstate New York before Victor Dedov captured her for the information he thought was in her head. A trial for treason certainly awaited her on US soil.

One question nagged as they winged across the Atlantic. *How had Julia known she possessed the one-time pad?*

No matter how many angles Kate examined, only one answer remained. What was it Sherlock Holmes said? *When you have eliminated the impossible, whatever remains, however improbable, must be the truth.*

When they landed, Kate was transported from the nondescript hangar at Reagan National to a rambling brick colonial revival-styled house situated on a twenty-acre horse farm far from Washington DC's Beltway.

The colonial in Northern Virginia might be described as a safe house, except it was more than that. It sat on a rise among a forest of towering jack pines and thick oaks. The main building had two wings, and several outbuildings littered the property. Tiny security cameras studded the exterior of the structures while armed guards with dogs patrolled the split rail fence around the perimeter and snipers were deployed in hidden locations.

After a nap and a shower, Kate dressed in fresh clothes provided by the Agency. She was led to the home's massive dining room that was converted to a mini operations center complete with LCD monitors, telephones, computers, and a row of coffee urns. Two men, both of whom she recognized, sat at the long conference table.

"Can I get some coffee?" Kate asked.

The man at the head of the table pointed at the bank of coffee makers. "Help yourself. I'll take a refill, black. Stephen?"

The second man nodded, and Kate served hot black coffee to the interim CIA director, Chester Wodehouse, and the Director of the Counterintelligence Center Analysis Group, Stephen MacCulloch.

MacCulloch, as he always did, resembled a homeless man after a weekend bender. Wodehouse's huge head and acne-marked face were hunched over a tiny laptop, on which he hunted and pecked out a message while his coffee sat steaming.

After a violent jab on the keyboard to send his message, Wodehouse banged his laptop closed. "Our friends at the BND tell us you've been on quite the walkabout the past few months." He consulted a thick dossier, its cover marked with red classified tape, and thumbed through a sheaf of pages. "Consorting with rogue FSB agents. Kidnapped and interrogated by the Belarusian KGB. Selling your services to MI6. All while a fugitive from your own country. These are serious allegations, any one of which might be considered treason."

Kate sipped her coffee. "Don't forget about the Belarusian KGB director who abducted me from your custody."

"Do you want to set the record straight? Shall we record our conversation?"

"That's a joke if you think I believe this room isn't recording everything we say."

Both men laughed.

"I assure you it is not," MacCulloch said. The shaggy man cupped his coffee in both hands like it was his lifeblood.

Wodehouse tapped the thick file. "You want to fill in the blanks?"

"Depends," Kate said.

"On?"

"On whether the CIA is going to violate my rights again by incarcerating me for months with no due process. And whether the CIA is going to use illegal interrogation and torture methods on me again."

MacCulloch chuckled as he sipped his coffee.

After tasting his own coffee for the first time, Chester Wodehouse, a consummate operative who rose through the ranks to deputy director on the back of an unblemished record in the field, slammed the file shut and tossed it on the table. "Look, we all regret the Montgomery affair. It put a huge black mark on this organization and all that it stands for. In a few months, she undid what we worked our entire careers to build. Now the White House and Capitol Hill have serious trust issues, which makes it difficult to get funding and to carry out our mission."

Kate snorted. "Funding? That's all you care about? Since when does the great Chester Wodehouse pander to the Hill?"

"Not my idea of a good time, believe me." Wodehouse adjusted his trademark black sport coat which he always wore over a black T-shirt. "But I didn't spend thirty years of my career in the trenches only to let this organization fall into obsolescence. You may not believe me, but I had nothing to do with what happened to you, Kate. Montgomery had me buried in so much bureaucracy and chasing so many rat holes that I was on the outside looking in. You may judge me for it, and indeed others will, but she had me fooled like the rest of the organization."

Across the table from her, MacCulloch nodded. "She had a lot of us fooled, Kate. If we sit back and let the country think the CIA was Piper Montgomery, we're doomed. We might as well fold up our tent and go home."

The coffee in her cup was cold. She grabbed the carafe and poured herself a new cup. *There is some reason I'm not behind bars.*

The interim CIA director stared at the silver carafe. "Kate, I have an opportunity now to make right everything that Montgomery fucked up."

"Are they going to let you? When's your confirmation hearing?"

Wodehouse rose and strolled to the row of coffee urns and filled his mug. With his extra-large head resting on broad shoulders and narrow hips, Chester Wodehouse was far from a handsome man. Still, he exuded the kind of charisma that appealed to the teams in the trenches. He had executed hundreds of successful operations behind the Iron Curtain, in the Middle East, and in other theaters. Known as brash but a straight shooter, Wodehouse was the opposite of the sort of man one expected to excel inside the Beltway. Yet here he was, tasked to right a sinking ship.

"There is a group of people in the White House who are backing my candidacy with Stephen here as my deputy. They want to resuscitate the old CIA, the effective CIA. The one that used tested techniques to generate real intelligence while deploying modern technology. As you know, Montgomery came from Congress. She was a politician. There is a growing tide of insiders who want to see the old CIA back in business. A CIA that takes risks and cuts through the bullshit and red tape to get real intelligence. Intel that can be acted on." Sweeping his arm around the room, Wodehouse beamed. "We're a huge organization with tremendous resources that should be put to good use."

Kate rubbed her hand on the table. "Why am I here?"

Wodehouse gulped his coffee, strode to the table, punched a button on an intercom, and barked an order. As he took his seat, the door opened and a staffer delivered a massive tray of pastries. Both men helped themselves.

Wodehouse munched a bear claw. "A wise man once told me to never apologize. It shows weakness, Kate, and that maxim has remained with me my entire career. But the CIA treated you poorly, and a woman of your skills and track record deserves better." The bear claw disappeared in a hail of crumbs.

Oh, God.

Thumping his hand on the folder, Wodehouse went on. "We're willing to make a trade, Kate. We can make all of this disappear. It'll all be expunged from your jacket."

"In exchange for what?"

"In addition, we'll reinstate you with full benefits and tenure, like you never left."

This can't be happening.

"All I have to do is forget about how the CIA treated me?"

"With Stephen in the role of deputy, his position will vacate. We'd like you in his former position reporting directly to Carla Han, the deputy director of the National Clandestine Service."

"How's Carla going to like that?"

Wodehouse shrugged. "Doesn't matter. Carla, as you know, was a Montgomery appointee and is concerned about her future right about now. She will benefit from your years of operational expertise."

"You want me to keep tabs on her."

"Listen, this organization needs a deep cleaning. Carla is on the bubble. I need people around me I can trust."

"Still searching for the mole?"

Sighing deeply, Chester eyed the pastries, apparently thought better of it, and sipped his coffee.

MacCulloch picked up the storyline. "Unfortunately, yes. We know Montgomery was a bad seed. We also know there are elements of a broader conspiracy still buried in our ranks. As we smoke them out with a series of disinformation campaigns, we'll cull the ranks. Because of the leaks we experienced while you were out of commission, we know you can't be the mole." With both hands on his coffee mug, MacCulloch leaned on the table. "Kate, we have the president's chief of staff and his national security advisor's support on this."

They need me.

"You must want something in exchange," Kate said.

"Right," Wodehouse said. "You're a no-bullshit person, Kate. I like that about you." His gaze pierced Kate like lasers. "We need two things. The first is a signed contract putting all this behind us. We'll forgive all your transgressions subsequent to your...ahem...incarceration, and you agree to waive any claims you may think you have against the Agency. I have the document already worked up. You can take as long as you want to read through it."

"And the second?"

I can guess.

"We need your help with the Vienna Archive."

There it is.

"While you were over the Atlantic, I talked to MI6's chief." In as few words as possible, Wodehouse briefed her on the operation in Stockholm, the empty box uncovered by Stepanov, the three-star general's subsequent disappearance, and Max's recovery. He also told her about Julia Meier's kidnapping and subsequent rescue by the joint BND and Austrian team. Chester Wodehouse let her absorb the news while he refilled their coffees.

Max is okay.

The news made her realize she worried about him more than she thought. Another notion sank in. Andrei had used her to expose Julia's treachery. The one-time pad she risked her life to retrieve was a fake.

So much for loyalty.

"Where is the Vienna Archive?" Kate asked. "Is it even real?"

"We believe, as do our friends at MI6, that your friend Mikhail has it."

"If that's true, why do you..." It hit her. "You want me to..." She couldn't form the words.

The two CIA men stared at her.

"You want me to convince Max to give it to us."

Wodehouse leaned on the coffee credenza. "Max has to do something with the files. What are his choices? Go public with it? Leak it to some do-gooder organization like WikiLeaks? Nothing will come of it if he goes that route. It will get washed away in the next news cycle. Instead, he can work with us and MI6 and we can make real change."

Blackmail. Sign the paper and I get my life back. Betray a friend in the process.

"Look, Kate. You're either on our team or you're not. Time to make a decision."

Kate tasted the coffee and eyed the donuts. Why would Andrei Asimov bury an empty box, create a false trail, including the coded message and the one-time pad, and send her on a wild-goose chase? *He didn't know who to trust.* All the intelligence agencies fell all over themselves to retrieve the archive while he sat back to see who betrayed him. The CIA was left on the outside, and now they wanted to buy their way in.

"I have two terms of my own."

Wodehouse snatched a cruller. "You're not exactly in a position to bargain, Kate."

Kate stood. "I'll take my chances with a lawyer."

The cruller disappeared and Wodehouse licked his fingers. "Let's not get hasty, Kate. We're all friends here. Tell me your terms."

"Get Kaamil Marafi released from the Emirates and

reinstated onto my team. Full benefits, tenure, and back pay."

Wodehouse laughed. "Do you think I can work miracles?"

"Listen, you have a mole problem. Kaamil is one of the few people you can trust. He was also incarcerated the past few months, and if there's still a leak, you know he's clean."

"I'll admit I didn't see that one coming," Wodehouse said between chuckles. "What else?"

"Full pardon and reinstatement of full retirement benefits for Spencer White."

"That was predictable. I thought you were going to ask for clemency for your Russian," Wodehouse said as he slid a document across the table.

Kate picked up the densely worded contract. "He's Belarusian. And that ship has sailed."

FORTY-SEVEN

Bath, England

The reunion, such that it was, took place in the operations room at the cherry orchard, where a small fire burned in the hearth. The housekeeper bustled in the kitchen to prepare a feast of roasted meat and vegetables while Tom served drinks. Alex, bundled in a winter jacket, roamed outside among the orchard trees with Spike bounding along near him. Max and Baxter sat in one corner with a bottle of Irish whiskey between them. Cindy, for once not buried in her laptop, sat with Goshawk and shared a bottle of Pinot Grigio. Noticeably absent was Badū, who had remained in Vienna, Spencer and his dog Charlie, who had returned to Colorado, and C, who was embroiled in a budget meeting in London. Max's calls to Kate went unanswered and unreturned.

Absently, Max toyed with the SD card in his pocket, where it had been since his return from Vienna. While on the MI6 jet between Vienna and Heathrow, Max examined the contents long enough to determine there was nothing but an old family picture of him, Arina, and his father. He had stared at the image for a long time and remembered when he found a memory card hidden in a family photo right after the explosion that leveled his childhood home. This image was from when Max was in high school. It showed Arina sitting on a horse while Max held the reins and his father rested a hand on the horse's flank. Arina's smile was radiant. *Happier times.*

Baxter received a call and ducked out. Max watched Cindy and Goshawk talk and he overheard words like *proxy server* and *spoofing.* Since their hurried departure from Vienna, where Badū remained behind to clean up the mess in the apartment, Goshawk attempted to apologize several times. It was too soon. The betrayal was too fresh, even if it was at the behest of his father.

The cursed Vienna Archive. A fabled cache of documents that caused so much death and ruined lives.

Of course it exists, my son. And you have everything you need to find it. All the clues. Only you can figure it out. It was the only way to keep it safe.

In the days since his father's death—Andrei's actual death—Max racked his brain in an effort to decipher his father's clues. He played back everything that happened since the bomb exploded in Minsk. The family picture retrieved in the barn. The picture of Julia uncovered in the butcher shop floor. The video on the miniSD card found in Raisa's locket that unearthed Kate's role in his father's scheme. The empty box buried in a farm outside Stockholm. The book retrieved from Stepanov's compound. Max tried to connect the dots and so far had failed. Ordinarily Goshawk's quick and analytical mind was an asset, but trust issues lingered.

Next to the bottle of whiskey sat the book of fairy tales he brought with him from Stepanov's compound. He thumbed through it absently before tossing back a shot of the whiskey as he rose and left the room. He shrugged on a down jacket and strode out into the cherry orchard. Dark branches, naked of their leaves, swayed in an invisible breeze. A dusting of snow piled around the tree trunks, and the pathway was an uneven track of frozen mud. He mulled the sequence of events as he walked. The attack on the cabin in Colorado and their subsequent flight to England. Kate's travels into Russia. The attack on Fedorov's chalet, where Max witnessed Stepanov's triumphant acquisition of the message, which contained directions to the empty box in Stockholm. All orchestrated by his father to expose Julia's treachery and take down Ruslan Stepanov.

A ten-minute stroll took him to the end of the tree row where a waist-high fence of stones lined the orchard perimeter. Beyond the wall was an undulating expanse of rolling moors, now murky in the evening gloom. He skirted a tree and started back to the farmhouse. Stepanov's operation to nab the one-time pad from Professor Euler stuck in his mind. Markov got there first and retrieved it but had a fake one in his pocket. Kate pickpocketed the fake, which was subsequently stolen by Julia. All with help by Goshawk.

Goshawk. She betrayed him at the behest of his father. *Why?*

For your own good, maybe.

He pushed her from his thoughts.

The scheme was an elaborate plan to flush out a possible traitor. It had the added benefit of taking out Stepanov, but still...

Max stopped next to a tree. A drop of sleet hit his head

but he didn't notice. The timing wasn't right. If Andrei had used the one-time pad to encrypt the message with the directions to the documents a year ago, as he said, he couldn't have predicted this sequence of events back then. Even Andrei, with all his operational wisdom and brilliant mind, couldn't have anticipated it.

That meant the message possessed originally by Fedorov, and that led Stepanov to Stockholm, was a fake planted by Andrei and his team. How had Fedorov obtained the fake message?

And where was the original message?

Another drop of slushy rain hit his face and soon it was a downpour. Max hurried into the house, shook out his jacket, and stood by the fire to warm up. The book of fairy tales caught his eye.

"Heading to bed." Max grabbed the book and disappeared up the stairs. Once in his room with the door locked, he examined the book. It was about eight inches by five inches and the light blue fabric cover was frayed in several places. Instead of thumbing through the pages, Max inspected the insides of the front and back cover. The fabric wrapped around the cover edges and was held in place by yellowed paper glued to the hardcover's cardboard.

He ran his finger around the paper's edge and compared the front to the rear.

Was the front paper more yellowed than the paper glued on the inside of the back cover?

Max retrieved the Kizlyar knife he had removed from Stepanov's office and slipped the point between the paper and the fabric on the inside of the back cover. Slowly, with care, he slid the knife around the paper's edge and eased it away from the fabric.

A slip of onionskin paper fluttered to the ground.

When he picked it up, a string of Cyrillic characters written in his father's distinctive handwriting stared back at him. The letters were organized in five-character blocks with hand-drawn boxes around each block.

A one-time pad.

––––––

I can't do this by myself.

He carefully placed the onionskin between two pages in the middle of the book and stuffed it under his arm. In the hallway, he pulled his door closed and went down the dark corridor. The house was silent. Everyone had gone to bed.

Next door to Max's room was Alex's. Max peeked in and saw the boy in a deep slumber with Spike curled at the end of the bed. He closed the door and walked to Goshawk's room at the end of the hall and tried the handle. It was unlocked. Time to bury the hatchet.

The lithe computer hacker sat on the bed in the dark room with her face lit by a laptop screen. When Max stepped in, she shut the lid and crossed her arms over her chest.

Max leaned against the closed door. "How did Fedorov find the message? The fake one that Stepanov stole that led to the empty box in Stockholm?"

"Andrei and I ran a little operation."

"Tell me about it."

"We let some intel slip out to one of Fedorov's people. Just like with the one-time pad held by Professor Euler. We created a trail of clues that led Fedorov to both hiding places. It was simple, really. Fedorov was desperate for leverage over Stepanov, to take control of the consortium. He took the bait."

"Where was the message hidden? The one with the directions to Stockholm."

"In Andrei's desk in his office at the KGB in Minsk. After we let the intel slip to his people, Fedorov ran a black bag job to snatch it."

"Where in the office?"

"His former office, actually. Someone took Andrei's role as assistant director. The message was hidden under a false bottom in one of the drawers."

Max paced to the window, which overlooked the dark orchard. "How did it get there?"

Goshawk placed the laptop on a side table and sat in a cross-legged position. A gauzy camisole hung on her shoulders. "What do you mean?"

"Part of your operation had to be to place the fake message in a place where Fedorov could retrieve it, no?"

She shrugged. "I assume Andrei had someone put it there. Gabrieli, maybe."

"Maybe. But what if it was there all along? What if the drawer was the message's original hiding place?"

Her brows scrunched together. "I'm lost."

Max handed her the book. "Open it."

When she flipped the book open, the onionskin fell into her lap. "What is... Is this what I think it is?"

Max peered through the window and half expected to see a team of Spetsnaz infiltrating the orchard below, but the bare cherry trees sat silent. "Is it possible a message can be written once but decrypted twice to reveal two different messages?"

"You mean the message hidden in Andrei's desk was the original—the one he placed there a year ago—and there are two one-time pads? Each one reveals a different message?"

"Is that possible?"

"One way to find out." Goshawk flipped open her laptop and clicked a few keys. When she turned her screen, the message was displayed. She held the onionskin out to Max between two manicured fingers.

Max pulled over a chair and took the one-time pad. "You read each letter in the message, and I'll find the corresponding letter on the one-time pad."

"You sure you don't want to do this yourself? Keep it private?"

Max smiled at her and shook his head. "What's the first character?"

Goshawk returned the smile. As she read each character, Max found the correct letter on the onionskin and jotted it down on a scrap of paper. When they were done, Max held the decrypted message up and her eyes widened.

"Oh, my God."

————

Minsk, Belarus

"Does it feel weird to be here?" Goshawk rode in the passenger seat while Max drove.

Pellet-like flurries swirled outside in the wind under a metal-gray sky, the kind of weather he remembered from his childhood, the kind of weather that sapped your will to accomplish anything and drove men to drink. His father had a quip for the snow. *What good is the warmth of summer without the cold of winter to give it sweetness.*

The old man's ever-present positivity wasn't something Max inherited. "Weird is one word for it."

The residential streets were empty as they motored

slowly up a hill and around a bend. The homes in this neighborhood were palatial in size and surrounded by wrought iron fences or stone walls. Down the street from Max's childhood home lived the CEO of a broadband company, a cabinet secretary, and an oligarch. No one was quite sure how the oligarch made his money.

"How's Arina?"

"Still suffering from memory loss. They say if she recovers, it might take a while."

"How is Alex holding up?"

"He's doing okay. Seems to understand his mother needs time to get better."

They drove in silence until Goshawk spoke. "I was pregnant, once."

Her comment made him realize how little he knew about his computer hacker friend. "What happened?"

"Miscarried. Can't have children now."

Max touched her arm. "I'm sorry."

She shrugged. "It's okay. I've come to terms with it."

The comment made him realize he had a unique opportunity to be part of Alex's life.

If only I can put this consortium thing behind me.

Max turned the car into the drive and stopped at the wrought iron gate, where he rolled down the window. A forest of oaks and pines towered overhead and lined the winding drive that led to the house. "This was the first inkling I had that something was wrong."

"How did you know?"

Max pointed at the street near the driveway. "There was a van with tinted windows parked over there. There was a telephone company logo on the side. It was a logo I didn't recognize." He leaned out the car window and punched a code into a keypad. The gate rattled open on its track, and they pulled up the drive while the gate closed.

The grounds were as Max remembered them. The crater where the main house had been was littered with shards of charred housing materials from the explosion. Crumbled concrete, rusted rebar, and jagged wood were all that was left of the building. Pockets of snow swirled on the ground, and ice covered the foundation.

"Jesus," Goshawk said. "That was a large bomb."

Max parked near where the home's front door had been and popped the trunk. Goshawk, dressed in jeans, hiking boots, and a down jacket, removed a backpack filled with computer gear while Max carried a bag with bolt cutters, a shovel, and a few other tools. He slipped a pistol in his waistband.

He led her past the bomb crater and down a trail through dormant trees to the barn. A memory flashed of his encounter there with Victor Dedov, his father's boss at the Belarusian KGB. At the barn, they took a right and set off through the woods.

"Is this a trail?" Goshawk followed easily on her long legs.

"It was at one time."

"How big is your property?"

"Three acres. We're almost there."

Max stopped next to a towering jack pine. Trees extended in all directions and the snow, heavier now, accumulated on the ground.

"There's nothing here," Goshawk said as she turned in all directions.

"Exactly. That's what he wanted people to think." Max thrust the spade into the frozen ground. "We should have brought a pickax." Before long, Max was covered in sweat and he shed his heavy jacket. It was twenty minutes before the shovel hit metal. It was another twenty minutes before they were able to clear enough dirt away to heave open a metal door.

"Flashlight, please."

Goshawk handed him a big black Maglite and Max shined the beam though the opening. A set of concrete steps went down.

"Coming?" Max ducked as he tromped down the stairs, where he found another set of doors. These were made of heavy steel and secured with a large padlock. He stuck his hand out behind him. "Bolt cutters, please."

When no bolt cutters slapped into his hand, he turned. Goshawk was nowhere to be seen. Max went up the stairs and found her standing in the cold. "What are you doing?"

"I'm not good in small spaces. What's down there?"

"It's fine. Nothing to be concerned with. It's an old nuclear bomb shelter from the sixties my father refurbished."

She hopped up and down to stay warm and peered at the trees.

"Don't you want to see the archive?"

"If it's even there," she said.

"Suit yourself." Max took the bolt cutters and went down the steps. After he snipped the padlock, he pushed open the door and sensed someone behind him. He turned to see Goshawk. "Curiosity killed the cat?"

"Something like that."

A musty smell permeated the small room. The bright flashlight illuminated a bunker-style room with pipes running overhead, concrete walls, and a concrete ceiling. The furnishings were modern, and a leather chair sat in front of a desk. A leather couch ran along one wall. Metal shelves contained canned goods and bottled water. A silk rug in reds and blues covered the floor. Clean, neat, and orderly, it resembled a modern Scandinavian apartment.

"Not exactly your grandfather's bomb shelter," Goshawk said.

"Before it was renovated, we used to play in here as kids. After the renovation, I was only in here one time." They moved into the room and the hacker wiped a thin layer of dust from the couch. "So where are the files?"

Max went to the desk, opened the drawer, and removed a remote control. He rummaged in the backpack and replaced the remote's batteries. He pushed a button and a rumble came from behind a wall. "Hit that switch on the wall."

Goshawk flicked the light switch and an overhead fixture snapped on and bathed the tiny space in a warm glow.

Max touched another button on the remote and a whirring sound began. A moment later a door swung open on the side wall near the end of the couch.

"Holy shit!" Goshawk leaned over to peek inside.

When Max swung the flashlight into the opening, the beam flashed over stacks and rows of stout metal archival boxes. After glancing at Goshawk, he entered the small chamber. The metal boxes were stacked six high and two deep in four rows.

"Forty-eight boxes," he called out. Max broke the seal on the closest box and flipped up the lid. Inside was a row of densely packed hanging files. With the flashlight in one hand, he plucked out a random file and opened it with the other. The contents included a set of bank statements for an offshore account. They went back a decade and showed amounts in the millions of dollars.

"We should have brought a second scanner," Goshawk said. "This is going to take us a week." She opened her backpack, removed a portable document scanner and a laptop, and set the system up on the desk.

Max pointed at the stacks of canned goods. "At least we have provisions."

FORTY-EIGHT

Grozny, Chechnya

The package was awkward and oblong and the trip was long and boring, but Max didn't care. There was plenty to occupy his mind while he traveled. There were two errands to take care of, both equal in importance.

This time when he crossed through Georgia and into Russia, he was met by one of Doku's men. Doku would have accompanied him, the man explained, but Doku's son's hockey league had an important game against the crosstown rival that night. They encountered no Russian patrols, and Max was safely delivered to Doku's house in Grozny in time to join the hockey team's victory celebration.

As the sun struggled over the horizon, Max sped north in a truck he purchased for cash from a used car lot in Grozny. A box of food made by Doku's wife was on the passenger seat, and Max munched on nicotine gum and sipped coffee. A Glock 9mm borrowed from Doku's collection was in a holster under his down jacket, but he didn't expect to need the pistol on the first leg of his journey. Maybe for the second errand.

Except for the scar that itched under a newly grown beard, he was mostly healed from the beating he endured in Stockholm, but the cold made his bones creak in a way he wasn't used to.

I guess this is just the way it is now.

The trip north from Grozny to Zurgan Military Prison was just over ten hours. There were no towns to stop in, no roadside hotels like in the US, and petrol stations were sparse. The truck's bench seat made for a moderately comfortable place to catnap.

There was nothing around the prison but a bleary white expanse of fields and the small closed town that would require credentials to enter. He didn't intend to get anywhere close to the town's border. When concern about his close proximity to the prison popped up, he pushed it away and thought about Alex, or Badū, or Arina.

Arina, Baxter had told him, transferred to a long-term care facility located in a town not far from Aspen. She still suffered from memory loss, but she was alive.

There's hope.

Alex seemed to adjust okay. The groundskeeper and his wife had grown close to the boy, and his schoolwork was top-notch. Still, Max worried that Alex needed friends his age and, of course, his mother.

The sun was low in the rear window when Max slowed the truck. A half-dozen ramshackle homes were clustered along a desolate road about ten kilometers from the closed town and the prison. He parked in an area off a side street that had been cleared of snow. No one was around, but a curl of smoke trickled from a metal chimney at his destination. A low gray sky stretched in all directions.

Snow squeaked under his boots as Max trudged up the walk. Someone had made a half-hearted attempt to push the snow aside. The wood creaked as he stepped onto a rickety deck. The home's faded red door hung askew on a single hinge with a rawhide thong loop where the handle should be. A boot imprint was in bas-relief near the doorjamb.

Before Max could rap on the decrepit wood with his knuckles, the door opened to a familiar old man. Weather-darkened skin covered a craggy face. The man's nose had been broken, and his lower lip quivered, but his blue eyes danced as he stood on two shaky legs. Anger simmered as his eyes registered recognition.

Max held out the long package. It had been wrapped tightly in oilcloth and held together with twine. Max wondered if the old man had the strength to take the package but remembered the energy with which the old man had first brandished the shotgun.

The old man took the package in one hand, removed a corroded blade from his pocket, and sliced the twine.

After an agonizing few moments while the old man struggled with the packaging, the paper fell away. Inside was a long gun case made of leather. With quivering hands, the old man unzipped the case and removed a gleaming but ancient double-barreled shotgun. The two barrels gleamed in the pale sunlight and the wooden stock shone with polish. A second package, about the size of a brick and wrapped tight in plastic and tape, thumped as it fell to the porch. The old man ignored it as he caressed the gun's stock, worked the bore axis hinge, and sighted along the barrel.

A tear rolled down the old man's deeply wrinkled cheek as Max turned and walked back to his truck.

The second errand was less enjoyable. A six-hour drive took him to the outskirts of Rostov-on-Don, where he consulted his new Blackphone for directions. It was 3:00 am when he found the address. Wired on caffeine and adrenaline, Max sat in the truck and screwed a long black suppressor onto the barrel of the Glock.

The residential street was desolate. Squat cinder block homes sat in a row. They were erected in the Soviet era in an attempt at public housing. Forlorn when they were built, now the structures sat in various states of disrepair and disuse. Not exactly slums, the housing units, along with the ubiquitous gray apartment buildings that lined every Soviet-era city, were all that working-class Russians might expect out of life. A tiny car rested on blocks in the driveway of his target.

According to the short employment dossier Goshawk retrieved from the Rostov-on-Don police files, the man lived alone in this house. After several discipline problems during his army career, he'd been drummed out of the military and landed here, in a corrupt local police force. Somehow, the man had risen to a position of power.

After he watched the street for a while to ensure no one was around, Max exited the truck, crossed the home's front yard, and stopped in the rear next to a chain-link fence that sagged in several places. The neighborhood was silent, the house dark.

With the gun in his waistband, he picked the rear door's lock and stepped into the house. Rancid oil and decaying vegetables assaulted his nose. In the largest of two tiny back rooms, he found his target snoring loudly under a dingy comforter. Max stood over him and pressed the suppressor's muzzle hard into his nostril.

The man's eyes opened and went wide at the dark shadow who stood over him. "What the fuck—"

"Where is my lighter?"

IF YOU LIKED THIS BOOK ...

IF YOU LIKED THIS STORY...

I would appreciate it if you would leave a review. An honest review means a lot. The constructive reviews help me write better stories, and the positive reviews help others find the books, which ultimately means I can write more stories.

It only takes a few minutes, and it means everything. Thank you in advance.

-Jack

ACKNOWLEDGMENTS

As I write this, I learned of Sean Connery's passing from my wife. She said, "It's sad, but he lived well." In these difficult and divisive times, his death and my wife's comments led me to ruminate on what it means to "live well." Max Austin would not be the man he is today without Mr. Connery's work to bring 007 alive. Yes, the actor was a man with charisma, grace, masculinity, and vitality. He was a rags to riches story who grew up in the slums of Edinburgh to win an Academy Award. He remained true to his heritage and core self, something we can all aspire to.

To me, living well means a constant practice of gratitude. Especially now, while a pandemic rages and partisan divisiveness threatens to tear the country apart, I remain thankful for so many things. My health, my relationship with my beautiful wife, and my community of friends and colleagues. I'm also hugely grateful for each and every one of my readers.

In no particular order, the following gracious, witty, and highly intelligent souls on my Advanced Reader Team deserve credit for helping to hone the story: Wahak

Kontian, Keith Kay, Bob Kaster, Scott Barnett, Mchael Levitz, Ralph Whittle, Robin Eide Steffensen, Gabrielle Ritchie, Ken Sanford, Ben Bergwerf, Judith DeRycke (and MJ), David Weil, Wayne Barnard, Chris Chase, Jason T, Bryce Bunting, Terri Sones, Portia Shao, Scott Koopman, Todd Friedman, Pat Ellis, Katherine Robinson, Marsha Rotheim, Philip Ammerman, Julie Petrovic, Emilee's Grandpa, Patricia Love, Kathy Mischka, Stephen J Potter, Brian Sullivan, Stefan Koziolek, EJ Dale, Bill Hess, Shay Morton, Catherine Baldwin-Johnson, Paul Hassell, James Rutherford, Janine Flynn, Robert Cox, Matthew Gregory, Bruce Bornstein, Philip Taylor, Karen Flannery, Rhonda W, Mike Davies, Grant and Raelene, Jeffrey Benham, David Bures, Molly Anderson, Ken Mompellier, Lance Kovar, Cindi Linville, Vince Gassi, Gerry Mullin, Doug Christ, John Heaton, Andy Perla, Bob Schiffman, Ron McDaniel, Charles Goldstein, Sharon Cameron, John Kelly, Tim Dickenson, Ralph Whittle, Cynthia Murphy, Buddy, Nancy Jamison, Joel Kaufmann, Henry Lavender, Mark Thomas, Mikael Sandeberg, Keith Tobias, Ken Cockrill, David Skinner, Casimir Stankiewicz, Mark Bertagnolli, Brian Thomson, Kerry Kehoe, Gregg Backemeyer, Jeffry Richman, Preston Trotter, Bill Hidek, Terry McEachern, Dave Cook, Donna Van Meer, Bob Vilardi, Lee Gregory, Robert Wivagg, Gary Needham, Tom Miller, Kevin Rensink, Sonya Rumer, David Parker, Michael Bugosh, Melissa Anderson Craig, Kimberlee Bachand, Carrie Salomone, Daniel Young, James Farmer, Jeff Raelson, Judie Desrochers, and John Rozum.

A writer's relationship with his editor is like one between siblings: Familial affection mixed with the occasional domestic spat. Long periods of distance while knowing they are available any time and have your back.

Martha Hayes has been my editor for the past three novels and you, dear reader, have her to thank for the quality of prose. She's a coach, a confidant, an ally, an agitator, and a wicked smart editor. More than anything, she's a friend. Thank you, Martha.

Last but not least, I have my wife Jill to thank. She knows why.

JOIN MY MAILING LIST

If you'd like to get updates on new releases as well as notifications of deals and discounts, please join my email list.

I only email when I have something meaningful to say and I never send spam. You can unsubscribe at any time.

Join my mailing list at www.jackarbor.com.

ABOUT THE AUTHOR

Jack Arbor is the author of six thrillers featuring the wayward KGB assassin Max Austin. The stories follow Max as he comes to terms with his past and tries to extricate himself from a destiny he desperately wants to avoid.

Jack works as a technology executive during the day and writes at night and on weekends with much love and support from his lovely wife, Jill.

Jill and Jack live outside Aspen, Colorado, where they enjoy trail running and hiking through the natural beauty of the Roaring Fork Valley. Jack also likes to taste new bourbons and listen to jazz, usually at the same time. They both miss the coffee on the East Coast.

You can get free books as well as prerelease specials and sign up for Jack's mailing list at www.jackarbor.com.

Connect with Jack online:
 (e) jack@jackarbor.com
 (t) twitter.com/JackArbor
 (i) instagram.com/jackarbor/
 (f) facebook.com/JackArborAuthor
 (w) www.jackarbor.com
 (n) newsletter signup

ALSO BY JACK ARBOR

The Russian Assassin, The Russian Assassin Series, Book One

You can't go home again...

Max, a former KGB assassin, is content with the life he's created for himself in Paris. When he's called home to Minsk for a family emergency, Max finds himself suddenly running for his life, desperate to uncover secrets about his father's past to save his family.

Max's sister Arina and nephew Alex become pawns in a game that started a generation ago. As Max races from the alleyways of Minsk to the posh neighborhoods of Zurich, and ultimately to the gritty streets of Prague, he must confront his past and come to terms with his future to preserve his family name.

The Russian Assassin is a tight, fast-paced adventure, staring Jack Arbor's stoic hero, the ex-KGB assassin-for-hire, Max Austin. Book one of the series forces Max to choose between himself and his family, a choice that will have consequences for generations to come.

The Pursuit, The Russian Assassin Series, Book Two

The best way to destroy an enemy is to make him a friend...

Former KGB assassin Max Austin is on the run, fighting to keep his family alive while pursuing his parents' killers. As he battles foes both visible and hidden, he uncovers a conspiracy with roots in the darkest cellars of Soviet history. Determined to survive, Max hatches a plan to even the odds by partnering with his mortal enemy. Even as his adversary becomes his confidant, Max is left wondering who he can trust, if anyone...

If you like dynamic, high-voltage, page-turning thrills, you'll love the second installment of The Russian Assassin series starring Jack Arbor's desperate hero, ex-KGB assassin-for-hire, Max Austin.

The Attack, The Russian Assassin Series, Book Three

It's better to be the hunter than the hunted.

A horrific bombing rocks the quaint streets of London's West Brompton neighborhood and Max Austin finds himself the target of an international manhunt the likes of which the world hasn't seen since the hunt for Osama bin Laden. The former KGB assassin must put his fight against the Consortium on hold while he seeks redemption.

As Max chases the bomber from the gritty streets of London through the lush Spanish countryside and into the treacherous mountains of Chechnya, he's plunged into a game of cat and mouse with a wily MI6 agent determined to catch Max at all costs.

Can Max find the terrorist and clear his name before it's too late?

The Attack is the third installment in The Russian

Assassin adventure thriller series that pits Max Austin against his arch-enemy, the shadowy consortium of international criminals that will stop at nothing to kill Max and his family. If you like heart-pounding, page-turning thrills, grab this adventure starring Jack Arbor's grim hero, the ex-KGB assassin-for-hire, Max Austin.

The Hunt, The Russian Assassin Series, Book Four

Friends are the family we chose for ourselves.

A man on a mission to save his family. A friend missing and presumed dead.

Max Austin is no stranger to mortal danger and hard decisions. But when the former KGB assassin is confronted by the choice to rescue a friend or save his family, he'll have to dig deep to keep those he cares about alive.

Haunted by a mysterious shadow that dogs him at every turn, he journeys through the treacherous Turkish desert, the harsh confines of Washington, DC, and the dirty alleyways of Cyprus searching for clues from his past. Along the way, he finds himself a step behind his adversaries who are intent on eliminating Kate Shaw before she can reveal her secrets. This time, failure in Max's quest will mean death for his friends and family alike.

Will he find Kate Shaw, or will this be Max's last mission?

The Hunt is the gripping fourth installment in Jack Arbor's Amazon bestselling series, The Russian Assassin, staring his stoic hero Max Austin. With a barreling pace, lovable characters, and unputdownable action, you'll see why Arbor's books sell like hotcakes and why readers clamor for more.

Cat & Mouse, A Max Austin Novella

Max, a former KGB assassin, is living a comfortable life in Paris. When not plying his trade, he passes his time managing a jazz club in the City of Light. To make ends meet, he freelances by offering his services to help rid the earth of the world's worst criminals.

Max is enjoying his ritual post-job vodka when he meets a stunning woman; a haunting visage of his former fiancé. Suddenly, he finds himself the target of an assassination plot in his beloved city of Paris. Fighting for his life, Max must overcome his own demons to stay alive.

Made in the USA
Las Vegas, NV
21 March 2021

19888222R00215